LADIES IN WAITING

LADIES IN WAITING

Linda Hudson-Smith

BET Publications, LLC
http://www.bet.com

NEW SPIRIT BOOKS are published by

BET Publications, LLC
c/o BET BOOKS
One BET Plaza
1900 W Place NE
Washington, DC 20018-1211

All Kensington Titles, Imprints, and Distributed Lines are available at special quantity discounts for bulk purchases for sales promotions, premiums, fund-raising, and educational or institutional use. Special book excerpts or customized printings can also be created to fit specific needs. For details, write or phone the office of the Kensington special sales manager: Kensington Publishing Corp., 850 Third Avenue, New York, NY 10022, attn: Special Sales Department, Phone: 1-800-221-2647.

ISBN: 1-58314-295-9

First Printing: August 2002
10 9 8 7 6 5 4 3 2 1

Printed in the United States of America

This book is dedicated to my firstborn, my beloved son:

Gregory Lee Lewis Smith

May you find love, joy, and peace wherever your journeys may take you. May you always seek God's approval in all that you do. The heart of your mother's deepest and purest love is forever with you. I love you.

In loving memory of my dear friend:

Lorna Thomas Trapp

Gone too soon, but never to be forgotten.

Sunrise: July 26, 1949
Sunset: October 17, 2001

ACKNOWLEDGMENTS

My Heavenly Father: Thank you for your holy presence in my life. Thank you for granting me grace sufficient enough for me to bravely meet the challenges of each new day. As you continue to lead, I will surely follow.

My loving husband, Rudy: Thank you for teaching me the true meaning of patience and the gracious art of waiting on God. Your knowledge of the Bible truths that you shared with me was invaluable in writing this book. Thanks for all your help and for allowing me to tap into your beautiful spirit as you and I created the sermons.

My dear friend, Elester Latham: A very special thanks for granting me the opportunity to cultivate the seed that you planted. While these magnificent characters took this story in a totally different direction than the original intent, the basic concept remained the same.

Deloris Williamson: Thank you for loving and supporting my son, Greg, and for taking such good care of my grandchildren, Gregory III and Omunique. You are a wonderful woman and an extraordinary mother. I love you dearly.

My editor, Glenda Howard: Thank you for your patience, your encouragement, and your most valuable input. I truly appreciate your open-mindedness throughout this entire process.

My fellow author, Ken Vann: Thank you for the sound professional advice you've offered me throughout this journey. May God continue to grant you peace and prosperity.

If

If you desire me,
you must be able to inspire me.

If you want us to become closer,
you must not take my distance personally when I need my space.

If you desire to hold on to me too tight,
you must know that my free and loose spirit will fiercely rebel against suffocation.

If you want to possess me,
you must be able to differentiate between possession and obsession.

If you desire to make me happy,
you must realize the responsibility for my happiness lies solely with me;
you can only enhance it.

If you want to make me cry,
you need to know that my tears will be tears of joy because I've set myself free from you and your desire to inflict pain upon me.

If you desire me to be less than your equal,
please understand that I will not lose my individuality or give up my identity just to take on yours.
I must have the freedom to accomplish all of my personal goals.

If you want to love me,
you must first love yourself.
Only then will you be capable of loving me as I deserve to be loved,
the same unconditional way in which I love myself.

If you desire to make me your spouse,
you must possess all the aforementioned characteristics in order to win my heart and my hand.

If you see the reflection of your dreams in someone's eyes,
to find love, it's never too late,
especially if you're still out there searching for your soul mate!

—Linda Hudson-Smith

CHAPTER ONE

"I've got to go, Mrs. Wiley. Reverend Jesse's waiting for me to visit him today. See you in church tomorrow. And I haven't forgotten that I need to take you grocery shopping first thing Monday morning. I thoroughly enjoyed our prayer session. Bye for now."

Marlene Covington hung up the phone, snatched her black leather purse off the sparkling kitchen counter, and rushed into the guest bathroom. Removing her makeup bag from her purse, she opened it and took out her compact. While she applied a creamy foundation to her mahogany brown skin, her dark brown eyes crinkled with laughter as she thought back on her phone conversation. Mrs. Wiley, the widowed senior member of her husband's church, First Tabernacle, had lived a lively eighty-two years and had a sense of humor like no other.

A frown suddenly crossed her features as she examined the dark circles under her eyes. "Girlfriend, you got more bags under your eyes than Ralph's grocery store. We have to fix that. No forty-eight-year-old woman, even one with a full figure like yours, should look sixty-plus. Lord, if you don't bring Jesse Covington out of the darkness of hell, I'm going to look older than this by the time this whole mess is finished."

Marlene stuffed everything back into her purse and went out the door off the kitchen that led to the garage. She then dashed back inside, grabbed an apple and napkin off the round oak table, and disappeared through the door again.

Settled inside her late-model midnight blue Lincoln town car, she carefully backed out of the garage of her upper-middle-class Ladera Heights home. This would be her and Jesse's first time together in over a month. It was a long, hard drive, but she'd find a way to fly to the moon to see her loving husband.

Marlene had met Jesse on the bus one evening in Washington, D.C. Both of them had been government employees during that time. An instant attraction had occurred between them. After dating exclusively for nine months, Jesse had asked her to marry him. Three years into the marriage, Jesse had heeded his call into the ministry. It had been a difficult transition for her, going from career woman to the preacher's wife, but she'd soon learned that the rewards of being in service to the Lord were endless.

But she had no doubt that what was now happening to her and Jesse had been whipped up by the prince of darkness and sent straight up to them from the dark caverns of hell.

Inside her inner-city Los Angeles apartment, which was clean and neat but crammed tight with modern furnishings and baby furniture, twenty-three-year-old city-college student and welfare mom Keisha Reed hurried to change the diaper of her one-year-old daughter, Zanari. Grabbing some baby bottles out of the refrigerator, she packed them in the diaper bag. She then grabbed hold of her four-year-old son, Zach. Flinging the diaper bag over her shoulder, she picked up a large sack lunch from the sofa. Eager to get going, she hustled her kids out the door and locked it.

Outside, where the early morning air was cool and crisp, Keisha strapped both kids into their car seats. After waving at a neighbor from across the street, she checked the trunk to make sure she had everything she needed in case the trip to the desert turned into an overnight stay. Before settling herself in the driver's seat, she looked up the street for her carpooling, Hispanic best friend, Rosalinda Morales.

Keisha laughed while watching twenty-four-year-old Rosalinda's long black hair swaying in the breeze as she shot out of the next-door apartment complex and ran down the street. Out of breath, Rosalinda slipped into the passenger seat of the rental car they'd gone half on. The two women exchanged smiles as Keisha looked enviously at Rosalinda's flawless nut-brown complexion. Loud rap music played on the radio, the type of music they both loved.

"I was beginning to think you weren't going to make it." Keisha nervously pushed a strand of her sable hair behind her ear. "Getting ready to make this trip to the high desert is always a stressful time for me. I wish Zach didn't insist on me bringing the kids every time. The long drive is hard on them. I hope I didn't forget anything this time."

The size of saucers, Rosalinda's jet-black eyes twinkled with amusement. "Like the last time, when you forgot the baby's food? The time before that you left the kids' pajamas and we ended up spending the night, as usual. If you think you got it all together, let's rock and roll."

"Yeah, can you believe I did that dumb crap? Zanari sure wasn't too happy about me leaving her food behind."

Rosalinda giggled. "Oh, how well do I remember. Little homey back there let out some screams that would wake the dead. She lets everyone know when she's hungry."

Keisha looked at her daughter in the rearview mirror. She couldn't help smiling. Her kids were the joy of her life even through all her struggles. "But that's the only time she really cries outside of when she's wet."

"And when little bad butt Zach decides to pop her upside her head with one of them dangerous toys you spend your money on."

Running a finger across her full wine-colored lips and then down the side of her caramel brown cheek, Keisha looked over at Rosalinda. "Speaking of money, how much you got?"

"About a hundred and ten dollars. And you know what I got to do with most of that. My mom is also going to need her medications refilled within the next week."

"I got paid yesterday, so we're in good shape for this trip, but I hope we don't have to stay overnight. I got a lot of extra things to do with my money this month. The kids both need new shoes. Zach's feet are growing like bad weeds."

"Tell me about it, Keisha. I don't know how I'm going to keep my bills current with my present situation. Working two jobs still isn't enough to make ends meet, especially when you consider that I have to take care of my sick mother and all the things I do for that no-account boyfriend of mine."

"Girlfriend, I don't know how we do it, either. But something's gonna have to give real soon. I can't keep this up much longer. I might have to join you in getting a second job."

"All we're doing is talking smack, Keisha. Our guys mean the world to us or we wouldn't be breaking our backs and our banks just to keep them happy. 'Cause we both know they don't appreciate anything we do for them. We're just two sorry-ass women in love with two dumb, supersorry-ass men." Both women dissolved into laughter.

While piped-in jazz music played on the stereo in the bedroom of her posh Bel Air home, Alexis Du Boise twirled around in front of the full-length mirror, checking herself out with an extremely critical eye. With a figure to die for and *Halle Berry* looks, the thirty-three-year-old natural beauty had no problem turning male heads. Still dissatisfied with her appearance, she removed the seductive red dress and tossed it on the king-size bed already piled high with other discarded clothing.

Finally, she settled on a low-cut black blouse and a smart-looking calf-length skirt of the same color. After running fingers through the short waves of her light brown pixie-cut hair, she grabbed her purse and overnighter and went out to the garage, where she got into a late-model Rolls-Royce. While her sexy doe brown eyes smiled at the thought of seeing her husband in just a couple of hours, she backed the expensive car out of the four-car garage.

Slowly, Alexis drove through her grand country-club neighborhood, admiring all its extravagant beauty. While listening to her favorite Los Angeles jazz station, 84.7, she thought about her handsome husband and how she couldn't wait to see his charming smile. Richard James Du Boise was the love of her life, the first man she'd ever gone out with on a real date—and she'd been missing his presence like crazy, especially with his absence from their bed.

Alexis had met R.J. Du Boise at a fraternity party that she and a few of her girlfriends had crashed when she was twenty years old. Before she knew what had hit her, he'd already swept her completely off her feet. They'd eloped three months later, on her twenty-first birthday, much to the dismay of her Christian family. Alexis's family thought R.J. was nothing more than a straight-up heathen. Despite her family's feelings about her husband, being married to the highly successful stockbroker over the past twelve years had been quite a whirlwind for a girl who'd grown up in poverty in a New Orleans ghetto. Now that the whirl had suddenly been taken out of the whirlwind, she found herself all alone and hating every second of it.

Way up in California's high desert, the afternoon sun blazed like a normal day in hell. Situated in what seemed like the middle of nowhere, the multistory, gray, brick, privately run men's correctional facility gleamed under the pounding sun. A few buildings on the seemingly endless desert acres of prison grounds also served as interim housing for inmates when overcrowding occurred at other California facilities. Lines of people, mostly women, wrapped completely around the place like a human bow. Loop after loop of shiny, razor-sharp barbed wire fencing fiercely protected the building's exterior.

Marlene was knocked for a loop by the ominous fencing as she took inventory of the line in front of the correctional facility where her husband lived as an inmate while waiting for an appeal that might overturn his conviction. Amazed by the presence of so many young women, women much younger than her forty-eight years, Marlene couldn't help wondering how many lost souls were in this line. She shielded her eyes from the sun as she zeroed in on a young woman arguing with a six-foot-four black male prison guard wearing a ranger hat and tinted sunshades.

Keisha Reed had a hand on one hip and a baby on the other. She held the hand of her male toddler as she argued over the guard's refusal to allow the women and children inside.

"Just doing my job, ma'am. I can't control the weather."

"I don't recall asking you to control the weather. I asked if we could step inside out of this heat. These kids are melting under this blazing sun."

"Sorry, ma'am, but you must already know that it's against the rules. I can only let you in when it's time to register for your visit."

"What you trying to say here? That I should know the rules? It sounds to me as though you're assuming that I've been here before."

"Not at all, ma'am. Just stating the facts."

Rosalinda Morales stepped out of line and put a comforting arm around Keisha's shoulders. "Don't do this, girl. You can't afford to have him deny you entry to the prison for popping off. You know how some of these guards are so insensitive. They don't need much of an excuse to send you packing. Cool your jets. Think about how much you want to get inside to see Zach. We can't afford to waste the money we've already spent on the rental car."

Keisha managed to smile at her friend. "You're right. I'm cool now."

Out of the blue it began to sprinkle. Marlene saw that no one in the line seemed to notice or care as they stared straight ahead at the locked doors. It started to rain harder, yet no one moved a muscle for fear of losing their place in line. Even as hairstyles crumpled and makeup melted, not a single person abandoned her position. Marlene could clearly see the deep sadness and obvious disappointment etched on the faces of these young women. The rain appeared to soak their spirits as well as their stylish clothes. Most of the women were dressed to the nines.

A blaring siren suddenly pierced the silence, causing the prison guard to immediately abandon his post. Marlene's insides quivered at the offensive sound. Before she could ask a question, the guard returned and readily slapped a VISITATION CANCELED sign on the front door—without explanation. She then read the sign, which also said the visitors could return the next day under the special-circumstance rule.

Marlene watched in silence as one of the female visitors ran up to the door and pounded furiously on the glass. Tears barely distinguishable from the raindrops rolled down the young woman's mocha brown face. Marlene's heart went out to her and all the other women in line. Each of them looked as if her heart were breaking. Bowing her head, she made a quiet supplication to the Lord on their behalf.

The line slowly dissipated as everyone headed for the parking lot, with heads hung low. It was a sad sight to behold. These women appeared bitterly disappointed. It seemed that there was no one to hold accountable for all their misery.

Back inside her car, terribly unhappy over not getting inside to see Jesse, Marlene started the engine and drove out of the parking lot. As she thought about her situation, she couldn't decide whether to go home and come back the next day or to go to the only hotel located in this miserable little town. She'd found the hotel on the Internet when she'd logged onto Yahoo! in order to map out driving directions. But she'd never dreamed of spending a night there. It was already enough that she'd had to drive this distance alone. She had asked their twenty-one-year-old son, Malcolm, to accompany her on the drive, but he hadn't wanted to make the trip.

These days Malcolm Covington only thought of himself. He'd been self-centered since he'd turned sixteen, five years ago. But he'd turned his self-serving ways up quite a few notches over the past couple of years. The boy had gotten into the habit of always smelling himself. He just didn't realize that the horrible stench of his egotistical funk stank to high heaven.

The little voice inside her heart, which she always referred to as the Holy Spirit, had convinced her that her she should stay over instead of going all the way home. A good night's rest would help prepare her for driving back the next day. Since it was already midafternoon, she was glad she'd listened to her inner voice, glad the hotel was only another few miles away.

Marlene suddenly spotted a disabled car as she drove down the deserted strip of highway en route to the hotel. Recognizing the young people as two of the women in the prison line, she immediately pulled over onto the shoulder of the road and rolled down the window.

"I stopped to see if I could help. What seems to be the problem?"

Keisha kicked one of the tires. "This damn rental just quit on us. We don't know anything about cars. The people charged us a fortune for this lemon and it won't even go another yard. Do you by chance have a cell phone?"

Marlene held up her cell phone for them to see. "Give me the number off the contract to the rental place and I'll call them. Where are you headed?"

Rosalinda pointed down the road. "We're going to the only hotel in this dismal desert town. Where you going?"

"I'm going to the hotel, too. Get all your things together and I'll give you ladies a lift. We can call the rental place about the car on the way. The rain has only stopped for a short time. Let's get those babies somewhere safe and dry."

Marlene eagerly introduced herself. She learned the women's names as she popped the trunk from the inside of the car. She then helped the two young women store their things and position the babies in the transferred car seats.

With everyone settled in comfortably, Marlene pulled the car back onto the highway. Marlene turned the radio down as she placed the call to the car place using the number off the rental contract. After a short conversation with customer service, she put her cell phone away.

"They'll pick up the defective car and drop off another one. I told them you'd be at the hotel. The *Budget* drivers will ask for you when they get there."

Keisha smiled at Marlene. "Thanks. It was real nice of you to stop. You don't find many people nowadays willing to help out. I don't know what we would've done if you hadn't happened along."

"I didn't just happen along. God sent me. Everything happens for a reason. I was going to go home and drive back tomorrow, but I was compelled to stay on. How old are your babies?"

Wondering what they'd gotten themselves into, Keisha exchanged nervous glances with Rosalinda. "Zach is four and Zanari is not quite two yet. Zanari's birthday is next month. These are my only children."

"Do both you and Rosalinda have a loved one in prison?"

Rosalinda gave Keisha a doleful glance before responding to Marlene's question. "Two best friends in love with two men who can't seem to get it right. Can you believe that? Sometimes I wonder about us, but we stick by our men because we love them. Is it your man that's in jail?" Rosalinda inquired as she wondered whom this sophisticated-looking woman might be visiting inside the prison.

"He's more than just my man." Warm thoughts of Jesse made Marlene blush. "He's my husband and a God-loving minister. And he's innocent."

The two women laughed at Marlene's last comment.

"Yeah, right," Keisha retorted. "That's what they all say. To let my man tell it, he's never so much as spit on the sidewalk. If he thought I believed that, he'd try to sell me the moon."

Rosalinda shrugged her shoulders. "Her man could be innocent. Mine is. That is, this time. He just got set up."

Keisha sucked her teeth. "That's the lie you keep telling yourself. Your man is guilty as sin, as he's been of all the other crimes. He just has your silly ass completely snowed under this time around. And, girlfriend, you should own the moon by now."

"Ladies, you have to watch your language. These kids shouldn't hear that kind of talk. As a Christian woman, I can't have that kind of talk around me, either. Let's call a truce."

"Out of all the people to get stuck with, we end up with a Christian woman," Keisha mumbled under her breath. "Out of respect for you, Rosalinda and I will agree not to use any more foul language. At least, not in your presence."

The afternoon was just about gone as they came upon the *Desert Inn Hotel.* A Rolls Royce parked in front of the entrance piqued everyone's interest. The three women got out of the car and walked to the rear. Marlene opened the trunk for them to unload their belongings.

Keisha whistled. "I wonder who that phat ride belongs to! Whoever it is, they got to have plenty of chips. That mug had to cost a grip."

"Maybe it's the warden's car or some other high-up prison official," Rosalinda said. "But I doubt it. Don't nobody come to this hotel but us ladies in waiting."

"*Ladies in waiting*? Is that what you young women call yourselves? What does it mean?"

"It's a joke among us dedicated ladies that come to the prison every single weekend, come rain or shine. We stand by our men, no matter the circumstances," Keisha explained to Marlene. "The guards dubbed us with that name 'cause it seems we're always left waiting."

Marlene looked astonished. "No offense intended, but it sounds more like low self-esteem than dedication. I don't get it. Why would anyone come out here in the middle of nowhere every weekend? Don't you all have lives?"

Keisha snorted. "I'm going to give you the benefit of the doubt—'cause this got to be your first time out here. Let me ask you this: Are you saying you're only going to visit your husband this once? That you're never coming back out here after this weekend?"

Marlene looked puzzled as the three women walked toward the entrance of the hotel.

Reaching out for the baby girl, Marlene took her in her arms while studying her pretty little vanilla-wafer-colored face. "I'm not saying that. Jesse's a loving husband and a God-fearing man. He shouldn't have been arrested in the first place. I'm going to visit him until he's released, no matter how long it takes."

"That's exactly Keisha's point. You're going to support your man, especially if he's innocent. His circumstances may be different, but the fact that you're going to hang in there makes you no different from us," Rosalinda interjected.

"Welcome to the Ladies in Waiting Club!" Keisha and Rosalinda said in unison.

Marlene looked perplexed. She didn't like being referred to as such, but she decided it was in her best interest not to make an issue of it. She didn't want to make any enemies.

Inside the lobby of the Desert Inn Hotel, soft music played overhead. Marlene, Keisha with the two children, and Rosalinda checked into the hotel. The two best friends pooled their money to get a room. As they left Marlene at the lobby desk, they asked her if she'd like to meet up with them later in the hotel bar. Much to their surprise, Marlene agreed.

Dressed in a flattering paisley robe, wearing leather slippers on her feet, Marlene picked up the phone in her room. Using a calling card, she placed a call to her home. The deep voice of Malcolm Covington came over the line. And then she heard the extremely loud rap music playing in the background. That didn't please her in the least. Marlene sighed wearily.

"Hi there, Malcolm. You sound like you're still asleep. You should be up by now, boy, and out looking for work. Half the day is already gone."

Malcolm's long, lean frame was stretched out on a twin-size bed. All the blinds were pulled together tightly to block out the sun. Out of respect for his mother, he turned the volume down on the radio. Malcolm possessed the most beautiful droopy bedroom eyes. His ebony eyes were what all the young women were attracted to—and he knew it. The women also kept his phone line hot morning, noon, and night.

Malcolm sat up in bed. "It's all good, Mom. I was getting up anyway. I got an interview at Wal-mart at three o'clock. Where you calling from?"

"I'm supposed to be at the prison, but they canceled visitation without telling us why. I'm at the Desert Inn Hotel, where I'm going to spend the night so I can visit your daddy tomorrow. Good thing I keep all sorts of clothes and shoes in the trunk. You know me, I'm always prepared for the best and for the worst."

"Are you going to be okay way out there by yourself?"

"It seems pretty safe. You could've come with me if you're so concerned. I've met a couple of nice young women that I'm going to meet up with later."

"Young women! How young?"

"Probably close to your age, give or take a few years. Their boyfriends are in prison."

"Oh, them type, huh? These young girls be trippin' behind these guys in jail!"

"What do you mean by 'them type'?"

"A lot of the sister-girls I know are into jailbirds and ex-cons. There's a bunch of dumb honeys out there. They think the cons are sexy. They also give them all their hard-earned money and let them run up their phone bills by accepting their collect calls."

"Is that why you've been trying your hardest to get locked up this past year?"

Malcolm sucked his teeth loudly. "Mom, you didn't have to go there. I've made a few serious mistakes, but you don't seem to think I've changed, when I really have. I'm not down with that kind of stuff anymore. Could you please give me some time off?"

"When you start taking responsibility for yourself, you can get all the time off you need. You could get a permanent vacation from my mouth if you get a job. As long as you're under my roof, dependently so, the mighty tongue will be right there wagging itself in your face."

"Okay, Mom, I got the message. Is there a number where I can reach you?"

Marlene gave Malcolm the name of the hotel, the phone number, and the room number. "My cell phone will also be on. I'll be home tomorrow. If my plans change, I'll call back. Don't have anyone in my house while I'm gone. That includes your little nappy-headed girlfriends, current and past. And make sure you get to that interview on time."

Marlene hung up the phone. Exhausted from the long drive, she stretched out on the comfortable-looking bed to take a short nap.

* * *

Already settled into the nicely decorated room with the two double beds, dresser, and a round table with four chairs, Keisha was busy changing Zanari's diaper while Rosalinda dressed Zach in a clean set of clothes.

"What do you think of the lady who gave us a ride, Keisha?"

"I think she's really nice. I just hope she's not one of those Bible-thumping sisters that you can always find on the first pew making goggle eyes at the preacher, while trying to reform the world and all its sinners. I'm not trying to hear no sermon way out here in the desert."

"She *is* the preacher's wife! I kinda like her, though. She's good with the kids, too. Little Zach seems to like her also. You know that there aren't too many people that little Zach cares two cents for. Are we taking the kids to the nursery or are we going to take turns going to the restaurant bar?"

"I got enough money for the nursery. They have good food and nice toys. Zach loves it there. I'm near broke, but I don't want to deprive my kids. It's tough enough on them already, especially with their daddy in prison and all."

"How's your college computer-training class coming, Keisha?"

"I love it so far. It's going to help land me a decent job. I'm actually glad for welfare reform. Otherwise, I'd still be on my butt waiting for that Mother's Day check to roll up in the mailbox. I like the idea of bettering myself."

"I hear that's a good program you're in. I'm glad you're taking advantage of the opportunities. I bet that in the next several years there'll be no welfare."

Keisha nodded. "That's the way it looks. But I'm going to love giving my babies more than I had. Welfare was passed down from generation to generation in my family, even though my mom got it under special circumstances. Hopefully I'll be the one to stop the vicious cycle."

Rosalinda stood Zach on his feet to tend to his hair and tie his shoes. When he backed away from the soft-bristled brush, she pulled the toddler in closer.

"I'm sorry you have to work two jobs, Rosalinda. Taking care of your sick mom is a job in itself. Do you think Ricardo appreciates what you do for him?"

"I'm not sure. But like we said earlier, something's got to give. I'm going to have to see Ric's lawyer sometime soon. I need another extension on this month's payment. Zach is ready to go, Keisha. You want to take them down early so we can come back and freshen up?"

"Yeah, let's do that."

Looking a little disheartened about their futures, Keisha and Rosalinda gathered up the children and left the room.

Easy listening music was playing in the dimly lit bar. A cool blanket of dusk had settled over the desert, smothering the insufferable heat of the day. Smiling and talking amicably, the three newly acquainted women were comfortably seated in a booth in one corner of the room. There was only one seat left in the entire place—and it was at their table.

From the bar window, the women could see a beautiful woman as she put something in the backseat of the Rolls-Royce they had spotted earlier. The stunning woman locked the door of the car and came inside the hotel. Seconds later, she walked into the hotel bar.

Rosalinda nudged Keisha, directing her attention to the doorway. Keisha then nudged Marlene. "Looks like the Rolls belongs to that sister. She sure is high-class. Look at all her gold and diamonds," Rosalinda whispered.

"She appears to be looking for a seat. Since there's only one chair left in the whole place, we should invite her over. What do you two think?" Marlene asked.

The three women started waving. When Alexis Du Boise finally looked in their direction, she seemed to gaze right through them. She totally disregarded the friendly gestures when a chair at the bar suddenly became available.

Keisha grunted. "Did you see that? That rich heifer completely blew us off, as though we wasn't nothing. Who in the hell does she think she is?"

Marlene clucked her tongue disapprovingly. "You shouldn't be talking about that woman like that. You don't even know her. Maybe she just wants to be alone."

"Sorry, but a bar is the last place a person goes to be alone," Keisha huffed. "She saw us offering her a seat. She could've at least acknowledged us. By the way, Ms. Christian Woman, ain't it against your religion to be in a bar, of all places?"

"Was it against Jesus' religion to go the places He went? It's places like this that a good Christian can do the best soul saving. Jesus is my best friend, my Savior. Jesus didn't turn His back on anyone. I believe in His commandment that we should love our neighbors as we love ourselves. Now, I admit I have a few neighbors that I find very hard to love, but I do the best with what I have to do it with. I simply let Jesus deal with my enemies and those I find myself wanting to have nothing to do with. You have to learn how to pray for your enemies, those known and unknown."

"Is that why you befriended us?" Keisha looked insulted by the whole idea. "If so, you're wasting your time. We don't need a sermon, especially from just another sinner. We're not trying to hear nothing about no Jesus. We already know what's up with that, but we're still young yet."

"Youth is simply a state of mind. So don't let your young age fool you. More youth are dying than any other age group. The church is filled with the elderly and the cemeteries are filling up with young people. I remember a time when it used to be the other way around. Now, with that said, I befriended you because you needed help. There are plenty of other souls out there for me to try and rescue. I don't ram my beliefs down anyone's throat. I try to lead by example. I respect your agenda. I just ask that you respect mine."

Keisha leveled an admiring glance at Marlene. "You're okay, Marlene. I really like talking to you. A lot of what you said makes sense. I don't know enough about your friend, Jesus, one way or the other. But I do know the state of my affairs. I barely have enough money to feed my kids—but I do see that it might get better soon. So please don't mind if I reserve my judgment on whether I should give any more thought to the man you refer to as your best friend, your savior. Let's just enjoy one another's company tonight. Our jailed men at least give us something in common. Let's drink on getting in to see them tomorrow?"

"I second that," Rosalinda chimed in.

As her mission from God was steadily becoming clearer, Marlene smiled at the two young women. She saw that a big challenge lay ahead of her, but she was up to it.

Smiling at each other, everyone clinked their iced-tea glasses together in a toast.

CHAPTER TWO

Early morning light streamed in from the outside, casting a bright light on the window table, where the small group of women and two children were preparing to eat breakfast. Keisha's head bobbed up and down to the soft music as she repositioned each one of the babies in the high chairs. After breaking up Zach's toast into manageable pieces, Rosalinda placed the saucer in front of him on the high chair tray. Keisha sat down next to one of the high chairs and Marlene immediately said a blessing over the food.

Rosalinda sat quietly, marveling at Marlene's ability to pray so effortlessly.

Marlene raised her head. "I hope the prison line isn't as long as it was yesterday."

Keisha laughed. "You better pray for something that's likely to occur. I've never been out here when there hasn't been a long one. We just have to get there super early."

"That's still no guarantee," Rosalinda said. "Some of the women camp out in their cars all night. With their kids."

"Why would women do something like that? Is it really that serious?"

Keisha nodded. "That serious, Marlene. Desperate people do desperate things. I'm one those people. So I understand the desperation. Getting in to see our men is our top priority."

"What are you so desperate about? You're so young."

"Youth has nothing to do with it when you have two kids, no husband, and are on welfare. Welfare and food stamps are barely enough to keep my head above water."

Marlene shook her head. "But didn't you realize that after the first baby? Why have another if it's so hard?"

Keisha gave Marlene a hard look. "It sounds like you're judging me. If so, you need to mind your own business. I don't need another judge and jury. My momma has both jobs covered, all the way from Atlanta. She even acts as the executioner on occasion. She sure as hell would love to execute my kid's daddy."

Marlene covered Keisha's hands with hers in a soothing way. Her eyes easily conveyed how sorry she felt for upsetting her. "No, sweetie, I'm not judging you. I'm trying to understand. I work with the youth at our church. They don't seem to know why they do certain things, either. I can't help out if I don't understand. I'm just amazed at the loyalty that all you young women display for these men behind bars. In fact, it's mind-boggling."

"Loyalty is only half of it. Going back to welfare, people often become a product of their environment. If all you've ever known is welfare and poverty, what are you supposed to do?" Rosalinda asked. "Who are you supposed to learn from? Who are your role models when everyone you know is in the same boat? Everyone talks the talk, but no one wants to walk the walk. I'm not on welfare, but I have a terribly hard time of it. I can't even get county assistance for my mother because I make over the limit. Since when are children financially responsible for their parents? That's a bunch of bull they've been feeding me. I'm appealing their decision, too."

Marlene was eager to learn more from these two fascinating young women. By understanding them, she felt she could be much more effective as a Christian, not to mention more understanding in her job as mother, friend, and foe to her troublesome adult son.

"She can't understand us, Rosalinda. She probably hasn't had to do without a single thing in her entire life," Keisha lashed out.

"Now who's being judgmental? You don't know any more about my life than I know about yours, Keisha. But I'm trying to learn. I'm trying to understand why some have so much and others have so little. I'd like to know what this world is coming to. I already know why."

"Why don't you ask the God you speak of so often? I believed in

God, too, once upon a time, once upon a blue moon," Keisha countered. Anger reigned supreme in her brown eyes.

Marlene smiled gently. "I used to feel that way. When I lost my first child, a little boy, to SIDS—Sudden Infant Death Syndrome—I actually cursed God. I know better now, but I had to learn to surrender my will to a power greater than myself. It wasn't at all an easy feat."

Keisha was astonished at how peaceful Marlene had remained when confronted. As she wiped off Zach's hands with a napkin, her eyes never left Marlene's face. She didn't know what the older woman had, but she knew she'd like to have some of it.

Rosalinda lifted Zanari out of the high chair. She also appeared amazed by Marlene's quiet spirit.

"I'm sorry about the loss of your baby, Marlene." Keisha briefly touched the older woman's hand in a soothing manner. "Real sorry."

"Me, too," Rosalinda remarked, feeling bad for Marlene's loss.

Keisha stood up. "We'd better get going. If we get there too late, we won't get in at all. This is the weekend, when everyone seems to come out in droves. It'll be a zoo up in that joint."

Keisha looked over at Marlene. "By the way, if your man is so innocent, how did he end up being imprisoned at CCF?"

"I wish I could answer that one, but I can't. It's an awful situation." Marlene's expression showed her pain. "That's why we have to get Jesse out of there in a hurry. I feel confident that we will win the appeal. I also believe that God has this matter firmly in hand. Jesse has been His good and faithful servant since he was barely out of his twenties. And nothing has changed in all these years. Jesse would never do the things he's been convicted of. Let's have a word of prayer before we take the journey right into the heart of the black man's hell on earth."

The prison visitor parking area was already loaded with cars by the time Marlene pulled her car into the lot. Keisha and Rosalinda followed right behind her in their new rental. The morning sun blazed with a scorching heat. The line of visitors was longer than the day before.

Marlene, Keisha, and Rosalinda finally took their places in the unending line.

Keisha then saw Alexis a few steps behind them. "No, she's not in this line! I can't believe Miss High-and-Mighty got a date with a prisoner. Maybe she's not as prim and proper as she'd like everyone to think."

Rosalinda snickered. "I don't know who she thinks she is, but I know she's not getting into this prison with that low-cut blouse on. Someone needs to tell sister-girl the truth of the matter. Showing all her boobs might work in other places, but not up at this joint."

Before turning to Keisha, Marlene eyes gave Rosalinda a gentle scolding, but she didn't verbally call her on her distasteful remarks. "Why don't you go tell her about the rules, Keisha? I have some nice things in the trunk of my car. We don't want her to get up to the front of the line only to find out she can't get in for the visit."

Keisha bristled. "If you're so concerned, why don't you tell her? Why should I do it?"

"Because she might appreciate it more coming from someone younger. If she's anything like what you two already have her pegged as, she won't be expecting it, period. You'll do a great job. Go ahead and show her how big your heart is. You'll feel real good about yourself afterward."

A reluctant Keisha looked doubtful about her mission. She didn't want to do it. But she couldn't seem to refuse Marlene. "I don't know about this, but I'll give it a try. I hope you're gonna be responsible for what happens if she catches an attitude. If that's a weave on her head, she'll be wearing it around her neck. No, that can't be a weave. It's way too short and cute."

Laughing, Marlene and Rosalinda watched Keisha as she walked back to talk with the beautiful Alexis Du Boise.

"Excuse me, miss, but we thought you should know that you can't get inside with the blouse you're wearing. It's too revealing. The prison has rules about inappropriate clothing. But I was told to offer you something else to wear."

Alexis looked down her nose at Keisha. "I don't recall asking for a fashion consultant. No one tells me what to wear. I'm Mrs. Richard James Du Boise III. Thank you for your offer, but I can assure you that I won't be needing it."

Keisha clenched and unclenched her jaw. "Shame on me for dropping in on your planet! If you'll excuse me, sister-girl, I'll just mosey on back to the real world." Keeping her anger in check, Keisha turned around and walked the short distance back to the line.

"We had that heifer pegged just right. She's lucky I didn't snatch her bald. She got her nose stuck so far up her butt trying to smell me that she can't even smell her own funky breath. She had the nerve to talk down to me. The same way she looked at us last night in the hotel bar."

Rosalinda started cursing in Spanish. Looking back at Alexis, she rolled her eyes. But Alexis wasn't paying her any attention. Her eyes were trained on the front of the line. When loud shouting occurred, everyone's attention was drawn to a prison guard having a heated debate with a young black woman.

"How you going to turn me away like that? How was I supposed to know that you couldn't wear a sleeveless blouse? Why don't you all tell people these things before they come way out here?"

"You'll have to take that up with the inmate you're visiting. They get a copy of the rules. It's up to them to pass on the information," the guard informed the visitor.

Alexis looked to Keisha. Her expression said that she'd like to take Keisha up on her offer, but it appeared that she didn't know how to voice it.

Reading Alexis's expression perfectly, Marlene handed her car keys to Keisha. "Take these and go to the car. Get something out of the trunk for both women. We really need to help one another out. We're all sisters in the Lord. Hurry so they don't lose their space. We've already been waiting a long time."

Keisha reluctantly took the keys from Marlene. Keisha told the other woman what she was doing, but she only nodded to Alexis, who followed her to the car without comment.

At the back of the car, Alexis slipped the sweater over her blouse. "Thank you for your help. I'm sorry about earlier. I've been on edge ever since my husband got busted and convicted for something he's not guilty of."

Keisha quickly decided not to address Alexis's husband's guilt or innocence. "You're welcome, but you need to thank the lady in the line with me. This is her car, her clothes, her suggestion. She says we have to stick together. I think she's right. She was glad to help out."

"I'm glad, too," the other woman said. "I would've been crushed if I hadn't been able to get inside. I have to catch the bus way out here.

My boyfriend would've had a fit if I hadn't shown up. I'll thank the lady for the top and give it back to her after the visit."

The three women hurried back to the line. When they stepped back into their original places, no one seemed to get upset.

The metal detector was one thing, but getting patted down like a criminal by the women prison guards was the hardest part for Marlene. She'd visited Jesse when he'd been located in the county facility, but it didn't compare to this unsettling affliction. She detested the way the guard had tugged at the underwire on her bra. Her hands had roamed and stayed a little longer than necessary on her person. Visitation was a humiliating process. Marlene would be glad when this was all over.

Immediately, Keisha noticed that Alexis didn't have a clue about what to do. Assuming it was her first time, Keisha stepped out of line to show Alexis the ropes. "Take your driver's license up to that desk. They'll give you a visitor's pass. You'll get a locker key and then they'll show you where to lock up your things. I'll see you in the visiting room."

"Thanks again." Alexis frowned. "Do you bring your kids with you every visit?"

Keisha nodded. "I can't afford a baby-sitter. You never know what's going to happen out here. One day can turn into two or three. Do you have kids?"

"No, we travel way too much for that. We've always thought of kids as a drawback. But I wish you the best of luck with yours. And I do appreciate all the help you've given me."

"See you later, but take good care of yourself if we don't." *Drawback? You and your husband are probably the drawbacks.*

Noon had come and gone by the time everyone began to settle down in the cafeteria-style visiting room. Marlene took inventory of the row after row of long tables and metal chairs set up for the visitation. Lined against one wall all sorts of vending-machine foods, snacks, and drinks were offered for sale. Three microwave ovens were stationed on one long counter for thawing and heating the frozen foods sold to the inmates and their visitors.

Marlene's heart fluttered when she saw her husband coming toward her. Dressed in dark denims, official prison visiting garb, Jesse Covington stood six-foot-one. In his early fifties, he was a dignified-looking black man, with nice salt-and-pepper hair, even white teeth, and a muscular body.

Adoringly, she looked into Jesse's eyes, stifling a giggle. "When we got turned away yesterday, I feared I might not get to see you at all this weekend. What was going on in here?"

"A fight broke out between some rival gangs." Marlene shuddered. Discreetly, he pointed out a few of the bad seeds in the bunch. "There are a few tough guys in here. They try to run everything and control everyone. But I'm not worried or afraid."

"Even though I saw a lot of things at the county level, Jesse, I'm surprised to see how beautiful and young some of these women visitors are. I don't understand what they see in some of these men. I just can't see why they'd drive way out here every single weekend."

"They probably can't help the way they feel any more than you and I. I don't think they'd fall in love with a criminal if they had a choice. Maybe they fell in love before their guys got into trouble. Love doesn't discriminate, Mar. People do."

"You always see the good side of everyone and everything. That's what I love most about you, Jesse Covington."

Marlene pointed out Keisha, Rosalinda, Alexis, and their men to Jesse. When her eyes fastened onto six-foot-three, sinewy, and extremely handsome Richard James Du Boise, she was momentarily fascinated with his good looks.

"I met the two younger ones yesterday, when I gave them a ride to the hotel, after their rental car broke down. I just met the classy one in the lobby. Have you met her husband? I can see that he's really good-looking."

"I rarely see any of these men. Many of them are not on my floor. I haven't met anyone officially. I hear names called, but I don't try to memorize them. I stay to myself to steer clear of confrontations."

With tears in her eyes, Marlene squeezed Jesse's hand affectionately. "That's probably wise, Jesse. I want you to keep yourself safe."

While glancing at the three women and their mates, she mentally formed questions she'd like to ask later. For one, how Keisha's man had gotten that deep scar in the back of his head. Marlene saw that Keisha looked thrilled to see her boyfriend. He was a fairly nice-looking young black man, tall and skinny. Marlene had seen that he had a deep gash at the back of his skull when he'd first walked in. His light brown complexion was rather red and patchy with a slight case of acne.

Keisha smiled broadly while Zach Martin played with his son and daughter. She glowed as he kissed and hugged each. "Don't I get some of that sweet affection, Mr. Martin?"

Zach grinned. "Are you trying to tell me you're jealous? Come here and let me give my best girl a hug. The right guards are in here today. Otherwise, hugging wouldn't be cool. Unless you coming or going. You know how it works, baby girl. You been through here enough times."

"I know. Just thought I'd mention it." Keisha leaned into Zach for a hug. "I aced all my tests at school last week. I'm actually computer literate now."

Zach scowled. "I don't see why you're all into that school mess. You need to have your big black butt at home taking care of my babies. Education ain't all that. There are folks up in here with master's degrees, but what good's it doing 'em?"

Keisha glared at Zach in exasperation. "No school—no welfare checks, no money on your books. Welfare reform is no joke. I thought you'd be happy for me. I can take much better care of the kids with a good job. Sometimes I feel like I have three kids when you say stupid stuff like that. You need to come correct."

Zach gave Keisha a venom-filled look. "Speaking of my books, did you put any cheese on them? I'm down to my last five dollars. I can't stand that damn dog food they expect us to stomach in here. It looks like gravy train after liquid's been poured over it."

"Your finances are straight, Z. But back to talking about getting better prepared. What's going on with the classes you were signing up for?"

Zach tuned her out. When Keisha looked ready to cry, he gave her an emotionless hug. Then the kids interrupted the anything but a Mahogany moment with crying. That irritated him.

"Can't you stop them from all that crying? You're spoiling Zanari and making Zach soft. This racket is getting on my damn nerves."

"You're the one who insists they come every weekend, so you can play daddy for a few hours. But all you do is rag on me. Nothing I do seems to please you."

Zach hugged her again. This time, with feeling. He hoped to quell her rising anger. Keisha was known to cut off his money supply when she got perturbed. But it usually didn't last long.

Keisha got the strangest feeling, one that chilled her to the bone. She somehow began to see Zach in a different light, especially when she looked over at Marlene and saw how much she and Jesse appeared to be into one another. They seemed so happy. Then she looked at Rosalinda and Ricardo, who held hands as they chatted quietly.

Around five-eight, Ricardo was an attractive Hispanic in his early twenties. He wore his long black hair in a ponytail. The tattoo skulls and crossbones on his reddish-brown arms were done in black and white. The other numerous tattoos were very colorful. His neck was also etched with what appeared to be small blue numbers.

"I miss you so much, Ric. I wish we could drop down on this floor and make love like we've never done it before. I'm so happy to see you I could cry."

"Don't talk like that, 'cause you know I can't do nothing about it in here. This place sucks. The food is terrible in here and I'm tired of being locked up like an animal. Did you bring some money? I got one cigarette left and I'm out of hair products and deodorant."

It hurt Rosalinda when Ricardo didn't bother to ask how she was doing or even to inquire about her mother's health. Instead of confronting him, she inhaled the searing pain and stored it inside her belly. Lately, every time she tried to get romantic with him, he made her feel silly.

"Don't I always bring money? I work long hours, Ric. Then I come home and take care of Mommy. She's not getting any better. Between the money I'm paying for her care and for your lawyer, I'm practically bankrupt. But do you even care?"

"Don't start that 'poor me' crap, Rosa! The few dollars you give me is not bankrupting you. How can you tell me you love me and complain about helping me out? Another thing, you haven't been at home to accept my calls the last two times. What's up with that?"

Rosalinda started to feel guilty, as usual, even though she saw that all Ric did was blame her or someone else for his problems. But she loved him too much too say anything else to upset him. Their times together were few and far between. Besides, she had another whole week to get through without him. She didn't want to face that week with him the least bit angry at her.

"I'm sorry, Ric. I didn't mean to upset you. About the phone calls, I've been working overtime at my second job. One of the employees has been out sick. I don't get home till late."

Rosalinda wanted to tell Ricardo that she was tired of the large phone bills every month, but that would also bring on his anger. Like Keisha, Rosalinda couldn't help noticing how loving Jesse seemed to be with Marlene as she stole a covert glance in their direction.

Rosalinda smiled at Marlene when she caught her looking their way.

"Jesse, the three women I pointed out to you are a real challenge for me. I somehow get the impression God has orchestrated our meeting. I'm still waiting to find out why. I sense that He wants me to help them in some way. In all the time I visited you downtown, I never felt compelled to get involved with the other women."

"Be careful now, wildflower. Don't go jumping to conclusions. He may have sent them to you for an entirely different reason. But you'll have all the answers in due time, His time."

A fight suddenly broke out between two inmates. In a matter of seconds it became ugly and brutal. As one of the inmates punched the other one in the kidneys and ribs, cursing and shouting came from the other prisoners. When the two men went down to the floor in a bloody battle, loud sirens sounded and armed guards came running from every direction.

Many of the visitors stared in stunned disbelief as the guards scuffled with the two inmates. From the comments being shouted back and forth between the two men, it sounded as if the girl visiting one inmate was the ex-girlfriend of the other one involved in the fight.

"All visitors line up against the far wall until some sort of control is obtained!" a guard shouted. "Stay calm but move quickly. This is a volatile situation that could turn deadly."

Scared and fearful for themselves and their loved ones, the women were shaking uncontrollably. All visitors were rushed out of the prison.

An immediate inmate lockdown was inevitable.

Out in front of the prison, visitors scattered about the grounds, heading for the parking lot. Keisha and Rosalinda anxiously waited for Marlene to show up. They were happy to see that she was okay when she finally exited the building.

Marlene was still shaking. "This place has given me the absolute jitters. It's been horrible. I can't stand the thought of what Jesse has to endure in that wicked place. Dear Lord, please keep my husband safe." With tears in her eyes, she looked back at the entryway.

Keisha stepped forward and embraced Marlene. "Calm down. You look really shaken. This happens a lot. If a fight or something breaks out, they put everyone on lockdown. It's hard to get used to. But if you're going to come here, what you just saw is one of the things you'll come to expect. Since this has happened, are you going to spend another night at the hotel?"

Marlene cringed inwardly. "I have to. If I don't, I won't know how he's really doing. But I'm not so sure my heart can take much more of this. This is something I can't ever come to expect. I don't know how you do it." She took a moment to compose herself. "Are you two going to spend another night at the hotel?"

Looking totally stressed out, Alexis joined the other three women, as they discussed another night of accommodations at the hotel.

"We really don't have the money," Keisha explained. "We'll just have to come back next weekend. The guys will call us and let us know they're okay. They always do."

"Since you all have been so nice to me, perhaps I can help out," Alexis said. "I'll pay for the extra night."

Surprised by the offer, Rosalinda frowned. "It's not just the price of the hotel. We have a rental car that has to be turned in. We're just about tapped out."

"My entire check for next payday is already spoken for," Keisha added.

Alexis smiled, showing off a beautiful set of even white teeth. Marlene thought that her beauty was breathtaking. More so when she acted the same way she looked.

"Not to worry. I can afford to take care of everything. Let's go back to the hotel and get something to eat. We can visit with one another over a hot meal. I'm sure the kids are extremely tired and hungry." In an awkward attempt to show compassion, Alexis briefly touched both Keisha and Rosalinda's hands. She only warmly embraced Marlene with her eyes.

Keisha was skeptical about the offer, but she agreed at least to discuss it. Keisha, the kids, and Rosalinda got inside the replacement rental vehicle. Marlene and Alexis walked to their own car. The three vehicles departed the parking lot at the same time.

Seated in the front seat of the rental, Rosalinda rolled down the window, allowing the hot air to rush through her fingers. "What do you think of the change in Miss High-and-Mighty, Keisha? She certainly turned humble all of a sudden."

"She seems nice, but I can see that she's not used to coming to any prison. I wonder what her man did to get himself locked up. Like everyone else, she swears he's innocent."

"So, do you think we shouldn't let her pay for the room and car?"

"I'm not saying all that. 'Cause I do want to see Zach again. I think we can let her pay, but we'll pay her back. I don't want us to be beholden to anyone. Is that cool with you, Ms. Rosa?"

Rosalinda grinned. "Cool! The guys will be surprised. I can hardly wait to see the look on my man's face when I roll up in there again tomorrow."

"How was Ricardo? Was he happy to see you?"

"If I'm honest with myself, I think he's happier to see the money I put in his commissary account. He said he only had one cigarette left. He says it's not healthy to borrow anything from the other inmates. They just might want something he's not about to give in return if he can't pay the loan back in a reasonable amount of time."

Keisha laughed. "Yeah, like his virginity."

"His virginity? Ric been knocking boots so long, he don't know what that word means."

"Not from his booty he hasn't!"

"Girl, Keisha, you didn't have to go there. Those are fighting words. They'd have to kill Ric if they try that on him. It would definitely be on up in there. He ain't going out like that. Ric ain't no one's punk."

"Are you sure they haven't already succeeded? Ric's been in and out of jail just like Zach has. He wouldn't tell you if it happened. No man is going to share something that deep with his woman. His so-called manhood would not allow it."

Rosalinda scowled. "I don't like this conversation. He says there's no way it can happen to him, but I know it's just his ego talking. I don't like to think about it. That makes me sick. Let's talk about something else. What do you have a taste for in the way of food?"

"Ugh, how can you think about food after talking about sex? At any rate, we're not going to have much of a choice there. The hotel menu's very limited. Burgers and fries are good. Since Miss Thang is paying for it, I should order a T-bone."

"Have you forgotten that we promised to pay Miss Thang back, Keisha Reed? At your suggestion!" Both women dissolved into laughter.

The three cars pulled into the hotel parking lot, one right behind the other. After parking, the women got out and walked toward the hotel entrance, each lugging one of the children. Keisha and Rosalinda stayed a few steps behind Marlene and Alexis.

The sun had already settled behind the desert's mountain range by the time the foursome met up again. Having ordered their individual meals, the women looked somewhat relaxed seated in a booth inside the hotel restaurant. The kids weren't with them. Alexis had paid for them to go to the hotel nursery. Instead of the soft music normally piped in, the music sounded livelier. It had a definite urban flavor.

Keisha folded her hands on the table. "Our men have been in and out of jail ever since we've known them, but what about you two? I get the impression that this is the first time that you two have been faced with something like this."

"Jesse would never do the things they've accused him of. They stopped him for a traffic violation. Said our church van had been used in a crime. When they searched the car, they found an empty 7-Eleven bank bag hidden behind the tire well. Several bags of money were stolen from the store during an armed robbery. Jesse would never commit such a crime as that."

"Are you sure? I never thought Ric did the things they said he did. But he had. He's been in and out of jail six times or more in the last two years. I don't think he's guilty this time."

Alexis raised a perfectly arched eyebrow. "If he's been in jail that many times, what makes you think he's anything *but* guilty? What makes you stay with a man like that? You could do much better, I'm sure. You're not an ugly woman by any means."

Rosalinda felt as though Alexis had talked down to her. Her body language said that she didn't like it one bit. As the waiter appeared, Rosalinda decided to wait until he set the food down before she told Alexis exactly what she thought. Rosalinda had to wait a bit longer when Marlene insisted on saying the blessing.

Rosalinda looked at Alexis with unveiled hostility. "Have you forgotten that your man is in the same place as mine is, behind bars? What gives you the right to judge my man or my reasons for being with him? What does it have to do with looks? You're unbelievably beautiful, but your man is still in jail. Isn't that so?" Rosalinda's head bobbed up and down and jerked back and forth as she talked.

Alexis was clearly offended by Rosalinda's cutting remarks. Throwing her napkin in the center of the table, she jumped up from her seat, prepared to walk out. Marlene stayed her with a gentle hand. Looking ready to defend herself if necessary, Alexis sat back down.

"Let's talk this out calmly. We're all in the same predicament. We can discuss these things without being at one another's throats. We can't resort to judging. We need to help one another through this difficult time," Marlene reasoned in a gentle tone. "We all have a burden."

"I thought she dropped in off another planet, but you two must come from the same place," Keisha said to Marlene. Her tone became harsh. "She thinks money makes her better than us and you think you have a monopoly on loving Jesus. News flash! Guilty or not, your men are in jail, too, subject to the same ugly conditions as ours. Godliness and wealth do not separate them from anyone else inside that hellhole. Okay?"

Marlene moaned. "I don't think I have a monopoly on loving Jesus. And you're right about the situation our men are in, but we don't have to tear each other down. We have to be supportive of one another."

Alexis looked uncomfortable. "I'm sorry. I shouldn't have said what I did."

Keisha sucked her teeth. "Why not? You meant it! You've been uppity from the start. We've tried to be nice to you because of Marlene. We've been in your shoes before as a first-timer. But people like you think they're a cut above the likes of us."

Alexis rose from her seat. She then removed several twenty-dollar bills from the pocket of her pants. Folding the money in half, she threw it in the center of the table and pointed at it. "That should take care of everything. As for being a cut above the likes of you, you're wrong. I'm a cut above most. As you might crudely put it, I'm outta here. *Ciao,* ladies!"

With their mouths gaping wide, the three women watched as Alexis walked away, strutting her fancy stuff as if she owned the world.

Rosalinda blew out a huffy breath. "The nerve of her!"

Keisha picked up the money and counted it. When she saw that there was way more money there than needed, she whistled. "The snooty heifer is rich! Gotta give it to her."

Marlene looked solemn. Her expression caused Keisha to apologize for her vulgarity. "At least she kept her word," Marlene commented. "I wish that hadn't happened. I'm glad I've met all three of you young ladies. I had high hopes of us becoming friends. Maybe it can still happen, once cooler heads prevail."

"Don't count on it," Keisha interjected. "But I'm curious as to what she's going to do at the prison tomorrow without someone there to guide her silly behind. I suddenly feel used."

Rosalinda took the cash from Keisha's hand and waved it in the air. "As long as she's passing out the mean green, she can use me up. Don't feel bad, Keisha. You've been nice to her, considering you've wanted a piece of her from day one. Helping her out made you feel good. That's what counts."

"Ladies, let's get back on track. We can go on as though nothing bad happened. We'll just continue to pray for Alexis. Now that we have that taken care of, Keisha, why is your children's father in jail?"

"Running a bootleg CD and video operation. Before you ask, he's guilty. He's supposed to be applying for a computer class so that he can eventually get into a work release program or get released to a halfway house."

Marlene was puzzled. "What's a work release program, Keisha?"

"He can work during the day but has to be in lockup at night and on weekends."

"I had no idea such things existed. What about your friend, Rosalinda?"

"Selling drugs, mainly marijuana, but he's not guilty this time. He was set up. Someone stashed crack cocaine in his house and called the police. Selling crack cocaine carries a mandatory sentence while powder cocaine gets those white boys a slap on the wrist and possibly probation. He thinks one of his homeboys is in on it. I hired a private attorney to appeal."

The waiter served coffee and dessert and then he quickly disappeared.

"That lawyer is way too expensive. Rosalinda already works two jobs and takes care of her sick mother," said Keisha. "In my opinion, she's crazy to be paying that much money out for Ricardo."

"Who asked your opinion? You've had your phone cut off numerous times for accepting Zach's collect calls from hell, which probably adds up to way more than Ric's legal fees. Ricardo was set up. End of story."

"Stay calm. You are best friends. What's wrong with your mother, Rosalinda?"

"She has renal disease. Her kidneys are in terrible shape."

"I'm sorry about your mother. I'll keep her lifted up in prayer."

"Thanks, Marlene."

"Jesse is innocent. He wouldn't even consider a deal when it was offered. I think I may know who's responsible. But I'm not sure. I'm working on getting the truth—and I will."

"Who?" Keisha asked.

"Like I said, I can't say for sure. I don't want to call it until I can."

Loud salsa music penetrated the room, startling the three women.

"Would you ladies mind having a word of prayer before we separate? That's if you can hear me above the loud music."

Without comment Keisha and Rosalinda exchanged uncomfortable glances. They bowed their heads out of sympathy for Marlene, who looked ready to break into tears. Once the check was paid, they stepped into the corridor.

At the elevator, they bade Marlene a good evening.

CHAPTER THREE

Even though the prison visiting line was extremely long, as anticipated, Marlene, Keisha, and Rosalinda had gotten there early enough to commandeer a spot close to the front. The sun was hotter than it had been the day before. Not even a slight breeze stirred the air. Cheerless faces sweated trickles of water as the heat swarmed and wrapped around the visitors' heads like a wool turban. Babies were crying and the older children looked downright miserable as they fought to withstand the high desert temperature.

Marlene looked around for Alexis. She felt disappointed when she didn't see her in the line. She had hoped that amends could be made between the four of them before the actual visiting occurred. Tempers had been short the previous evening. Marlene attributed it to everyone being tired and frustrated. It had been a long wait to get inside. In her opinion, the abrupt end to the visit was probably what had caused the women to become edgy and moody.

Once the doors were open, the line moved quickly. The visiting processing didn't seem to take nearly as long as the day before. Marlene was grateful for that. Outside of her dislike for being patted down like a common criminal, the wait to process through was the part she had hated the most about the visit.

Unlike before, Jesse had already picked out a table for them when Marlene made it to the visiting room. He smiled when he spotted her at the doorway. Lifting his hand, he waved so that she could see him. Smiling, she made a beeline to where he sat. His brief embrace, all that the rules allowed, left Marlene hungering for more.

"Thank God you're okay, Jesse. If Friday hadn't been a work holiday for some of these women, they wouldn't have seen their men at all. This can't be easy on you. Two days in a row of inmates fighting has to be hard on a person. Is it like this all the time?"

Quietly observing the other males, he took a quick look around the room. "There's something going on in here pretty much all of the time. There aren't so many physical altercations as there are verbal ones. Somebody is always jawing at someone. It's usually about a bunch of nothing. They fight over card games, sports, what's on television, the phone lines, and anything else they can think of. It doesn't take much for someone to get a verbal battle going."

"Like it is sometimes down at the church." They both laughed.

"Thanks for that bit of humor, wildflower. But I'd trade the nonsense at the church over this madness any day of the week. I do admit that there are times when I think our church folk are going to come to blows. It can get pretty rough when some of those Christian egos clash."

"Christians, my foot! Some of our members have got nothing but the devil in them, Jesse. They're always spoiling for a fight about something, at least a couple of times a month."

It felt good for Jesse to laugh. Marlene's sense of humor always brought a good chuckle from him, especially when she was coming down on the few troublemakers in his congregation. For the most part, she handled the troublesome group with kid gloves. But there had been a few days in the past twenty-plus years when she'd taken off the gloves completely.

"If it's not too upsetting for you, can you tell me what a normal day is like in here for you? I just want to know how you spend your time."

He shrugged. "Some of us wake up pretty early around here, but it's not a requirement. You know me. I've always been a morning person. Can't get a thing done lying in bed. If you want to eat breakfast, the guards take you down section by section, until everyone is brought in. The same goes with lunch and dinner. Nothing formal about getting there or the setting after you're in the dining hall. We can sit anywhere we want. Me, I find a table off to myself. I wonder if some might consider it rude of me, but I'm just trying to play it safe.

The most worrisome part for me is when the guards do the head count. But they have to make sure everyone is present and accounted for. That's their job."

"Besides during meals, do you stay in your cell all the time?"

"I've been to the library a couple of times. I was interested in knowing how much of the reading materials in there are inspirational. I was surprised and pleased to find that they have quite a few books on Christianity, as well as many other forms of religion. The Muslim community has a heavy presence inside and outside of these walls. The few that are inmates are always trying to convince others to convert. They're still demonstrating what happens inside your stomach when you eat pork. From what I've heard from a couple of the guards, the Muslim prison ministry is one of the best ones offered."

"The guards actually talk with you about stuff like that?"

"There's some pretty decent guys that work here. They also know I'm a minister. And they're privy to my record, which lets them know I've never been in any legal trouble in my life until this incident. They're pretty smart at figuring out who's who and what's what."

"I thank God that you have someone to talk to. Being isolated from the outside is horrible enough, but for you not to have someone to talk to on the inside isn't a pretty thought for me. But there are some women that I've heard talking while we're waiting in the line to get in—and they seem to have nothing good to say about the guards. Why do you think that is?"

"Just like with anything else, there can be bad ones among the good. I figure if I don't do anything to provoke any of them, I won't get to find out firsthand who the bad ones are. There are inmates in here who purposely like to aggravate those in authority. They're not satisfied unless they're being yelled at or worse. I can hear a lot of it going on all during the waking hours. There's more trash-talking going on between the guards and inmates than I could've ever imagined. You won't find me talking trash to either group, that's for sure. I'm going to sit here quietly until the good Lord sees fit to sign my release papers."

Marlene's eyes filled with water. "That's something I never stop praying for. I can't wait for the day to come. Do they have any type of educational programs?"

"Interesting you should ask. Just this morning, I did a little reading up on all the things they offer as incentives to the inmates. For one, they offer computer business applications. I've signed up for that one, but I may never get it. There's a long waiting list, and I don't plan to be here for any long length of time. Since we're living in the age of high tech, I thought I could benefit from learning to use the computer, especially instruction on Internet usage. I never had time to learn it because I've been too busy running the church. Now I have nothing but time, but the classes are full. The irony of it all. The prison offers both commercial cleaning and horticulture. The self-help groups include Alcoholics Anonymous, Narcotics Anonymous, marriage and family counseling, and an alcohol chemical treatment series."

"Sounds to me like you did more than a little reading."

"You could say that. Some of the statistics I read were rather startling. Out of a population of 873 inmates, 432 are white as opposed to 317 African-Americans, 34 Hispanics, 85 Indians, and 2 Asians. That leaves the race of two other inmates unaccounted for."

It was hard for Marlene to smile as her mouth turned down at the corners. It saddened her that her once extremely busy husband was reading prison manuals to while away the lonely hours. "Is the entire prison population mixed in together?"

Knowing what she was really asking, he smiled softly. Do you have to come in contact with people who have committed extremely violent crimes such as murder? He was sure that that was the question she hadn't been able to bring herself to ask.

"Violent offenders are housed in separate units. Armed robbery is considered a violent offense. No one being killed is what kept me out of that unit. Still, this prison does house other types of violent offenders. Yes, they're mixed in with the nonviolent prison population. Please don't worry about that. I wear the full armor of God every waking and sleeping moment."

"I would be lying if I said I don't worry about you, about what goes on in here, but I try not to. This is an alien world to you, Jesse. You don't speak the language, you don't know the culture, and you're totally unfamiliar with the fast and hard rules played by the others in here. You're a very intelligent man, but you're completely ignorant of the things that govern this particular world. It seems to me that ignorance can get you killed in here."

"It's very true what you have said, wildflower. But He knows all things of all worlds. It is in Him that I put my faith and trust. This is a place where I don't dare to walk alone. 'Be still and know that I am God.' Psalm 46:10. That verse stays with me at all times. Every single day I read the story of one of Jesus' followers who was wrongly thrown into jail. Not too much different than the one Daniel survived, this is simply a modern-day lion's den. A falsely accused Joseph also ended up in a place like this. You know the stories by heart, Marlene. I just ask that you keep them in mind when you begin to worry. Do you believe wholeheartedly in my innocence?"

She would've been highly offended by his question under normal circumstances. "Of course I do. That's something you never have to doubt."

"As it is the same with God. His word should never be shrouded in doubt."

"Amen, Jesse. Amen."

Marlene looked up just in time to see Alexis come into the room. She smiled at her, but Alexis didn't even bother to acknowledge her presence. Marlene was sure Alexis had seen her. How quickly some people forget. Marlene wasn't one to make people feel beholden to her, but she wished Alexis could've shown some appreciation for how everyone had rallied to assist her with her predicament just a short time ago. A smile and a friendly hello didn't cost a thing. They were the least expensive things in the costly world of today.

Alexis sat down at the same table with Rosalinda and Ricardo, but she acted like Rosalinda didn't exist, either. Marlene observed Rosalinda's reaction to Alexis's direct snub of her. Rosalinda leaned over and said something to her boyfriend, something that made him laugh and look at Alexis. Marlene was glad she wasn't within earshot of the comment. But she hoped that Rosalinda hadn't been too unkind. Marlene was also glad that Keisha hadn't been the one Alexis had ignored in such an obvious way. Keisha was more verbally explosive than her best friend was. There was plenty of hard work for her to do if she was ever to get Rosalinda and Keisha on the path to righteousness. Hard work, but also a labor of love. It was looking more and more like Alexis could benefit from it, too. Marlene took another look at Alexis.

R.J. looked at his wife and smiled. "You are one beautiful woman. What did I ever do to deserve you?"

"I still haven't figured that one out yet," she joked.

He grinned. "What took you so long to get in here? Visiting started over twenty minutes ago. You had me thinking you weren't coming at all."

She shook her head. "You obviously have no clue what's it's like to get in here. The lines are longer than the ones Mama used to have us standing in when they were handing out surplus cheese. These women that bring their children out here are also clueless. I wonder how many of those kids have suffered with sunstroke? It's hot out there. There's not a shady spot or a single shade tree on the entire grounds. There's nothing out here but desert dust, hot concrete, and menacing barbed wire. Neither the outside or the inside of this place is fit for humans."

"Lighten up, Lexy. You're breaking my heart. I got to live in this place."

"I'm sorry. I just can't stand it out here. I've seen more strange-looking bugs outside of here. I'm surprised I haven't seen a snake." Just thinking about snakes gave her the willies.

R.J. laughed at the expression of utter distaste on her face. "It's too hot for them during the day. But I'm sure they come out to play at night."

"Maybe we should change the subject. You know how I hate those creepy crawlers." She suddenly looked disheartened. "I miss you. I miss us. My life just doesn't seem right without you being right there in the midst of it. You've always been there to carry the load. I don't know how I can keep this up." She looked into his eyes. "I'm sorry. I shouldn't be talking like this." She really didn't know what else to say. Everything that came to mind seemed so insensitive.

"How was your last trip to the salon? Your favorite place for taking a time-out."

"I couldn't seem to get as relaxed as I normally do. It seems that Paul hasn't heard about our predicament yet. He hasn't mentioned a single word about it. If he knew, he wouldn't be able to keep his tongue from wagging. During the massage therapy, all he talked about was how he and his lover are considering adopting a child. Do the courts really allow two men to adopt children?"

"I don't know. It probably has happened more than we know. I know that single people are adopting children all the time. I'm glad that we decided never to have them. Kids go through too much today.

Do you ever wish that we'd gone back on our decision not to have rugrats?"

"I never think about it. Our lifestyle has always been too fast-paced. We wouldn't have had the chance to do half the things we've done. I can't imagine dragging a couple of screaming kids to Paris and Rome. Seeing the misery and hearing the screams of the kids that these women bring way out here is enough to make any childless woman vow to never have them."

"Why don't you just come out and say it, Lexy?"

"Say what?"

"That children are nothing less than a pain in the rear." They both dissolved into laughter.

"Yeah, we're far too selfish to have kids. They would've done nothing but be in the way. I can't imagine me running to soccer or T-ball practice or being a member of the PTA. God forbid. Combing hair and packing lunches isn't something I could ever see myself doing. My nails would stay in ruin. What would I've done with them when we played tennis at the country club or when we took a cruise to the Mediterranean last year? I certainly would've had to give up my bridge club meetings. No, we've had way too much to do to be saddled with bratty kids."

Alexis knew that she didn't believe a word of what she'd just said. R.J. had long ago made the decision that they'd never have children. When he made a decision, it was usually final. Alexis rarely challenged him on anything. Life was simpler that way. She just went along with the program. The money and the lavish gifts he always presented to her had kept her content. Contentment had flown right out the window with his conviction. She wasn't sure she would ever find contentment in anything again. Money had suddenly become her worst enemy. It was the love of money that had caused the troubled flood waters to rise up and take R.J. down under.

In many ways Alexis felt sorry for R.J. Her husband was a man who didn't think he needed anyone or anything. She understood a lot of what drove him, but there were also things about him that she'd never come to understand. Still, that didn't stop her from loving him.

Bounced between his parents' homes, during their bitter divorce, R.J. had felt as if he'd been forced to take sides. He could never tell either parent that he'd had a good time with the other after the visits. It had been an awful situation when both parents, traveling together, had been killed in a car accident on the way home from what had been reported as a bitter day in court.

Relatives had taken R.J. in, but after the insurance money ran out, no one had seemed to want him. It was then that young Richard James Du Boise had taken to the streets. Nothing had come easy for him after that. R.J. had learned every street hustle and scam that was out there. It was the money from those activities that had put him through college. R.J. saw himself as a self-made man.

"What's up, Lexy? You seem to be lost somewhere in outer space."

She laughed away her insecurities. "Just thinking about the things we're going to do when you get out. We'll have so much catching up to do. Paris in the spring sounds divine."

"Yeah, that's what I'm talking about. Kitten, continue to believe that it's going to happen. No one can keep a good man down. Money is power, baby. You wait and see. Don't worry your pretty little head. I got it covered."

Alexis wanted to throw up. It seemed to her that R.J. still didn't get it. If money was so powerful, then why had things gotten to this point? Why hadn't he been able to walk away from the embezzlement charges before a conviction was handed down? Money wasn't as powerful as he'd made her think all these years. Those were the questions she longed to ask him, but she already knew the answer. *Don't worry your pretty little head about anything. I got it covered.* That was his answer to every question she had about this case and about their personal finances.

For a brief second Alexis allowed her gaze to encompass Marlene and Jesse. She then scanned the room for Keisha and Zach. Seeing them laughing and holding hands made her wonder if she and R.J. would ever sound that happy again. Since they were sitting at the same table, she could hear Rosalinda and Ricardo's conversation. They sounded happy enough.

But was everyone really as joyous as they appeared? Didn't appearances have a way of being deceptive? How could anyone be happy being locked in a room that they couldn't get out of until the locks were electronically released? With no way just to walk out the doors without assistance, the visitors also became prisoners. Alexis felt like a prisoner with no way out.

Another glance at Marlene and Jesse was all it took to have Alexis wishing that she and R.J. could get back what those two seemed to have despite the bars separating them.

Marlene noticed Alexis looking at them. Before Marlene could smile at her, Alexis jerked her eyes away and turned her attention back to her husband. That bit of attitude from Alexis made Marlene become more determined to warm such a cold heart. Alexis wasn't as unaffected by or as immune to people as she wanted others to believe. Behind that snobbish, smug, self-assured attitude was a woman scared of her own shadow. Marlene would bet her last dime on what she thought was a very accurate assessment of one Alexis Du Boise.

"Marlene," Jesse called out to her, snapping her out of her thoughts. "How are things financially? Are we getting by okay?"

"You know how thrifty I am, Jesse. We're more than okay financially. I've socked away more money than you are aware of. I called it saving for a rainy day, but I didn't expect this type of stormy weather to hit our lives. I knew we'd more than likely have to weather a few rain showers. If they were to come, I never imagined them turning into major storms, or for them to last more than a short period of time. Finances are the least of our worries. God has also blessed us in that area. I've done a little investing over the years. It's been paying off."

Jesse frowned. "The appeal process is a costly one, wildflower. Major Townsend doesn't come cheap. He's only one of the best defense attorneys in the business. Despite our defeat, his legal representation is still very much sought after."

Marlene wished she could tell Jesse that Major wasn't charging them, but she'd promised not to. It had been a condition Major had placed on her in taking the case. He had told Marlene that, as a lawyer, he believed wholeheartedly in Jesse's innocence. As a member of Jesse's congregation, he believed unequivocally in Jesse as a true and faithful servant of God. Above all, he believed that God would crown them victorious in the appeal process. She had also been sworn to secrecy regarding the appeal defense fund that the various church committees had started in Jesse's behalf.

"Townsend is getting assistance from God in mounting a great defense for the appeal. We can't lose with that combination. As you've said on numerous occasions, there are reasons for all this darkness, reasons for the false conviction. We just have to wait for God to shine His revealing light down on us."

Jesse massaged the back of his wife's hand. "You have no idea how much better your comments make me feel. I can wait on the Lord. Knowing that you're willing to wait on Him, too, means a lot to me. I know you probably think this is harder on me than on you, but I'm withstanding the rigors of prison life. I couldn't do that without God. It also makes things even easier for me to endure when you're here to support me in every way possible. In other words, I couldn't do this without you, either. We're going to be okay, wildflower."

"I believe that, Jesse. If I didn't, I would have lost my mind by now."

Jesse bowed his head and Marlene did the same. Hearing her husband praying with such reverence immediately calmed her fears. She missed sitting in church listening to him deliver profound messages, missed his presence in their home and in their bed, missed them having morning and evening prayer together. Jesse had led them in devotion every single morning and had closed out every evening with prayer and song of praises.

As Jesse lifted his head, his troubled gaze met with his wife's. "There are some things that I need you to do for me. Things that I should have taken care of long before."

"Anything for you, sweetie. You look so concerned."

"In all these goings-on, I forgot to appoint someone to look after Sister Childress and her seven kids. I don't have to tell you the state of poverty in which they live. Then there's the Rucker family. They've come to count on the weekly food baskets. And don't forget Brother Boone and his need for transportation to the dialysis treatments. I hate to admit that lately I haven't thought much about anything but my appeal."

Marlene squeezed his fingers. "It's all been taken care of, my love. Has been since shortly after you were brought up here. We all knew that you had a lot on your mind. What things I didn't know about, I looked up on your personal calendar. Everyone is getting what's needed. I'm taking care of most of your extra duties, but I've also solicited help from several of the deaconesses."

Tears escaped from his eyes as he blinked hard to hold them back. "This is why we're so good together. We're always able to anticipate each other's needs. We can count on each other no matter the circumstances. You have always been my soul mate. Thank you, wildflower, and thank you for remembering all those things that I temporarily forgot."

She wrinkled her nose. "You're welcome. Everybody that you've mentioned sends to you best wishes. As for us, we have always been good together. Riding the bus the night I met you had been the only option I had in getting home. I remember being furious with my cousin when he didn't pick me up as promised. But after I started talking to you, I would've been mad had he showed up at the next stop, like he usually did when he was running late." She giggled. "I'm telling you this story like you haven't heard it a thousand times already."

"That's okay, sweetheart. I could stand to hear it a few thousand times more. Besides, your sweet voice has a way of lulling me into a state of euphoria. Marlene, you are my hope. You're all that my dreams have been built upon. As the old saying goes, you can't lose with the stuff you use."

She blushed. "Go on now, Jesse. You're starting to act a darn fool in here. You don't want these people to see me swoon at your big feet, do you? If you keep coming on with it, my big behind is going to lift out of this chair and land right in your lap. You always know how to jet me up to cloud nine."

Gripping each other's hands tightly, they succumbed to their laughter, which instantly caught Rosalinda's attention.

"They seem so happy, while I'm over here thinking about how rough my week was at work," Rosalinda told Ricardo. "So many people have called in sick. That meant I had to work twice as hard."

"Hard work never hurt anyone."

Rosalinda blinked hard, unable to believe what Ricardo had said. That was a strange statement coming from a man who never did a day's worth of hard work in his life. He thought selling dope was a hard enough job. Well, considering how dangerous it was, and the worry of getting caught, she guessed it could be hard.

Ricardo Munoz came from a great family. If anyone should've succeeded in life, it was him. But he'd gotten messed up with some people who were always involved in something illegal. Ricardo had barely graduated from high school. Immediately after graduation, he'd become a tough guy. He'd begun to hang out with street gangs until he was jumped into one as a bona fide member. His family had tried numerous times to pull him back from the brink of destruction, but it seemed that he didn't want to be rescued.

"Rosie, I need you to make contact with one of my homeboys for me. I haven't heard from J-Loco in a while. He owes me some money."

"Ric, I don't want anything to do with J-Loco. That dude is as crazy as his name suggests. His name also speaks of his character."

"I don't have anyone else on the outside to do it for me."

"What if I tell Little Jesus to make the contact for you?"

"That'll work. I didn't think about your cousin, my best dog. I'm trying to be patient with J-Loco, but he's got to pay up. I don't want to have to sic my boys on him. He could get hurt pretty bad."

"Don't do that. You're in enough trouble already. Let me pass the word to my cousin first. Little Jesus will make the contact."

"Thanks, baby. I tried calling my momma today, but she wouldn't accept the charges."

Rosalinda put her hand on top of his. "I know that has to hurt."

"Naw, it don't bother me no more. She has her reasons. Every blue moon she'll accept my call. But it's all good."

Ric would never admit to Rosalinda that it did hurt. There were times when he called the house knowing she wouldn't accept it. Those were the times when he just wanted to hear her voice. He used to get his calls through when his siblings answered the phone, but she had stopped them from accepting the calls after she'd gotten a five-hundred-dollar phone bill. His siblings had been accepting the calls when their parents weren't home. Now, no one accepted them.

"Those calls are expensive, Ric. The phone companies are straight-up robbing people. I'm sure these prisons get some sort of kickback for installing certain company's pay phones. It's a shame how they're making millions off of prisoners' families."

"Don't start complaining, Rosa. I don't want us to start arguing about your high phone bills. We enjoy our phone conversations, so let's just leave it at that."

Not wanting to upset him in any way, she smiled. "Okay. I do enjoy our conversations, especially when we make love." She blushed.

"Don't start that, either. My flagpole can't take it. It feels like it's going to break in two when it gets so stiff, and I can't do nothing about it here in this visiting room."

"Okay, Ric. I'm feeling you. You see that lady over there?" She pointed out Marlene to Ricardo. "When the rental car broke down, she gave us a ride to the hotel. She's really nice. Her husband is a preacher. She says he's innocent."

"Yeah, right. Just like me."

"I thought you were innocent this time."

"Oh, I am. But practically everyone in here says they're innocent. What's the preacher up in here for?"

Rosalinda filled Ricardo in on what Marlene had told her and Keisha about Jesse's conviction. Once she finished telling him the story, he looked over at the couple.

Marlene felt heartsick. The visit with her precious Jesse was ending all too soon for her. Emotional turmoil welled up inside of her every time she had to walk away and leave him behind. A day without Jesse was equivalent to a lifetime without sunshine.

CHAPTER FOUR

Like a caged lioness, Keisha paced the floor in the emergency room at Martin Luther King Hospital. Zanari had suddenly taken ill while Keisha had been putting her to bed. The ER doctor had told her that Zanari was having a serious asthma attack. She didn't even know her daughter had asthma. This was the first time something like this had happened. She'd never had any difficulties breathing before now. Keisha had noticed the rapid rise and fall of her little chest when she'd gone to cover her up. Her little heart had been beating like a jackhammer.

Wasting no time on trying to figure out her daughter's problem, Keisha had whisked her straight to the nearest ER. Zanari had been taken right in for treatment the moment the triage nurse saw her erratic breathing. Keisha was upset with herself because she hadn't thought to call an ambulance. But that had probably been for the best. Emergency response time in the inner cities left a lot to be desired. People needing immediate treatment had actually died because of such a delayed response to 911 calls.

While Zanari was in X ray, Keisha had plenty of time to focus on Zach not being there for his family. There'd been several emergencies that he hadn't been around for. She first thought about the thumbtack that little Zach had stepped on over a year ago. A few months back he'd sprained his little foot while chasing after a butterfly in the park.

Thank goodness she had county medical cards for the kids. Zach had only worked at odd jobs when he wasn't in prison. At any rate, those times were few and far between. He'd never worked at a job that offered anything akin to medical and dental benefits. Zach was a street hustler, one who believed in making lots of money, but with only minimum work input. Zach was into selling anything illegal he could find. If nothing else, he was a good salesman. She had once thought he was good at being her man. She wasn't so sure about that now.

Entering her apartment, Keisha was still in shock over the fact that they'd actually admitted Zanari to the hospital. Her little girl had been sleeping peacefully when she'd left her room in the pediatric ward. Keisha had been told that she should go home and get some rest, that Zanari would probably sleep through the rest of the evening and throughout the night as a result of the medication she'd been given. The nurse had promised to call her should Zanari's condition change for the worse. Keisha still had to find someone to keep little Zach for her. She hated to ask Zach's mom, hated asking her for anything, but there wasn't any other choice for her.

Lucian Martin was the kind of woman who thought her son could do no wrong. In fact, she was in such denial about her son and his criminal activities that it was pathetic. She couldn't count the times Lucian had bailed him out of jail using whatever she could for collateral. Keisha knew that Lucian didn't care much for her, that she thought she wasn't good enough for her son, but she couldn't let that bother her now. She needed a baby-sitter so she could be with Zanari. That was that. Lucian did love the kids, but not as much as she loved her son Zach.

Keisha called Lucian and set it up for her to keep Zach over there for at least a couple of more days. Then she called her own mother, down in Atlanta, another call she hated to make.

When Martha Reed answered the phone, Keisha told her all that had happened with Zanari. Then she prepared herself to hold her emotions in check as the usual lecturing began. Rolling her eyes to the ceiling, she sat back in the chair and listened to her mother break it down for her in no uncertain terms.

"But, Momma . . ."

"But Momma nothing! You need to hear what I'm saying to you for a change. Zanari is going to keep getting sick if you don't make some serious changes in your life. Asthma is often a symptom of emotional distress. If you keep taking those precious babies to that damn prison, things are going to get worse than they already are for those kids. Thank God they're not school-age. Little Zach would be coming home crying every day because of the teasing about his daddy being in prison. If Zach keeps getting himself into trouble, his children are going to have to fight their way through school. Is that what you want for your kids?"

Keisha felt like screaming. She knew her mother was genuinely concerned for the children, but she didn't have to exaggerate so much. Her kids were going to be just fine. Her very own circumstances as a child hadn't been too different from theirs. "Momma, the kids are okay. They love seeing their daddy. The playroom is full of toys and Zach really enjoys me bringing them there to spend quality time with him."

"Quality time! There is no such thing as quality time inside prison walls. You've got to be joking, girl. They love it 'cause they don't know any better, Keisha. Do you want your kids growing up thinking that prison is somewhere to go and play and have a good time? You need to get real. Zach has been in and out of the penal system since you've been with him. He's out for a few months and then he goes right back, leaving you pregnant each time. You got pregnant with little Zach right after he came out of prison before. Zanari was conceived his last time out. He's a habitual criminal. What are you going to do when he gives you AIDS on one of his vacations from behind bars?"

"AIDS! Now, Momma, you're taking this here lecture too dang far. I think I'd better hang up now before we get into a major fight. I don't want to disrespect you, but you can't be saying stuff like that to me. That ain't even right—and you know it."

"Somebody has to say these things to you. Those babies are defenseless. The harm that you do to yourself is your business. What danger you bring to my grandchildren is mine. I don't want to get social services involved in this, but I will fight you for those kids if it means a better life for them. Zach Martin is no good, has never been any good, and will never be any good. You owe it to your kids to give them a better life. There are statistics out there that prove heterosexual women are getting AIDS from their mates who've been in prison at one time or another."

"I'm going to go now, Momma. This is leading us nowhere. Please don't ever threaten to take my kids away from me again. I'm not trying to hear that from you. Do you understand?"

"I understand perfectly. It's you that needs to come to some understanding, Keisha Reed. I've already been where you are right now. I don't want to see you and your kids suffer the way you and your sister and brother did. What you need to understand is that I will intervene to keep that from happening!"

Martha Reed hung up without saying good-bye to her youngest daughter. That hurt Keisha. But she was glad that her mother had hung up on her instead of the other way around. She worked hard at not disrespecting her mother, but there were times when she did just that.

During those awful times, when her mother had berated her harshly, there had been many instances where she hadn't been able to hold back her smart-aleck retorts. Disrespecting her mother always left her full of guilt and remorse. She'd end up apologizing and swearing she'd never do it again. But she always seemed to repeat her bad behavior in the heat of their battles.

Keisha hung up the phone and stomped into her bedroom. Without turning on a light, she lay down across the bed and began to sob her heart out. A part of her knew that her mother was right, but the part of her that couldn't see Zach as others saw him was her biggest problem. That's what had her in as much denial as Lucian. However Keisha was just now starting to see that. What she was going to do about it was the question she couldn't yet answer.

Martha Reed seemed to forget that her own kids' daddy had been a convict. In fact, he'd died in prison at the hands of another inmate when Keisha was eight years old. She couldn't help remembering all those nights she'd heard her mother crying over the phone to her father, telling him how hard it was to raise three kids without him. Her mother had worked two jobs during the week and had also worked a third one on Saturdays. The hard work always left her bone-tired and irritable. Even then, she'd still found time to nurture her kids.

Whoever had said that the apple didn't fall far from the tree sure knew what they were talking about. She'd never compared her children's situation to her own. Her dad had died before she was old enough to really understand his absence from the home. It was true that her mother had never taken them to the prison. But there were times that Keisha wished she had. All she ever had of her father were his letters and the pictures he'd sent home periodically. To this day, neither she nor her siblings even knew why Dublin Reed had been incarcerated. There were probably ways of finding out, but she'd convinced herself that she'd be better off not knowing. It must've been pretty bad, since Martha had refused to talk about it with her kids all this time.

Zach and Zanari deserved to know their father and to spend as much time with him as possible. How could she deny them at least that much? She would've given anything to have had the pleasure of getting to know her own father.

Determined not to let anyone run her life or her children's lives, Keisha decided that she and her kids were doing just fine the way things were now. And the next time Martha Reed brought up the pitfalls of taking her kids into the prison system, Keisha was just going to have to tell her that at one time she herself had also catered to a man in prison. How soon people forget, Keisha thought in irritation. Highly agitated with the things she had to face alone, she put in a call to Marlene, hoping they could chat before she went back to the hospital.

When Keisha had called to tell Marlene she was feeling really depressed over her daughter's illness, Marlene had invited her over to her house so she could have someone to listen to her vent. Marlene didn't invite a lot of people into her home, at least not until she got to know them really well, but she had really taken quite a liking to Keisha and Rosalinda. While seated in Marlene's kitchen, they were deeply absorbed in discussing Keisha's numerous issues.

"There is so much bad stuff going on in my life, Marlene. My baby getting sick has gotten me down something awful. I just don't understand how God can let some of these bad things happen to people. There's homelessness and all sorts of horrible things going on in this world. My money problems are one half of what's wrong with me. I must admit that Zach's issues are more than the other half of my problems. Doesn't God see that we're in dire need down here?"

"I used to blame God for all the bad in my life. One day, when I couldn't stand the hurt anymore, could no longer take the jagged pain of grief and bitter disappointments, I finally realized that God and Jesse were the only good things in my life."

"I understand what you're saying, Marlene, but why do you keep trying to make me believe that your God is so great? What's so great about Him?"

"There are not enough hours in a ten-year span for me to tell you about His greatness. Besides, I promised I wouldn't preach to you or ram my beliefs down your throat. But if you'll trust me, I can show you His greatness. Come to bible study with me. Give it a shot. What have you got to lose?"

"My mind, which is already totally screwed up. My mom is threatening to take my kids away from me. She's serious about it, too. But if God is so good, why is He allowing her to mess with me like this? Why doesn't He put her big mouth and her sinful thoughts in check? Talking about taking kids away from their mother is nothing less than evil."

"I don't think this is between you and God. He doesn't have anything to do with this. Your issues are with your mom. Anyway, why is she trying to take your kids?"

"Zach! What else? My taking the kids up to the prison pisses her off. She just doesn't get it. Those are Zach's kids. He has a right to see them. She says, 'If he wants so badly to spend time with his kids, he should've cared enough about them not to get into trouble in the first place'."

"I see your point. But I also see your mother's point."

Keisha bristled. "How's that?"

"How many times has Zach been in jail since your kids were born?"

"That's beside the point."

"That's exactly the point I think your mother is trying to make."

"Whatever. She should just mind her own business. These are my kids!"

"Do you think your mother loves you and your kids?"

"Of course she loves us. But that doesn't give her the right to interfere in our lives. For your information, my daddy was in prison. He also died there."

Marlene gasped in horror. "I'm sorry. I didn't know."

"Very few people do. That's not something you find yourself talking about over a drink or dinner with your girlfriends. My mother catered to my father in prison just like I cater to my man. The only difference is she didn't take us to the prison for visits. To this day, we don't even know why he was there. That's something she would never talk about. If it was good enough for my mom to look after a man in prison, why isn't it good enough for me to take care of Zach?"

"I see your point."

"Do you really? Do you even care about me as a person? Or are you just feeding me a line of bull to get me down to your church?"

"Keisha, baby, I'm going to care about you if you never step foot inside my church. Caring about other people isn't just about being inside the church. In fact, I think it's more important what you do for people outside of the sanctuary. Jesus loved and cared about people everywhere he went. If He was into picking and choosing, we'd all be in big trouble."

"I don't see myself sitting on no hard-behind pew watching some preacher frantically pace back and forth across the pulpit while frothing at the mouth. Besides, black folks stay in church too doggone long, anyway. What do you all do in there for four and five hours at a time? Don't even try to tell me you're praying all that time. No one prays that much."

"We only stay in for two hours at our church. Forty-five minutes is for bible teaching and then we have a fifteen-minute break between services. The other hour is used for praising in song, prayer, and for preaching. The Lord's day is a day for rest, a day for regrouping and preparing for the next six. The Lord knew what he was doing when he designated a day of rest."

"Two hours? I doubt that! I never heard of no black church ever having a two-hour service. I've been to church a time or two, back in the day."

Marlene laughed heartily. "Back in the day? What do you know about back in the day, girl? You weren't anywhere near being born yet."

Keisha laughed, too. "I mean the seventies when I say back in the day. My mom talks about it all the time. I learned a lot from her about that time."

"For the most part, those were good years. But they go back further than the seventies. Back in the day takes in part of the sixties as well." A sentimental look settled in Marlene's eyes. "The music was sweet back then—and you could clearly understand what the singers were saying. In the seventies silky-smooth-throated Marvin Gaye owned the heart of every woman. 'Distant Lover' brought tears to your eyes. Rufus featuring Chaka Khan upset the rhythm-and-blues charts with their funky style of music. And we can't leave out the soul-stirring Al Green, who is now singing praises to the Lord. 'How Can You Mend a Broken Heart' was one of my very favorites."

"Yeah, I bet them hot grits had something to do with Al Green's music-style changes. That sister worked the brother over with them grits."

"I remember that incident well. It was the talk of the town. Al had the Lord in him before that incident, before he ever became a pop singer. He just returned to what he'd been taught as a youngster. That woman did what she did 'cause she had the devil in her."

Keisha cracked up.

Marlene smiled broadly. "Those Ohio Players had hips moving and swaying every which way with songs like 'Skin Tight' and 'Fire.' Girl, we had some all-night clubs back then. We ushered in the sunrise on many a weekend. I remember when my best friend, Bev, and me practically went to work right from the club on Saturday mornings. Good thing we only had to work a half-day on Saturday. We would've never made it through a full day. After work we'd rush home and lay down for a short time. By nightfall we were right back out there doing our thing. We partied hearty on Saturday nights since we didn't work on Sunday."

"My mom still talks about those days. She cherished them as if they had gold in them."

"They did! Those were golden moments, never to be relived but never to be forgotten. That's why we have those wonderful 'golden oldies' to remind us of what used to be."

Keisha's eyes began to grow misty. Hearing Marlene talking about her memories stirred up her emotions. She remembered all too well how Zach had treated her in the beginning. He'd brought her candy and flowers and had always been on time or early for their dates. She couldn't even count the number of movies they'd gone to as a couple. Zach didn't know how to cook, but he'd bring over pizzas and other fast food when he came over for a night of watching television and listening to good music. If Zach had been doing illegal things then, he'd kept it separate from their relationship.

"Have you ever had a broken heart, Marlene?"

"For sure. That's why Al Green's song about a broken heart was one of my favorites. I was twenty when it happened. It was the only time I ever had my heart broken. That guy did a tap dance, the cha-cha, and the Harlem Shuffle right on my heart. Then I had the nerve to let him come back and do it all over again. This time he tap-danced all over me. I was too through with love after that episode. Our story read like one of those crazy daytime soaps."

"Zach has broken my heart a few times. Unlike me, you only took the guy back once. I can't tell you how many times I've taken Zach back. I don't know what happened to his romantic nature. He still butters me up, but it's not the same as it used to be. Things changed drastically after little Zach came. It got even worse once Zanari was born. I guess I had something to do with that. It was hard for me to have sex with him while our baby was in the same room. He didn't understand that. He said the baby didn't know what was happening. I disagreed. Babies learn what they learn by seeing, hearing, and feeling. Besides, Zach and I get so loud and crazy. If nothing else, our screaming and panting would've probably scared the Pampers off the baby."

Marlene was somewhat embarrassed by their conversation. Her skin had paled a little. The difference in their ages made her a little self-conscious about discussing such a delicate topic as sex with Keisha. She was certainly old enough to be Keisha's mother.

Recognizing Marlene's obvious discomfort, Keisha smiled. "I know the trend that our conversation has suddenly taken is awkward for you. But that's what I like about you. You can open up to me even though you're much older than me."

"Watch your mouth! Don't hold my age against me, girl."

"I don't. As I was saying, it's easy for me to talk about sensitive things with you. Even though I haven't known you all that long. There are times when you are completely nonjudgmental."

"Times?"

"Yes, times! Will you stop interrupting me? I'm having a hard time getting this out as it is." Marlene zipped her mouth with her forefinger, but not before she smiled endearingly at Keisha. "You not only listen to me, I think you actually hear what I'm saying. When I talk to my mom, she only hears her next thought. She doesn't cut me any slack whatsoever. We used to be so close. That is, BZ."

"BZ?"

Keisha doubled over in laughter. "Before Zach!"

Marlene gave a belly laugh. "You're crazy, Keisha!" Her eyes softened as she looked at the young lady sitting across from her. "You're right, I am much older than you. But I'm sitting here with you like I would, back in the day, with one of my best girlfriends. We used to talk about life, politics, sex, men, and more men for hours on end. We seemed to never run out of things to discuss. That's some of what I like about you and me as friends. We're able to open up to one another. I'm old, but I'll never be too old to learn. I feel as though we're learning from each other. We both have something to bring to the table, something very worthwhile. I might get a little embarrassed when we touch upon certain subjects, but I'll get over it. If I had a daughter, I would hope that we would be able to be as open with each other as you and I are being right now. Love is born out of respect. Although I may not always agree with you on how you see things, I need you to know that I will always respect you and your views."

Keisha wiped the tears from the corners of her eyes. "Thank you for that. Rosalinda and I are like that with each other. I love Rosalinda. She's so sweet, so very loyal. She's having a hard time with her mother being so ill. On top of diabetes, she just learned that her mother also has lupus. I didn't ask her exactly what that was or what it meant because I felt stupid not knowing."

"Remember that the only stupid question is the one not asked" Marlene said. "Lupus is a disease that causes the immune system to attack the body's own tissues and organs. There are three types of lupus: systemic, discoid, and drug-induced. The most serious of the three is systemic. It can be very serious and there's no cure for it to date."

"Wow! Maybe I need to find some information on it if I'm going to be there for my girl."

"It can't hurt. I'll give you the 800 number for the Lupus Foundation of America in Rockville, Maryland. When's the last time you saw Rosalinda?"

"A couple of days ago. As you know, the buildings we live in are right next door to each other. She was supposed to come over last night, but she didn't. Ric's lawyer called and wanted to see her right away. Something other than her mother's illness is bothering her, but I don't know what. I'm going to find out, though. Rosalinda has a tendency to stuff lots of garbage before she decides to exhale."

"Don't we all!"

"Since we've talked about Zach and me, I want to hear about you and Jesse."

"As I said before, I was too through with love. I didn't fall in love again, promised myself that I would never be that stupid again. Fell in and out of infatuated lust a couple of times, but never in love. Not until I met tall, dark, and handsome Jesse Covington. Girl, that man stole my heart without my even knowing a thief was in my presence. It didn't take me long to realize my heart was MIA—missing in action. The only time it would beat was when he was around. It was like he carried my heart deep inside his shirt pocket. The only time I came alive was when Jesse was there with me. However, I was smart about love this time around."

"What do you mean?"

Marlene giggled like a schoolgirl. "I played hard to get. I had that boy's tail going in circles. Believe it or not, 'You Got Me Going in Circles' became our favorite song. He'd call me up and sing the lyrics over the phone. He could sing, too. No, the boy could sang! Those were the golden days back in the day." Looking like she had found the pot of gold at the end of the rainbow, Marlene got to her feet. "All of a sudden I'm hungry. I've fixed some potato salad and baked beans to go with the beef ribs I barbecued early this morning. Would you care to eat with me? I know you have to get back home before long, but I'd love your company a while longer." Marlene handed Keisha the portable phone. "Call the hospital to check on the baby."

"Beef ribs? I've never had them." Keisha dialed the hospital number and waited for someone to answer.

"In that case, you're in for a real treat. They're good, especially with my special sauce. Would you mind getting the plates while I warm the food?"

"Not at all." Keisha got to her feet.

Marlene pointed at the cabinet where she kept the dishes. "The silverware is in the center drawer. Thanks for your help."

While Keisha talked with the nurse in charge of Zanari's care, modern technology allowed Marlene to warm the food and place it on the table in less than twenty minutes. Keisha learned that Zanari was still asleep. She promised the nurse she'd return to the hospital at the first light of dawn. Before sitting down with Keisha, she retrieved a fresh pitcher of ice-cold lemonade from the refrigerator. Seated at the table, Marlene passed the blessing.

"Is everything okay with Zanari?"

"She's still sleeping, as was predicted." Keisha lifted her fork and picked a large piece of egg out of the potato salad. "So, what's your son, Malcolm, like?"

"That depends on who wants to know." Malcolm dropped down into one of the chairs at the table. He extended his hand to Keisha. "I'm Malcolm. Maybe you can find out what I'm like for yourself. I've got nothing but time."

Marlene raised her eyebrows sharply. "Boy, if you don't move away from her, you're gonna be sorry you have me for a mother. This is girl talk up in here."

Malcolm roared. "Girl talk! Mom, in case you haven't noticed, you haven't been a girl for nearly half a century."

Marlene swatted Malcolm's face with the back of her hand. "Shush your disrespectful mouth, boy. For sure, you're getting way out of line." All three of them busted into laughter.

"Ain't you gonna hook a brother up with a plate, Mom? Them ribs got my name written all over 'em."

"The only thing I'm going to hook you up with is a right hook to your eye," Marlene countered pertly.

Despite her flip remarks, Marlene jumped right up and began fixing Malcolm a plate. She loved waiting on the two men in her life. In the absence of Jesse, all she had was Malcolm to pamper and baby. And Malcolm loved to be waited on, loved not hearing his father fussing at her for lavishing too much attention on their only child.

"I've been sitting here for several minutes now—and I still don't know your name."

"Keisha Reed. Pleased to meet you, Malcolm."

"Oh, you're the one in love with the convict!"

Marlene could've died on the spot. She got so nervous that she actually felt her heart thumping forcefully against her ribs.

"Yeah, I am. And you're the one who's stuck on himself, the one who thinks he's all that and a bag of something or other," Keisha countered with sarcastic pleasure.

"Who told you that?"

"The same person who told you that I'm in love with a convict."

Simultaneously, their eyes turned on Marlene.

Embarrassed to no end, Marlene smiled sheepishly. "Malcolm Covington, that wasn't a very thoughtful or nice thing to say to Keisha. You owe her an immediate apology."

Malcolm turned to face Keisha. "Don't you think my mom should be the one to apologize since she's been gossiping about both of us?"

When Keisha began laughing, Marlene and Malcolm followed suit.

Covertly, Malcolm studied Keisha while they ate. He was used to women swooning at his feet. Age wasn't a factor, either. Older women loved him as much as the younger ones did, if not more so. In fact, at sixteen, he'd lost his virginity to a woman ten years his senior. But here he was sitting across from the one fine sister who hadn't so much as given him a second glance.

"What's up with you, Keisha, girl? What do you see in men behind bars? Can't you get a real man to come on to you? You're fine enough."

Keisha cut her eyes at him. When she saw Marlene about to interject, she held up her hand. "I got it, Marlene. First off, it's none of your business what I see in any man. Second of all, if you're going to step to me, you better come correct. I don't know what you're used to from other women, but you don't phase me with your Michael Jordan wanna-be black behind."

He looked at her in disbelief. "Girl, you trying to dis me? I ain't going out like that."

"You may not go out like that, but you're going out of my kitchen. Finish that food and go somewhere and find someone who wants to listen to your bullcorn!" Marlene shouted.

"You better listen to your mother if you want to stay healthy. Neither one of us is trying to hear the noise you're talking, Malcolm Covington. For sure, I'm not listening. You don't impress me in the least."

Malcolm got up. "Girl, you want me. You want me bad. And we both know it. Stop fronting for my mom." He walked over to the kitchen counter and scribbled something down on a napkin. He carried the napkin back over to the table and laid it beside Keisha's plate. "Here's my private number. It only rings in my bedroom. Call me later."

Before Keisha or Marlene could respond, he took off running. They could hear his loud laughter as he sped through the hallway.

"Where'd you get him from? He really thinks I could be interested in him. He's sure enough handsome, but far too immature for me."

Marlene smiled. "You're right about my son. He's got more confidence in his looks than he should. A man who cares only about his looks is usually a man of little substance. I can't wait for the day when Malcolm comes into his own. If he turns out to be half as good as Jesse is, he has a chance at being a great man." She couldn't help wondering what his chances at life really were. Malcolm was constantly dancing on the outer edges of hell.

Marlene got a strange look in her eyes. Keisha had seen that look in her eyes before. She wished she knew what it meant. Something told her not to intrude upon Marlene's deep thoughts. She respected the fact that some things were very private, no matter how good friends you became with someone.

Keisha thought Zanari looked so tiny lying in that big hospital bed. It had been a nightlong ordeal for both her and the baby. Zanari had suddenly taken a turn for the worse, but the doctors on duty had worked hard to get her asthma back under control. Keisha had never feared anything like she had last night. Losing her daughter to death would have been her undoing. The fact that Zach wasn't there for her and Zanari made her feel even worse.

Glad that Marlene had come to offer her much-needed comfort, she felt compelled to say a prayer; Marlene had said plenty of them since she'd arrived in the early hours of the morning.

Looking frazzled, Keisha scowled. "I want to communicate with your God, but I don't know how to pray, Marlene. How do I start? What words do I say?"

Marlene smoothed Keisha's hair back from her face. "He's real easy to talk to, Keisha. Talk to Him like you're talking to your best friend, Rosalinda. Without the profanity, of course."

Keisha relaxed enough to laugh, which Marlene was happy to hear.

"Just let go of the worrisome things you're thinking, the bad stuff you're feeling inside. Just let go. Give it to Him. It works."

"People always close their eyes. Why is that?"

"Just one form of meditation. Closing your eyes helps you to relax and get in touch with the higher power. But you don't have to close your eyes to pray. I pray with my heart and my brain all the time, with my eyes wide open. I'm in constant prayer. You have to be nowadays."

"I can't imagine that. I'm usually cursing someone out in my head and in my heart. For instance, take Zach's mother. That woman can make me cuss a blue streak. But I'd never curse her to her face. I would never disrespect her like that. She sure can make me mad as hell. Oops, sorry. I keep forgetting that you're a Christian."

"What you need to do is stop cursing and then saying you're sorry. You do it out of habit. When Zanari and Zach start saying those same exact words, you're going to go upside their heads. Just remember that kids live quite a bit of what they learn at home. As for cursing people, it doesn't matter whether you do it to their face or not. The sin is in thinking it. If you're thinking it, it's just the same as saying it. The penalty for such is also the same. Speaking of Zach's mother, why can't you get along with her? She's the kids' grandmother."

"It's not me that can't get along. I have tried repeatedly to find some common ground with her. She doesn't even bother to try, period. She gets along with very few people. But she still doesn't realize that she's the major portion of the problem. Zach says his father left her for another woman cause she was so darn evil all the time."

"How awful for her. She's probably hurting, too. Perhaps you should be the bigger person. Continue to reach out to her if at all possible. She may eventually come around."

"Huh! And get my head bit off? I don't think so. Anyway, been there, done that. Trust me, the lady's bites are filled with poisonous venom. To change the subject, purposely, how's your jive-behind son, Malcolm?" Keisha laughed. "See, you can be proud of me. I controlled my tongue that time. I'm sure you can guess what word was on the tip of it."

Marlene laughed, too. "The boy thinks he got a job. Finally! If he gets it, he'll only be working four hours a day. Nonetheless, he'll be working. For how long is the question. He gets a job, but after a couple of paydays he finds a reason to quit or he gets himself fired. He's been dropping in and out of city colleges since graduation from high school, but he still has a long way to go before he can even think of finishing. Things haven't been good between us. I'd put him out if I could."

"If you could? Why can't you?"

"Why can't I what?"

"Put Malcolm out!"

"He's my child."

"So what? It just so happens that he's an adult child."

"Some needy woman would just take him in, anyhow. He's always had a soft cushion to fall back on. Someone will rescue him."

"That someone is you. It's my guess that you don't know how to let go of him. He's never going to grow up if you keep treating him like a baby."

Marlene shifted her eyes. "As young as you are, what do you know?"

"More than you think. You and Zach's mother are a lot alike but also a lot different."

Marlene and Keisha turned around when Rosalinda entered the private hospital room carrying a large, stuffed white monkey.

Smiling, Rosalinda hugged both women. She then went to stand over Zanari's bed. "I see that our little angel is sleeping. I was hoping she'd be awake." She put the monkey at the foot of the bed. "I hope my get-well present doesn't scare her to death. What were you all talking about when I came in? It sounded a little heated."

Keisha shrugged. "Marlene's son, but it wasn't nothing bad." Keisha filled Rosalinda in on their conversation up to the point of the subject of Zach's mother.

"When you said Zach's mother and me were a lot alike, what did you mean?" Marlene asked.

"You believe in your God and she believes that Zach is God. You both think you're helping your sons, but you're not."

"The same way we're helping Ricardo and Zach?" Rosalinda questioned Keisha. "We aren't doing any different with our men than they are with their sons. What we do for those hardheaded busters is not helping, either. We've bailed them out of more situations than a lot of mothers would do."

Keisha eyed Rosalinda with curiosity. "What you talking about, Rosa?"

"Okay, Arnold!" Everyone laughed at Rosalinda's reference to the old television sitcom *Diff'rent Strokes.*

"I just think we've done too much for our guys, Keisha. They don't appreciate it. We've known that for a long time, but we still continue to go for broke in supporting them."

"Yeah, that's right, but what I'm talking about is somewhat different. I'm talking about Marlene's inability to let go." Rosalinda didn't see any difference in the two situations, but she decided not to say any more to Keisha.

"I think I could really let go of Malcolm if circumstances were different." Marlene fiddled with a hangnail on her left hand. "I'm ready for it now. But I fear for him. What if he gets hooked up with the wrong people? He's easily influenced by other people, mostly the ones who don't want anything out of life. He goes along with whatever the in crowd is doing. He can't seem to make his own decisions, even in how he dresses. He doesn't stick with anything he attempts for any length of time. It seems to me as if he thinks he has to fit into a certain mold in order to be accepted.

"It sounds to me like he's already hooked up with all the wrong people and he's doing it right from your house. Malcolm chooses his friends, good or bad, just like everyone else does. Malcolm chooses to do what he does. And you choose to shelter him from the real world. It's that simple. You've told me enough about him for me to know that you've spoiled him rotten."

"Maybe. Your comments are certainly worthy of much thought. I do know it's time for him to grow up and take responsibility for himself. I can't do this forever. Jesse Covington has to be my main focus in life right now. I've let too much time slip away already. Yeah, Malcolm is going to have to start fending for himself. No more enabling from me is the answer."

"It's easy to talk the talk, but hard to walk the walk. I say the same thing about Zach all the time. I threaten to kick his butt to the curb at least four to five times a week. But as you can see, I'm the only one that has her back pressed up against a cold hunk of cement. While standing in the line out at that prison, I see so many women that are in the same cramped-up place as I am."

"I've been thinking about that very thing," Marlene interjected. "I see the same thing you see every single weekend. I have to include myself in that, but not because of Jesse. I'd like to talk with each and every one of them. Just want to offer them some encouragement. Some of them look so defeated, like they've given up on life. I have talked to quite a few women out there, but I have this strong desire to do much, much more. Women supporting men in prison are in dire need of something."

"You could make an announcement inviting everyone to come to your church," Rosalinda suggested. "Or even pass out invitational flyers in the line."

"I got it." Marlene snapped her fingers. "What do you think about starting a support group?" Both smiling, Keisha and Rosalinda nodded. "A support group for women loving men in prison. A place where people can come and share their feelings without being judged."

"It's a great idea, Marlene, but how will you get women to come?" Rosalinda asked.

"The suggestions you made a second ago would be a great start," Marlene remarked.

"Yeah," Keisha jumped in. "There's a lot of ways to advertise the group. For getting the word out, colorful flyers are the in thing nowadays. For sure."

"Area newspaper ads," Marlene added. "We could place ads in the local papers as well as in the area and free community papers. Creating an Internet message board or chat forum is just another possibility. I think this could work. I'll see if we can have the meetings at the church to start out with. Nothing goes on there on Thursday evenings. I'll run it by the church council. I'm sure they'll approve it since we already have a prison ministry in place. This could really go over big with the three of us running it. I'm getting more and more excited about the idea."

Keisha put her forefinger to her temple in a thoughtful gesture. "Any suggestions on what name we should give to the group?"

"Ladies in Waiting," everyone responded simultaneously. Laughing, they gave one another high fives.

"Jesse is going to love this idea. I can't wait to tell him about it."

"I'm sure both my Zach and your Ric will hate the whole freaking idea. For sure, they don't want us to change and stop doing what we're doing for them. I think a lot of the inmates might hate the idea. It could interfere in all the scams they got going involving vulnerable women."

"I know that's right. I'm going to call Alexis tonight and ask her to join us. What do you think about that?" Marlene eagerly awaited their response.

"That sister don't want no part of us." Keisha rolled her eyes in a dramatic way. "She's already shown us that. We're not classy or sophisticated enough for her to hang around with. She's been running hot and cold since we first met her. I think she has more serious issues than we do. But I also think she's been deprived of something more important than money. Love. Maybe you should call her. I guess it can't hurt."

Rosalinda whistled "As rich as she is, she couldn't have too many issues. Isn't money everything?"

"Not if you believe in God," Marlene interjected. Moaning sounds from Zanari kept Marlene from going any deeper into her answer to Rosalinda's question.

Keisha picked up Zanari to soothe her. "Momma's right here. My, you look much better. Her breathing sounds pretty good now." She kissed her daughter on the forehead. "Are you hungry, little momma?" Wiping her eyes with her tiny fists, Zanari nodded. "Okay, big Momma's going to see that her little momma gets fed."

Marlene took Zanari from Keisha. She kissed both of her cheeks. "Auntie Marlene is going to run now, sweetie. You feel better now." Marlene hugged the little girl, squeezing her diapered bottom gently before handing her to Rosalinda. "I'll see you both in a few days. If there's any change in our Sunday travel plans, Keisha, let me know as soon as you can."

"I know I'll be going if you still think you can arrange for someone to stay with Zanari. Zach needs to know that his daughter is in the hospital."

"Consider it done. We'll leave right after I get out of church, but I'll call you with the details. Bye, girls." Marlene waved at the two friends as she exited the room.

CHAPTER FIVE

Keisha finished filling out the booking number to see Zach and handed it to the guard.

He raised an eyebrow. "The woman that just walked away has already registered to see Zach Martin. Do you want to go in at the same time or wait until she comes out?"

Keisha looked shocked. "Are you sure I'll be able to get in later? Our daughter has suddenly taken ill and I need to speak with him about it."

True to her word, Marlene had found someone from her church to sit with Zanari while Keisha visited with Zach.

"You'll definitely get in, but the other visitor processed through first. You don't have to wait until she comes out. You can always go in at the same time once the visiting room is open."

"I can wait for a while." She handed the guard her driver's license.

Keisha walked over to where Zach's slightly obese mystery woman was seated and sat down beside her. She sat little Zach down on the floor at her feet to play. Deciding to introduce herself to the other woman, Keisha thought it best to give her real name so she could see if the other woman reacted to it.

Keisha smiled. "Hi, my name is Keisha! I haven't seen you here before. Is this your first time to visit?"

Keisha's friendly demeanor delighted Tammy Arnold. Weighing in at one hundred seventy-five pounds, she had a lovely face and beautiful dark brown hair. Her smile revealed nice teeth. "I'm Tammy. I come every Sunday for the late visit because I don't work on Mondays. At any rate, I was told that Sundays were the best day for visiting."

That figures, Keisha thought. She and Rosalinda would already be back home by then. They always did the early visit on Sunday when they stayed over, and rarely came back for the late session because of work on Monday morning. "Nice to meet you, Tammy. Do you have a relative up in here?"

Tammy giggled. "Just my man, Zach. Who are you here to see?"

Keisha held her temper in check. She had to get as much information as possible so she could bust Zach upside the head with it. Since Tammy hadn't reacted to her name, Keisha figured that she didn't know about her and the kids.

Smiling cynically, Keisha crossed her legs. "My kid's daddy. What a coincidence, my son's name is Zach, too. Do you have any children?"

Tammy's face broke into a huge smile. "We're gonna go half on a baby when he gets out. We talk about it every night when he calls. I can't wait. I'm about broke trying to keep that Negro in cigarettes and food. I'm gonna have to get another job if he's not released soon."

Keisha felt like throwing up, but she tried hard to hide her inward feelings. She was now sorry that she'd given her real name just in case Tammy told Zach about their meeting. Just as Keisha started to tell Tammy she had to go to the bathroom, Tammy got to her feet.

"Time for me to go in. What did you say your name was? I'm terrible with names."

"Misha," Keisha lied. "I know you've got to hurry, but could you write your phone number down for me? Maybe we could carpool out here sometime. You do live in Los Angeles, don't you?"

Tammy reached into her purse and handed Keisha her business card. Tammy was employed as a beautician. According to the name of the shop, she was also the owner.

"I live in Inglewood. I'm sure you know where that is. Please call me sometime. It would be nice to have someone to talk to who knows what it's like to have a loved one in prison. My family and friends are totally against my coming out here to see the man I love. It's hard when you have no one that understands. Also, maybe I could hook you up with one of the latest hairstyles. With a discount, of course."

"Of course. I'll ring you up real soon. Count on it." Keisha was disgusted and sickened by the whole scenario that Tammy had painted for her. Zach was a dead man!

Keisha pulled little Zach up from the floor and they went off to look for Rosalinda, whom she hadn't seen since they'd registered. When Keisha realized that Rosalinda was probably already inside, she took a seat to ponder the incredibly painful events of the past few minutes.

While looking around the visiting room, as she waited for Jesse to appear, Marlene noticed the Du Buoises seated on the back wall, near the microwave ovens. Looking like a frightened rabbit, Alexis appeared to be holding on to her husband's hand with all her might.

Richard James squeezed Alexis's hand affectionately. "It's good to see you, beautiful. How's my baby holding up?"

Alexis smiled with adoration. "I'm fine. It's you that I'm worried about. More so, after the horrible things I've witnessed out here. I'm always glad to know that you're all right."

R.J.'s jaw clenched tightly. "I'm sorry you have to witness these things. It seems to be an everyday occurrence in here. Someone's always got a beef about something."

"Has anyone tried to mess with you?"

"They don't get a chance. I don't hang out with the masses. I stay in my cell and read a lot. I'm glad for the variety of magazines they have in the library. *Money Market* is my favorite."

His comment sparked an unexpected anger inside her. "That's strange, don't you think? Money is what landed you in this godforsaken place."

"We're not going to get into that, are we, Alexis? We discuss this every day on the phone. I just want our visit to be a pleasant one."

"You haven't convinced me that you're not guilty of embezzling all that money from the brokerage firm. I still have a lot of questions," she whispered. "Questions that you still refuse to answer. Questions that I need the answers to if I'm ever going to have any peace."

"I've answered them a thousand times already. But you still ask the same ones over and over again. What's the point in that when the answers are not going to change?"

Alexis recognized the intolerant look her husband was giving her. She decided to let things rest. He wasn't going to tell her any more than he already had about the charges of which he'd been found guilty, the charges that had landed him in prison. It was a no-win situation for her, as it always was. She didn't know any more about Richard James as it pertained to his business dealings than she knew about some stranger. He never confided in her about business.

"How's your appetite? You look like you've lost a few pounds, R.J."

"There's no way you can work up an appetite in here. I've dared to venture to the gym a few times, but that doesn't even do it. The food they serve looks and tastes like vomit."

Alexis cringed at R.J.'s description of the food. She chewed on her lower lip, wondering if she should ask the question that had just popped into her head. She didn't want him to think her insensitive to his plight. But her future on the outside was at stake. "Do you know how much longer our liquid assets are going to be on hold?"

R.J. wrung his hands together. "I talked with Tom on Friday. It shouldn't be much longer. Lexy, you're going to be just fine. You can always use the money from the accounts no one knows about. Every single dime of that money is legit. I promise you that."

"How can it be legit? You didn't declare it when you listed all our assets. I'm afraid to even look at those bank accounts let alone touch the money in them. I don't want to end up in prison, too. The police are still watching the house as well as stalking my every move." She snorted. "I can just see me standing in the employment line if Tom doesn't clear your name soon. I'm sure there aren't any job openings for a career arm ornament."

"You need to stop worrying about that. That money is yours to use however you see fit. I wasn't going to leave you alone with nothing to live on. The hell with what I did or didn't list. I'm serving time for my alleged crimes. Every day I sit in here, they're getting more than their pound of flesh off my yellow, black behind."

"Are you sure Tom is the best lawyer for you? He doesn't seem to be getting things done in a timely fashion. Has he even filed the motion for appeal?"

"Tom Goldstein is the only lawyer that can handle this. He's been our lawyer for years and he's always come through. His firm handles every conceivable kind of law. An appeal was filed immediately after the verdict. We're in good hands. I'll be out of here before you know it." The look on his face belied the confident way in which he'd spoken.

Alexis couldn't stand to see her husband looking so anxious. "I sure hope so. Our bed is not the same without you. I really miss us having breakfast together out by the pool. It's that time of year, you know. The plants and flowers have all come to life on the property."

"What about our nightly skinny-dipping ritual? Sweet Lexy, I can almost taste your delectable flesh in my mouth. When aroused, you're as sweet, ripe, and juicy as a Texas watermelon. Oh, I can't wait to taste you again."

Alexis blushed. "We shouldn't be talking like that. It's only going to make it harder for us when I have to leave. Do you think we'll ever be together like that again? I get so scared that we may never be together beyond this concrete jungle."

Glad that he was in a prison where at least minimum contact with visitors was allowed, R.J. placed his forefinger against Alexis's full lips to quiet her. "We can't even entertain those type of thoughts. You have to remain positive. I know it's hard, but that's the only way we're going to make it through this."

Briefly, Alexis looked over at Marlene. "Do you see that middle-aged couple over there by the vending machines?"

"What about them?"

"I don't know. They seem to have a serene aura around them. They look as though nothing dark and evil can touch them or penetrate their joy. It's as if they hold a secret that will keep them together forever."

"I think we also have a special aura. Don't you?"

"Not like that. What's between us is damn good. But those two have a golden glow about them. I've never before seen that kind of light. What do you think is missing from our lives?"

"Lexy, where's all this uncertainty coming from? You still believe in us, don't you? I don't think anything's missing from our lives. But from that comment, you obviously do."

Alexis shook her head. "I'm being sentimental and silly right about now. Of course I believe in us. I just feel lost sometimes, especially when I have feelings of abandonment. It's as if I've somehow lost my spiritual connection. I don't know what it is. Do you get to go to church in here?"

"They have services twice a week, but I don't attend."

"Why not?"

R.J. looked from Alexis to the middle-aged couple she'd pointed out to him. Did they have something to do with his wife's strange behavior? "Baby, it's safer to stay right in my cell as much as possible. Is that a good enough answer for you? Or do you want me to be graphic?"

Alexis pulled a quarter from her pocket and spun it around on the table. "I guess it's good enough. If you'd go to church, don't you think things might be easier for you? I feel as though I have some real serious soul-searching to do. Our lives have changed so drastically."

"Would it make you feel better if I went to church, Lexy? Is that what you want?"

"It's not about how I feel or what I want, but it might make you feel better. I remember a time when we went to church every week. It now seems like eons ago."

"I can't remember why we stopped going, Lexy. Do you?"

Alexis shrugged her shoulders. "I don't. I just want to know how we got here from where we once lived and played every day. It's frustrating, R.J."

R.J. raked a hand through his wavy hair as he studied his wife's odd expression. "I don't know, kitten. I just don't know."

Alexis cut her eye sharply at him. "I think you do know. I've witnessed some questionable things, but I put blinders on because I didn't want to deal with the bad stuff. I love you so much. That's what allows me to keep my blinders in place. You need to know that I'm taking them off. I'm also losing the rose-colored glasses that I've been seeing the world through. When are you going to remove yours, R.J.?"

Richard James ran a trembling hand across his forehead. "What are you going on and on about, woman? Something's eating you up on the inside. Give it to me straight, Lexy."

"I've just been thinking about a lot of different things. The people I met have me questioning my lifestyle. I actually thought I was much, much better than they are. That is, until one of them told me I was no different from them."

"Different from them in what way, Lexy?"

"They told me that regardless of my wealth and position, my man is still in jail, just like theirs. Who can argue with the truth?"

"Who are these people?"

"Some women I met outside the prison my first time out here. I later spent some time with them at the hotel. They tried to be friendly to me before that, but I had my rich-snob hat on. Then they turned around and gave me something to wear because they knew I couldn't get inside with the type of clothes I had on. I gave the younger black woman a lot of attitude about her suggestion, but she turned out to be right. I wouldn't have gotten in that day without their kindness. I would've had to go all the way back to the hotel and change clothes. I probably wouldn't have made it back in time to see you. The visit ended prematurely anyway."

"All that doesn't answer my question. Who are they? What is their social standing? Or are they a bunch of ghetto hood rats?"

Alexis gave her husband a look of disgust. "That remark would've made me laugh a couple of weeks ago, but now it only affirms that I don't like what I've become. I guess I'm a hood rat, too, since I also grew up in the ghetto. Or have you forgotten?"

"That's different, Lexy. You may have grown up there, but you never belonged. You've always been a million times better than your environment."

"No." She shook her head. "That's just what you've taught me to believe. You bought me this fake ID with your millions. You molded me into your perfect idea of what a woman should be like, what Richard James Du Boise III's woman should be like. This outer package is a blatant lie. I've decided to go shopping for a new inner wardrobe. Only then will the outer appearance change. And all it's going to cost me is a badly needed emotional release."

"What the hell's gotten into you? You sound like a damn walking advertisement for social change. Are you suddenly turning into a poster girl for morality and such?"

"Like always, you haven't been listening. But R.J. you'd better start. When and if you get out of here, you need to know that I'm not going back to the old lifestyle. I'm not putting my blinders back on. With the naked eye, I want to see you and the world for exactly what they are. I just hope you'll decide to join me in the real world. I love you, but I hate what you've become. I hate what I've allowed you to mold me into."

He looked dumbfounded. "You're serious about this, aren't you? Lexy, I don't know what to say, other than to tell you I think you're being down right ungrateful, not to mention unfair. You've had no problems in the past spending the millions I make, no matter how I've made them. You can't drive that Rolls-Royce in the ghetto. Not without getting jacked. But that's exactly where you'll end up if you make the decision to abandon me. Who do you think is going to take care of you in the style you're accustomed to? I still have the ability to cut your finances completely off. You might want to remember that."

She didn't even flinch at the anger in his tone.

"I guess I'll have to learn to rely on God again. In the same way I did when I was growing up. For sure, you can't take care of a single one of my needs, physical or emotional, locked up in this monkey cage. In all your attempts to flee the jungle, you've landed right in the middle of it. As you can see, there are plenty of Tarzans but no Janes to swing on the bars with. Don't you see that alone as a wake-up call?"

Angry at his wife's comments, R.J. leapt to his feet. "I think this visit is over. You come back when you've cleaned all that hazardous debris out of your pretty little head. This is the one time I need you to be strong for me, but it sounds like you're wimping out on me, Lexy. These people you've been talking to sound like a bunch of Jesus freaks or something much worse. We'll talk later."

"Don't be so sure about that. Like always, you talk, I listen."

In stunned disbelief, R.J. sat back down. "What did you say?"

"You heard what I said, but you don't ever want to hear what I have to say. I talk; you put on earmuffs. And it doesn't even have to be winter. May your dreams be filled with all the evils of money, money, and more money. Money that you damn well can't spend in here."

"Out of all the people I expected to turn on me, you never once came to mind, Lexy."

"I'm not turning on you. I'm only telling you how I feel. Why is it that you have to make all the decisions in my life? Don't you think that I'm capable of making my own?"

"I think you got that wrong. You've always looked to me to make the decisions. I never thought you cared one way or the other to be involved in making the decisions. If you did care, you never spoke up about it."

"Well, I'm speaking up now! If this is the only way I can get my voice heard, then so be it. But I'm tired of listening to your bull. I never said anything back then because you wouldn't have listened if I had. But you have no choice but to listen now. You are a captive audience."

"So, it's like that, huh? I guess we'll just have to see who the captive really is."

Just to prove to her that he did have a choice, that he was still in control, he got up. After giving Alexis a long glare, Richard James walked away and disappeared behind a door that clanked shut once he passed through.

Sorry that she'd treated her husband that way, especially given their circumstances, Alexis dissolved into tears. R.J. simply wasn't used to her thinking for herself or voicing those thoughts. She was sure that stating her opinion was what had made him the angriest. He didn't think she should have one. Now that she'd messed up her visit, what was she to do?

Alexis's eyes were drawn to Keisha when she entered the room. Through her tears, she watched as Keisha and her son sat in the far corner of the visiting room and wondered where the little girl was. Alexis couldn't help feeling something deep inside for both of Keisha's pretty children. When Keisha sat down and settled Zach at her feet, Alexis's heart skipped a beat.

With his last visitor gone, Zach sat across the table from Keisha. For several seconds he watched his namesake playing next to his mother's chair. He then turned to Keisha. "How are you doing, baby girl? I've missed you like crazy. I was surprised to learn that I had a visitor. I didn't expect you today."

"Missed you, too, love." Keisha seethed inwardly but was careful not to show it. "I came out here today because Zanari has been admitted to the hospital. She had an asthma attack, but she's doing much better. I thought you should know."

Zach looked genuinely concerned. "Asthma? When did that start?"

"This is the first attack she's ever had."

"My baby's going to be all right, isn't she? I couldn't stand it if something happened to her. I don't think I could take that."

"The doctors think she's going to be fine. I'm just going to have to watch her more closely, especially for signs of breathing distress. How are things going in here?"

"What can I say? Every day in here is totally unpredictable, but I'm trying to make the best of a bad situation. Sorry I wasn't there for you when Zanari took sick. How are things going otherwise?"

"The same. The kids are a handful when they're well, but when they get sick it's even harder for us. I get frustrated every time I think about you not being there to help me carry the responsibility of home and your kids. Zach, it shouldn't be this way! No woman my age should have to go through this alone."

Zach patted her hand to soothe her. "I know, baby girl, but it's gonna happen for us. Just give me a little more time. The deal's in the mix, baby. Anything new happening?"

Deciding it was time to set him up for the kill, Keisha coughed to clear her throat. "Not really. Oh, I've met several very interesting women during some of my visits, but the most interesting of them all is the real nice lady I met today. She's a cosmetologist. She even offered to do my hair at a discount. I liked her." She closely watched Zach for any sign of discomfort.

When he scratched the back of his ear, something he did when nervous, she knew she'd hit a sensitive spot.

"A hairdresser, huh? Where'd you meet her?"

"Out in the lobby, just before I came in here. I think she'd just finished her visit with her boyfriend. It seemed as though she was on her way out," she lied to throw him offtrack. "She was immediately drawn to little Zach. She and her boyfriend are going to have a kid when he gets out. She said something about them going half on a baby. R. Kelly song, no doubt."

Zach scratched behind both ears now. "What's her name and where's homegirl's shop?"

Keisha was momentarily distracted when little Zach started to cry. In an attempt to quiet him, she lifted him off the floor and positioned him on her lap.

"I'm sorry, Z, what did you ask me?"

Zach looked irritated. "I asked you the lady's name and where's her shop? Why can't you ever pay attention, Keisha?"

Keisha cut her eyes at him for using a sharp tone. "You try doing what I have to do twenty-four-seven with your kids, and I don't think you'd be asking that dumb question. Don't piss me off. I'll walk out of here and never look back. I'm fed up as it is."

Zach drummed his fingernails on the table impatiently. He tried to calm himself before speaking again. "I'm sorry for snapping, Keisha. It's this freaking place. But do you mind answering the questions I asked you?"

Keisha decided to let him stew in his own juices since he'd already confirmed the truth for her by his persistent line of questioning. "I'm sorry I mentioned that I met someone. It seems to have put you on edge. I can't remember her name. I think it starts with a *T.* Sounds like a name for a white girl. It's on the card she gave me, but it's in the locker in my purse. Her shop is in Inglewood."

Keisha sat back and watched Zach squirm in his seat. The game was so good that she decided to play it a little longer, or perhaps even let him figure it out for himself. She knew he wasn't going to stop questioning her until he got the information he was after.

"That sounds like it could be my homeboy's girl. If it is, you need to stay away from that stank-ho and her shop. She's trouble with a capital *T.* She sleeps with anybody who asks her."

Keisha raised one eyebrow. "How would you know that?"

Still scratching both ears, Zach looked uncomfortable. "Rumors! How do you think?"

"What's this so-called tramp's name? Maybe I'll remember if I hear the name called."

Zach struck his temple with his palm, as though he was trying to remember. "Tori, Tamara, or is it Tammy? I know it's something like that."

Keisha frowned. "I'm still not sure. It could be one of those. I just don't know. At any rate, I'll find out because I plan to go to her shop next week. But I don't think we're talking about the same person. This woman didn't seem like a tramp to me. She seems real sensitive."

Zach slammed his fist down on the table, startling Keisha. His son started to cry again.

"I forbid you to go around that dumb heifer. You stay away from her until I find out where her shop is. If it's the person I'm thinking about, you stay out of there. I hear they deal seriously illegal shit from that shop."

"You'd know about the illegalities, wouldn't you? Sure you aren't the supplier?"

Zach gave her a warning look. "You wouldn't be talking that trash if these guards weren't around. Who you been talking to out there in the world, anyway? Whoever it is, baby girl, they giving you bad advice. Advice that could get your pretty face cracked wide open."

Keisha stood up. "Yeah, like I'm about to crack your face with this here good-bye. Since I haven't had the chance to put paper on your books yet, don't bother to check, 'cause I ain't leaving your black behind squat. Say good-bye to your no-account daddy, little Z." Keisha walked out with her son in her arms, leaving behind a highly perturbed Zach.

Keisha nodded at the two custodian inmates as she passed by the security area. When she heard them say Zach's name, she slowed her progress toward the exit in an attempt to listen in.

"That Zach Martin is some dog. I hear that both of his ladies are here today," one inmate said.

"That's nothing, dog. Zach got four other ladies in waiting tramping up in here. A couple of them are big, leggy white chicks. I hear they keep his books tight with the paper."

Having heard enough of the conversation, Keisha sucked in a deep breath, fighting her tears as she looked over at Rosalinda and Ricardo. Lifting her head high, she walked to the front of the lobby, hoping she'd find the strength to kick her worst habit, Zachary Martin, to the curb. No sooner than she'd finished her thought, she stepped up to the U.S. mail slot and placed inside the box the postal money order she'd purchased to put on his books. She hoped it was enough to last him until she came again.

Seated near the vending machines, Rosalinda and Ricardo weren't having an easy time of it, either. Rosalinda sighed heavily. "I'm about tapped out of money, Ric. I have to keep some money to pay for my mom's prescription medicine. She's due for a refill. Your lawyer hinted that I could pay your fees by having sex with him. I should go to the Bar Association about that."

He scowled. "If you do that, we can forget about me getting out of here. I don't think it would be so bad when you think about why you're doing it. I already know your heart is mine."

Rosalinda's expression went from one of shock to downright distress. Out of all the unreasonable things he'd asked her to do during their time together, he'd never asked her to give up her body to someone else. That hurt her deeply. "You would actually want me to sleep with him? It sounds like prostitution."

"I don't think of it like that. I just think we have to do whatever it takes to get me out of here. If you do it this one time, I promise you won't ever have to do something like that again. You love me, don't you, baby?"

"Of course I love you." Rosalinda had tears in her eyes. "I'll consider it, but I'm not at all comfortable with this proposition. Sleeping with a stranger sounds screwed up, but my man asking me to do that for him makes it even worse." Just the thought of it made her feel ill.

Ricardo leaned into her. "Baby, just think of what you'll be doing for us. Think of all the nights that we'll spend making love when I get outta here. In fact, think of me while you're with him. That shouldn't be too hard for you since you think about me all the time, anyway."

She looked at him as if he had two heads. "You want me to imagine that I'm with you while he's doing me? That's so sick! I don't know about this, Ric. I'm not sure I could go through with something like that. I don't know how you can even ask me to do that."

His eyes narrowed in disgust. "Rosie, you don't love me. I can see that now." His use of the nickname Rosie caused her to flinch. He only did that when he was extremely agitated with her. "You just talk a good game. 'I love you, Ric. I'll do anything for you,' " he mocked. "If you don't do this for me, then that makes you a liar. If you won't do anything for me, stop saying it. I bet you're screwing somebody else, aren't you, you little trick? If I find out you're messing with someone else, I'm going to sic my posse on you. When they get through with you, you'll wish you'd screwed that lawyer. You already know what my boys are capable of."

Why couldn't she ever attract the good ones? Why did she always end up with the no-good con artists, the career criminals of this world? Ric's threat to have his boys do her bodily ham scared her. Yes, she knew exactly what they were capable of. She'd already seen some of what they could do to someone they perceived as getting out of line. While brushing away her tears, Rosalinda looked over at Marlene with envy ablaze in her dark eyes.

Marlene was looking at her preacher husband in an intimate way. While smiling at each other, their love shone brightly through. Both of them closed their eyes when Jesse began to pray out loud softly. Jesse smiled at Marlene after the prayer.

Gently, Marlene smiled back. "We've been sitting here chitchatting for a while now, but I want to know how you are really doing, darling. You look so tired."

Jesse let out a sigh. "I'm okay, sweetheart. Not much sleep will leave a man looking haggard, but we're not to worry. God has my back in here. There's a lesson in this somewhere. He'll reveal it when it's time. What's most important is how you are, sweetheart."

Marlene put her hand over his. "God's got my back, too. I miss you. I miss you most when I turn over to catch your warmth—and end up turning into the dreadfully cold spot where you should've been to heat it up. It won't be much longer. God not only hears our prayers, He'll answer them."

"That's my girl. I thank God every day for bringing such a beautiful spirit-filled creature into my life. You complete me, Mar."

"We complete each other, my darling husband. I love you so much. Have you seen your lawyer yet? I haven't heard a word from him since you were sent up here."

"Surprisingly enough, Major came early this morning. I didn't think I'd see him again until Monday. He feels confident that once the appeal process is granted, he can prove that those aren't my drugs and guns. It's a good thing my fingerprints are nowhere on those items. But what good did it do me? The jury still convicted me of a crime I didn't and couldn't commit."

"I know that has to hurt, but they're not there because they're not yours. This shall pass, too, Jesse. We have a lot of challenges ahead of us and a lot of obstacles to hurdle. Even with all our problems, I can't help thinking about the young women I pointed out to you before. It seemed we were on the right path, but the air hasn't completely cleared from the explosion we had with Alexis. I find myself almost back at square one. I'm determined to bring us all together again, but I'm not sure where to start."

Jesse smiled tenderly. "If there's a way to accomplish your mission, I have every confidence that you'll find it. Keep your faith, my angel."

"I try hard not to let my faith waver. The moment I feel fear creeping in, I close my eyes and pray it away. As well as having God in my life, I'm used to having you there to shelter me in troubled times.

Sometimes I have to pray a long time to keep the fear at bay. My biggest fear is that I may never again see you outside these concrete walls. That's the one fear that I must find a way to conquer." She shuddered at the thought of never being in her husband's arms again.

As Jesse took her hand in his, his warmth spread through her. "We're not going to talk or think like that, wildflower. We have to believe that I'm coming home real soon. You have to claim it in His name before it can happen. You already know that."

Jesse fought not only his desire, but also his need to break down and cry. Marlene needed his strength and his courage right now. She was a woman who'd never lived a day alone in her life. She'd gone straight from her father's home to his. Now she was forced to live her life in his absence. With all her strengths, there were times, like now, when she was very fragile. He saw himself as a strong man, a man of God. In God's service, he was a man of power with unlimited resources. But he had to admit that his courage had waxed and waned over the past couple of weeks. He was counting on God to restore his strength and endless power. He'd promised never to forsake his children. Jesse Covington believed in the promise, believed he was a child of God.

As he thought of his own child, he was sure that Malcolm wasn't very much comfort to his mother. The boy was far too wrapped up in himself and his good looks to think about anyone else. Malcolm had broken Marlene's heart on so many occasions. But she was the ultimate in mothers. She'd immediately forgive his wrongdoings. Then she'd put her heart right back out there for him to trample on all over again.

Jesse felt bad that he hadn't taken hold of his son a long time ago despite his wife's objections. The types of discipline he'd had in mind to administer to young Malcolm had never worked for his wife. She'd never failed to come between them in their heated verbal battles.

Marlene's eyes clouded with distress when the guard shouted that the visiting time was up. She gripped Jesse's hand tightly. "Oh, Lord, where does the time go? I've got to get through another whole week without seeing your face, Jesse. How am I going to do it?'

Careful not to provoke the guards, who were known to take away privileges at the drop of a hat, he gave Marlene a quick hug. "By praying, wildflower. That's how. This will be over soon." He believed that with every breath in him, but he didn't know how long she would continue to believe in him. He could only pray that she wouldn't have too long of a wait.

Marlene had a lot of faith, but she feared the system and how severely it dealt with men of color. Often, he'd heard her tell Malcolm that he could end up behind bars for merely spitting on the sidewalk—and that there was no such thing as justice for black men. While she hadn't wanted to make her son fear the police, she'd had to pound into him to respect the laws. The jails were full of innocent people, but the laws seemed to have no way of protecting them from the corruption that ran rampant in law enforcement agencies all over the country. But just as there were innocent men in jail, there were plenty who deserved to be right where they were. A world without law enforcement agencies wasn't the kind of thought he cared to entertain. There were far more good cops than bad ones.

Jesse had a hard time keeping his tears from flowing as he watched the woman he loved disappear on the other side of the door. A door that had just set her free, but kept him locked inside the darkest dungeons of hell. Satan was the ruler of this place, but the long reign of the prince of darkness was coming to an end very soon. Jesse had not a smidgen of doubt about that.

CHAPTER SIX

Despite Zach's objections, Keisha was having her hair done by Tammy. It had already been washed and conditioned. Tammy was now blow-drying it. Nearly filled to capacity, Tammy's modern deco beauty shop, Tammy's Hair Biz, had lots of tasteful black art on the walls. Music from one of the top black radio stations could be heard drifting from the overhead speakers. All ten of the hair dryers were in use, except for the one that was broken and had a FOR REPAIR sign on it. There was one dryer in the shop that everyone referred to as the incinerator because it got hot enough to melt a person's scalp.

"This is a nice place you have here, Tammy. I'm really impressed. How long did it take you before you got your own shop?"

"This was my grandmother's shop, her lifelong dream come true. She willed it to me when she died last summer. I was already working here, so I know all the customers. I split up my grandmother's clientele between all the stylists. However, there were a few customers that only trusted me to do their hair. If my grandmother couldn't do her clients for one reason or another, I always filled in for her. So many of them were already used to me."

"You must be good then. Sorry to hear about your grandmother."

Ready to curl Keisha's hair, Tammy put the large curling iron on the electric heating element. "Thanks, Misha. Who has your kids today?"

Keisha felt guilty that she'd lied about something as simple as her name. "Their grandmother is keeping them for the weekend. My little girl, Zanari, just got out of the hospital. She has asthma. It's only Thursday, but since I was coming out here to get my hair done today, she decided to take them a day early."

"I'll keep your daughter in prayer. Is it your mom that's keeping them or their dad's?"

"Their dad's. My mom lives in Atlanta."

"Are you married to your babies' daddy?"

"No. We don't even live under the same roof, but we're still together."

"Well, that's better than him not being around his kids at all. I know so many women that got children where the man just up and left them."

"How'd you meet your man? I remember you saying something about you two going half on a baby. R. Kelly song, huh?"

Tammy laughed. "Girlfriend, it ain't gonna happen no time soon. Don't laugh, but I met Zach through a *singles* ad in the local newspaper. We started out by writing one another."

Unable to believe her ears, Keisha was truly astonished. "You got to be kidding! Did you know he was in prison when you first answered the ad?"

"Yeah, I did. The ad read, 'Lonely brother in jail, unjustly so. Needs outside cellmate. Looking for someone to kick it and keep it real with.' I thought his ad was kinda cute, so I wrote him, and he wrote back. A week later I went to see him. That's when he started telling me he might not be able to write anymore 'cause he couldn't even afford stamps."

Keisha looked horrified by what Tammy had told her. She couldn't help wondering how many other women may have answered Zach's con ad as she thought about what she'd overheard at the prison. Keisha not only felt like a fool, she knew she was the biggest one of all. Zach had been playing her just as he was playing all the rest.

Tammy put the finishing touches on Keisha's hair by spraying it with a light oil sheen. She then handed Keisha a two-sided mirror. "Check it out and see if you like it."

Keisha looked in the mirror at the front and the back of her new hairstyle. Smiling, she primped and patted at the same time. "I love it." Pausing a moment, Keisha looked at Tammy with concern. "Tammy can you take a break? I'd like to talk to you about something serious."

Tammy looked curious. "Sure. We can go into my house. It's connected to the shop by that door over there." She pointed at the entrance to her house. "Let me tell Connie to hold things down for me. Be right back."

Keisha and Tammy seated themselves on the forest green leather couch in Tammy's comfortable living room. The decor was warm and friendly. Just as in the shop, she had an abundance of black art on the walls. The coffee table and end tables were done in dark wood. A bookcase held hardbound books of African-American authors. There were also numerous framed photographs of smiling people and pictures of a host of Tammy's satisfied customers.

Keisha looked nervous as she played with one of the sofa pillows. Tammy couldn't help but notice how antsy Keisha had become. That made her wonder what her new friend could possibly want to share with her.

Keisha finally turned to face Tammy. "I hope you won't get upset with me, but I've kinda been deceiving you. I like you and I don't want to tell you any more lies. You see, we're actually sharing the same man. Zach Martin is the father of my children."

Tammy could've been knocked over with a feather. Wondering if she'd heard Keisha right, she sat there with her mouth gaping wide. "Did you say that Zach Martin fathered your kids? That we're both seeing the same man?"

Feeling sorry for Tammy, who now had tears swimming in her eyes, Keisha nodded. "It's the truth, Tammy. Zach and I have been together for many years. I was just as surprised to learn about you and Zach as you are to learn about me. And my name is not Misha. It's Keisha Reed. I didn't want you to know who I was just in case Zach had told you about me."

Tammy looked more hurt than angry. "Why did you act as if you really liked me and wanted to be my friend? People always do that to me. Being fat makes me a target for every evil person alive. I should've known better than to think that you could be a true friend to me. I feel so stupid. I can't believe I trusted you so easily. You and Zach have made a big fool of me."

Tammy started to sob. Keisha moved over closer to her and put her arms around her. Keisha lifted Tammy's head and looked into her tearful hazel eyes. "The truth of the matter is, I do like you, a lot. That's why I could no longer front you like this. Zach has burned both of us. I don't think we should let him get away with it. He just can't go around hurting people like this. I'm truly sorry, Tammy. I hope you can forgive me. It wasn't my intention to cause you pain."

"Then what was your intention, Mish . . . Keisha?"

"To get as much information from you as possible, so that I could confront Zach. When you said you met him through a newspaper ad, I saw that both you and I are possibly suffering from low self-esteem. Why else would we let a con man like Zach play us this way? Meeting someone via a newspaper ad is a seriously dangerous thing to do, especially for the woman. How did you get caught up in something crazy like that?"

Tammy wiped her eyes with the heels of her hands. "Loneliness, plain and simple. A fat girl like me doesn't have her phone ringing off the hook, or have men lining up at the door wanting to take her out. I hate to admit it, but I've never had a serious boyfriend before now. And now I know that Zach wasn't at all serious. What are you going to do about Zach? He's cheating on you and your children."

"The question is, what are *we* going to do about Zach? We can't let him get away with this." Keisha grinned. "I have a plan if you're willing to listen."

"I'm all ears, but it has got to be good."

"Trust me, it's going to be better than good. It's going to be better than the bomb. It's going to be the explosion!" Keisha and Tammy started laughing uncontrollably, giving one another high fives. Deep down inside, both women were in pain, but neither of them wanted to let the other know how much Zach's deceptions was costing them emotionally.

On the way home from Tammy's, Keisha found herself doing a lot of soul-searching. They'd come up with a good plan to get back at Zach, but she wasn't sure she could go through with it. She loved Zach. Would Tammy give him up if she told her that she couldn't play him like that? Would Tammy walk away from Zach for the sake of their kids? Keisha realized she had so much more to lose than Tammy. But the fact remained that Zach was no good. What was she to do with that bit of truth?

What she'd always done: continue to be there for him, come hell or high water.

Marlene, Keisha, and Rosalinda were having dessert in Marlene's brightly lit kitchen. Marlene had invited the two young women over to her house with the hopes of further discussion about the support group. Unfinished slices of blueberry pie sat on dessert plates in front of each woman. The other half of the uneaten pie was in the center of the table.

"You've been awfully quiet since you got here, Keisha. Is there something on your mind?" Marlene inquired. "You look downright troubled."

Tears immediately sprang to Keisha's eyes. Quickly, she dabbed at them with a paper napkin. "I haven't said much because I've been so upset. I found out that Zach has several other women visiting him and giving him money. I met one of them the last Sunday we were there."

Marlene looked mystified. "He had you both come there at the same time?"

Keisha frowned. "No, not really. Rosalinda and I hardly ever go there for the late visit on Sunday. I actually talked to this woman that day, but I didn't tell her that I was there to see Zach. I wanted to get all the 411 on her and Zach's relationship so I could confront him with it. That is, if it turned out that she was there in any other capacity than just a friend."

Marlene eyed Keisha intently. "How did you find out about her in the first place?"

"From the prison guard who registered us that day. He told me that the lady who was just in front of me had already registered to see Zach. He wanted to know if I wanted to go in at the same time she did or wait until she came out."

"You should've gone in right behind her and made Zach look like the fool he is," Rosalinda interjected. "I can't believe you kept this from me."

"Like I said, I wanted to get the facts first. Tammy—that's her name—did my hair a couple of days ago. But when I found out that she met Zach from a singles ad in the local newspaper, I got real concerned for her. He later ran a sob story down to her about being broke, and she fell for it."

"A singles ad? How's he able to do that from behind bars?" Marlene asked.

"Easily! Newspaper ads purchased by inmates are one of the biggest scams going. I just didn't know Zach was into it. It's a way of getting money, clothes, electronics, and other stuff from vulnerable women."

"Does Tammy know who you are now?" Rosalinda asked.

Keisha picked at her pie with a fork. "Yeah, I had to tell her the truth. She's not to blame for this. This is Zach's mess—and he's going to pay for it, too."

Standing at the sink, Marlene turned around to face Keisha. "How'd she react?"

Keisha thought about Tammy's reaction. "She was upset with me at first. She didn't like the fact that I had deceived her by pretending that I wanted to be her friend. I told her she was right, but that I needed to know what was up."

"What did she say to that?" Rosalinda queried.

"She was cool after I told her that my kids belonged to Zach. I felt worse for her than I did for myself, especially when she started crying real hard. She thinks people use her because she's fat. I tried to tell her that Zach didn't know what she looked like until after she went to visit him. That didn't make her feel any better. The fact that he was using her still remained."

Marlene sighed. "Oh, dear, this is horrible. How can one human being do that to another one? Have you talked to Zach about all this, Keisha?"

"Not really. I strung him out that day, but I only gave him tidbits of info to chew on. Tammy and I are going to set his ignorant ass up real good. Oops. I'm sorry, Marlene. I know you don't want me talking like that, especially in your home. Forgive me?"

Marlene's eyes softened as she walked over and hugged Keisha. "All's forgiven. I appreciate the effort you two have been putting forth in respecting me in and out of my home. But you've got to learn to respect yourself. Only then will respect for others come easily to you."

Rosalinda took a bite of her pie. "Have you decided what you're going to do about Zach and his doggish ways, Keisha?"

Marlene held the palm of her hand up in a stop sign position. "Excuse me. I don't want her to think about Zach. She has to focus on herself and the kids, because it's clear that Zach's not. He's out for himself—and himself alone. This is about you, Keisha Reed, and how you really feel about yourself. What has happened in your life to make you think that you deserve to be treated this way?"

"I know there's an answer to your question, but I don't know exactly what it is. I now know that I'm suffering with the same thing I saw in Tammy. Low self-esteem. But I love Zach. He's the daddy of my two babies. Where do I go without him?"

"Up, young lady. Way up to the top." Marlene smiled gently. "You've just taken the first step toward solving the problem. You've identified it. Recognizing the problem is a big part of the solution. Now that you've done that, you can start working on it. I don't know Zach, but I know that he's disrespecting you. By letting him do that, you're bringing dishonor to yourself."

"I don't see how loving someone is dishonoring myself," Keisha responded.

"You may love Zach, but love is not what he feels for you. Love doesn't take advantage of others. Love won't try to make a fool out of someone. When you learn to love yourself, unconditionally, you'll begin to understand what I'm saying." Marlene picked up *Acts of Faith*, an inspirational book by Iyanla Vanzant. She began to read from it. Softly, she read the entire text of one of the pages that had to do with relationships.

"Keisha, she's right. We're both caught up in something we don't understand. Zach and Ricardo aren't acting like real men." Feeling ashamed, Rosalinda lowered her lashes as she took another tiny bite of her pie. "I need to talk about something, too, but I'm not sure I should. I don't think Ricardo would want me to discuss it with anyone."

"Damn Ricardo!" Keisha shouted. "Damn both of them to hell." Marlene scolded Keisha with a mere look. Keisha put her hand over her mouth. Her eyes apologized to Marlene for cursing. "If something's bothering you, Rosalinda, you need to let go of it. That's why we've been friends all these years—because we can tell each other anything. I'm sorry I didn't do that."

Nervously, Rosalinda rubbed her thighs with the palms of her hands. Looking from Keisha to Marlene, she ate the last sliver of pie and then put the fork down. "I met with Michael Hernandez, the lawyer I hired for Ricardo, some time ago. I told him that it was getting harder and harder for me to continue paying his fees. Before I could ask him about getting a public defender, he hinted to me that I could pay him in flesh-rendering services."

Keisha jumped up and stood over Rosalinda's chair. "Are you saying that he asked to sleep with you? Why that sleezy bas—" The disapproving look Marlene gave Keisha cut her off in midsentence.

"Sit down, Keisha. You're not helping Rosalinda with all the theatrics. She needs us to be calm and rational."

Frowning, Keisha sat back down. She rolled her eyes at Marlene dramatically.

Marlene ignored Keisha's eye language. "Rosalinda, have you even talked to Ricardo about this?"

Rosalinda's shoulders trembled as she began to sob. "He told me to do whatever it takes. I told him it seemed like prostitution to me, but he said that he doesn't look at it that way. He says we have to do whatever it takes to get him out of jail."

"We?" Marlene challenged. "Did you ask him if he had a mouse in the pocket of his prison blues? Better yet, did you ask him what role he's going to play in this little back-alley scenario? It seems to me that it's up to you to take all the risks while he sits back and enjoys the free ride. There's not going to be any *we* when it comes to you lying flat on your back while some naked man you don't even know is hovering over you."

"Well, he really can't do anything to help his situation while locked up. He promised that he'd never ask me to do anything like this ever again."

Marlene took her turn to jump out of her seat and stand over Rosalinda. "Say what?"

Keisha wanted to mimic her by telling her to stop the theatrics, but she thought better of it, especially when she heard the thunder in Marlene's voice and saw the flashes of lightning in her eyes.

"I know you're not trying to tell me and Keisha that you're considering this insanity, are you? Pray tell, child, I hope not." Under her breath, Marlene began to pray really hard.

Keisha put her arms around Rosalinda and hugged her tightly. Marlene handed Keisha a napkin to wipe Rosalinda's tears and the tears falling from her own eyes. "You can't do this, Rosalinda. You're better than that. I'm better than that. Both of us are better than what we've been putting up with all these years. It seems like your visit with Ricardo was as rough as mine was. We're going to have to find a way to help each other get through this nightmare. I can't take much more of Zach and his doggish ways."

"The pressure has been mounting for me over the last couple of days," Rosalinda cried. "I sometimes feel that I have to go through with this or lose Ricardo all together. But I'm scared to death of sleeping with a man I don't even know or like. Hernandez and I come from very different places in life. We are total opposites."

Marlene looked at both women with grave concern. The fact that both of these young women had allowed no-good men to abuse them and bring ruin to their lives brought her no comfort whatsoever. She could clearly see herself in their place more than anyone could ever imagine. Because she, too, had allowed herself to be manipulated by a man whom she loved as much as life itself: her twenty-one-year-old son, Malcolm Covington.

It seemed that Malcolm had been manipulating her from his early days in the crib. Because of the loss of her firstborn, she'd acted irresponsibly in raising him, often giving in to his unreasonable demands and presenting him with expensive material things. Most everything pertaining to Malcolm had been done against Jesse's wishes.

When Malcolm had started skipping school and hanging out with unsavory characters, she'd ignored some of the obvious signs of his troubled state by telling herself that he was just going through a phase. Then her teenage honor student had quickly become an outright failure in his studies, even flunking out of gym. Disrespecting his teachers had been an all-too-often occurrence, as well as getting expelled from school. It hadn't been long before smoking and drinking followed his numerous other bad habits. Jesse hadn't been informed of many of his son's escapades. Marlene had convinced herself that he was too busy to bother and that she could handle them effectively.

Feeling extremely nervous, Rosalinda sat in Michael Hernandez's plush inner office suite. It appeared that quite a bit of money had been spent on the interior decoration. Rich mahogany accents and soft leather furnishings brought to the cavernous space a fair amount of warmth and coziness. There were numerous Spanish-themed oil paintings on the wall.

Though she'd pretty much made up her mind to sleep with the

lawyer to pay Ricardo's legal fees, she wasn't at all pleased with her decision. Thoughts of Marlene's and Keisha's reactions had stayed with her all through the past evening and all through this entire day.

Unsure as to how to present her decision to Hernandez, Rosalinda looked like a woman in deep agony. How was she going to tell him that she was going to go to bed with him—and then later have him believe that she was enjoying it?

Her hands began to shake as Michael Hernandez stepped into the room. No matter what she thought of him as a man, he was terribly handsome. Still, his good looks weren't going to make a difference when it came to sleeping with him, not when it went against everything she'd been taught. But then again, her being with Ricardo went against everything her mother had ever told her about what characteristics and qualities she should look for in a mate. He wasn't anything like the man her mother had hoped she'd one day find. She imagined that her loving grandfather had probably turned over in his grave when she'd first started dating Ricardo Munoz.

Immaculately dressed, Michael Hernandez wore an expensive dark blue double-breasted suit. It looked fantastic on his tall, slender frame. The powder blue shirt was striking against his dark complexion. His keen features and coal black orbs were very pleasant to the eye. He reminded her of the rich, swarthy, extremely virile Spaniards she used to read about in period romance novels. For a brief moment she imagined him riding up on a white horse and sweeping her off her feet. Off into the sunset they would ride as they galloped toward his remote castle. As for his physical attributes, he was a wonderful specimen about which to daydream or fantasize.

"Hello, Rosalinda. It's so nice to see you again." Just short of openly flirting, he smiled at her in a knowing way. "I was surprised to learn that you'd made another appointment to see me so soon. How can I help you out today?"

She picked pieces of non-existent lint off her skirt. "I came to see you about Ric's fees."

He raised a thick, dark eyebrow. "I already gave you extra time to pay on the account. Wasn't it enough time? Do you need more time to come up with the money?"

She had hoped he would've given out the same sexual payoff hint that he'd alluded to before so she wouldn't have to be the one to bring up the subject. Had she misinterpreted his remarks the other day? With his dark eyes trained intensely on her face, she could see that he wasn't going to make this easy for her.

Completely unnerved by him and his good looks, she dug around in her purse and came up with her checkbook. She wrote out a check for one hundred dollars, knowing that it would bounce. But it was all she could think of to do. She had to get out of his presence. She would call his secretary when she got home and tell her she'd just learned that she didn't enough money in the bank to cover it. She'd also ask if they could hold it for a week or two.

As she practically threw the check down on his desk, she got to her feet. "I've got to be going now. I'll try to send you more money next paycheck."

He stood up. Before she could get to the door, he was there, blocking her exit.

"You seem very upset, Rosalinda. Has something bad happened since we last spoke? I'd like to help you out anyway that I can."

She tried to step around him, but he moved right back in front of her.

"Why don't you let me take you out for something to eat. I know a place where we can talk about what you're feeling. I can only imagine how hard Ric's incarceration must be on you. I think we should discuss other options for him. What do you say to my offer? There's a nice place with great Mexican food right down the street. We can even walk down there if you prefer that to riding in my car."

Rosalinda breathed in deeply. Was this the sexual hint she'd been looking for? Perhaps he'd make the arrangements for them to sleep together over dinner. "I am hungry. Thanks for the generous offer." If she was going to do this, she wanted to get it over with as soon as possible.

"My pleasure. Give me a moment to clear up a few matters with my secretary. Then we can be on our way. While you're waiting, you can decide if you want to walk or ride."

The Mexican restaurant was cozy, romantic, and dimly lit with candlelight. An odd choice for talking business, Rosalinda mused. Seated in a red leather booth, Michael sat across the table from her. She studied him closely while he checked out the menu.

He looked up at her. Being caught watching him so closely made her blush. “Is something bothering you, Rosalinda? You don’t seem yourself. You can trust me with confidence. I guess having no one to confide in isn’t easy.”

She sighed with impatience. “What makes you think I don’t have anyone to confide in?”

“Well, most people who are romantically involved with someone usually confide in their significant other. We both know that yours isn’t around to hear you out. That’s all I meant.”

“Ric and I talk every single day. Often we talk several times a day. What’s your point?”

He raised an eyebrow. “That must cost you a pretty penny since he has to call collect.” Although his comments were presented in an extremely subtle way, the blaring truth of them grated on her nerves. He was being coy, cagey, and she hadn’t yet come up with the formula for how to break it down to him for playing this silly little cat-and-mouse game with her.

Sighing deeply, she twirled a strand of her hair around her forefinger. Then tears suddenly came to her eyes. She didn’t have the strength or the desire to play this scenario out. “Will you get to the point of why you brought me here, Mr. Henandez. We both know that you have something on your mind other than business. Why don’t you get right down to the heart of it? I don’t have time for childish games.”

Nonchalantly, he shrugged his broad shoulders. “I’m sorry, but I thought we came here to eat and to talk about Ric’s options. Why don’t we go ahead and get the waitress over here. I’m as hungry as you probably are.” Looking as innocent as a newborn babe, he summoned the waitress with a slight wave of his hand.

Despite how he looked, she didn’t think there was one virtuous thing about him. He was setting her up like a clay pigeon. Though she was sure of that, Rosalinda didn’t know what to think now. He was playing a clever game with her. She knew it, but she didn’t know how to become a participant in it. What was he waiting for her to say? That she was ready to screw his brains out? She could plainly see that he wanted her. His desire for her was burning in his eyes like an uncontrollable inferno. Her wanted her in bed in the worst way.

Without even asking her what she’d like to have, he took the liberty of ordering for them. His arrogance further frazzled her nerves. Once the waitress stepped away, he turned his attention back to her.

For several minutes he only stared at her. No matter how hard she tried, she couldn't read the odd expression in his mysteriously dark eyes.

"Would you mind if I asked you a personal question?"

Rosalinda's eyes grew as dark as his. "I don't mind you asking. I just hope you don't mind if I choose not to answer."

He grinned. "That's your prerogative. I don't know if it matters to you or not, but I would really like to have you respond. What do you see in Ricardo Munoz? Why does a beautiful woman like yourself waste your time on someone who can't seem to stay out of trouble?"

"Hey, that's two questions!"

"So it is. Fine. Answer whichever one you wish."

She chewed on her lower lip. "Would you believe me if I said I don't know the answer to either of your questions. That is, if I had the desire to respond."

"I would have no reason not to believe you. Did you believe me when I said you were beautiful?"

"Truthfully?" He nodded. "No, I didn't believe a word of it. I'm not ugly, but I'm not beautiful, either." Experiencing feelings of deep shame and embarrassment, she put her head down for a brief moment. "I feel anything but beautiful, outwardly and inwardly. Don't you have to be beautiful inside for it to reflect outwardly? Doesn't beauty wear a halo inside?"

His breath caught at her enchanting questions. He didn't know how he'd expected her to respond. It certainly hadn't been in that way. "Have you ever heard the saying that beauty is in the eye of the beholder?"

"Yes, I have, but you didn't answer my questions. I'd like to know why not."

He shook his head. "I don't know. Perhaps I didn't expect that type of emotional depth from you." He looked deep into her eyes, as if he could see her soul through them. "Yes, to both questions. But everyone can't always see their own inner beauty. Therefore, they can't know that it's wearing a glowing halo for the world to see. I really do think you're beautiful. I can clearly see the brightness of your halo as it sits above your heart. It's such a shame that you've managed to trick yourself into believing you don't have any such inner beauty."

Her laughter was filled with cynicism. "Mr. Hernandez, you don't have to try and make me feel good in order to seduce me. It's not that kind of party—and we both are very much aware of that. Speaking of hearts, let's get right down to the heart of the matter. During our last meeting you hinted to me that I could pay Ric's fees by sharing my sweet, tender flesh with you. Is that offer still open?" She couldn't believe how bold a statement she'd just made.

Those hadn't been his exact words, but her flesh did look sweet and tender. Not sure of how to answer her very pointed question, he swallowed hard. "What if it is? What would your answer be to that offer?"

Leaning forward with a seductive smile on her pouting lips, she placed both elbows on the table and entwined her fingers. "Just let me know when and where I can fulfill your desires. I already know how." Although her actions were totally out of character for her, she found herself enjoying the slutty role she felt she'd been forced to play.

He was saved from a response when the waitress appeared with their food order. Wishing he knew how to sweat only from within, he mopped his brow with a white handkerchief. Glad that she'd gotten that over with, Rosalinda dug into the food as if this whole scenario didn't bother her in the least. It disturbed her more than she'd ever let him know. This rich SOB expected her to sleep with him—and it was obvious that she'd given him the answer he desired. The next move was up to him.

As wealthy as he was, she didn't expect anything more from him than a lousy roll in the hay, in a cheap motel in a sleazy part of town. That seemed to be his exact opinion of her: cheap and sleazy. Why else would he proposition he in that way? There was a moment there when she actually thought she'd misjudged him. Unfortunately, he'd disappointed her. Bitterly so.

Despite all his good looks and tons of money, he was a despicable human being. He was no different from the man she'd chosen as her first lover. Ric seduced people into buying drugs and other illegal goods. Michael Hernandez seduced women into sleeping with him in lieu of his legal fees.

In her opinion, both were criminal acts.

The second after she took her final bite of the cheese enchilada, she sipped the last of her iced tea through a straw. Wiping her mouth on the linen napkin, Rosalinda looked straight at Michael. "Thank you for dinner, Señor Hernandez."

"You are indeed welcome, Señorita Morales."

Looking and feeling as if he'd just been run over by a steamroller, Michael summoned the waitress to pay the check. After handing her his American Express card, he settled back in his seat to ponder the intriguing time he had already spent with the beautiful Señorita Rosalinda Morales. He suddenly found himself afraid to make further direct eye contact with her.

It bothered him that this stunning woman was in love with a no-good punk, a punk who would surely one day bring her world completely down around her ears. But he wasn't convinced that it was love in the true sense of the word. He was certain that Rosalinda didn't even know what love was. If she did, she wouldn't be so willing to sell her most intimate treasures to the highest bidder. And the fact that she was willing to do it for a man who couldn't possibly love her set his teeth on edge. *Man* was a poor choice of wording to use for Ric. There was nothing about his client to suggest that he was anything but a two-bit punk.

More important, if Ricardo loved her, he could never ask her to do something so vile.

"I'll wait to hear from you on when and where." Rosalinda got to her feet. Without looking back, she walked out of the restaurant.

Rosalinda's hands shook so bad that she had a hard time unlocking her car door. Michael Hernandez had worked her into a ball of confusion. Her nerves were completely frayed. No matter how much confidence she'd displayed back there, she didn't think she could go through with such a cold, unemotional act. Sleeping with someone for the reasons she was considering was crazy. What was she to do? She loved Ricardo, and this was what he expected of her. How could she be sure that her sleeping with Hernandez would get him out of jail? If he could get him out of jail so easily, why hadn't he been able to keep him from being convicted in the first place? What guarantee did she have that it would actually happen?

Was this something that could even be guaranteed? For whatever reason, she seriously doubted that it could be guaranteed or even achieved. Part of her wished it were impossible.

* * *

Inside the nursing-rehabilitation center, Rosalinda went straight to her mother's room. As she walked down the plush carpeted corridor, she looked at her watch. It was dinnertime. She'd gotten there just in time to see that her mother ate her food. Paulina's appetite had nearly been destroyed during her illness. She often told Rosalinda that she didn't seem to have taste buds any longer. Nothing tasted good to her. But Rosalinda always insisted that she eat anyway, to keep up her strength. Paulina did at least drink the Ensure, a supplemental health drink given to her.

Paulina smiled when her daughter entered the room. *"Hola,"* Paulina greeted cheerfully.

"Hola, Mommy."

CHAPTER SEVEN

As he sat far back in a corner, at a long table in the cafeteria, Jesse thought about how he'd never dreamed he'd ever find himself in this particular world. Behind bars was an altogether different world, a world made up of concrete, steel bars, anger, bad attitudes, and the deepest of sorrows. The stench of pain and anguish in this place was so thick you could almost pluck it right out of the air.

Although he'd been wild in the early years of his life, he'd settled down before he'd reached age thirty. Marlene had easily settled him down. She had a way about her that made him want to do everything in his power to keep her happy, contented—and in love with him. As he turned the pages of his photo album, the sweet but sometimes bitter memories seemed to engulf him. Tears came to his eyes when he looked at a picture of baby Mason.

Their first child had come much earlier than planned or expected, but they'd joyously welcomed the new addition to the Covington family. In the beginning, when the doctor had made the announcement back then, Jesse had been really honest with himself. He had admitted to himself that he could've used more time alone with Marlene before settling down with children. But never had there been a day that he regretted having Mason as a son. Even when Marlene had focused the majority of her attention on their baby boy, he'd never wished for things to be any different.

It was the death of Mason that had sent Marlene into a depression from which no one thought she'd ever recover. Her grief had completely overwhelmed her, causing her to curse God and vow never to believe in anyone or anything ever again. Their marriage had suffered under the strain of all the coarse emotions that had come after the baby's untimely death. Marlene had been emotionally unstable and had become totally uncommunicative for months. When she'd finally begun to come around, she'd immediately sought solace in her husband's arms. Malcolm had come as a result of the nights they'd spent making love, seemingly making up for lost time.

Feeling eyes on him, Jesse dispelled his thoughts as he looked up. He smiled at the man Marlene had pointed out to him during one of her visits. He remembered her telling him that he was the wealthy stockbroker married to the classy beauty.

"Is there something I can do for you, young man?" Jesse closed his photo album. Rarely did he get into conversations with other inmates. Something seemed to compel him to talk to the tall, handsome, fair-skinned brother.

R.J. Du Boise stared at Jesse but said nothing. That alone caused Jesse to immediately experience waves of discomfort. Hard staring and malicious looks from one inmate to another were high on the list among the main causes for outbreaks of verbal arguments—ones that often turned into physical altercations.

Without taking his eyes off Jesse, R.J. sat down across from him. Continuing to stare at the middle-aged preacher, R.J. folded his hands and rested his elbows on the cafeteria table.

"If you have something to say, young man, perhaps you should just come out with it. I don't like being stared at. I don't want any trouble, either. That's why I'm over here in this corner all by my lonesome." R.J. frowned.

That joyless expression pushed Jesse's caution button. He steeled himself to remain calm.

"Is your wife always up in other people's business?"

Jesse was a little taken aback, but he smiled anyway. "I don't know. Maybe you should be asking her that question. But what makes you think that my wife has been in your business?"

"Because she's filling my wife's pretty little head with a lot of Christian BS." R.J. snickered. "Forgive me. I forgot I was talking to a man of the cloth, a nonsinner."

Jesse laughed. "I beg to differ. I've no problem with admitting that I'm a sinner. I've been a sinner all my life. Will always be one. Will eventually die as one."

R.J. shook his head in disbelief. "You trying to tell me that you don't think you're perfect—that you actually commit sins? Or are you just trying to pull my leg?"

Jesse didn't laugh again. He saw the serious expression R.J. wore. The questions asked were what Jesse couldn't believe, but he'd heard them loud and clear. "Exactly. No man in the flesh is perfect. No mortal man is without sin. I must say that I'm genuinely surprised by your questions. You seem like a very educated man to me."

"Educated bookwise, streetwise, and to the world? Yes. Educated in Christianity? Hardly! Even though I used to go to church every weekend, I didn't get much out of the services. Didn't get much at all out of it. There were times when I truly thought it was a waste of time."

"Why do you think that was? Before you answer that, is it against the rules for us to exchange names? If not, I'm Reverend Jesse Covington?"

"R.J. Du Boise here." Pondering Jesse's question, R.J. stroked his chin. "You black preachers tend to get on your soapboxes. So many of you seem to think that the services are all about you. About what you think and about what you want from this life."

Jesse raised an eyebrow. "Care to expound a little more on that for me?"

"Would love to. Preachers don't teach anymore. They only preach nowadays, but the problem is that you can't understand them half of the time. They get to whooping and hollering all over the place. They lose me at that point. That is, if they haven't already done so by then."

"Lose you how?"

"Man's attention span is only so long to begin with. It's real hard for this man to sit still for an hour, let alone four or five. And what about the poor little kids? Our church went straight from the bible lesson study into the regular service, which went on and on and on. They lost me somewhere in between the second to fifth hour, along with a host of others. When I finally did wake up and take a look around, I saw that everyone else had nodded off, too. Eyes were closed and mouths had fallen open all over the place."

"I see what you mean."

"Do you? Do you keep your parishioners in church all day?"

"I was guilty of that at one time." Jesse laughed from deep within. "I thought it was what people wanted. That's how it was when I grew up. I shouted and hollered because I thought it was what was expected of me, especially from the older people in the congregation. I later found out that, after an hour or so, all they wanted me to do was shut up and sit down. And they wanted it even more than the young people did." Both men laughed at that.

"We now have a forty-five-minute lesson study," Jesse offered. "The first half hour of the church service is used for singing and praising. I try very hard to get my message across in the last thirty minutes. I may go over by ten minutes or so, a time or two, but I try to stick close to the allotted time. We don't pass the plate. Wooden offering receptacles can be found at each entrance to the sanctuary. We found that people give more that way. We don't stand on ceremony, period. I learned a lot of valuable lessons from the Sagemont Church in Houston, Texas. It took me a long time to realize that the seventh day was a day for rest."

R.J. seemed more relaxed now to Jesse. His demeanor had gone from threatening to amicable in a few minutes. The unexpected conversation had turned out to be okay, as far as Jesse was concerned. For a man who, he thought, looked as if he might be spoiling for a fight just a short time ago, Jesse found himself actually liking R.J. It was kind of nice to have someone to talk to, especially after all the time he spent alone in his cell. Reading the Bible and other inspirational works was what helped Jesse to get through each day. It also kept him out of harm's way. Mingling with the others was a sure way to find oneself in difficulty.

R.J. smiled at Jesse in an admiring way. "I like you, brother. You seem to have your thing altogether. But if that's the case, why are you in here?"

Jesse rocked his upper body back and forth as he thought about the question. "It's a long story, but since we have nothing but time, I'm going to share my woeful tale with you. I usually stay off to myself, but I don't mind telling you that I'm enjoying the company. A man can go stir-crazy locked up in this wicked place for too long. Here are the facts of my case: I was stopped by the police because the vehicle I was driving was supposedly used to commit a robbery at a 7-Eleven store located a few miles from the neighborhood I live in."

Jesse went on to explain how he'd been locked up in the first place.

Then he talked about all the unbelievable things that had followed his arrest.

"So, I guess you're saying that you're innocent."

Jesse eyed R.J. with curiosity. "Is that a statement or a question?"

"Are you innocent?"

"As innocent as they come. I'm still in shock at being found guilty of a crime that I know I didn't commit. God and me are the only ones who know for a fact that I'm innocent of all these trumped-up charges. Ever heard of the expression 'stopped while driving black'? That's what I think happened to me. Someone had committed a crime and they needed someone to blame quick, fast, and in a hurry. Who better to blame than a brother? They said I fit the description of the perpetrator. According to the particular police department that patrols my neighborhood, all brothers fit the description."

"What about the vehicle you were driving? Do you believe it was involved in a crime?"

"I don't know how it could've been. The church van was in my possession that weekend. I had taken it home after delivering food baskets to several families in need. When I went to bed around eleven o'clock that evening, that van was still parked in my driveway. The vehicle in question was only described as a white church van. They didn't even have the name of the church. How many white vans with church logos are out there on the streets of L.A.?"

"I see your point. That's a tough break. Are you appealing your conviction?"

"Most definitely. I just have to remain patient with the long process."

The two men stayed silent for several minutes, each surveying the buzzing activity going on around them. Two inmates were arguing heatedly. As usual, they were loud enough for everyone to hear them. Jesse and R.J. would be surprised if the angry exchange didn't end up in a bloody battle. If that were to happen, a total inmate lockdown was sure to occur. Jesse, for the most part, didn't mind the isolation. Lockdowns nearly drove R.J. insane each time they happened. He hated feelings of seclusion.

R.J. turned his attention back to Jesse. "Aren't you going to ask me the reason why I'm locked up in here?"

Jesse shrugged his shoulders. "I figured that if you wanted me to know, you would tell me without my asking. I'd never ask you something like that. It's really none of my business. I also respect your right to privacy."

"Oh, so you think I was wrong for asking you that?"

"Not at all. The only difference between us is that you wanted to know—and I don't care to know one way or the other. As it stands, I've got enough to deal with on my own behalf. However, the truth is, we're both locked up in here, innocent or guilty. It doesn't matter what anyone else thinks we may have or may not have done to get inside of here."

R.J. studied Jesse for several seconds. He couldn't believe this brother might actually be for real. Practically everyone in the place had asked him, at one time or another, "What you in for, man?" R.J. had stopped counting the number of brothers who'd said they were innocent, falsely accused, or framed. The ones who were most certainly guilty of their committed crimes seemed almost proud of the fact. As the guilty ones talked about why they were in prison, they did everything but pound their chests in a King Kong–like gesture. They seemed to wear their guilt like a badge of honor.

For a reason he didn't understand, R.J. somehow believed that Jesse really was innocent. The man seemed totally unaffected by the dark world surrounding him. It was like he had an invisible shield around him, like nothing evil or bad could penetrate the fortress of peace that he'd erected for himself. He seemed immune to everything and everyone with which he came into direct contact. R.J. had to admit to himself that he was in total awe of the way Jesse dealt with his situation. He also admitted that he was ashamed of why he'd been sentenced to prison.

The reason for his imprisonment could only be defined as greed.

"Have you ever thought of volunteering some of your time to the chaplain's office?"

"Doing what, R.J.?"

"What you must do best. Preaching! I think there's a few people up in here who might be interested in what you have to say. Preachers come in from the outside and hold services all the time. I'm sure there are more than a few other preacher inmates in here. If so, they haven't made themselves known. I think you might have something good to share with the brothers."

"You think so, huh?"

"I do. I'd come to hear what you had to say."

Jesse was pleasantly surprised by R.J.'s comments. "For a brother who came over here ready to take me to task over something you think my wife is doing, I'm surprised to hear you say that. Perhaps I'll look into it. I must admit that I have thought about talking with my counselor about holding a weekly bible study with other inmates who might be interested in it. But then I thought it would better for me to stay off to myself. I can't afford any more trouble than what I already have."

"Have you ever heard this saying—what would Jesus do? WWJD?"

Jesse was once again surprised. "I've heard it many times. Thanks for the friendly reminder. I'll see what I can cook up."

R.J. stood up. "I'm not going to shake your hand because I'm not sure of how that'll be perceived by some of the others in here. Like you said, we don't need any more troubles. I'll see you around. It was a pleasure getting to know you."

Jesse smiled. "I could ask you the same question you asked me earlier. Does WWJD ring a bell? But I won't go there. Perhaps the next time we talk, you'll be able to tell me a little bit more about what my nosy wife has done to tick you off." Both men laughed, glad that they'd reached at least a plateau of amicable acceptance with one another. "Check you later, R.J."

"Later, Reverend Jesse."

Seated at her kitchen table, Alexis studied the five-carat oval-shaped diamond she wore on her right hand. She couldn't help thinking about how such an expensive trinket had been paid for—and if she might have to pawn it one day to make ends meet. Concerned about the exorbitant amount of money it took to maintain their home, the expensive cars, and other valuable assets, Alexis couldn't help but worry about their suddenly dire financial situation. It was starting to look as if the money well could very easily dry up.

In the twelve years they'd been married, R.J. had never made her privy to all the ways he'd earned his money—big money—outside of the six-figure salary he made as a stockbroker. All she'd ever had to concern herself with was the bank account that he'd opened exclusively in her name. It wasn't that she hadn't asked plenty of questions about their finances, because she had. But R.J. would just tell her not to worry her pretty little head over such, that his financial advisor had everything under control. Still, she was sure that some, if not most, of the money he made wasn't legit.

Marietta Grainger, the Du Boises' maid, came into the kitchen. "Missy, would you like a fresh refill on your coffee?"

Alexis looked up and smiled at the pet name by which Marietta called her. "Please. Thank you."

Marietta refilled the cup and returned the glass carafe to the coffeemaker's heating element. She turned and looked at Alexis, whom she absolutely adored. "You seem to have a lot on your mind this morning, missy. Is there something you'd like to get off your chest? You know I always have a spare ear for you to shout into." Despite her long tenure in the United States, Marietta's Caribbean accident was still thick and spicy.

Alexis was grateful to have Marietta around. It kept her from being totally alone when R.J. was away on business—and now that he was locked up. Though she lived in the maid's quarters located at the back of the property, Alexis found comfort in the fact that she could call on Marietta any time of the day or night when she wasn't off or away on vacation. She'd even been thinking about having the sixty-three-year-old Marietta move into one of the downstairs bedrooms until R.J. came back home . . . if that was ever going to happen. There were times when she had her doubts about his conviction being overturned. And he wasn't even eligible for parole for three years.

Alexis took a sip of her coffee and set it back down. "Why don't you pour yourself a cup of coffee and join me at the table? I do need your understanding ear."

Marietta smiled endearingly at her employer. Possessing beautiful long salt-and-pepper hair, which she kept brushed straight back in a thick bun, Marietta was a native of the West Indies. Medium in height, she didn't appear to have an ounce of fat anywhere on her body.

Although she was the maid and the motherly type, there was nothing about the widowed Marietta that suggested she didn't have anything less than a very active life. She belonged to all sorts of social clubs, dated often, and loved to travel in her off-duty time. But she also wore a pager when on duty, so Alexis would have no problem locating her.

Alexis watched as Marietta fixed her coffee to fit her own taste. She always took two teaspoons of sugar and a dash of fresh cream. "I've been thinking about my parents the last couple of days. I didn't realize how much I missed them until I found myself alone. I didn't know that when R.J. took me out of the ghetto, he never intended for me to return there. My parents have been hurt for years because I never come home to visit with them. How do you think they'd receive me if I suddenly popped up on their front porch?"

"With open arms, missy."

"You're probably right. But my three sisters and two brothers won't welcome me there. They refer to me as the family sellout, among other undesirable names. And they're right. As close as we were, I was able to walk away from them and never look back. I was actually very ashamed of where I came from, but I do love my family. R.J. found every excuse in the book for us not to go back for a visit, and he didn't want me to go alone. Then I stopped trying to get him to go, period. But I can't blame him. That's my family. I'm now more ashamed of myself than I am of where I came from. I wittingly let R.J. and his money come between us. I would love to hear my mother's voice. It's been over a year since I last called their home."

"Call her. I'm sure she'd love to hear from you. Your parents aren't getting any younger. Why'd you stop calling in the first place?"

Alexis gave a minute of thought to the question, but she knew there was no legitimate excuse for cutting them off from herself. It was an act of uncaring selfishness. She had to admit that she'd only begun to really think about her family when she first began to realize that her financial circumstances could change for the worse. It was a real possibility that she could end up not far from where she came. Wouldn't her siblings just love that?

Nevertheless, she hated the bad attitudes her siblings gave her when she did call. The names they'd called her by were none too pleasant: rich bitch, snooty heifer, family traitor, uptown whore with a pimp for a husband, a kept woman, etc. Rarely had her mother answered the phone, but she'd often prayed for that to happen before she'd placed each call.

Alexis had also sent her mother and father lots of money in the first year of her marriage. But it seemed as though when they'd realized she wasn't ever coming home to see them, they'd decided to send it all back. She'd never asked them their reasons for doing so, because she already had a pretty good idea of why.

"Clara and Jacob Gautier had once been dirt-poor but extremely proud. My father worked as a farmhand until he landed a great job with the railroad. The benefits that came with the job meant that he could now provide medical and dental benefits to his wife and six children. I can clearly remember the family celebration that took place the day he came home and said he'd been offered the job."

"I bet that was some celebration."

Alexis's fingers tightened around the coffee mug. "It certainly was. The only position Clara Piccard-Gautier ever held was that of wife and mother. Clara is a genteel woman who has a kind word and a genuine smile for everyone she comes into contact with. Both of my parents are wonderful people. Even when they had very little to offer, they never failed to share it with others less fortunate them themselves."

Marietta patted her employer's hand. "I don't think you should delay in making that call. You need your parents at a time like this. In due time, your siblings will also come around."

Marietta got to her feet. "I'm going into the laundry room to tend to the wash now. If you need me, just holler."

Alexis smiled. "Thank you for the ear." Marietta placed a tender kiss in the center of Alexis's forehead before leaving the room.

Alexis stared at the telephone. Her fingers itched to dial the New Orleans number that she didn't even remember, but fear of the chilly reception she would more than likely receive kept her rooted to the chair. If Jacob Jr., Carolyn, Tracey, or Victor, the eldest of the six children (Alexis being the fifth child) answered the phone, they'd probably hang up on her. One of her siblings were almost always there. Her parents rarely answered the phone when their kids were around. But if she was lucky enough to get Tamara, the youngest, she might have a shot at talking to her parents. Unless the family had managed to turn Tamara against her, too, she would probably call one of her parents to the phone. Jacob Jr., the eldest child, had detested R.J. from the moment he'd first met him, and had never wanted him to marry his little sister in the first place.

Jacob Jr. would definitely not be an ally for her.

The thought that one or both of her parents could be dead struck her like a lightning bolt. It wouldn't be hard for her to believe that her siblings would have a funeral without including her. She began to tremble at just the thought of such an occurrence.

Leaping from her seat, she rushed over to the phone and looked up the number in her address book. Her fingers trembled as she dialed. After allowing three rings, she hung up, as if the receiver had burned her hands. With tears running down her cheeks, she left the kitchen. Sure that her call wouldn't be a welcomed one, she decided to abandon her mission.

Chewing on her lower lip, Alexis stared at the phone on her nightstand. All alone in the house since Marietta had gone out, she felt lonely and desperately wanted to call Marlene. Though she hated to admit it, there had been a soul-stirring spiritual connection between them. The two young women were also on her mind. They'd been kind to her. In turn, she'd been her usual snobbish self. In her solitude, Alexis had convinced herself that she didn't know who she was anymore. If she was honest with herself, she'd lost her identity a long time ago.

Alexis had been a fun-loving girl, had seen the beauty in every living thing—everything but herself. While growing up in poverty, Alexis had learned to make the best of things. Being poor hadn't been a problem for her because she'd never been taught that she was. Food, shelter, and clothing made them wealthier than most. Their parents had taught them to appreciate the basics, the mere essentials for day-to-day living. Somehow, Alexis had forgotten what she'd been taught. Money had become her god and had turned her into an evil, snobbish sinner.

Only recently had she come to appreciate her own natural beauty. Before that time had come, it had only been the expensive clothes and jewelry that she'd seen as beautiful. Pre-R.J. she'd loved to plant flowers and greenery and then watch them grow. The feel of dry or wet soil in her hands always excited her. The great outdoors had been her playground back then.

Post-R.J., Alexis wouldn't think of sticking her hands in a pile of dirt. Dishes weren't on her daily list of things to do. In fact, Alexis didn't do anything domestic. The housekeeper made her bed and took care of every other mess she made throughout the house. Over the years, she'd grown more and more selfish and inconsiderate of others. Her playground had become the world.

Even though she loved the housekeeper like family, she could now see that she had taken the older woman for granted. Sure, she gave her lots of extra money and expensive gifts, but she'd never really told Marietta how much she truly appreciated her being there for her and

R.J. Now that her husband wasn't there, she had begun to show her gratitude a lot more. Still, she wasn't showing thankfulness as much as she should.

She looked at the phone again. Without second-guessing herself, she glanced at the piece of paper with Marlene's number written on it. After dialing, she counted the rings. Finally, when Marlene picked up on ring number five, Alexis couldn't find her voice.

"Hello. Hello? Is someone there?"

"Yes, Marlene. It's . . . Alexis Du Boise. . . . How are you?"

Marlene sat at her kitchen table in silence. Both eyebrows had risen when Alexis had given her name. She felt bad that she hadn't called Alexis about the support group, though she still had intentions of doing so. "I'm fine. How are you? It's been a while."

"I know. Sorry about that. I owe you, Rosalinda, and Keisha an apology. I was horrible to everyone the last time we got together."

"Yes, you do, and yes, you were." Marlene didn't believe in pulling punches. "But we all have days like that from time to time. I'm so happy you called. How's your husband?"

"R.J . . . . oh, he's doing as well as can be expected under the circumstances. I didn't see him last weekend. I was sick with the flu."

"I'm really sorry to hear that. You should've called. I would've been glad to come see about you."

"Marietta, our housekeeper, lives on the property. She always takes such good care of us. I didn't realize how good she was until R.J. went away. I guess I've had a lot of time on my hands to ponder so many things. How's Jesse?"

"Jesse's good. He's coping very well. Rosa and Keisha rode out to the prison with me last weekend. They're really financially strapped, but they always find a way. We spent the entire weekend at the hotel. We did look around for you. Are you planning to go this Saturday?"

"Absolutely. R.J. missed me not being there. He said it was a hard weekend to get through out there."

"I can imagine. Maybe we'll see you there. You have a good week. I enjoyed our chat. Thanks for calling, Alexis."

"You're welcome. But, Marlene, before you hang up, I'd like to know if the three of you would like to come over for dinner one evening this week? How's Wednesday?"

Unable to believe her ears, Marlene stuck her finger in one ear and twisted it around to make sure the canal was clear of wax. Alexis asking them to dinner was quite a shock. "Well, that's so nice of you to offer. I have prayer meeting every Wednesday evening. Perhaps we can do it another time. By the way, I'd like to talk to you about the support group we're starting for women who have loved ones incarcerated."

"That sounds like a great idea. What about Thursday?" Alexis persisted. "You could tell me all about the group then."

"I'm free Thursday night, but you'll have to check with the other girls."

"Could you call them for me?"

"I could but I won't. An invitation to your home should come from you, Alexis. It would be more appreciated that way. The girls deserve the respect of being invited by you."

"Yeah, you're right. I'm not very good at extending myself to others, but I want to be. When I was younger, my mother said that I brought more strangers home to dinner than all of her other children combined. I guess I didn't see them as strangers back then. A lot has changed since that time. A whole lot—and not all of the changes have been good."

"Change is a scary thing, Alexis. None of us like it very much."

"If you'll give me their numbers, I'll call them and extend the invitation to dinner. If they can't come, though I hope they can, I'd still like you to come. It has gotten pretty lonely around here. I haven't been able to talk to our longtime friends about anything . . . not that I'd talk to them about my situation, anyway. That's one of the reasons I like the idea of a support group. It seems that everyone has made themselves totally unavailable to me since R.J. got arrested. I guess I'm saying all that to let you know just how much I hope you'll come to my home."

"I'd be delighted to come. Let me have your address." As Alexis rattled off a prestigious Bel Air address, Marlene blew out a gust of breath. "Thanks, Alexis. Tell Rosalinda and Keisha that they can ride with me if they decide to accept the invite. Just have one of them call me. You take care. I'll see you on Thursday."

"Thanks, Marlene. *Ciao.*"

CHAPTER EIGHT

The drive to Alexis's place had been filled with laughter and a lot of down-home girl talk. Marlene, Keisha, and Rosalinda had grown so comfortable with one another. The two younger women had come to look to Marlene for guidance. She had become the female role model for the way they eventually wanted to live their lives. Each wanted what Marlene Covington had plenty of—love, faith, and tons of patience.

In turn, the two younger women had taught Marlene that being older didn't always mean wiser. Keisha and Rosalinda were a lot wiser than she'd given them credit for in the beginning. She had also found out a lot from them. She'd already found out that she had a lot more to discover about women loving men in prison, the system itself, and life in general.

"Damn!" Keisha shouted as Marlene turned the car on to the street where Alexis lived. "Look at these houses. I take that back. Get an eyeful of these mansions. Her husband must be a millionaire. People really do live like this. Imagining it is one thing. Actually seeing it is a totally awesome experience."

Marlene laughed. "Apparently so. But you need to watch your mouth."

Rosalinda hit her forehead with an open palm. "I thought you lived large, Marlene, but this ritzy area is almost too much to take in at one time. Alexis is snobbish because she can be. She doesn't need anybody or anything. She probably invited us out here so she can show off what she has—what Keisha and I will never have."

"I don't think so." Marlene shook her head. "She seemed very humble in asking us out to dinner. She has apologized to all of us for her past behavior. She has a live-in maid, but I still think she's lonely. She even liked the idea of the support group. Everyone needs somebody. And there are things that people need that money can't buy. Jesus is the only one who can fulfill every need and all desires. People may think because they have everything that they don't need anything. But if they don't have Jesus, they are poorer than the mice that live in the basement of the church. God supplies the needs of every creature He created."

"If she looks down on her maid like she did us, she probably is lonely. I only came out of curiosity. Seeing this neighborhood makes me even more curious. I can't wait to see the inside of the kingdom of her royal highness." Rosalinda's comment made everyone laugh.

Tucked away behind gates, the large house looked as if it had plenty of room for parking. Since Alexis hadn't mentioned where to park, Marlene didn't know what to do. Marlene's expensive town car greatly diminished in value when she considered the type of car Alexis drove. They hadn't seen anything but expensive cars since exiting the freeway. The parking dilemma was solved when Marlene saw the gates open and their hostess waving to her to drive into the secured parking area inside.

Smiling beautifully, Alexis came over to greet her dinner guests. "Hi, everyone. I'm so glad you could make it. Everything is just about ready for you." Alexis hugged each one of the women, surprising them in the process. "I'll take you on a minitour of the house while Marietta puts the finishing touches on the extraordinary dinner she prepared in your honor."

Playfully, Rosalinda nudged Alexis. "You mean you didn't cook for your good buddies? Man, I was looking forward to tasting your cooking."

Feeling an impish mood coming on, Alexis bumped into Rosalinda, the way she and her sisters used to do to one another. "Don't start with me, girlfriend. I'm not going to let you get under my skin this time. I invited you here for a good time. I've sheathed my claws for now."

Everyone laughed at Alexis's homegirl attempt. It had sounded dumb, even to Alexis.

Rosalinda smiled. "Okay. I promise not to get on your case if you promise not to scratch me with those long, designer claws of yours."

Alexis laughed. "The outside of your house is utterly marvelous. Can't wait to see the inside."

"I hope you all like it. It's our dream home. And we love it."

Marietta was introduced to the guests as she set the beautifully browned roast turkey on the table. "It's nice to meet each of you. I'm glad Alexis will have you for company this evening. I hope you'll enjoy the meal she had me prepare especially for you."

Keisha rolled her eyes dramatically. "Meal? This is more like a feast! In the absence of Thanksgiving and Christmas, Mr. Tom Turkey, along with all the traditional fixings, never made an appearance at our dinner table. But I'm sure glad he's visiting with us this evening."

"His visit will be short-lived," Rosalinda chimed in. "We're about to pick poor Tom clean. Those creamy mashed potatoes with that divine-looking gravy don't stand a chance of being around too long, either."

Keisha gave Rosalinda a cagey look. "What do you know about mashed potatoes and gravy? You're putting on airs. You know you guys only have burritos, enchiladas, and tacos for holiday meals."

"Whatever, Keisha! You always got something stupid to say."

The other women looked on in amusement as the two best friends continued dissing each other. It was nice to see that neither of them took the snide jabs seriously.

"I'm on my way out. I bid everyone a pleasant evening," Marietta said in parting.

Alexis bit down on her lower lip. "Uh, Marietta, why don't you join us? We'd love to have you stay. This is almost like a girls' night out, only we're dining in."

In all the years Marrietta had worked for Alexis, never even once had she been asked to dine with her in the presence of company.

Marietta winked. "This old girl got a hot date! I think he's the one. You know what I mean. The one I wouldn't mind settling down with. He's a handsome one, too. This dinner here is a hen gathering. Don't get me wrong. That's not a bad thing, but I'm looking forward to dining out tonight—and partying late into the night with the head rooster!"

Everyone cracked up as Marietta swished out of the room, her laughter filling the air.

Once everyone was seated, Alexis looked to Marlene to pass the blessing. Without a moment's hesitation, everyone bowed heads and held hands when Marlene requested them to do so. She then began praying over the meal. Afterward, there was silence as the dishes were passed around the table.

Marlene bit into a juicy slice of white turkey meat. "Tell us about yourself, Alexis. What were things like for you while growing up?"

"I was too cute for my own good." Alexis laughed softly. "I was a good girl in a physical way, but a bad, adventurous one in so many other ways. I went to places that I shouldn't have. Did lots of things that I knew were wrong. I got into a lot of trouble with my strict, religious parents. But the things I did were minor infractions considering some of the stuff you hear about today. I spent a good deal of time in our church. My sisters and me were all in the youth choir. It was a family requirement. After church, I became the biggest devil of all. I was the leader in calling people and asking them if their refrigerators were running. When they'd answer yes, I'd tell them they'd better hurry up and try to catch them."

Though everyone was familiar with that kind of story, laughter rang out around the table.

"How'd you meet R.J.?" Rosalinda asked.

"Ah, R.J., my hero, my knight in shining armor. I met him at a frat house. Somewhere else I shouldn't have been. He was my first for everything."

"Everything?" Keisha interrogated in a knowing manner.

"Yes, ma'am. My first date, my first kiss, and my first boyfriend were all the same man. He had me hook, line, and sinker at first sight. What about all of you? How'd you meet your guys?"

"Zach was a hunk when I first met him. He had the cutest, tightest butt, and a solid six-pack beneath the muscle shirts he liked to wear. His smile seemed to have wings. It had a way of lifting me right out of my shoes. I met him at a concert in the park near my cousin's house, where I lived when I first moved to L.A. We were there for a cookout. He was there with his homeboys. When I separated from my peeps to take a walk by the lake, he saw me and came down to talk to me. We've been inseparable ever since." She laughed. "Well, that's the way it used to be, before he started taking long vacations without me." She felt like crying at the memories. Instead, she laughed again.

"What about you, Rosalinda?" Alexis inquired.

Rosalinda frowned. "There was nothing special about Ric and me meeting. When I met him, I was in dire need of some attention. Ric gave it to me. I met him through one of my cousins, Little Jesus, a cousin who is always in trouble. I should've figured out what he was like by the company he kept. Birds of a feather flock together. At any rate, I fell in love with him despite his bad attitude and penchant for getting into trouble with the cops—serious trouble. I've tried to convince myself that he's innocent this time, but I know deep down in my heart that he's probably not. I guess that's called denial."

"Don't I know about denial," Alexis offered. "I've been there most of my life. I thought R.J. was the answer to all my questions about life. He was the one who could make a difference for a little ghetto girl from New Orleans. I suddenly find that I've been living in a dream world. Unfortunately, Sleeping Beauty has checked back into the real-world hotel. I'm alone. This is really hard for me to admit without feeling guilty and selfish, but there are times when I actually like being by myself."

Marlene raised an eyebrow. "Like it how?"

"I feel free for the first time in my life." Alexis folded her hands. "When you're alone with yourself, your thoughts dare to take you places that you didn't have the courage to visit before. I've been thinking a lot about my family and how I abandoned them for wealth and power. I deserted them for the outrageously fictional world of one Richard James Du Boise. I haven't talked to anyone in my family for a long time."

Keisha looked as if she was unsure of what Alexis was saying. "Are your parents alive?"

"I really don't know." Alexis looked ashamed of her admission.

"You don't know! Why not?" Keisha tossed back.

Alexis dropped her head down. "I don't know because I haven't bothered to keep up with them. I left them behind with my little back-water ways. R.J. was able to convince me that I never belonged there—that I was better than everything and everyone on the wrong side of the tracks. My siblings are terribly annoyed with me. So when I did call, depending on who answered the phone, I sometimes didn't get to talk to my parents. My family was never too keen on R.J."

"Why's that?" Marlene inquired.

"My father saw something in R.J. that he didn't like. My brothers have always thought that he was educated but just another slick-as-oil con man. I've been laboring over the idea of calling my mother, but I'm afraid that whoever answers will hang up on me. But I don't think my mother would do something like that if she were to answer the phone."

"Oh, how sad," Marlene commented. "Would you like me to call her for you?"

Blinking hard, Alexis pondered Marlene's question. "You'd do that for me?"

"If it means reconnecting you with your family, of course. You certainly need them at a time like this. Family is so important."

"You're right again. But everyone in mine is definitely going to have something snide to say about it. 'I told you so' will come in spades."

Marlene smiled with understanding. "If you want to talk with your mother, you'll have to endure whatever trouble comes your way. Which is worse? Enduring the snide comments or never talking to your mother again? We do have choices, you know. They probably feel abandoned by you, not the other way around. It sounds like you're the one who stopped calling."

A cloud of uncertainty settled in Alexis's eyes. "Would you be willing to call and ask for my mom right now?" Alexis glanced at the clock. "It's almost ten o'clock there."

Marlene nodded. "Right now! What's her name?"

"Clara Gautier."

Alexis's fingers trembled as she dialed the number she'd had to look up in the address book. Her guests were surprised and saddened by the fact that she didn't even know by heart her own parents' phone number. Alexis handed Marlene the phone. After crossing her fingers, Alexis held them up for Marlene to see.

"Prayer," Marlene softly mouthed. Finger-crossing meant nothing compared to a God who could see all the things written upon one's heart. "Good evening. I'm sorry to call so late, but could I speak with Mrs. Gautier?" Marlene listened to the caller as she was asked to identify herself. "My name is Marlene Covington. She doesn't know me, but I have some information that I was asked to pass on to her."

Marlene was told to hold on while the party checked to see if Mrs. Gautier was still awake. When Clara came on the line, Marlene gave the thumbs-up sign. An audible breath of relief gushed out of Alexis's mouth.

"Hello, ma'am. I'm sorry if I disturbed you, but I'm calling about your daughter, Alexis. . . ."

A muffled scream came across the line, cutting Marlene off in mid-sentence.

"Oh, dear God! Thank you, God, for answering my prayers. Is my child okay? Please tell me my baby girl is not hurt in any way."

Tears slid from Marlene's eyes. "I'll let her tell you that herself." When Marlene handed the phone to Alexis, she saw that her eyes were also filled with water.

Alexis put the speakerphone on when she saw how eager everyone looked. She also needed the support should it go badly. She somehow felt confident that the girls would come to her side if she needed them to. If the conversation got rough, they could hear it firsthand. Alexis may not have realized it, but she seemed to be looking for approval from her guests—and also to win their moral support.

"Momma," Alexis said in a childlike voice.

"Lexy, darling, is this really you, child?"

Tears trickled down Alexis's face. "Yes, Momma, it's me. How are you?"

"Whatever ails me will ail me no more now that I've heard from you. Where are you, dear child? Where have you been keeping yourself?"

"I'm still in California." Alexis delved deep down inside her heart in hopes of finding more courage. "Momma, is Daddy okay?" She held her breath in anticipation of the response. *Please let Daddy be alive, too.*

Clara's soft laughter rippled through Alexis, stirring up strong, soul-deep emotions. "Daddy's just fine, Lexy. I'd let you talk to him, but he's long since been sleep. If I wake him up and tell him you're on the phone, he just might have himself a heart attack. He's been pining over you for months. I'll tell Jacob over his first cup of coffee at breakfast. He's usually very calm during the early morning hours. How's R.J.?"

Alexis swallowed hard. "He's fine, too, Momma. He's away right now." She'd never tell her mother where her husband really was. At least, not over the phone.

"I know you're quite busy these days, but is it possible that you might come home for a short visit? We'd love to see you. And I could certainly use a big hug from my fifth child. We miss you so much, Lexy. Could you please fulfill an old lady and an old man's dream?"

"I'd love that, Momma. But I'm worried about how the rest of the family might feel. They've never been too happy about me leaving New Orleans."

Clara laughed again. "Daddy and I still run this family, Lexy. This home still belongs to your daddy and me. Besides, your sisters and brothers talk about you all the time, wondering if you'll ever come home for a visit. They'll be happy to see you. I'm sure of it."

"Are you really sure? I've called many times over the years, but they wouldn't let me talk to you. So I gave up trying."

"That's no excuse, Lexy. You could've called in the middle of the night, when no one would've been here but your father and me. But I don't want to get into blaming anyone for anything. We've all been at fault. If we'd had your number, we would've called you long ago. I tried to get it, but I was told it was unlisted. All I want now is to see my baby girl. Can you do just that one thing for your daddy and me, sweet Lexy?"

Alexis decided it would do no good to tell her mother that she had called and left the new number with one of her sisters. It was obvious from Clara's comment that it hadn't been passed on to her.

"Yes, Momma, I can. I'll call you once I've made all the arrangements. I love you, Momma."

"Momma loves you, too. That's something you never have to doubt. Please call back in the morning and talk to your daddy. I can't wait to see the look on his face when he hears your voice. I know it'll be priceless. I'm gonna have my camera handy so I can capture that glorious Kodak moment on film."

"Oh, Momma, I wish I could see that moment, too." Alexis chewed on her lower lip. "What if someone else answers the phone and won't let me talk to you?"

"Don't worry about that. It's not going to happen. I'll see to it myself. You just make sure you call. Be sweet, honey, until we talk again tomorrow."

"Okay, Momma. Good night."

Alexis's whole body shook with the force of her runaway, heartfelt emotions as she hung up the phone. The much-needed release had sneaked upon her, overwhelming her in the process. The other women cried, too, feeling deep compassion for the woman who was finally able to make some semblance of peace with her family. She hadn't made peace with everyone, but she'd made a great start by connecting with the most important people in her family: her parents. The four women embraced until all their emotions were reined in. Feeling more composed, they returned to their seats at the table.

"Thank . . . you, Marlene," Alexis practically sobbed. "I can't . . . believe how . . . easy this . . . was. And I can hardly believe that my mother still wants to see me after the way I've neglected them." She suddenly looked fearful. "I don't know if I can do this by myself."

Marlene waved off Alexis's last remarks. "Why not? That's your family."

Alexis shook her head. "I know. Regardless of what my mother said, there's going to be some opposition for me to deal with from my siblings. Trust me. My oldest sister is going to give me nonstop fire and brimstone over my lengthy absence from the family. She's going to dig her nails so deep into me—they'll probably break off beneath my skin."

Marlene shrugged. "You're going to have to face them no matter what. Keep yourself focused on your mission and don't let anyone deter you from it. Seeing your parents is all you should concern yourself with for now. Don't allow yourself to think about anything but them."

Alexis's smile came like a bright beam of light. "Why don't you all come with me. We could do it over a weekend. If you haven't already been there, you'll love New Orleans."

Rosalinda sighed with dismay. "We go to the prison every weekend. Ric would have a conniption fit if I missed one visiting session. But it does sound tempting."

Keisha brushed Alexis's hand with hers. "You can't use us as a buffer in this. Seeing your family is something you have to do alone."

"Oh, I plan to see them by myself the first time. But I need you guys for backup, for support. We'll get a large hotel suite and a nice luxury rental car. You all can take in the sights, sounds, and delicious smells of New Orleans while I'm visiting. Before we leave, I'd like to take you out to meet my family. That is, if all goes well with our initial visit."

"Maybe you should take this trip alone," Marlene suggested. "I'm sure everything will work out just fine."

Keisha frowned. "Marlene's right. Rosalinda and I couldn't afford a trip like that anyway."

"That's the truth," Rosalinda seconded.

"I'd be bankrolling the entire trip. I'd never ask you to pay for something I've invited you to," Alexis assured her guests.

"In that case, let's get to packing," Keisha joked. "No, I'm just kidding. I think we all agree you should go and see your family alone." The others nodded in agreement.

"Okay, okay" I think I'll just consider having my parents come here instead. It'll be easier for me to make amends with them first. I'll deal with the rest of the family later. Now that we have that settled, who's for sitting out by the pool for a spell? We can have our dessert and a glass of wine out there."

Marlene clapped her hands. "That sounds wonderful to me. What about you two?"

Both Keisha and Rosalinda nodded in agreement.

Keisha gave Marlene a strange look. "Are you going to drink a glass of wine?"

"I'm a saint, not a teetotaler." Everyone laughed at that comment and the comical expression on Marlene's face. "If I wasn't the designated driver, I might be tempted to have two glasses. How do you like me now?" If the truth were known, she needed a glass of wine to calm her nerves. Jesse's absence was starting to get to her, more than she wanted to admit.

"Wine for everyone!" Alexis sang out.

As Alexis poured her best wine into chilled, frosted wineglasses, she couldn't remember ever having been this happy to have guests over. R.J.'s friends were all stuffed shirts. All they ever talked about was money, money, and more money. Often, she was left alone to entertain the prim and proper wives while R.J. took the men into his special playroom.

Billiards, along with a variety of other high-tech games, were in the room that she'd only graced a few times. Even then, it had only been for a minute or two. R.J. said it was a man's room, no place for a delicate lady like herself.

As usual, whatever R.J. said was the gospel truth, according to him.

This was as good a time as any to see exactly what kept him in that room for hours on end. Without the fear of him catching her in the act, she could thoroughly investigate the room that was practically off-limits to women. It was something she'd wanted to do since the first day he was locked up.

R.J., what am I going to do without you here to squash my every thought and control my every move? She laughed from deep within. "Live it up!" she uttered under her breath.

Drawing everyone's attention, her happy laughter sailed onto the air, light and breezy.

"That phone call to your mother really did wonders for you." Marlene was happy for her. "If you can help it, Alexis, don't ever again let that much time pass between phone calls to your parents." Marlene studied Alexis's smug expression. "Your joy isn't just about the phone call. What's up with you?"

"I'll tell you once we're out on the patio. Everyone, follow me."

The out-of-doors decor was every bit as intoxicating as the lavish interior of the house. Kings and queens couldn't live any better than R.J. and Alexis did. The fully-covered patio was stocked with a full bar and all the very best barbecue equipment man had ever made. Several sets of the finest in patio furnishings graced the large redwood deck. There was even a built-in brick fireplace that burned real wood. The water in the pool and Jacuzzi was crystal clear. Plenty of colorful flower gardens and carefully tended lavish greenery completed the outside decor.

Marlene took a sip of her wine once everyone was seated around the glass table. "What had you looking so smug a few minutes ago?"

Alexis's laughter bubbled in her throat. "I was into mischievous thinking. R.J. has this room that he's particular about me not going into. In fact, he's made it clear that he doesn't want women in there, period. Without him here to stop me, I think I'll do a little investigative snooping. He can stay in that room for hours and hours at a time. So there must be something in there that's pretty darn interesting—and I think it is high time that I find out just what that something is. He keeps it locked up tight, but I now have all of his keys. I'm going on a scavenger hunt! Would you ladies care to join me?"

Marlene frowned. "That might not be such a good idea, Alexis. Some secrets are best kept. Don't go looking for something you might not be prepared to discover. Remember that curiosity kills."

Alexis widened her eyes. "Then I should already be dead. There should be no secrets between married couples, but R.J. never thought that rule applied to our marriage. That man has numerous secrets, intimate secrets, way more than Victoria. I'll think about what you've said, Marlene, but I'm not so sure I'll change my mind. I want to know exactly what's in that room. More to the point, I want to know what R.J. did in that room every single night for the past five years."

"I'll go in there with you if no one else will," Keisha offered. "You got me curious as hell over here." Marlene gave Keisha a warning look. "Don't look at me like that, Mizzzz Marlene! You want to know, too, and so do you, Rosalinda. You're all just too embarrassed to admit it."

Alexis jumped up. "Let's do it." Without another thought, Marlene and Rosalinda were out of their seats, following right along behind Alexis and Keisha.

Satisfaction was about to be achieved. The death of the curious cat seemed inevitable.

The room itself looked like one big enigma. All the modern electronic gadgets seemed to add to the mystique of the secret room. The built-in television appeared to be the size of an actual movie screen. Navy blue leather sofas and numerous reclining chairs faced the gigantic audio-visual center. There were several other comfortable chairs and also a couple of Vegas-style poker tables and stools in the room. The fully-stocked bar was even grander than the one on the patio. A variety of extraordinary African-American works of art hung from the pecan-colored wood-paneled walls in expensive brass and wooden frames. Several types of modern electrical fixtures provided ample but subtle lighting.

In Marlene's opinion, the icy feel of the room was somewhat eerie. She actually shivered from the unusual frigidity of the indoor atmosphere.

Roslinda's eyes bulged. "Look at all these pinball machines over here. This is some kind of an amazing arcade up in here. I wonder if you have to use money to get them to work."

Alexis shrugged her shoulders. "I don't know. Do you see coin slots anywhere?"

Marlene's eyes instantly fixed onto a metal panel built into one wall. An array of silvery buttons protruded from the shiny panel. Itching to push one of them, Marlene put her hands behind her back to still the desire. "I wonder what all these buttons go to?"

Alexis crossed the room and stood before the panel. "I've never seen this before. But I guess that's not so unusual since I've never gotten much further than the inside of the door. Wait a minute." Alexis picked up a magnificent picture that had obviously fallen off the wall. Then she saw the outline on the wall where the picture had once hung. "The earthquake," she announced, "the one we had a couple of weeks ago. The picture must have fallen then. It looks as if it was covering this control panel. Talk about mysterious. This room is that and a lot more."

Keisha came over to look at the panel. "Maybe we should push one or two of them and see what happens. They probably control all these electronic gaming machines."

"You're probably right." Though reluctant to do so, Alexis pressed her finger against one of the buttons. When nothing happened, she pushed in another one and then another one. Blue lights suddenly flashed and then dimmed. Slowly, one entire section of the wall opened up. The unexpected movement scared each of them to death, causing them to huddle together in fear.

Nothing could have prepared Alexis and her guests for what they found behind the wall. Astonished, trembling with trepidation, Alexis walked around the room, surveying its contents. Her heart nearly skipped a beat when she realized that the room held a variety of Vegas-style slot machines.

Inside the secret room, from behind that paneled wall, Richard James Du Boise had been running an illegal gambling casino.

Alexis began to tremble even more. Her eyes were filled with the brightness of unshed tears. "So, an illegal operation is what's been going on in this room for years now. How could I have been so blind? Why didn't I see what was going on in my own house? R.J. may not be guilty of embezzlement, but the evidence in this room clearly suggests that he's guilty of something even more sinister than stealing from clients. Illegal gambling and possibly income-tax evasion. I couldn't have even imagined that something like this was going on in our home."

"Are you saying you didn't know anything about this?" Keisha asked. Alexis was too numb to do anything but nod. "That's hard to believe. I can't imagine not knowing what's going on in my own house."

"That's 'cause you live in a tiny apartment and not a ten-thousand-square-foot house like this one," Marlene remarked. "What are you going to do about all this?"

Alexis shook her head. "I have no idea. Keisha's right. No one is going to believe I didn't know about this room. R.J. has some explaining to do. Our last visit didn't go so well. And from the looks of things, I don't think the next one is going to go any better. Let's get out of here. This room is starting to freak me out."

After the women filed out of the room, Alexis locked the doors, wishing she'd never gone into it. Marlene was right. Curiosity had killed the cat, along with her spirit.

CHAPTER NINE

Smiling sweetly, Keisha opened the door of her apartment to Marlene. The two women embraced warmly before Marlene came all the way inside. While taking a few minutes to catch her breath from the two flights of stairs she had climbed, Marlene's eyes gave the apartment a quick once-over.

"Oh, my, you do have a nice place here, Keisha. Very nice. I love it."

"You sound like you expected something else. Do you think all welfare recipients live like hood rats? Well, if you do, we don't. I take very good care of myself, my apartment, and my kids. Not only that, I take pride in the way we look."

"You are so defensive. Of course I don't think that, Keisha. I'm just happy to see that you manage so well with no one to help you. I wasn't sure what I expected your place to look like. It probably wouldn't have mattered to me one way or the other. I already know how clean and neat you keep yourself and the kids. There are a lot of people on welfare who have lots of pride."

"It may not seem like it at times, but I have a lot of pride."

"I know that, Keisha. Everyone on welfare isn't just looking for a free ride. There are people out there who have to use the system to help pull themselves up by the bootstraps. Just like you're doing. There are also a lot of people working to better themselves while getting the necessary assistance. I hope that settles it for you. Now, I'd like to see the rest of your place before it is time for us to get on our way."

Keisha hugged Marlene. "Sorry for being so sensitive. Just another result of the way I've been conditioned. It seems to me that everyone has a negative reaction to people on welfare. I'm trying so hard to break the welfare cycle. I don't want my kids to face the things I've had to because I needed county assistance. That's why furthering my education is so important to me."

Marlene pecked Keisha's forehead. "You're doing just fine. It won't be long before you'll graduate from your class and start earning decent wages. With all things considered, you've done the best that you can do. Don't forget that. Your kids certainly won't."

Keisha took Marlene down the hall and into her bedroom. It wasn't a large room, but it was neat and clean with plenty of room to maneuver around the furnishings. The full-size bed was without a headboard, but a large mirror hung above it. The apartment-size dresser also had a mirror. In the kid's room there were maple twin beds and a baby bed.

Keisha had bought the twin beds for when the kids were old enough to have overnight guests. Besides that, she'd gotten a good price. With the counter space filled by a variety of cosmetics and toiletry items, the one bathroom was sufficient for now, Keisha explained. She planned to look for a larger apartment in the near future.

The doorbell pealed. "That's probably Rosalinda. You can continue to look around while I get the door." Marlene nodded.

As she toured the rest of the apartment, Marlene couldn't help wondering if Malcolm would ever have a good job, his own place, and, at some point, a family. She was tired of seeing him around the house all the time since the job at Wal-mart had already fallen through. Malcolm had claimed that his supervisor was always on his case, the same played-out reason he'd cited for discontinuing work at other jobs. Now that Jesse wasn't there, Malcolm was at home more than he'd ever been. When his dad was in the house, Malcolm found every excuse in the book to be gone. Even though Malcolm was a preacher's kid, Jesse hadn't forced him to attend church after he reached a certain age. He was sure they'd instilled the right things in him. Jesse believed that parents were responsible for their children when they were young. He didn't think parents were responsible for who their children became as adults. It was about choices when a child reached adulthood.

With an enthusiastic smile on her face, Rosalinda skidded down the hall. "Hi, Marlene. How are you? I'm glad we're riding out to the prison with you. Thank you for being so kind."

Marlene embraced Rosalinda. "I'm fine. And you're welcome. You seem mighty happy for it being so early in the morning. Did you win the lottery?"

Rosalinda laughed. "No, but I got my personal loan approved. I can get some things done now that I have the extra money. I did a consolidation on all my bills. After the credit union takes that one lump monthly payment, I'll still have money left over to pay for my mom's medications. If I'm real careful with the extra cash money from the loan, I'll be in good financial shape for a while."

"That is, until Ricardo learns you got a loan," Keisha interjected. "If he finds out, he'll make sure that he gets his share of it."

"He's not going to find out. I'm determined not to tell him this time. I seriously need that money. He got me for most of the last loan."

Keisha rolled her eyes. "And he's gonna get you for most of this one."

"Keisha, I don't know why you always have something to say! You give as much money to Zach as I give to Ric. You've pawned every piece of decent gold jewelry that you owned just to put money on his books. You don't even have money for milk and diapers half of the time. You need to back off of me."

"Ladies," Marlene sang out. "We need to get on the road if we're going to get there in time for visitation. You two shouldn't forget that you're best friends, that you've always had each other's backs. Okay? I'm going to keep reminding you of that fact until you get it right."

Keisha rolled her eyes at Rosalinda. "You better be glad she's here to referee. I'm about sick of your flapping lips. My fist is just itching to connect with your pretty nut-brown face."

Rosalinda frowned as she shot Keisha an unpleasant hand gesture. "Same here, bi—"

"Uh, uh, uh," Marlene warned, stepping in between the two young women.

When Marlene starting laughing uncontrollably, Keisha and

Rosalinda looked at her like she'd lost her mind. She was laughing so hard that she had to hold her side to keep it from splitting.

"What's so funny?" Keisha finally inquired.

Marlene struggled to get her funny bone under control. "I guess I haven't learned my lesson yet. I just did it again."

"Did what?' Rosalinda asked.

"I just stepped in between two people who were trying to take each other out. I'll never forget the day Jesse blacked my eye, but good."

Keisha's mouth fell wide open. "You let your husband black your eye?"

"I didn't let him. I just happened to step in front of a big, ugly, hairy fist that was meant for Malcolm. By the time I finally came to, I had a black-and-purple burlap bag under my eye and a headache that wouldn't quit. Jesse was madder at me than he was at Malcolm. Said it was foolish of me to get between two full-grown men, especially with one of them angry enough to kill. Jesse was the one ready to commit murder. Malcolm was scared out of his wits. So scared that he went to his room and locked the door. Once inside, he opened the window and climbed out. He wanted to get away from the house until he was sure I'd come around. He called home a couple of hours later to see if it was okay for him to come back. He didn't want to face Jesse without me."

Rosalinda looked nonplussed. "What kind of preacher would want to murder his own flesh and blood?"

Marlene waved the question off. "Let's get out of here. I'll tell you the rest of the story in the car."

Marlene smiled as she pulled the car away from the curb. Keisha and Rosalinda had already gotten back to acting like best friends. They'd forgotten all about their heated exchange while they'd busied themselves packing their belongings into the trunk of the car. Marlene had brought along a cooler packed with sodas and luncheon-meat sandwiches. They were all going to spend the night in the same room. Marlene had booked one of the only three suites the hotel had. Keisha and Rosalinda would take turns spending the night on the pullout sofa bed. Zach's mother had agreed to keep the kids. Since Zanari's hospitalization, Lucian had been helping out Keisha more.

Gospel music played on the CD player. Keisha and Rosalinda kept exchanging frowning glances. They wanted to hear some hip-hop music, but neither of them had the nerve to ask Marlene to change the station. The gospel was kind of soothing to both of them, but after about an hour of it, they'd had enough. Their heavy sighs went totally unnoticed by Marlene.

"Marlene, you never finished telling us what happened between your husband and son," Keisha reminded her, hoping to block out the gospel sound.

Marlene glanced at Keisha for a brief moment. "It's not a pleasant story, but I was laughing because getting in between you two reminded me of that night. Jesse was ready to annihilate Malcolm because he thought he had stolen some money from his grandmother, Jesse's mother. When Jesse asked him about the missing money, Malcolm said he hadn't taken the money—that his grandmother was just a senile, old fool suffering with Alzheimer's disease."

"For true?" Rosalinda asked.

"For true. As if that wasn't enough to send Jesse into a red rage, Malcolm went on to say that he hated his grandmother and that he wished she didn't have to live with us. The shouting between them began. I remember Malcolm raising his fist at Jesse, telling his dad that he was an adult, that he wasn't taking another whipping from him. That's when this fool lost her mind and stepped in. If I hadn't stepped in, Jesse would've gone to jail that night. He surely would've hurt Malcolm that time. I don't think I could've stopped him. He's innocent of the charges against him now, but he would've been guilty of a crime back then. A serious crime."

"Did Malcolm take the money?" Rosalinda asked.

"He did, unfortunately. Jesse knew he'd taken the money when he first asked him. He was hoping Malcolm would come clean with him. But when Malcolm started lying and then insulting his grandmother to cover up his criminal acts, Jesse lost it."

Keisha looked perplexed. "How did Jesse know your son had taken it?"

"Under Malcolm's mattress, Jesse found the exact amount of money that was taken, along with Grandmother Covington's silk handkerchief. The same one that she kept her money wrapped up in. Malcolm didn't have a job at the time. He admitted his guilt to me later, but he's never told his dad the truth. I haven't either, but Jesse already knows the truth. That unfortunate incident happened over two years ago."

Keisha scratched her head. "I'm surprised at you, being a Christian and all, that you'd cover up for your son like that. That couldn't have helped him any. If he was doing stuff like that, he needed to face the music."

"I know." That's all Marlene could say. She didn't want to get any deeper into the topic.

She'd probably said too much already. When she covered up for Malcolm, she knew that she was as guilty of the crime as he was. There were times that even she couldn't see beyond his handsome face and beautiful eyes. He would be her baby until the day she died. Malcolm had cast his spell over her the first moment she'd held him. She hadn't been able to break the spell yet. Malcolm still knew how to manipulate her in so many ways. The loss of one child had been enough. The thought of ever losing another was just too much for her to bear. That alone kept her off balance where her only son was concerned.

As expected, it was hot and dry up in the high desert. Though she wore light clothing, Marlene sweated profusely as she scanned the visiting line for Keisha and Rosalinda. Though they had ridden out there with her, the two young women were nowhere to be seen. They'd somehow gotten separated between the parking lot and the prison building.

Ever since Keisha's line had been temporarily disconnected for nonpayment of the bill, knowing of their limited incomes, Marlene had come up with the idea of them riding with her. It had eliminated the cost of a rental and the gas to go in it. Although both women owned cars, they had no confidence whatsoever in their hoopty-style transportation, they'd told Marlene. The old cars were barely able to get them back and forth to work. There was no way their wrecks would withstand a long-distance drive.

As a Greyhound bus pulled up to the curb near the prison entrance, Marlene turned her attention to the people getting off. Several young women rushed the bus's exit doors and hurried to the back of the line. Nothing could have prepared her for the shock of what was worn by the young woman who seemed to be the last person getting off the bus. Her shock increased tenfold when two tiny white-tuxedo-clad boys and a cute little girl in a pink frilly lace dress came and stood right beside the woman.

Stunned out of her gourd, Marlene couldn't help staring at the young woman as she carefully came down the steps of the bus wearing satin heels. Dressed in a pure white wedding gown, with a full chapel-length train folded doubly over her arm to keep from dragging on the ground, the beautiful Hispanic woman gave soft commands to the little people who were apparently members of her bridal party.

Not caring about losing her space, Marlene followed the Hispanic woman to the end of the line and stood right behind her. She was so curious about what this all meant that she just had to have more information. She could hear the whispers and laughter of the other visitors, but it really wasn't funny. In fact, it was rather sad and somewhat pitiful if it meant what she thought.

Knowing she was being nosy and too bold for words, but unable to help it, Marlene tapped the young woman on the shoulder. "Do you speak English?"

She smiled at Marlene. "Oh, of course," the woman answered in a barely discernible Spanish accent.

"I guess it's probably obvious to most everyone in line, and I don't mean to pry, but are you getting married today?"

The woman's pretty face beamed as bright as a ray of sunshine. "I am. I'm so excited about it. The chaplain is going to perform the ceremony in the prison chapel."

Marlene looked down at the three children. Her heart nearly broke at the sight of them. She was sure they didn't have a clue as to what was about to happen. "Are these your kids?"

Smiling with pride, the woman tapped each child on the head. "This is my five-year-old daughter, Pietra, and my four-year-old twin sons, Orlando and Ramondo. By the way, my name is Mercedes Espinoza. In just a short while it will be changed to Mercedes Ortiz." She extended her hand to Marlene. "And your name?"

Marlene was so dumbfounded that she had a hard time shaking herself loose from the chaos she felt inside. She took Mercedes's hand for a brief moment and squeezed it gently. "I'm Marlene Covington. It's a pleasure meeting you and your children."

Marlene had to put her hands behind her back to keep from reaching down and picking up the kids, one at a time, to hug them. They were probably going to need a lot more than just hugs in the next few years. If Marlene was correctly assessing the situation, they were prime candidates for a future Montel Williams show.

"It's nice meeting you, too. I guess you're real curious about why I would marry someone in prison."

Wondering if her expression was that obvious, Marlene coughed nervously. "It had crossed my mind, but I wouldn't think of prying into your private affairs." *But only the Lord knows how much I want to hear whatever juicy tidbits you're willing to share.*

Mercedes smiled. "It's okay. I'm not ashamed of what I'm doing. Rolando is the father of my children. He's a good man, but trouble seems to find him wherever he goes." She actually giggled. "He was convicted for armed robbery. That carries a mandatory sentence in the state of California. The owner of the store was killed. That made him an accessory even though he wasn't the one who pulled the trigger. Rolonda was given twenty years to life."

This young woman was talking about armed robbery and accessory to murder as if she were discussing something as ordinary as the weather. And she was going to marry this man, an accessory to the murder—the same man who might possibly spend the rest of his life behind bars. That was something Marlene couldn't even begin to fathom. It just wasn't registering.

What is going on inside Mercedes's head? Marlene wondered. She felt terribly concerned about the horrendous effects this tremendously appalling situation would later have on these small children. Mercedes didn't look to be any older than twenty-five. Marlene had doubts that she was even that old. It wasn't too often that she was at a loss for words, but she certainly was at the moment. The truth was, she'd found herself at a loss for words a lot lately. She'd never known that so much high prison drama went on before Rosalinda and Keisha had come into her life. This was all too unbelievable for her.

Mercedes nudged Marlene out of her shocked state. "Are you okay? I'm sorry if I upset you. I wanted to answer the questions I saw in your eyes. I hope you don't worry about the children and me. We'll be fine. Rolando is finally making good on his long ago promise to me."

"I hope you will be, but I'm the one who's sorry. I just didn't know what to say. Were there certain steps that you had to take to marry an inmate?" Marlene put her fingers up to her lips. "Oh, there I go again. I'm sorry, I should've called your children's father by his first name. Please forgive my insensitivity."

"That's okay. We both had to take marriage counseling for six weeks. It went really well for us. We definitely needed the counseling and we learned a lot of good things. Rolando is now truly committed to the children and me. He's going to be a faithful husband."

I guess so. It's easy enough to be committed and faithful locked away behind bars, especially when you might not have much hope of ever living outside this concrete jungle. Conjugal visits aren't even an option for married couples inside this prison.

So, what is this marriage really about? Marlene wondered, amazed at the conversation.

"I see. I wish you only the best in your marriage." Marlene instantly berated herself inwardly for telling that blatant lie. All she wished for was that this young woman would get back on the next bus home and never come back to this evil place again. She wished that Mercedes would take her children home and keep them safe and warm, protected from such an ugly, unhealthy environment. Silently, she prayed for this entire family.

What in the world did these men behind bars have over these women? If it took her the rest of her days, she was going to make it her life's mission to find out. And what was the motivating factor behind these women who were so loyal to men who couldn't do a single thing for them? They had nothing whatsoever to offer, yet they had somehow managed to conquer these beautiful young women, had managed to suck their youthful lives right out from under them. That in itself seemed too deep for her to get to the bottom of.

Marlene Covington knew that she would rise to the challenge she'd been presented with, one way or the other. God's mission for her was becoming crystal clear with each visit right into the heart of hell.

Just as the line began to move forward, Marlene finally spotted Keisha and Rosalinda. They waved while quickly making their way to the back. Each woman embraced Marlene before getting into the line. Marlene didn't miss the strange looks they gave Mercedes and her little wedding party. When they got together for the late lunch they'd planned, after the prison visit, Marlene knew exactly what the first topic of their discussions was going to be.

If they didn't wake up soon and begin to smell the coffee, they could easily end up just like Mercedes. Married to men who could do nothing for their ladies, nothing but leave them alone and waiting.

* * *

Jesse looked a couple of pounds thinner than he had on Marlene's last visit. Only a week had passed since she'd last seen him, but she noticed a definite change in him. He was even walking slower than normal. Had something happened to him to make him look so dejected?

Feeling anxiety-ridden, she grasped his hand as soon as he reached the table. "Jesse, are you okay? You don't look like you feel very well."

Before seating himself, he bent down and hugged his wife. He then kissed her on the mouth and on both cheeks. "Hello, wildflower! I can't tell you how good it is to see you. You're looking as beautiful as ever."

"Jesse Covington, don't try to run that weak, predictable game on me. When you don't want to answer my questions, you do your best to try and distract me. It didn't work. Now, stop trying to put me off and tell me how you're feeling. Physically and mentally."

Jesse smiled weakly, too dispirited to do much more than that. His eyes blurred as he tried to keep Marlene in focus. He hadn't slept for two days. A lot of disturbing things had occurred over the last couple of nights. Jesse had stayed awake to make sure that he didn't become the next victim of circumstance. His frantic vigilance had left him weak and tired.

The loud, brain-piercing screams of pain and anguish he'd heard coming from the shower stalls had kept him awake the first night. Plain old fear had kept him from going to sleep last night—after he'd seen several guys practically drag one of the newer guys from his cell. He knew they'd have to kill him before he let them take advantage of him sexually. Outside of God, his size had become his biggest ally. He wouldn't think of sharing what had occurred with his wife. She already had more than her share of worries.

He covered her hand with his. "I'm tired as can be, but otherwise I'm just fine. I'm going to be real honest with you, even though I'm sure you already know what I'm about to say. This isn't a nice place to be. I wouldn't wish these horrific conditions on anyone, not even an enemy. I'm growing weary, Marlene. My faith in God hasn't diminished an ounce, but my strength is all but depleted. It is hard to sleep in a place like this. It's even harder to eat in here. My stomach feels like it's full of lead, not to mention acid, after I finish one of those unpalatable meals they serve."

He saw the tears in her eyes. "I'm sorry, sweetheart. I shouldn't talk like this in front of you. I can see how much I've upset you."

Lifting his hand, she kissed the back of it. "You haven't done a thing to upset me. It's the system that has me so distraught. There wasn't a shred of hard evidence against you, but the prosecutor was able to convince the jurors that you'd committed the crime." She blew out a ragged breath. Her heart was beating way too fast. She needed to calm down before her heart exploded inside her chest. Her blood pressure had a tendency to shoot right through the roof during stressful times. *My Lord, please deliver us from all this evil.*

"How are things going at the church, Marlene?" He thought it best to change the subject, seeing that his wife had gotten so upset. He was also concerned with her history of high blood pressure. The last thing she needed was to find herself lying flat on her back in a hospital bed. "No one's giving you a hard time, are they?"

She grinned. "Reverend Clay Robinson is doing a superb job in your absence, but he can't wait for your return. He has enough duties of his own. We're all eagerly awaiting your homecoming. There's not a day that goes by that someone from the church doesn't call to check on Malcolm and me. Everyone is being real supportive. They all love you so much, Jesse."

Her comments made him feel good, really good. Still, he knew some troublesome members of his congregation were going to get antsy about his absence before too long. He wouldn't be at all surprised if even a few members of the deacon board turned on him.

"Speaking of Malcolm, how's the boy doing? Is he helping you out around the house?"

Marlene sighed. "Malcolm is still Malcolm, the pretty boy. He does help around the house, but not if I don't get after him about it. That boy's so lazy he stinks. His room smells like a high school locker room. I'm sure I saw something green growing out of his sneakers the last time I dared to venture into that musty jungle."

They both laughed.

"All joking aside, he's doing okay. But there's room for improvement."

"Wildflower, he's never going to improve if you don't start kicking his butt to the curb. You shouldn't have to do anything in that house but take care of your personal needs. That's a grown man living off of us. He won't even run the vacuum or wash a dish unless somebody insists on it. And I can imagine what's happening now that I'm not there to stick it to him. I just know he's constantly taking advantage of you—because you let him do it when I am there. When are you going to let him fly free? When the mother bird kicks her young out of the nest, they either fly or splatter themselves all over the ground. It's time for you to kick Malcolm out of the nest, Mar. Whether he flies or not is entirely up to him."

"But he's still enrolled in the city college."

"And he'll continue to be a career student as long as we let him. He stays in school to keep from working. The problem is he's not doing anything while he's there. His grades are atrocious. He does just enough to keep from flunking out." He couldn't go to a university because of his failing grades in high school. Jesse shrugged his broad shoulders. "I'm sorry. I don't even know why I started this. We've only had this conversation a million times. It has yet to end on a pleasant note. That's not something either of us needs right now."

Marlene's eyes grew soft and liquid. "I feel you, Jesse. Things are changing at home. He's been out looking for a job practically every day. He got the job at the Wal-mart, but it didn't work out. His supervisor was always on him. You know how that goes. He'll have a job in the next couple of weeks. He's trying really hard."

How many times had he heard her say that? How many times had Malcolm made her believe that he'd been hassled on the job, that an employer had promised to call him for a job within the next couple of weeks? How many times had he told her there were no openings at the places he'd gone to? How many times had she fallen for the same old story? There were too many times to keep count.

Marlene was always trying to save the world, but she didn't have a clue how to save herself from Malcolm. Jesse had to wonder if that would ever change.

"You're not going to believe what happened while I was waiting in the line. I still can't believe it myself." She went on to tell Jesse about the bride-to-be and her three adorable kids.

Jesse raised an eyebrow. "Getting married in prison? I'm as shocked as you are. Is it becoming fashionable these days to marry an inmate?"

"Now that you mention it, I think it has. The Menendez brothers had fiancées after they were locked up behind bars. So did the Night Stalker, Richard Ramirez. I think Ramirez actually got married. That's too scary." Marlene shook her head. "It's also becoming fashionable for young women to hook up with inmates through their friends or family members on the inside. Can you imagine telling your sister or a female friend that you got someone you want her to meet the next time they come for a visit? And when she asks who it is, you tell her your cell mate. They're also hooking up inmates with people they know over the phone. What kind of mess is that? I'm doing my best to get it."

Jesse laughed. "Where'd you hear that one?"

"You hear just about everything while standing in that line. Malcolm seems to know quite a bit about what goes on in these places. When I told him about the three women I met, he wanted to know how old were they. Then, when he found out they had men in prison, he started to run it all down for me."

"How's your mentoring project coming with those young women?"

"We've been seeing a lot of each other, especially since they started riding out here with me. It's like having two daughters around. I've grown to love them. I also talk to both Keisha and Rosalinda on the phone a couple of times a week. We're going to have a late lunch after this visit. We plan on staying in the hotel tonight so we can come visit tomorrow. But that'll mean missing church again. We've also worked hard on pulling together the support group. Our first one is scheduled for next week."

"That sounds wonderful. I'm happy that's working out for you. But You don't have to come here again tomorrow. I know this has to be hard on you."

"Not as hard as it is on you. I don't mind coming here, especially when I see that it lights up your face. We're in this together. I'm in this for the long haul, no matter how long of a haul it turns out to be, Jesse Covington."

He swallowed the emotion-induced lump in his throat. Marlene was the best thing that had ever happened to him. She'd come into his life at just the right time. Before her, he'd been rather trifling—and he hadn't thought much of settling down with only one woman. If someone had told him back then that he'd end up in the ministry, he would've called that person a liar. As he looked over at the two young women his wife was hell-bent on saving, he couldn't understand why they were wasting their time in a place like this. He couldn't help noticing that Rosalinda looked like her young man had cast a deep, dark spell over her.

"Have you seen my lawyer?" Ric asked Rosalinda.

"Yes, Ric, I've seen him, and we talked."

"What did you talk about?"

"I needed an extension of the payment plan." She decided not to go into any details since she'd made up her mind to sleep with Hernandez. It wasn't something she wanted to talk about.

He sharply cut his dark eyes at her. "Why do you keep needing extensions? I'll never get out of here at this rate. What are you doing with your money, anyway?"

"I don't believe you asked that since I send you the majority of it. Ric, I don't make a lot of money. I work two jobs as it is. I had to pay for medication refills out of this check. Don't you believe I'm doing the best that I can by you?"

He heard the hurt in her voice, but he hated it when she whined and complained. "Can't you get them to give you a raise? You been at both jobs long enough."

She had been given a raise, a couple of them. But she didn't want him to know that. Even with the raises, there was hardly any money left over after she paid all her monthly expenses. The rising cost of her mother's medication practically took all the extra money she managed to save.

"Instead of that temporary rehab place, you need to put your mother in a long-term nursing home and be done with it. Won't Medicare pay for her medication if she's permanently placed in a nursing home?"

She looked horrified. "How can you even suggest something like that? I was brought up to take care of my own. The Morales family don't put their loved ones in no nursing facility!"

"That's your biggest problem, Rosie. You always put your family before me. When you gonna start putting me first?" He pounded his fist against his chest in anger. "If she's home from rehab when I get out, I ain't living with your damn momma. I'm not moving back into that apartment with her. She takes up entirely too much of your time. And that takes time away from us."

She tried to take his hand, but he pulled away. "I'm sorry, Ric. I hate myself when I upset you. Could you please hold my hand? I'm sorry, baby. I won't let it happen again."

He took her hand, but only because he needed her. He'd rather die than let her know how much he needed her. But he did, badly. She was the only person who hadn't lost confidence in him, the only person he could still manipulate into doing anything he wanted, the only person who continued to accept his collect calls. In fact, she was the only one there for him, period.

Rosalinda held the master key to his cell. It was her finances that might eventually set him free. As he looked at her, he thought he'd better be a little nicer to her. She'd been giving him a lot of lip on the last two visits, something she'd rarely done before. He saw some changes in her, changes that he didn't particularly like. Had they been on the outside, he would've just roughed her up a bit to get her back in line. But if he did that in here, it would mean going into the black hole—solitary confinement.

The hole was darker and worse than he could ever imagine hell being.

He squeezed her hand. "I love you, baby. I shouldn't talk to you like that. I just get so upset about being in here. I don't mean to lose control. You're the only one that cares about me. When I get out of here, I'm going to make it all up to you. I'm gonna get a job and buy you that engagement ring you deserve. Will you marry me when I come home, baby?"

Rosalinda's eyes shone brightly with tears. "Of course I'll marry you, Ric. But do you really mean it this time?"

He saw that he had her undivided attention. That made him grin. Talking about marrying her worked every single time. "I mean it this time. I know I've said it before, but I wasn't ready for it then. It's now time for me to settle down and take responsibility for myself." He leaned forward in his seat. "It's time for me to love you the way you deserve to be loved."

He grasped both of her hands. "Do you know what I'm thinking right now?"

She giggled. "No, but I know what I'm thinking."

"What's that?"

"You sure you want to know, Ric?"

"I'm sure."

"Do you remember when we made love in the men's bathroom at the Coliseum during a Raiders game several years ago? That's what I was thinking about."

His eyes grew bright. "Yeah, that was some game. The Raiders was scoring a touchdown while I was scoring you. You were pretty hot that evening. I'm getting hard just thinking about it. Too bad I can't do nothing about it in here. But we'll do it over the phone Monday night. What do you say to that? Make sure you're in bed when I call."

Blushing, Rosalinda smiled. "It's a date."

The scraping sound of a chair on concrete pierced the air, causing everyone to look in the direction of where it came from. Then loud shouting occurred.

"Bitch, don't tell me nothing about going to no freaking grocery store. You don't leave that house unless I tell you do so. You're my bitch. You don't eat or take a dump unless I tell you to. You been getting mighty defiant, and that's gonna get you hurt real bad."

Marlene turned around just in time to see a woman's backside slam hard onto the floor. Her baby, who had apparently been sitting on her lap, bounced up and then came down on top of her stomach. The man she'd been sitting with stood over her with a menacing scowl on his face, looking ready to pounce again. Before the guards could reach the scene, he bent down and punched her dead in the mouth. Blood flew everywhere.

Purely out of instinct, Marlene got up to rush to her aid, but Jesse pulled her back. "Let the guards handle this one, wildflower. You stay right here." He tightly gripped her wrist to keep her from moving. He knew Marlene wanted to help the woman, but this wasn't the same world she lived in. This wasn't a place where you could come to someone's aid without the possibility of severe consequences. No, he couldn't let her place herself in that kind of danger.

What ensued next caused Marlene to tremble as her husband buried her face against his chest. He didn't want her to see the guards beating the crap out of this guy with their sticks as they tried to contain him. The inmate, now in handcuffs, screamed a stream of obscenities as he was literally dragged from the visiting room by two burly guards.

Marlene was sure that the visit would end as she held onto Jesse with all her strength. She didn't want to look up and see them ushering everyone out of the room. She didn't want the time with her husband to end this way. Her tears scalded her cheeks as they ran down her face. When she finally did look up, and saw that no one had yet come to the woman's aid, Jesse couldn't have stopped her from going to the rescue. Not without the risk of hurting her in the process.

"Somebody please get some wet paper towels! This woman needs help!" Marlene yelled.

Keisha brought the paper towels and handed them to Marlene. Then she picked up the crying baby. "It's going to be okay, sweetie. Don't cry. Your mommy's going to be okay."

Zach had hit her, too. On more occasions than she could even remember. But she was the type that hit back. Their domestic fights usually ended up with both of them nursing flesh wounds and emotional hurts. Their children were probably the ones who got hurt the most, she considered. That baby was frightened to death. Seeing the holy terror in the little one's eyes made her think about what her children must've gone through when she and Zach had gotten into physical altercations and shouting matches in front of them. It was certainly a disconcerting scene to ponder. Perhaps Martha Reed knew what she was talking about, after all.

Marlene tried to talk to the young black woman, but her lips were too swollen for her even to open her mouth. The domestic violence that had occurred inside the prison made Marlene think that this young woman had more than likely been verbally abused and physically violated inside her own home, as well. She was beginning to understand that this thing of women being controlled and manipulated by men in prison ran much deeper than she would've ever imagined.

Visibly shaken, Rosalinda stooped down next to Marlene. "Someone is getting a doctor to come down here to look at her injuries." Rosalinda took the woman's hand for a brief moment. "I hope you're going to be okay. I'm so sorry this happened to you."

Tears pooled in Rosalinda's eyes as she thought of all the times that Ricardo had hit her or ferociously pulled her hair because she hadn't been in the place where he thought she should be. As though he read her thoughts, he shouted for her to get back to where she belonged.

Almost mindlessly, she obeyed his firm command.

Close to having an emotional breakdown herself, Marlene wiped the injured woman's tears with one of the wet paper towels. What was so amazing to her about this was that everyone had simply returned to what they'd been doing before this incident. It was like nothing as serious as this had happened. It seemed that once the inmate was escorted away, everyone had lost total interest. No one seemed to care a rat's behind about the injured woman and her crying child.

Jesse helped the two custodial inmates hold the door open for the gurney to be pushed through. Two men dressed in white lifted the woman onto the portable bed and put her baby in her arms. Then they were whisked away without so much as a word from the attendants.

Back in their seats, Marlene took Jesse's hand. "That's so sad what happened in here. And I didn't even get to find out her name. If this is heartbreaking to me, what must it be like for her and that baby?" She wiped away an errant tear. "I was so sure this visit was going to end. The thought of it made me tremble inside. But now I'm so ashamed that I had the nerve to think about that before I considered the woman's perilous plight."

Jesse patted her hand. "Don't be too hard on yourself now. You don't have anything to be ashamed of. Your thoughts were natural ones. I didn't want the visit to end, either. Visiting time is as good as it gets in here."

"I don't see Alexis," Marlene told Jesse. "She said she was coming today. Maybe she's coming for the late visit. She had us over to her house for dinner. Can you believe that?"

"Rich or poor, the woman is like everyone else. She needed someone to reach out to her. I'm glad you were there for her. Did you have a good time?"

"We had a wonderful time!" Marlene wanted to tell him what they'd found in her husband's secret room, but she feared that their conversations might be recorded. She then told him everything about their visit but that particular part.

"You never know, do you. Beauty doesn't always make you lucky or blessed. Sounds like she's had as hard a time as most. Not calling her parents all this time is a downright shame, but I'm not to judge her reasoning. I'm glad you put them back in touch with one another. The angels are smiling down on you, wildflower. Don't change. I love you just the way you are."

Marlene wrinkled her nose. "Love you, too, sweetie."

Jesse didn't want her to change, probably didn't think she needed to change, but she knew there were some things that she had to change. The nature of her relationship with her son was one of things that needed changing, drastically so. She had tried being the sweet little mother, but now it was high time for her to step in Malcolm's face as the big, bad wolf. It was time for her to take off the sheep's clothing and give both herself and Malcolm a reality check.

CHAPTER TEN

His hot hands entwined themselves in the length of her hair as he kissed her breathless. She closed her eyes, hating herself for what she was doing. His kisses were getting lower and lower. He had started with gentle kisses to her forehead. Then he'd sensuously brushed her ears with wet ones. When his luscious mouth had claimed her lips with feverish passion, she hadn't expected such wonderful sensations to fill her up. Now his mouth was at the base of her throat. That felt good, too, his tongue flicking in and out to taste her creamy flesh. This wasn't something she should enjoy. But she was—too much, in fact. By the time his mouth lowered to her cleavage, the insides of her thighs were hotter than they'd ever been in her life. Her inner core was ready to explode.

As he continued to seduce her, she tried not to respond to his heated caresses by thinking of the phone call she'd received from him earlier. The she remembered fidgeting with the dials on the car radio as she'd waited for him at the point of their rendezvous. At that point, she had checked her watch for the hundredth time. Michael Hernandez had told her nine o'clock. It had been two minutes after the agreed-upon hour—and it had gotten dark outside. Nervously, she had tapped her fingernails on the steering wheel, to keep from going crazy.

The insanity of the whole idea had made her sick with anguish.

But here she was, inside a sleazy motel, with a man who wanted her to trade sex for past and future services. In the absence of love, this picture was all wrong.

A sudden burst of raw emotions caused her nearly to fall apart. This was insanity. She couldn't do this. She couldn't sleep with one man to pay another man's legal fees. It was lower than immoral. It was worse than degrading. It was prostitution.

As if the devil were chasing after her, Rosalinda ran from the motel room, straightening out her clothes in the process. Out in the parking lot, she immediately got into her car, cranked up the engine, and sped out of the parking lot of the cheap motel he'd chosen for their repulsive rendezvous. Tears blurred her vision, but she kept driving. She didn't want to be anywhere in the vicinity if Michael happened to chase after her. Once she'd put a safe distance between herself and the motel, she pulled off to the side of the road, her heart beating erratically.

Hot tears flooded her face as she lowered her head to the steering wheel and cried with much bitterness and inner anger. Ricardo had gone too far this time. Asking her to sell herself to his lawyer was the last straw. Just as Keisha had told her, Rosalinda Morales was better than this. It was unfortunate that it had taken something this horrific to bring her to the honest-to-God truth about Ricardo. She was better than this. She'd finally come to the conclusion that Ricardo Munoz was the person who wasn't any good. And he had finally proven that he wasn't good enough for her.

As for Ricardo's lawyer, when she got through with him, he was going to wish he'd never heard of a woman named Rosalinda Morales. Michael Hernandez was in for a rude awakening; the death of his career was imminent.

Rosalinda was annoyed to find Michael Hernandez on the other side of the door to her apartment. When she tried to slam it shut in his face, he forced his way inside. Adrenaline rushed through her at breakneck speed. Fearful of what he might be capable of, she looked around for something to use in defending herself. Her trembling hands quickly wrapped around the base of a brass candleholder. If he dared to come at her, he wouldn't be able to tell his side of the story. At least, not until he came out of the coma.

"Rosalinda, you don't need to be afraid of me."

"I'm not."

"Liar. I see fear in your eyes. I just came here to see if you were okay."

"How did you get my address?"

"Off your checks. Checks that haven't been cashed, I might add."

That unexpected comment stunned her. It also explained why she hadn't yet gotten an overdrawn statement from her bank. Still, that didn't change her mind about his character.

"May I sit down so we can talk? It would be nice if you'd put down that heavy candleholder. You could kill someone with that thing."

"Someone?"

Smiling gently at her, he raised his hand. "I'm too young to die, Rosalinda. And I wouldn't want a beautiful woman like you to end up behind bars."

Although she saw him as evil as Satan, the charming son-of-a-she-dog was so lethally handsome it was frightening. Earlier, when he'd held her in a tight embrace, he'd made her flesh desire him like crazy. "Speaking of bars, that's where you're going to end up, when I'm finished. 'Disbarred attorney behind bars.' Has a nice ring to it, don't you think?"

He raised an eyebrow. "Ah, I see where this is going. Let us talk before this gets way out of hand. I think you'll understand me better once you've heard what I need to say."

"There's nothing for us to talk about."

"There's plenty for us to talk about." He edged toward the camel-back sofa. "In order to break the ice, you can start by telling me why you ran out on me." Keeping his eyes fixed on the candlestick, he slowly lowered himself onto the sofa.

Her mouth fell open. "You are insane! Ran out on you? You sound like we had a date, with something special going on." Keeping a close eye on him, she sat down in a distant chair.

"We did. We were going to spend the entire evening together."

"Letting you screw me in lieu of legal fees can hardly be classified as a date or as something special. I was there at that sleazy motel, Michael Hernandez. Earlier, while I waited for you to show up, I had plenty of time to give much thought to what I was about to do. More important was the reason why I was doing it. After being inside that room with you, I finally came to the conclusion that I had to be out of my mind for even considering degrading myself in that manner. You know something else? You and Ricardo Munoz are two of a kind, kindred spirits, evil ones. I hope you both burn in hell, which is exactly where you belong."

Michael exhaled a huge gust of breath. He hoped the relief he felt wasn't too obvious. Silently, he thanked God for bringing her to her senses. He'd tested her, and she'd proven herself worthy. Rosalinda Morales was exactly the kind of woman he thought her to be. A misguided woman who'd fallen in love with the wrong kind of man—that didn't make her a bad person.

Rosalinda Morales was worth saving from the likes of his loser client, Ricardo Munoz. Michael Hernandez had decided quite a while back that he wanted to be the one to rescue her.

"You may find this hard to believe, but I have a genuine interest in you. The kind of interest a man has in a woman he's wildly attracted to. You're beautiful and intelligent. You're sexy and intriguing." Now he just had to find a way to convince her of those very things. She had no idea of the unending charms she possessed.

Staring at him in total disbelief, Rosalinda was obviously shaken. None of what he'd said rang true for her. How could he be interested in her? He was educated, wealthy, and suave. Despite his impressive credentials, he was highly unethical and had the morals of an alley cat. His comments made no sense. If he'd had a serious interest in her, why had he tried to debase her?

"I think you'd better leave now. This has gotten way out of hand."

"Don't shut me out. Just think about what I've said here tonight. I know this is complicated, especially with my being Ric's lawyer and all. But I'll handle that. If you'll consider giving us a chance to get to know each other on a personal level, I'll take myself off his appeal case. I need to do that, anyway, no matter what you decide. Please think about it. I'll call you in a few days."

He quickly made it to the door, but turned around before opening it. "I dare to say that you wanted me as much as I wanted you. *¡Buenas noches, mi bella señorita!*"

Rosalinda stopped herself before she hurled the candlestick across the room. Since he'd already closed the door, she'd only cause serious damage. He was right. She had wanted him. Still wanted him. Never could she allow something like that to happen between them, not ever.

As Rosalinda dressed for bed, she looked at her naked body in the mirror. She could clearly see why a man would desire her. Beyond the physical attraction, she didn't think she had much else to offer. While pulling a nightgown over her head, she thought about the things Michael had said about her.

Intelligent—very much so, except when it came to dealing with Ricardo.

Sexy—a strong possibility. Men had certainly whistled and flirted with her before.

Beautiful—the jury would remain out on that one for some time to come.

Thoughts of her ill mother made her cry. All the time she'd spend running out to the prison would've been better spent by visiting with and reading to her mom. So much of her time had been wasted on a man who had no respect for her at all. She had heard that everyone had a breaking point. Finally, she had reached hers. Ricardo was history. If it had been love she'd truly felt for him, he hadn't valued it or her. With his disrespect, he'd lost whatever feelings she'd had for him. Just as he'd done with everyone else, he'd managed to push her away.

Although she was worried about what his homeboys might do to her, her mind was made up. Ricardo Munoz would no longer have control over her life. Come hell or high water, she was going to move on. Thank God she hadn't given in to him about having his baby. If she had, she would've been stuck with having him around for life. She was still young, and it pleased her that someone else thought she was attractive—even if that someone was a person she could never have. Still, Michael's assessment of her made her feel good about herself, inside and out.

Ricardo had to be told about her decision. But not in person. She didn't trust herself that much. He had a way of manipulating her with ease. Ric would have to be told over the phone. Then again, actions were supposed to speak louder than words. Her absence at the prison and a newly acquired unlisted number would do for starters. What about his homeboys? There was no doubt that he'd have one of them call her at work. But she could deal with that.

What he might instruct his homeboys to do in retaliation was what she feared most.

* * *

Marlene had not only worked her tail off, she had nearly worked Keisha's and Rosalinda's fingers to the bone. Getting ready for the support-group meeting hadn't been an easy feat. Once Marlene had gotten board approval to use the church, they'd jumped into the project with both feet. Ads had been placed in several newspapers, and all sorts of colorful flyers had been made and distributed to local churches, community centers, beauty shops, health spas, and numerous other places where women had a tendency to congregate. Rosalinda had even placed flyers in several different Weight Watchers centers. Keisha had taken some to her school to pass out.

They didn't know how the first meeting was going to turn out, but they'd sure had a lot of calls from women inquiring about the sessions. The church phone had practically rung off the hook over the past week and a half, but Marlene had transferred Jesse's private number to his study to her home so the calls wouldn't interfere in the church staff's regular duties.

The number of women who'd actually shown up for the first LIW support-group meeting astounded Marlene. The ad she'd placed in several different area papers had certainly reached out and touched quite a few people. It was almost unbelievable that these many women had relationships with inmates. Black, Caucasian, Hispanic, young, middle-aged, and even elderly women crowded into the church, each looking for an empty space on one of the pews. If they kept coming, they were going to have to open up the balcony. The crowd capacity might even reach SRO status. So far, she hadn't seen any children come into the sanctuary. She felt rather relieved about that, since she believed a lot of soul-baring could take place before the evening was all over. Many a tear was bound to fall.

The scene before her was actually a beautiful sight to see. Women from different ethnic backgrounds, probably from many different walks of life, were amicably coexisting in the same space. Marlene was eager to experience the interaction. For sure, they all had something in common. The one common denominator was the incarcerated men in their lives, the men they loved with maniacal passion. What had brought them together was rather sad, but she prayed that everyone would leave with a renewal of hope and faith after all was said and done.

By the time Marlene took to the podium, she could see that every space on every pew was filled. The balcony had been opened just in case there was a rash of late arrivals. Tears sprang to her eyes, but she held them back. This was a time for a show of strength. Being that she was the group leader, she had to remain stoic, unbiased. Remaining in control was a must.

"Good evening, ladies! My name is Marlene. It's so nice to see such a huge turnout. I'll be leading the group session tonight. As this is our first attempt at something like this, I hope everyone will be patient with the process. Keisha and Rosalinda are here to assist you in any way they can." She pointed out her two comrades. "This is an idea that the three of us came up with. By the number present, we're glad that you thought it was a good enough idea to come out. We thank you for your presence here this evening. All I ask is that when each person gets up to talk, that we give respect to the person who's speaking. You don't have to use your name if you're concerned with anonymity. I also ask that what is said here in this room will stay in the room. I'd like to break the ice in this session by telling you a little about my situation."

As Marlene covered the details of her story, she told the group why her husband was in her prison, that he was innocent, how much time he'd been sentenced to, and that the conviction was in the appeal process. The moment Marlene gave up the floor, several women got to their feet.

Seeing a need to oversee the speaking order, Marlene came back to the podium.

"So that everyone gets a chance to speak, we're going to limit each person to five minutes. We have such a large crowd here. Since this is our very first time, we should go down the pews and call on only those who have a desire to speak. We'll go from the front pew and then to the back. We'll start right here in the front row. If you don't have a desire to speak, just say pass."

The first black woman stood up. She seemed a little apprehensive as she kept her eyes focused on Marlene. "My name is Gloria, and my boyfriend is in prison for selling drugs to an undercover narc. He's a repeat offender. I don't know all that's happening to him on the inside, but I know I'm not going to abandon him. We have three kids together. The kids and me are the only bright spots in his day. Visiting time is as good as it gets inside of there. I love him. I hope that he'll change one day, but I'm not going to leave him. He's already down on the ground. I refuse to stomp on him while he's in that position."

Several people clapped as she returned to her seat.

"My boyfriend is also a drug dealer," the second black woman said. "Uh . . . my name is Margie. My man is somebody's son, grandson, brother, nephew, uncle, and a friend to many. He's not a bad person. Misguided? Yes, I'd say so. Black man sells dope, he gets hard time. White man sells dope, he gets slapped with a short probation, if that. The difference for time sentenced for rock cocaine or crack, the black man's drug, versus white powder cocaine, the white man's drug, is astronomical. Both are highly addictive, but the rules applied in sentencing are as different as night and day. If Denzel Washington did the things Robert Downey, Jr. does, he'd be incarcerated, no second or third chance. I stand by my man because I love him. But more than that, he's a first-time offender who simply had the book thrown at him. When he couldn't get a decent job that paid fair wages, he turned to dealing. He thought of it as a way to feed his family and to give them the things he never had. Still, there's no excuse for breaking the law. He's living with the consequences, but I do believe he won't go back to that lifestyle once he's out."

A lot of mumbling occurred after the last statement. Margie gave a hard look to the disbelievers before sitting down.

Anger clouded a petite black woman's face as she got to her feet. "You all can say what you want about our criminal misfits. And, no, I don't want to give my name. I'm just plain tired of the mess. Unlike what I've heard so far, I want out of this crazy relationship, and can't get out. My so-called man is a gang member. If I don't do what he says to, I may as well dig myself a hole and bury my own black behind. I'm a hostage. My family members are hostages. He threatens to hurt them first, so I'll suffer before he has me tortured and then killed. A man who has no freedom controls me because he has henchmen who do. His homeboys will do anything he tells them to. I constantly live in fear. . . ."

"Did you know he was a gang member when you met him?" someone asked.

"I didn't know for months. Then the evidence of his gang affiliation started popping up all over the place. You may be surprised at this, but I wasn't in love with him when I found out for certain, even though he'd shown me a totally different side of him when we began dating. When the other side came out, the controlling, abusive side, I was trapped in a nightmare I couldn't wake up from. If I left him, there would be serious consequences, he told me. I accept collect calls from a man that I hate. My hard-earned money is sent to someone I'm terrified of. Every week I visit a man that I can barely stand to look at. I'm already dead and buried, just without the dirt. In my opinion, giving up your life for a man in prison is downright crazy. They will eventually suck the life right out of you. When they get out, they'll probably leave you high and dry, anyway. And they may leave you with a death sentence. AIDS!"

A Caucasian woman slowly got to her feet. "That's your story, and I do feel for you. But my man is innocent, unequivocally. He would never hurt anyone, yet he was convicted of rape. I know that he didn't rape that woman, 'cause he was with me at the time it was supposed to have happened."

Everyone looked skeptical.

"I know what you're thinking. I see it on your faces. You think I'd lie for him, be his alibi to keep him out of trouble. Wrong! Thomas was a professional photographer, a very successful one, who didn't believe in mixing business with pleasure. He ignored the advances of one of his top models. She felt rejected by him. Then she screamed rape, several days after the alleged act."

Tears fell from the woman's blue eyes. Her shoulders shook as she let her emotions run free. "He didn't rape that woman. No way, no how. While trying to prove it, I may die as a lady in waiting. That's the term the guards use for those of us who stand steadfast by our men. I'm sure many of you are familiar with it."

"You see, that's the kind of loyalty most of us have. I'm Pearl. Some of us have men who are worth every waking moment and every dime we spend on their behalf. You women who have these no-good guys make me damn sick with your whining and complaining. If he was a no-good snake before he went to jail, chances are he'll be the same when he gets out." She looked upward. "Lord, please forgive me for my angry thoughts in the sanctuary. And I know that Satan didn't make me do it. I'm not saying every man is innocent, either. People make mistakes. That's part of being human. But the punishment is not always equivalent to the crime. Society has the tendency to think that all people in prison are bad, that they deserve to be locked up and have the key thrown away. The only mistake my husband made is giving a couple of his female students a ride home. A couple of weeks later, after seeing their failing class grades, they accused him of molestation. Said he fondled them when he gave them a ride home. He gave them a ride because it was raining cats and dogs. Those two thirteen-year-olds lied through their teeth and never so much as flinched while doing it. It was only recently that they admitted to lying. Said they'd seen a similar case on television and decided to use the same theory. My husband should be released fairly soon."

The crowd rose to their feet as they cheered and whistled.

"That's wonderful news!" Marlene enthused.

"Is it?" Pearl shot back at Marlene. "My husband's life is ruined. People will always wonder about him. He was a good teacher as well as a great athletic coach. Who's going to hire him since the story was all over the papers and the news? Who's going to believe that he's totally innocent, that two teenagers could be so malicious and evil? No, it's not wonderful. Yes, I'm glad he's coming home, but I dread what he has to face. For the rest of his life he has to live with those false allegations—allegations that led to a false conviction. Please pray for him. Pray for our entire family. We're going to need it."

Marlene walked over and embraced Pearl. "I'm sure we'll all keep your family lifted up in prayer." She returned to the podium and asked for everyone's attention.

"When we started this group, we had no idea how many women would show up. I must say that I'm amazed at the numbers in attendance. Before I was faced with the same situation that many of you have found yourselves in, I didn't know anything at all about the prison system. I can already write a book with the knowledge I've gleaned in just a few months. I'm trying to understand all the issues. I just didn't know there were so many. I always thought it was cut-and-dried—innocent or guilty. I've never really thought about some of the issues that have been brought up during the meeting. I never gave much thought to extenuating circumstances. And I've never experienced this type of loyalty from one human being to another before my husband went to jail. And I'm a preacher's wife. This has been an awesome experience for me. I hope to learn more and certainly to be more open-minded about all of these situations. I'm going to try not to assume anything anymore."

Another black woman stood up. "My son is in prison. He's guilty as sin, but he's my child—"

"Excuse me!" came an interrupting protest from somewhere in the middle of the room. "I think you've got the wrong group. This one is for women loving men in prison."

The woman standing put her hands on her hips and rolled her eyes at the speaker. "Exactly, Miss Thang! I'm a woman. My son is a man who's in prison. And I love him. From what I read in the newspaper, the criteria for the group simply stated that it was for women loving men in prison. I meet the criteria. Am I right, Ms. Marlene?"

Marlene stood up to address the crowd once again. "I must admit that this group was designed around male and female relationships that involved husbands and wives, girlfriends and boyfriends. But now that you've articulated your point, I can't think of a single reason why mothers shouldn't be included. You do meet the criteria, as it was written. Welcome to the group! How many others in here are mothers of inmates or somehow related in another way?"

Several hands went up.

"Okay!" Marlene was terribly excited about the new categories added to the group. "For those of you that raised your hand, I'd like you to clarify your relationship with the person in prison. But only if you want to. We'll start right here in the front."

Once the announcements were made, it was clear to Marlene that this group would reach a number of people with varying issues. Out of the group that had raised their hands, there were grandmothers, sisters, daughters, aunts, cousins, godmothers, and even best friends. All were in some way supporting men in prison.

"It appears that this group is off to a great start. Ladies, we didn't start this group so that we could stand in judgment of you and your reasons for supporting your loved ones. No one has the right to judge, period. We want this group to be a place where we can come together as concerned women, a place where we can openly share our feelings. We had no idea that so many of you would respond. We're just glad that you did."

An extremely young-looking black woman raised her hand. Marlene quickly acknowledged her, gesturing for her to stand.

"I just want to thank you all for doing this." Her distinctive accent was of one of the Caribbean nations. "I have no one to turn to. As my people are a very proud people, my family has exiled me because of my relationship with an inmate. You see, I'm a teacher at the prison. I fell in love with one of my students."

Audible gasps permeated the room. She ignored the uneasy glances that passed between the attendees. The whispering made her nervous, but she held her head up high. She was a black queen, a compassionate person, and a dedicated woman, one who loved the heart of her man.

"My involvement with my student resulted in me being fired. My peers have ridiculed me. I've been called every filthy name you can imagine. My parents are angry over the thousands and thousands of dollars spent on my education. Wasted dollars and useless energy, they said to me. They think I have dishonored them and that I'm degrading myself by being with this man. My heart doesn't see this man as anything less than a man. My heart controls my head, not the other way around."

"What was his crime?" someone shouted.

"I don't think that matters. What matters here is that people can change. Even those with hardened hearts can become different on the inside. Love does transcend all things. Women love hard. Women love for an eternity. We're forgiving. We understand beyond comprehension. But that's who we are. That's how the Lord made us. Man is somewhat weak in certain areas, though he doesn't think so."

Everyone laughed.

"I didn't mean that to be funny or as a put-down. Our men have been put down enough. Unfortunately, some people can only survive in a structured environment. Life these days is too hard for far too many men, especially our men of color."

"Why won't you tell us what he did if you believe what you're saying? If you're not willing to share that, why are you here?" An impatient voice came from one of the back pews.

"For support. To offer and receive it. To communicate with people like myself. As someone who loves a prisoner, do you need any less compassion because your man may have committed a worse crime than someone else's man? I don't think so. The jails are full of all kinds of people. Sometimes you have to look into the hearts of men to understand them. They don't wear their hearts on their sleeves as we women do. I'm not here for you to approve or disapprove of the man I love. I'm here because I need love and understanding as a woman alone in the world. Have I made a mistake in thinking I'd find that here among my sisters?"

As Marlene looked around the room, she saw tears in many eyes.

Discreetly, she wiped her own away. "Thank you for that. As for your last question, no, you haven't made a mistake. Though our circumstances may be different, love and understanding is what we're all seeking at this difficult time in our life. I hope that each and every one of us will get our needs met, as they pertain to this group's function. Because there are so many of us, I see the need for rules and possibly bylaws. Tonight, we'll just wing it. As the three original members of this group, Keisha, Rosalinda, and myself, we're going to work on getting those things done before the next meeting. However, I need to get a feel for how many even want to meet again and for how often we should do so. Does someone care to make a suggestion?"

"Once a month is the norm for most types of support groups," one woman offered.

"Because of our special needs, I think we should meet once a week," someone suggested.

"That's probably too often," another person interjected, "especially for those of us who work. How many would agree with twice a month?"

The majority of the women raised their hands in support.

Marlene slammed the side of her fist onto the podium. "Twice a month it is. I think it would be a good idea to set up an emergency hotline. There may come a time between meetings that someone might need to talk things through with another member of the group. How many of you would be willing to volunteer a small portion of your time to man the phones?"

Marlene was pleased with the number of hands that went up. "That's great! Thank you. I'll have a volunteer hotline sign-up sheet ready for our next meeting. I'll also have an additional phone line installed in my home. The line can be transferred to whoever is on call. That way no one has to compromise her home phone line. Does that seem like a workable solution?"

The loud clapping was all it took to approve the hotline idea.

"All right, ladies, we're on our way." Marlene took a moment to consult her watch. "Wow! The time has really flown by. Before we close this session, is there anyone else who has a burning desire to share?"

"I do," a small, raspy voice responded.

All eyes immediately turned to the rail-thin, sickly-looking black woman who sat in the very back of the room. Slowly, seemingly with much difficulty, she got to her feet.

"Out of all the things said here"—she coughed—"only one of you has addressed the issue I'm about to speak on." She had to stop to clear her throat. "I believe it was said . . . that your man might leave you with a death sentence. I'm here to inform you that a man who said he would love me to death has done just that. At the time it was said, I didn't know that he meant it literally. I'm dying from AIDS. At birth, our newborn was also sentenced to death. He's infected with the virus, too. The saddest part about this is that my lover knew he was infected when we were together physically, numerous times, the last time he was set free. He's now back inside prison walls, where condoms are considered contraband. My question to you all is this: Should I continue to support him? Should I support the man who has cost me my life?"

Questioning glances were passed around the room, gasps came hard, and tears flowed unchecked. When no one stood to answer the posed question, Marlene saw that she had no choice but to speak. The only problem was she didn't know what to say—and she didn't know what to do in this highly sensitive situation. Prayer was the only response she knew how to give.

"I would like everyone to bow their heads. We need to consult our Creator for the answer to the sister's question." She licked her dry lips. "Lord, we stand before You today, as we are Your loving, misguided children. There is no one but You that can direct us to the right path. As You have witnessed here today, there is much anguish, turmoil, and suffering here in Your house. Every woman in this room has a burden to bear. One of our dear sisters has been infected with a deadly disease. She has asked a question of us that only You have the answer to."

Marlene had to stop for a moment to gain control of her surging emotions.

"Lord, we pray that You will provide her with the answers she is seeking. We pray for her strength and courage. Dear Lord, help us to stand united in our mission, in the mission You have appointed us for. May each and every one of us reach out to her in her time of need. Help us to understand and to know what it is that You would have us do. If it is Your most holy will, we ask these things in Your precious name. Amen."

Several hearty amens rang out, simultaneously.

Marlene smiled gently. "I wish I had an answer for you, but I don't.

However, the answer is forthcoming from the Lord. Do you still love this man?"

The sick woman nodded as tears filled her eyes. "I have loved him since forever." Her threadbare voice trembled with trepidation. "We grew up together. We played in the sandbox as toddlers. We fought with each other, as kids will do. We shared puppy love as preteens. We challenged one another at everything as teenagers. Our feelings kept growing stronger. As adults, we fell madly in love. Well into manhood, he started getting into serious trouble with the law."

An elderly lady stood up and put her arm around the sick woman's bony shoulders.

"I'm here for you, my sister. How long ago were you diagnosed?"

"When I was six months pregnant, I found out I had been infected. My baby is three months old now. After I found out, I had to give up my job as a registered nurse. My lover has no one but the baby and me. His family has long since turned his back on him. He's one of those career criminals you hear so much about. I've been considering abandoning him for weeks now. Recently, in one of our heated discussions, he revealed to me that he knew he was infected the last times he *poked* me. Those were his trifling words, not mine. I thought he was just talking out of anger. But then he told me in painstaking detail how he'd planned for us to die together. We'd done everything else together, so he thought we should die together, too. He contracted the disease after being gang-raped as an inmate in another prison a few years ago."

The room was silent as death. Even Marlene couldn't find the right words to say. For several minutes everyone just sat there, lost in their own thoughts, absorbing into their souls the words of the woman who was losing her future, her very life. All because of her love for a man.

Finally, Marlene came to the conclusion that this meeting needed to be adjourned. Quietly, she slipped to the podium. Before ending the meeting, she gave the time and date for the next one. As the women filed out of the church in an orderly fashion, Marlene pressed into the dying woman's hand the piece of paper on which she'd written her phone number.

Shortly after the meeting had been adjourned, Marlene, Keisha, and Rosalinda were the only women left in the building. Keisha and

Rosalinda sat quietly as they watched Marlene running around the sanctuary making sure that all the doors leading to the outside were locked.

Marlene plopped down on the front pew across from where the other two women sat.

"Whew, that was some first meeting! I'm overwhelmed by the numbers in attendance, but I'm disappointed that Alexis didn't show up, as promised. When I talked with her this morning, she said she was still trying to decide whether to contact the authorities about what she found in R.J.'s private room. She's thinking of having the illegal items removed without further jeopardizing R.J., but she doesn't know anyone that she can trust. Just before we hung up she assured me that she'd be here." Picking up a cardboard fan, she rapidly waved it back and forth, hoping to cool herself down. "What did you two think of the meeting?"

"In my opinion, Alexis is still a flake. She's still running true to form, hot and cold. As for the meeting, I thought it went very well. But I hadn't expected so much high drama." Keisha dragged her right palm across her forehead. "That's the kind of stuff A movies are made of. My heart broke for the dying woman. All these different situations are serious. I have a lot more soul-searching to do when it comes down to my relationship with Zach. I don't know what to do after hearing all those heart-wrenching stories. What did you think, Miss Rosa?"

"There are so many thoughts still going through my head. Listening to everyone that had the guts to speak made me realize that I've come to the right decision about ending my relationship with Ric. After hearing that woman talking about AIDS, I know I'm doing the right thing. But it's not just the fear of the disease."

"What?" Keisha screeched. "When did you decide all that?"

"Some time ago. After I rendezvoused with Ric's attorney at some sleazy motel."

"Say what?" Marlene jumped to her feet. The fan she held was taking a beating as she repeatedly hit it against her left thigh, moaning and groaning in despair. "You slept with that attorney? Please tell me I didn't hear you say that you went to bed with that wicked mercenary, sweetie. Oh, God, please help us." Marlene was breathing so hard, she had to take a minute to allow her heart rate to slow down. Emotionally worn out, she slumped back into her seat.

"Relax, Marlene, I didn't sleep with him." Rosalinda shook her head in dismay. "As much as I hate to admit it, it wasn't because I didn't want to. He had me ready to go there for a short while. At the last minute, I couldn't go through with it. You should've seen me high-tailing. I was such a nervous wreck that I had to pull my car over to stop shaking."

Keisha was so weak with relief that she began to cry and laugh at the same time. Her arms went around her best friend in a tight embrace. "I'm . . . so glad . . . you didn't . . . do that." Keisha began to sob hard. "I'm glad you ran away from there. Oh, Rosa, what are we going to do about the men we love? You said you were going to end it with Ric. Did you really mean that?"

Anxiously awaiting Rosalinda's answer, Keisha started sobbing all over again.

Pulling Keisha's head to her chest, Rosalinda gently stroked her friend's hair. "Calm down, now. I meant it, Keisha. I have to let go of him. He doesn't mean me any good. But it's not all his fault. I've let him do these things to me. I have you to thank for my decision."

"How's that?" Keisha wiped her eyes. "What did I have to do with it?"

"You told me I was better than that. You said we were both better than that. I thought of your remarks before and while I was with Hernandez. Ric isn't good enough for me. I've made my decision. Now you have to make yours. No matter what you decide, I don't want it to affect our close friendship. I'm here for you, just as you've always been there for me."

Rosalinda wasn't ready to tell them what Hernandez had said about his feelings for her. Nor did she want anyone to know that she was actually considering his mad proposal of getting to know each other on a personal level.

"I haven't made a decision yet." Keisha frowned. "Zach is the father of my children. That makes our circumstances completely different from yours and Ricardo's. If I didn't have his kids, well, maybe I could walk away. I can't say for sure. But you and I, we're best friends, Rosalinda. We'll always be together, for life."

"Thank you for that. Even though I'm certain of our friendship, I needed to hear you say that. As for Alexis, she's got big problems. There's no way she could've spilled her guts here tonight. She has to be very careful that she doesn't end up getting locked away herself.

Who's going to believe that she knew nothing about her husband's illegal operation? Nobody will, not when it was going on right in their own house. I'm still having a hard time believing it."

Quieter than she'd ever been in her life, Marlene listened to the two young women, women she'd come to think of as family, vowing to stand by each other. Before they could notice her falling tears, she quickly wiped them away.

Who was going to stand by her? When she told Keisha and Rosalinda the entire truth about her situation, as it pertained to her loving husband, Jesse, would they lose total respect for her? Or would they still want to be there for her, the same as they'd vowed to be there for each other? *God, I hope so,* she cried inwardly. *I surely hope so.*

CHAPTER ELEVEN

Seated at the conference table in the pastor's study, Marlene stared at the fourteen active members of the church's deacon board like they were martians or some other alien beings. The pain in her heart made her wince. Out of all the things she'd imagined this special afterchurch meeting would be about, she would've never guessed it to be what the deacon board had just presented to her. The fact that Jesse had recently asked her about how she was being treated at the church was running through her head.

As she sat in stunned disbelief, she couldn't help thinking about how a few of the people in the church had begun to stare hard at her. An onset of rude whispering had occurred when she and Myrna Jacobson had walked into the sanctuary for worship services a couple of hours earlier. Although it had made her wonder if they'd been whispering about her, she hadn't given but a minute of thought to it. These strange occurrences had been new to her since she had always been so welcomed by the members. Were those events a preamble to what was happening now? Thinking about these things would have to be put aside for now, since the deacon board was waiting for her to respond.

She got to her feet. "I can't believe what I just heard. You say you want to remove the pastor from his ministerial position, the same man who literally built this church with his bare hands, stick by stick, brick by brick. I don't think so. This is Jesse Covington's church. I'm not trying to hear any of this. There's not one of you sitting in this room that Jesse hasn't been there for at some time or another. Are the church members behind this ridiculous idea?"

"It hasn't been presented to them yet, Sister Covington," Deacon Ralph Gray said. "We wanted to talk with you before we informed the church members of our decision."

"That's what I thought. Who brought this atrocity of an idea up in the first place?" All eyes fell on Deacon Raynard Clark. "Ray, I can't believe that you, of all people, are the one that started this malicious crap. You're the last person I would've expected this from. It seems to me that evil doesn't miss a beat. And to do this on the Lord's day, right after worship service, proves just how much evil is working overtime in this thing."

"Sister Covington, I didn't intend for you to take this personally."

"How did you expect me to take it, Ray? I know you haven't forgotten that Jesse is my husband, my best friend, and he's certainly been yours. And why aren't the deaconesses in on this? You don't have to answer that, 'cause I already know why. I could stand here and rattle off all the amazing things he's done for you, the numerous ways he's rescued each and every last one of you, but I know for a fact that you don't want me to go there. It could prove embarrassing to the lot of you. Your memories can't be that short. But if that's the case, I can sure help you remember all the times he's had your back. Like you, I hope we don't have to go there. There's not one of you that has any room to stand in judgment of Reverend Jesse, not a blasted single one of you. If there are any of you who don't agree with the idea, this isn't meant for your ears."

Marlene's heart was beating so fast that she had to take deep breaths to calm down.

"Now, Sister, ain't no need in getting yourself all worked up over this," Brother Charles Carmichael remarked. "We're just—"

"Now, Sister, hell!" Marlene interjected, on the very edge of completely losing her composure. "Don't you know that this is my husband's very life that you're tampering with? The church is his life."

"Sister, we know the church is Reverend Jesse's life. You don't have to tell us that."

Marlene stepped out of her shoes. Looking like she might hurl something at the deacons, she bent down and picked up one of her shoes. "I can tell that you're all surprised at my behavior, but at the moment I don't care what you think. I'm sure I'll regret things later, but I'll deal with that when the time comes. Perhaps you all have gotten too used to my soft-spoken words and gentle demeanor. Well, that's about to change. You need to know that I'm no tissue-paper woman. At the moment, you all sure aren't acting very appreciative of the numerous things Reverend Jesse has done for you personally, financially, and otherwise. You'd be crazy to think that I'd just stand by and let this board get away with something as outrageous as this."

Marlene took a moment to catch a breath. She hadn't finished her say, not by a long shot. While waving her shoe back and forth in the air, the glassy glare in her eyes let everyone know that she had a lot more to say.

"Don't you old coots dare try to patronize me. I'm a darn good Christian, but I can whip a little Satan out of me whenever I find it necessary to do so. Don't underestimate me because of my good nature and the fact that I'm a woman. That would be a big mistake. I'm the force that you're going to have to reckon with for now. I'm taking this entire deacon board on—and anyone else who gets behind you on this silly suggestion. I have the Almighty on my side."

"Sister Covington, this church needs a leader. Reverend Jesse's going to be gone away a long time. What are we supposed to do in the meantime?" Brother Jacob Carlton asked.

"Jesse is this church's leader! Has been for the past twenty years. And don't you forget it. Young Reverend Clay Robinson has been doing a fine job in Jesse's absence. He's filling in for Jesse very nicely. It sounds to me like you all have lost faith in your pastor and in the power of your God's tender mercies. Jesse won't be gone as long you think. Ask the Lord if you don't believe me. With all that said, you need to hear this. I won't allow you to put your plan into action without putting the measure to a vote. Every member in this church has the right to have his or her own say in this matter. I can call everyone on the church roster and have them come in this evening for a special meeting. If not this evening, then perhaps tomorrow, or even the next day. Nothing is going forward without the vote of the entire congregation. Are we clear on that issue, brother deacons?"

Brother Willie Bowen got to his feet. "Your plan has my vote, Sister. I'll even help you call on all the members." Brother Bowen had been as outraged as Marlene was now when the idea had been first presented to him. He hadn't done anything to try and stop it, simply because he'd known the pastor's wife would not let something as serious as this go unchallenged. Besides, he hadn't wanted to break rank with the deacon board until it became apparent that he should. She had certainly proven him right about her reaction to the ludicrous idea.

Marlene looked to Brother Clark. "What about you, Ray? Do I have your vote?" Intentionally, she had put him on the spot, since he was the one who came up with the idea. She smiled inwardly as he fidgeted in his seat. If he decided to challenge her, he'd be more than fidgety.

"Well," he said in a lazy drawl, "I think this measure of getting the congregation involved should be what we put to a vote first."

The look Marlene gave him could have easily cut glass.

Without uttering a single word, Marlene went into Jesse's right-hand desk drawer and pulled out a phone message pad. After tearing off several sheets, she handed one to each deacon. She knew this was risky, but she had a pretty good idea that she had a tad more support in the room than she had opposition. Now was the time to separate Jesse's friends from his enemies.

"The Lord is my shepherd, I shall not want. . . ." came Marlene's whispered prayer as she went about her business.

While their names wouldn't appear on the voting sheets, she'd know the ones who had opposed her idea. It would be the look on the faces of the opposition that would give them away. If this maneuver failed, she'd insist on the deaconesses being in on the vote as well. She didn't think there was a woman in Jesse's church who would vote for him to be removed from the church roster as their pastor. The female members of the congregation truly loved their pastor, but then she again thought about the whispers and stares that had come from some of them.

"Brother Gray, now that everyone has voted, could you please collect the votes?" She went to the chalkboard and made two columns, one FOR, one AGAINST the measure.

Seconds later, when the counting was finished, there were ten votes for, but only four against soliciting the vote of the entire congregation.

She hadn't expected to win by such a wide margin. Marlene smiled triumphantly. Looking right into the eyes of Brother Ray Clark, the instigator, Brother Glenn Amos, Brother Donald Jones, and Brother

Mitchell Thompson, the deacons who hadn't yet spoken a word, she made them aware that she knew they'd been the opposition. "Let's get these phone lines busy. This matter needs to be settled ASAP." With nothing more to say, she picked up her purse and left the conference room. Smiling smugly, Brother Bowen followed her out of the study.

Tears of joy and sorrow fell from her eyes as she went into the church office to begin calling the members. She felt joyous that Jesse had plenty of allies, but her sorrow came at the attempt to get rid of her husband in the first place. Bowing her head, she thanked God for allowing her to prevail. Then she asked His forgiveness for cursing and acting like a heathen inside the sanctuary. She had allowed someone other than herself to dictate her actions.

For committing such an egregious indiscretion, she felt deep regret.

This battle of wills was far from over—and she could only hope that the church would come out the victor. For that to happen, it meant leaving Jesse in his rightful position. It wasn't as if she didn't know that Jesse could possibly be away for a long time. She just wasn't going to allow herself to think negatively. She had faith that he would soon be released, and that was all she was going to entertain for now. Though he'd been found guilty, in her opinion, he was an innocent man. That was a fact of which she was certain.

Marlene had to rush across town to Sister Wiley's house to take her grocery shopping. The phone calls to the church members had just been completed on this Monday morning. When she hadn't been able to get ahold of everyone, they hadn't been able to hold the meeting during the Church's evening service. She'd had to leave detailed messages for those members who she still hadn't been able to reach.

After making sure Sister Annie Wiley was safely secured by her seat belt, Marlene went around to the driver's side and slid behind the wheel. She gently patted her elderly companion's hand before pulling the car out of the curbside parking spot.

As the car rolled down the street, Marlene began to tell Sister Wiley about the meeting she'd had with the deacon board. She held back her tears, as difficult as it was. Marlene didn't want to inflame the situation any more than necessary.

"Can you believe they're trying to kick Jesse out of his own church, Sister Wiley?"

"Hmm, that's how many so-called Christians work. There are way more advocates for Satan in the church than there are for the Lord. Not all the board members are followers of Satan, but there are a few seriously evil ones in our midst. If you want, I can help put all of them in their places. Using my proven method, I can guarantee you they'll stay there, too."

Marlene couldn't keep from grinning. "That sounds like you got something devilish on your mind. That could make things even uglier than they already are. I don't know about doing something like that. It seems rather sinful."

"Okay. It's your call, Sister Covington. If you don't want to know how to muzzle that worrisome deacon board, I understand. If you change your mind, I'm the one to come to."

"I do want to know. Now!" Marlene screeched, giving into a wave of laughter.

Sister Wiley cracked up. Marlene looked like a fox that had managed to find a foolproof way into the henhouse.

"I thought so. There comes a time when we have to call out the big dogs and sic them on the unruly trespassers. We'll have them singing 'Who Let the Dogs Out.' Now, here's what we're going to do. When we get back to my house, I want you to stay over for a bit. After we put the groceries away, over a cup of hot mint tea, I'm going to give you the 411 on that deacon board—so much so that you're going to have to write it down to remember it all."

Marlene giggled. "Oh, Sister Wylie, we're going to have to put in lots of overtime on our prayers this week. I've already had to ask for forgiveness for cursing in the sanctuary. I felt like I could tear Brother Clark limb from limb. I've been the big bad wolf all day today, for sure."

"Yeah, I know what you mean. Besides wanting to tear my kid's head off, I done cursed a few times this week myself. Just because I'm eighty-two years old, people have a tendency to think I'm a darn fool, and that I'm on my last go-round. I don't have dementia and I don't have Alzheimer's disease. What I still have is a sound mind and a healthy appetite for the opposite sex—and that makes me mentally unstable in my children's eyesight. Sara Leigh got upset because she thought the cable show I was watching was a bit too risqué. She really got mad at me when I asked her how she thought she got here."

"Pray tell, what were you watching on cable, Sister Wylie?"

"*Sex and the City!* It isn't all that risqué. When my husband was alive, our bedroom escapades would've put that show to shame. I admit that watching it gets the blood boiling a bit, but that's what it's supposed to do. The Bible is filled with stories of love and lust. The problem is, my children don't read the Bible like they should, or they'd know them kind of stories exist. I done told my three kids a million times to mind their own business," Sister Wylie huffed.

"I hear you, Sister Wylie. I'm feeling you, too."

"All of them got enough to worry about with their own spouses. Sara Leigh can't keep her husband at home, yet she got time to be all up in my business. Carrie Louise is two steps away from divorce court, and trifling Reginald's situation is too scandalous to even mention. At eighty-two, I earned the right to watch anything I want on television, and to go anywhere I darn well please. Including Las Vegas. They're going to have a fit when they find out I'm considering living with Brother Paris Shelton. I'm going to tell them that they can blame Social Security for our arrangement. If we marry, we lose our pensions. Neither of us can afford to do that."

Marlene had a hard time holding in her laughter. "Sister, you're too much for me. I hope that when I get your age I'm just as spunky. Not only did I have to take the deacon board to task, I'm seriously considering giving Malcolm a swift boot out the front door. That boy and his nonexistent work history is starting to push all my buttons."

"Sister Covington, you're going to kick Malcolm out of the house? Sure enough?"

"Sure enough thinking about it!"

As they rode along, Marlene told Sister Wylie about how well the support-group meeting had gone. She was no longer sure she'd be welcome to continue have the meetings in the church after the earlier episode with the deacon board, but that wasn't going to stop her. She would hold the support group elsewhere if necessary, but she was going to have her group. The Lord didn't send her on a mission if He hadn't planned to back her up.

The Lord had always made a way for her. And He'd make a way this time, too.

* * *

Sweat poured from Marlene's body as she tossed and turned in her king-size bed. Visions of Jesse being wrestled down to a cement shower floor by several faceless men caused her to thrash about in the bed. As one of the men sexually tore into her husband's body while the others held him down, she screamed again and again. Awakening, trembling all over, she sat straight up in the bed. Realizing it was just a bad dream brought not a dash of solace to her heart. The fact remained that something as horrible as a man being raped by another man could happen inside the prison walls. Riddled with numerous unsavory conditions that no human being should ever have to endure, the prison was such a cold, inhumane place for anyone to be.

"Oh, Lord, please don't let anything like that happen to my dear Jesse. He couldn't bear it and neither could I. Please, Lord, hear my prayers. We've got to get him back home."

Unable to go back to sleep, Marlene thought about all the unpalatable things her son had been involved in over the past year. Things about which she hadn't told her husband.

The friends he'd chosen to hang out with seemed not to care an iota about anything or anyone. The style of clothing that Malcolm had turned to wearing almost made her ill at times. With his pants and boxer shorts hanging down off his behind, nearly showing his bare crack, he often looked like a dangerous thug. A pretty one, but a thug nonetheless. She'd found a blue head rag mixed in his dirty clothes, the type gangs wore, but he'd denied ownership of it. She couldn't even entertain the thought of Malcolm being a gang member, but she couldn't deny that there were obvious signs of such. Actual proof of her son being gang-affiliated would, for sure, send her heart into cardiac arrest.

Then there had been a couple of run-ins with the police; he'd barely escaped criminal charges simply because there hadn't been enough evidence. She wouldn't allow her mind to take her to the worst of what she thought he might've done, or at least know something about. No, she couldn't get there just yet. But facing the facts of what might turn into a reality couldn't be put off. While she'd been seriously anticipating kicking Malcolm out, she'd gone into his room to start packing his things. What she'd found in his gym bag had shocked her beyond comprehension. Knowing she was in dangerous waters, Marlene got up, raced into the master bathroom, and turned on the shower full blast. Lowering herself onto her knees, she began to pray for guidance where her son was concerned.

Freshly showered, Marlene sat on the spare twin bed in Malcolm's bedroom, looking none too happy with her son, who had dressed in baggy pants and an oversize sweatshirt. His room was decorated with dozens of model airplanes. The room had an overall aviation theme. There had been a time when Malcolm had talked of nothing else but wanting to be a commercial airline pilot. He'd even considered starting a career in the air force. Then he'd found out that his good looks were a valuable asset. It hadn't taken him long to learn that he could get paid without lifting a finger. He somehow always managed to find just the right type of women, the kind who were willing to bankroll his every whim.

"Momma, why are you looking at me like that? What's up?"

"We need to talk, Malcolm—and I don't want any of your attitude. You understand?"

Malcolm looked strangely at his mother. He'd hardly ever heard her raise her voice. The look in her eyes told him that she had something serious on her mind. "Okay, Mom. I understand."

"I need to know what you know about the moneybag that was found in the church van. We both know those things don't belong to your father. I want the truth this time."

"I told you the truth the first time you asked me about this. I don't know how those things got in the van. I swear to that."

"I know what you told me before, but I don't think you were telling the truth. Were you inside that van before Jesse was arrested?"

Malcolm played with the edge of the bedspread, unable to look his mother in the eyes.

"Boy, if you know what I know right about now, you'd better look me in the eye and tell me the truth. You've lied so much, I don't think you know when you're actually telling the truth. Have you been in that van?"

"I borrowed it one night when Dad brought it home."

"Borrowed it? From who?"

"Well, I didn't actually borrow it. I took it while you guys were asleep."

"You mean you stole it! Boy, you better come at me straight, because no one will be able to hold me responsible for what I'm about to do to you. You think them pants are hanging off your behind now? When I get through whipping through them, you won't even recognize them as pants. Are you feeling me?"

"All right. You win. I stole the van and I went over to my girl's house."

"What's Sheila got to do with this?"

"If you'll let me finish, I can tell you the whole story."

"Okay, I'm going to let you finish. But let me warn you, I'm not up for no bull. You got it, boy? This is one time I will hurt you."

"I got it, Mom. I picked up Todd before I got to Sheila's. After we got to her house, I let Todd take the van to go pick us his homegirl. This stuff happened before Dad got arrested. I brought the van back to the house just before the sun came up the next morning."

"And?"

"And what?"

Marlene jumped up and slapped Malcolm upside the head. "I told you not to play with me, boy. Did you all rob a 7-Eleven while you had that van out joyriding?"

Malcolm protected his head from another slap. "Mom, I ain't committed no dang robbery. I was at Sheila's the whole time. Todd and his girl took a long time getting back to Sheila's house, much longer than I ever expected. But they didn't say nothing to me about robbing nobody."

Marlene now suspected the very troubled Todd Jacobson of perhaps accidentally dropping that moneybag in the van as she chewed on Malcolm's statements about how long Todd had taken to get back to Sheila's. This was a sticky situation at best. And she hoped Malcolm was telling the truth.

She threw the blue 7-Eleven bank bag down at his feet. "Then explain this being found in your gym clothes."

Surprised at seeing the bank bag, his eyes dilated with fear. He shrugged his shoulders. "I don't know nothing about that thing. I've never seen it before now. I swear to you, Momma. You got to believe me on this one. I'm telling the truth. You're gonna have to ask Todd about this."

"I intend to. The Lord Jesus is going to have to help us all if you're lying to me again. As members of your father's congregation, I imagine Sister and Brother Jacobson are going to have a lot to say about this, too. It's probably going to cost Sister Jacobson and me our longtime friendship. 'Cause I'm sure going to tell Jesse's lawyer what I just learned. That means Todd will surely be implicated in this nastiness. What did I do to deserve a troubled godson and an even more troubled son?"

Marlene got up from the bed and gave her son one last hard look. "It's late, but I'm still going to call the lawyer. He needs to know this information as soon as possible. This is hardly over, Malcolm. I'm going to have to tell your father the truth about everything you've gotten yourself into over the past year. If you're planning on running away from home, you best do it before he gets out of jail. I promise I won't ever try to stop you from running away from home again. In fact, I encourage you to do so. A twenty-one-year-old man should be on his own, anyway. It's time that I should be able to walk around in my house naked without having to worry about where your sorry black behind is."

Malcolm was shocked to learn that his mother wanted him out of her house. He could tell that she meant what she'd said, simply because she'd never talked to him that way before, ever. He knew that now was not the time to challenge her, but he needed to try to get back on her good side. He was a pro at melting her heart.

"I'm sorry, Momma. I can see how upset you are. I don't know if Todd used the van to rob someone or not. But I need you to know that I didn't know anything about it. He's never breathed a word to me about no 7-Eleven robbery. Momma, I'd never hurt you like that."

Marlene looked worn down. "Save your apologies for someone who gives a damn, Malcolm Covington. I don't care about nothing or nobody but your daddy right now. Forgive me, Lord, but that's just the way I feel at this moment in time."

"Momma, why you hating on me?"

"Hating? That's too mild a word for what I'm feeling right now. I don't hate you, Malcolm. Just some of the things you do. A mother's love is without conditions. But my love is not going to help you when you find yourself behind bars. Keep right on taking the destructive path you're on, and you'll find out just what I'm talking about. In fact, you're going to the prison with me this weekend. You need a reality check, my brother."

"I'm not going out to that prison. No way!"

"Fine. Let me know your new address and phone number so that we can stay in contact."

"What you talking about, Momma?"

"The move you're about to make. Today!"

"I can't believe you're going to make me go out to that dang prison. I don't want to see Daddy locked up in there like that."

"I can't make you do anything. You've already proven that to me time and time again. To go, or not to, is a choice. Just hope you make the right one."

"This is stupid. It's blackmail. If I don't go with you out there in that hot desert, I got to move out. Now how Christian-like is that?"

Marlene's razor-sharp glance had Malcolm hand-checking his throat to see if it had been slit. "Don't you dare question my Christianity, fathead boy! I'm not an angel. I've got many faults, Malcolm. The things I've let you get away with over the past year are my biggest ones. Now, I'm not going to hear no more smart-mouthing from you. I want you to march right into your room and pack your damn stuff. In fact, I already started packing for you. That's how I came across that gym bag."

His eyebrows appeared to grow wings.

"Yeah, I cursed. I answer to a high authority. I don't answer to you, period. Once you've packed your gear, leave my keys to my house on the hall credenza. Then quietly close the door behind you. Thank you."

Unable to believe that his mother was actually throwing him out of her house, Malcolm continued to stare at her with a defiant look on his face. *She has to be crazy if she thinks I'm leaving here. This is my house, too.*

"Do you need an escort, boy?"

"What kinda escort?"

"A police escort! If you don't move your black tail from in front of me, that's what you're gonna get. I'll slap a restraining order on you if I have to. If I haven't made myself clear by now, let me do so. Get the hell out!"

Malcolm saw no chance whatsoever of placating Marlene. She had proven to him that she was indeed crazy—and that he was going to have to leave her house this night, for sure. Many thoughts ran through his head, but he thought better of voicing any of them. With the mood his mother was in, it was a risky proposition for him all the way around. With his head hanging as low as it could without hitting his chest, he left the room.

As she cried softly into the bed pillow, Marlene's heart sorely ached. Throwing Malcolm out hadn't been an easy thing to do, although it had been necessary. She had to regain control of her life and her home. Malcolm had ruled for far too long. He now had to become the master of his own destiny. She'd be there for him if he fell, but he'd never know his full capabilities if she didn't let go of him. Her work was done in raising him; it had long since been over. She had to step back, had to step into the role of adviser, but only give advice when asked. Parenting was a lifetime ordainment. It didn't end when children became eighteen. Enabling should never become a part of the process.

Standing at the bedroom window, she looked out at the pine trees in her front yard. Jesse had planted them, had nurtured them right along. Then he'd let them mature while he'd kept a close eye on their continued growth. She'd have to learn to do the same with their son. It was time for Malcolm to become a man.

There was much work yet to be done in obtaining Jesse's release. They weren't getting any younger. She had to fight for whatever time they had left on this earth to be together. Marlene had no intention of loving her husband from behind bars for the rest of their days. *Till death do us part* was the vow she'd taken, the vow she fully intended to keep—up close and personal.

On the other hand, if Malcolm were guilty of the crime Jesse was paying for, she'd have to deal with that, too. The thought of her young son—her pretty, young son—behind bars was as unattractive a scenario as any she could ever imagine. He wouldn't fair well in jail. He had a smart mouth and a quick temper. The combination of those two could prove deadly inside of a place like that. Malcolm Covington would experience seriously hard times if that were to occur.

Kneeling down beside her bed, Marlene began to pray for her family, for an abundance of strength and courage from the Almighty.

Tears flowed unchecked as she communicated with her God. A God who knew all and understood all, a God who would never forsake His children.

A God who delivered His very best, according to His will, according to His purpose.

And we know that all things work together for good to them that love God, to them who are the called according to his purpose.—Romans 8:28

CHAPTER TWELVE

Marlene was extremely nervous about telling her best friend that she thought her son might have committed the crime for which Jesse was in prison. Friends since grade school, she and Myrna Jacobson had a long history. Myrna's reaction was what concerned Marlene most. Just as Malcolm was her and Jesse's only child, Todd was Myrna and Raymond's.

Her eyes were wet as she watched Myrna devour the lunch Marlene had prepared for them to talk over. Her dear friend loved to eat. More than that, she loved to pig out on anything Marlene cooked. Her face stayed in the plate. The smothered steak, mashed potatoes, and golden-brown gravy had Myrna coming up only occasionally for brief snatches of oxygen.

"This is *soooo* good! Why aren't you eating, girl. Grab one of those biscuits and soak up some of this delicious gravy. You aren't gonna gain that much weight."

"Huh! Just looking at that calorie-laden food it is enough to make me gain weight. I'm going to stick to this here chicken salad for now. My hips are up on my back already."

Myrna laughed. "Suit yourself. I'll even take the leftovers home if you don't want them around. There's enough steak and potatoes left for me to have for lunch and dinner tomorrow."

"Malcolm will have a fit if I don't leave him some. . . ." Remembering that Malcolm wouldn't be coming home to eat any of her meals brought tears to Marlene's eyes. With that in mind, she allowed her comment to go unfinished. Myrna didn't need to know all her business.

"Okay, girl. Just trying to help you out. Don't want you to go throwing all this good food into the garbage, not when you got a human disposal around to toss it into. I know Reverend Jesse must be missing him some of your black-eyed peas in cornbread and those killer barbecued beef ribs. I know he's not eating like that up there in that pen."

When Marlene flinched, Myrna realized what she'd said. But it was too late.

"I'm sorry, girl. I'm always running my big mouth. Forgive me for what I just said. I wasn't thinking, as usual. By the way, you invited me over here 'cause you wanted to talk to me about something serious. Is it anything to do with Jesse?"

"I'm afraid it has everything to do with Jesse. Please allow me to finish all of what I have to say before you jump in. It's important for you to listen to me, Myrna. And I promise to listen to you when I'm finished. Just remember that we've been friends a long time."

"How could I ever forget that. Girl, I'm here for you. You should know that by now. We're been through a lot of firestorms together. We're going to get through this latest one, too."

"I truly hope so."

Once Myrna finished polishing off the contents of her plate, Marlene got right to the point, telling her what Malcolm had told her about the night the church van had been involved in a robbery. When she got to the point that involved Myrna's son, Todd, she prayed inwardly for strength. There was no delicate way to tell her best friend that her son could be arrested once Jesse's lawyer took the new evidence to the district attorney. She had asked Major Townsend, Jesse's lawyer, to wait until after she'd had the opportunity to talk with Myrna about everything.

"You've known Todd since the day he was born. How could you think he'd do something like that? Marlene, we're godmothers to each other's children. How can you believe this?"

"I never said I believed it. I don't know what to believe anymore. I know this is hard for you. This isn't easy for me, either. I'm just giving you all the facts, as I understand them."

Marlene looked thoroughly distressed. Myrna Carson-Jacobson had been her constant companion through life's ups and downs.

More than just a few pounds overweight, especially for someone just a little over five feet tall, Myrna had a lovely brown sugar–colored face. The anguish now filling her tea brown eyes made Marlene feel horrible about the entire situation.

"Facts or speculation? What makes you believe that Malcolm is telling the truth, after all the tremendous lies you've already caught him in? I hate to say this, but we both know that Malcolm is a habitual liar. Has always been one. He's also been known to steal a dime or two."

Cutting her eyes sharply, Marlene sighed hard. "Myrna, you and I have been friends for most of our lives, but if you think I'm going to sit here and listen to you defame my son, you'd better think again. I could bring up a lot of really bad things that Todd has done, but what would be the point since you're already quite aware of them. The problem is you and me. We've covered our sons' butts for so long. And now Jesse is paying for our ineffective parenting."

"Jesse's paying for his crime of seriously neglecting his son. He's so busy at the church that he forgot Malcolm even existed. How many times have I heard you say that yourself?"

"Numerous times, but I never thought I'd hear you use it as a weapon against me. That was a low, coldhearted blow, Myrna. I think we'd better end this conversation before irreparable damage is done. Words can be lethal when used as ammunition. I was hoping it wouldn't come down to us acting like this. We'll talk again once things cool off a bit."

"Don't count on it. I may never talk to you again. If you try to implicate my son in your son's crime, don't be surprised when you find your clothesline loaded down with your family's dirty laundry. Malcolm does not have the bright future that you seem to think he has. He's been at the root of all the problems in your life since he was fifteen. And, furthermore—"

"That's enough from you," Marlene said with deadly calm. "I'll see you to the door."

"Don't bother. I don't want you to have the satisfaction of slamming it behind me. I can find my own way out."

* * *

Marlene had already started crying when she heard the door slam shut. The closing door was symbolic of her being shut out of Myrna's life for good. She'd tried to approach the subject with lots of sensitivity, but that probably meant nothing to the woman who thought her best friend was possibly going to be responsible for having her only child brought up on criminal charges. No one would be the victor in this situation. A lot more heartache was ahead.

Glad that she was seeing Keisha and Rosalinda later on in the evening, Marlene hoped their company would help lift her funk. It was becoming more and more apparent that she was going to have to deal with the loss of a loved one. She and Myrna loved each other like sisters. While gravely concerned about her relationship with Myrna, Marlene couldn't help wondering what her loving husband was going to say when he found out she'd been sitting on this for over a month now. If Myrna flipped out, she didn't want to think about what Jesse might do or say.

Waiting for a pay phone to use to call his wife, Jesse Covington closely watched Zach Martin as he talked into the phone. Jesse wasn't trying to listen to what was being said, but Zach's voice was loud enough for everyone to hear.

Zach put his hand over his left ear, trying to drown out the loud noises coming from the recreation room. Dressed in dark blue denim jeans and a powder blue shirt, the normal prison garb, with a cigarette stuck behind his ear, Zach leaned against the wall as he tried to charm Keisha. He hoped to regain the control over her that he somehow seemed to be losing.

"Come on, girl. What you talkin' 'bout? How you gonna dis me like that? Why you talking about skipping out on me all of a sudden? Outside my mother, you know you're the only one I got to rely on out there in the world."

That wasn't true. Tammy was living proof of that. And there were several others, from what she'd overheard the custodial inmates saying.

"Zach, I didn't like your attitude on my last couple of visits. It's been over a year now since you've been gone. I need a man who's got my back. Our four-year-old son is growing like a bad weed and he needs a positive role model in his life. Little Zach needs a responsible daddy."

Zach drew in a shaky breath. "Listen, baby girl, you know I love you. We done been through thick and thin together. How you gonna act like this? You know I'm working on getting outta here. My classes should come through any day now. Can't you hang in there a little longer? Come on, sweet thing, tell me you love me."

When Zach heard the familiar sigh, which normally meant that Keisha was softening, he knew he had her right where he wanted her. "Baby girl, just think about that first night of freedom. We're going to bring down the house. I'm gonna take you to paradise."

Keisha giggled. "If you promise me it's going to be as good as them nights on the last three times you got out, I might reconsider." Keisha had to cringe at the sound of that.

Keisha tried to keep herself from giving in, but she couldn't do it. Zach had her heart wrapped up tight. Giving him up wasn't going to happen, at least no time soon. She was sure that Tammy wasn't going to be too happy with her decision to hang in there with him. Tammy seemed to be looking forward to them busting him but good. But they had kids together, and that changed everything. She had to stop a minute and ask herself as if she was just using her kids as an excuse to stay with their no-account father. Probably so, she concluded.

Relieved that he had her back in check, Zach sighed inwardly. "It's gonna be better than that, baby, 'cause I been in here longer than on those other times. Girl, I'm a starving man. I can't wait to lick you up and down and all around. You're so sweet. For my dessert, I'm gonna suck on you like you was a chocolate lollipop. Can you feel me, baby girl?"

"Oh yeah, Z, I can feel you," Keisha cooed. "I'm already wet. When you going to talk to your counselor again about taking the special classes?"

"I got my request in. It ain't gonna be long now. Hold on to those memories, baby girl. I got to run. All the lines for the phones have gotten long." He made a kissing noise into the receiver. "That's for you, little Zach, and my princess Zanari. Keep it hot for me, baby girl. I'll try to call later. And don't forget to put some more money on my books before you register for the next visit. My account is practically bone-dry."

"I'll do what I can, but Zach needs some new shoes. See you on the weekend. Love ya."

As Keisha disconnected the phone line, she felt herself cooling off. Zach's last statement had brought her back to the realization that all he wanted from her was money. She knew for a fact that he was lying about her being the only one he could depend on, knew that he more than likely had money on his books. Knowing wasn't the problem for her.

Being able to stop loving him was.

Ricardo looked like a refugee from a roughneck gang. He wore a black wave-cap on his head, tied tightly in the back. He passed by just as Zach hung up the phone.

"What's up, dog?"

Zach laughed. "Just getting one of my five broads back in line. Now I got to call Tammy and work on her fat behind. But she's gonna be a lot easier than Keisha. Tammy girl wants to go half on a baby when I get out of here. What kind of crap is that? She been listening to too much R. Kelly. And she loves them bullcrap love poems I send her. I'm all inside that fat tramp's head. You know I got to be about my paper, dog. I got five women putting that cheese on my books. And I'm sending most of it to my mother to put in the bank for when I get outta here. I should have a grip by the time I blow this hellhole. Then I'm going to find me a fresh new broad."

Ricardo gave Zach five. "That's how you got to work them silly hoochies. If they stupid enough to give up the chips, we got to be smart enough to take it and make it work for us. It can be real lucrative up in here for a brother. Besides Rosie, I'm working three hoochies myself."

Loud shouting caused Zach and Ricardo to turn around and see what all the commotion was about. When three guards came running down the hall, they moved out of the way with lightning speed.

"The Crips and Bloods must be at it again in the rec room. That's why I stay the hell out of there. You gang-bangers be crazy, dog. Your posse's gonna get us all locked down again. I'm probably gonna have to wait till later to call Tammy. Damn, them suckers be messing up my enterprising gig. I wish they'd calm down for a minute till I get my groove across to Tammy."

* * *

Unable to believe the disrespectful way in which these two young men talked about women, Jesse shook his head. He'd never heard such blatant contempt coming from a man regarding the mother of his children. It boggled Jesse's mind to hear Zach referring to his lady with such dishonor. Ricardo's comments weren't any better. Marlene definitely had her hands full in trying to get those two young women to take a hard look at the men in their lives, to take a look at what they'd become a part of. Sorry that he couldn't put his call through to Marlene, Jesse moved quietly back to his cell when several guards initiated a lockdown.

This was a hard way to live one's life, especially for an innocent man, Jesse thought. The moment his cell door clanked shut, Jesse kneeled in prayer. With tears in his eyes, he bowed his head.

"Lord, I don't know why I ended up in a terrible place like this, but I know that You do. I don't know how long You intend for me to stay here, but I am patiently waiting for You to reveal Your will in this matter. Lord, I know You love me, that You won't ever forsake me, but I miss my family something awful. I crave for the time to come when I will be back in the pulpit. I miss my church family and my neighbors. Please ease the dagger-sharpness of the pain of missing them so much, as well as missing the normalcy of my life on the outside. I pray that I might endure this separation until You see fit to return me to the woman, the son, and the job that I love. Thank You for keeping me safe from the unending turmoil that goes on inside these cold, concrete walls. Thank You, Lord."

Keisha looked up when she saw movement at the window outside her apartment door. When the bell rang, she jumped up. She couldn't believe her eyes. Her mother stood there, looking twenty years younger than her actual fifty-two.

Keisha leapt out of her seat. "Mom, what are you doing here? I just talked to you on the phone in Atlanta last night. Look at you. You've lost a lot of weight. I'm so proud of you."

Martha Reed embraced her daughter. "I know you've heard of planes. I came to see about my babies."

Keisha helped Martha bring her bags inside. For the time being, Keisha stored them in the hall closet.

"Oh, there she is. There's Grandma's little angel." She reached down and picked up her sleeping granddaughter from the sofa. "Come to Grandma, Princess Zanari."

Keisha eyed Martha with suspicion. "Why are you really here, Mom?" *To be all in my business. I'm sure of that.*

"I've already told you my reason for being here." She kissed Zanari and laid her back down. Taking the blanket that Zanari had kicked off of her, Martha covered the baby up.

"I hope you didn't come here to get all on my case about how I'm raising my kids. I got enough drama going on in my life as it is."

"Relax, Keisha. I'm only here to support you. I know things are tough for you right now. I have no intention of adding any more drama to your unbelievable Lifetime-channel style of living. Where's Grandma's big boy?" Martha sat down in the only other chair.

"He's with Zach's mom. She's been keeping him a lot more since Zanari was admitted to the hospital."

"It's about time she did something to help you out. Oh, well, I guess everyone can't be the grandmotherly type like me. How's Zanari coming along?"

"The doctor says she's much better. I just have to keep a close eye on her. Her breathing isn't a hundred percent, but it's getting there. How'd you get here from the airport?"

"A taxi that nearly cost me an arm and a leg. The driver was nice enough to carry my bags up those steep steps of yours."

"That was nice of him. I was glad when Zanari was released from the hospital. I was tired of spending my nights there and going to school from there in the mornings, but I didn't have to miss a single class or miss any hours from my job. I'm really happy about that. The lady that I told you about, Marlene Covington, she made arrangements for someone from her church to come sit with Zanari while I was at school and work. She has been a real blessing in my life. Someone's going to come and sit with Zanari while I attend the support-group meeting tonight. The one I talked to you about over the phone."

"Where'd you tell me you met her?"

"I didn't. I met her at the prison."

Martha snorted. "Another lady in waiting, huh?"

"Don't be so cynical, Mom. This is a wonderful lady. Her husband's a minister. It seems that he's been wrongly accused and convicted of a serious crime."

"Isn't that usually the story? I can't tell you how many women told me that their men were innocent when I used to visit your daddy in prison."

"Was daddy innocent?"

Martha Reed appeared to shrink several inches right before her daughter's eyes. The look on her mocha brown face made Keisha wish she hadn't given voice to her thoughts. The next look Martha gave Keisha leveled her on the spot. If she didn't know better, she would think her mother hated her. Keisha didn't understand why it had to be this way between them.

"Let me tell you something, little girl. I don't answer to you. You answer to me. Whatever happened with your daddy is none of your business. You understand me? Furthermore, don't ever ask questions that you don't want the answer to."

"But I do want the answer. I've always wanted to know." Keisha stood up. "You tell me it's none of my business what happened with you and your man, but you try to make my business with Zach your own. Why was it good enough for you to support Daddy in jail, but it's not good enough for me to do the same with my children's father? Can you tell me that?"

Martha crossed the room and roughly grabbed Keisha by the arm, then pushed her back down in the chair. "Look, little Miss Thing, Dublin Reed was my husband at the time of his incarceration. Are you married to Zachary Martin?"

"What does that have to do with anything?"

"Everything! I took a vow to stand by that man through the good and the bad. Back then wasn't like it is now. You got married first and then you had the kids. There were exceptions, but they were rare where I came from. Even then, accident or not, a marriage usually happened, even if it was a shotgun wedding. You young people don't know the first thing about commitment. Everything you do is backwards. 'I'm an independent woman,' you scream. Independent fools are what you are. Only a misguided fool brings a child into the world with no means to care for it. And a lot of you don't just stop at giving birth to one. The world is full of children with irresponsible parents like you and Zach. You and that sorry man of yours don't know the first thing about parenting. But you're going to learn. I'm going to be the one to teach you. Real good."

"I thought you came here to support me?"

"I did. But you started this—and I'm going to finish it. Don't step in my kitchen if you can't stand the heat, because my oven is always on. If you don't want your goose cooked, stay out of my dang kitchen. The temperature in there is rarely lukewarm, and never cold."

"Mom, I ain't trying to hear this from you. You can turn around and take this noise right on back to Atlanta. I'm all grown-up now. I don't have to listen to your put-downs any longer."

Martha pulled Keisha up from the chair and hit her hard across the behind, several times.

"Why you hitting me on my behind like that?" Keisha's face darkened like a thundercloud.

"You better be glad it was your behind, 'cause I feel like slapping your silly face." Martha pushed her daughter back down in the chair. "You need to get something straight inside that thick head of yours. I'm the parent. As long as I have breath in me, I'm going to parent my kids. It's a lifetime job, a career. God help the parents that let their kids run them into the ground. I'll slap you all the way to Atlanta and back if I see that you're out of line. Are the issues clear?"

"Yeah."

"*Yes, ma'am* is what you've been taught. Don't risk saying *yeah* to me again. We're not on any telephone now. You're right within my grasp. You feeling me, girl?"

"Yes, ma'am."

"That's better."

Martha pulled up the other chair and got right in her daughter's face. She was so close to Keisha that their knees touched.

"This is something I swore I'd never do, but I can see that I don't have any choice. I don't want to see you make the same mistakes I did. Even though you've already started on the same path I took, I'm here to redirect you. It's never too late to switch paths, especially when you realize you're on the wrong one."

"Where are you going with this? Can it wait until after the support-group meeting? There are people counting on me to help out. I don't want to disappoint them. And I don't want to be late."

"I can wait. I got nothing but time. And I'm going to use that time to make sure that time doesn't run out on your fast behind like it did mine. That you can count on."

An hour into the support group, the look on Keisha's face was none too pretty. Her mother had gotten up to talk in front of the support group. That realization didn't make Keisha the least bit happy. What was her mother going to say now? She hoped Martha wasn't going to insult these women like she'd insulted her today by calling them fools. Keisha leaned forward in her seat so she could hear Martha's every word.

"I'm an out-of-town visitor and I'm glad that I got a chance to come to this meeting. I wish I'd had somewhere to go for support when my husband was in prison. I'm speaking because I'm hoping by sharing my past that I can help out others with their future. I'm afraid if I wait any longer to tell my story, that someone very close to me may walk in my very footsteps. The shoes I wore back then were not fit to walk in. That's why I don't want to see them on someone else's feet today."

Keisha couldn't stop her eyes from filling with tears, because she knew Martha Reed was talking about her, as well as the other people like her. Still, she wished this wasn't happening.

"The only crime my husband committed was that of being a Casanova. Some of you all may know my husband. He may be living at your house today, or might have lived there at one time. I know you hate to admit to it if you do know him. I've lived in denial, too. I've forgotten more of his women than I can remember. And I remember plenty of them. But he wasn't any criminal. His only crime was having an affair with the chief of police's wife. He had more than an affair with her; he got her pregnant. The woman died while having an illegal abortion."

Keisha was positively mortified. This was not something her mother should be airing out in public. She could see that her mother had meant it when she said she was going to finish what her daughter had started. Martha's kitchen wasn't just hot. It was on fire.

"I forgave that indiscretion just like I forgave all the rest. It was much later in life that I came to understand that a woman didn't have to stay with an ungodly man, and vice versa."

Martha ignored the shocked expression on Keisha's face. She had to get through this right now or she never would. She had to do this for both herself and her daughter. Outside of her husband's numerous affairs, this was the hardest thing she'd ever had to stomach. This was a secret she'd carried inside of her for too long. Before Keisha had started following in her footsteps, this was one story she had vowed to never reveal. It would've been a dishonor to her deceased husband. Things had changed. Dublin was dead. Keisha was alive—and in big trouble.

"If he didn't commit a crime, why was he in prison?" someone in the crowd asked.

"Weren't you listening to me, honey? Having an affair with a cop's wife is a crime. We're not just talking about a regular cop's wife. This was the chief. It didn't happen right away, but he eventually got my husband. Busted him on trumped-up charges. The chief got his revenge. There are guilty men in jail and there are innocent ones. But it doesn't matter one way or the other. Once they get in the system, their life is no longer their own. What bothers me the most is when young women stay with or get involved with men who use the system like a revolving door. My husband never came home from prison, so I don't know if he would've ever gone back. But I doubt it. He didn't belong there in the first place. He hated it. He was killed in prison, leaving me as a permanent lady in waiting. It seems like I'm still waiting for him to show up. I don't want to see any woman wasting her life away while waiting for someone that may never come home. But I also understand that for many of you there isn't a choice. Love is the most addictive of all habits, the hardest one to break. Thank you for allowing me to share. May God bless each of you."

A healthy round of applause followed Martha's remarks. Keisha could only glare at her mother. No one knew it was her mother, but she was still embarrassed by the whole thing.

Keisha knew that Martha's last statement had been meant especially for her. How could she be upset with her mother, when she was only trying to spare her the pain of the same fate? But her mother couldn't live her life for her. She'd made her mistakes, but they'd been hers to make. Keisha had to make her own, too. She couldn't live her life based on her mother's.

Just as Dublin Reed had been Martha's fate. Zachary Martin was hers. Only Keisha could change the course of her life. This was her life to run, her kids to raise up, her man to support, her decisions to make, and her consequences, good or bad. No one else could live her life for her.

Just as Marlene reached the podium, a lot of commotion broke out in the back of the room. Everyone had stood up, so she had to crane her neck to see what was happening. She could hear the loud shouting and cursing, but she couldn't see from whom it was coming. When the crowd shifted just enough for her to catch a glimpse, she saw two pretty young women going at one another with a vengeance. Words were flying and anger was raging between them.

"That's my man! You stay away from him. If I catch you up at the prison visiting him again, it's going to be on! And you can believe it will be much worse than this here."

"He ain't thinking about you, girl. When you going to get that through your thick head. I'm the new leading lady in his life. I'm dating him now. So what you got to say about that?"

As the other woman went to swing at the one who'd just spoken her mind, Martha Reed caught her hand in midair. "That's enough of this. This is the house of the Lord. What is wrong with you two? You shouldn't be acting like this in the church. In fact, you shouldn't be carrying on like this, period. Show some respect for yourselves."

"You better get your hands off me, old lady. I will dust this room with your fat behind."

"Oh, hell, no, she ain't talking to my mother like that."

Marlene snatched Keisha back by her belt. "Your mother?"

"Yes, ma'am. I'm afraid so. I'm sorry she got up there and said the things she did. I'm embarrassed by it, but she's still my mother."

Realizing that the woman had been talking about Keisha as the person following in her footsteps, understanding flashed in Marlene's eyes. "You stay right here, young lady. I'm going to end this nonsense inside my church right now. This ain't happening in here," Marlene huffed. "Not the house of worship. They have to take that loud noise away from here."

Before she left the dais, Marlene suddenly turned and went back to Keisha. "You don't have anything to be sorry about. Instead of being embarrassed, you should be proud of your mother. She showed a lot of courage."

Marlene practically ran to the back of the room. The next thing

Keisha saw was Marlene escorting the two women out into the hallway. She was glad Marlene had gotten there before Martha had taken that chick out for talking to her like that. She might have been a pushover for her man, but she wasn't the type to take anything from those young girls. Keisha cringed at the thought of having to bail her mother out of a Los Angeles County jail for beating the crap out of those two hardheads.

The crowd was all abuzz when Marlene came back into the room alone. She hurried to the podium and picked up the microphone. It took her a few minutes to quiet things down.

"We're sorry for that interruption. But something good has come out of it. The two young women agreed to talk to one of our counselors. We don't want this to be just a place to come and air things out. We're prepared to offer counseling and prayer to anyone who needs it. I was really caught off guard when those two young women told me they were blood sisters fighting over the same man. I was stunned to hear one of them use the term *dating* in reference to visiting an inmate. But apparently that's how it's seen by many. That's what I was told when I asked."

"That's why people get all dolled up when they go to the prison, especially them young ones," someone offered. "They also get the hair and the nails done for the occasion. Some of them actually see going out to the prison as going on a date."

To keep from crying, Marlene shook her head from side to side. "It's in situations like this that we all need to rally together and try to see what we can do to help. This group can do great things if we all pull together. Because my vision for this support group goes beyond airing out troubles and finding support, love, and understanding among ourselves, I invited a guest speaker to join us this evening. Dr. Lorna Trapp is here to uplift and inspire. Please give her a warm welcome."

Sporting a healthy head of reddish-brown sister-locks, Dr. Lorna Trapp made haste in getting up to the podium. Fair-complexioned, medium in height, she was a very attractive sister. Before speaking, she took a moment to adjust the microphone.

"Good evening, ladies. It's an honor to stand here before you. I'm not going to bore you with my credentials and a whole lot of talk about myself, because that's not what's most important. I will hand out business cards to those who are interested in knowing more about me.

"When Mrs. Covington came to me and asked me to speak with her group, I was more than a little surprised to hear what this support group was all about. Once she explained the objectives and goals of the group, I saw that she was on to something wonderful and inspiring. The topic I'd chosen for my talk tonight has completely changed. After seeing what just went on in the back of the room, I was inspired to go in another direction. I'm not going to talk about what you can do about your situation with the men you're supporting in prison. I'm here to talk about you and what you can do for you. It all begins with you and it will all end with you."

Dr. Trapp took a sip from the glass of water that Rosalinda had just handed her.

"The love for self is what I decided to speak on. How we feel about ourselves is how others will see us. How we treat ourselves is how others will treat us. There are a couple of specific points that I must bring out first. Please hear this if you don't hear another word I say.

"We give people permission in how to treat us. No one can do anything to us that we don't give them permission to do!" To stress her comments, she repeated them again and again.

"Write those words down and read them over and over. Read them until they sink in, until they're etched into your brain, until they become a part of your soul. Once we have these words locked into our memories and have made them a part of our souls, then we can begin to ask questions of ourselves. How do we see ourselves? How would we like to see ourselves? How do we treat ourselves? How do we want to treat ourselves? The answers lie within us, therefore we're the only ones who can answer them. No one can answer them for us. I can't answer them for you, either, but I can help you learn how to find the answers for yourself. Once we've done an in-depth study on self, we'll move on to the engaging topic of setting boundaries.

"I'm going to leave you with those words and that simple assignment. If you're interested in working on improving self, keep coming back. I believe that getting in touch with self will help you deal with whatever comes your way. It is in knowing and loving self that we can come to experience triumph and deal effectively with failure. I am committed to helping us help ourselves. Because I truly believe in the needs and the mission of this group, I am going to make myself available as often as my professional schedule will permit. Thank you for being such an attentive audience. May God bless you and yours."

Clapping and cheering roared until Marlene brought everything under control. She'd been worried that some of the women might reject the idea of her bringing in professional speakers, or the mention of counseling. It was apparent that there weren't any obvious objectors. But that didn't mean she might not receive written or caller complaints or even lose a few members before all was said and done. She would cross that bridge when and if it loomed in front of her. By all indication, tonight's meeting was a success. It would do her no good to borrow trouble.

Not a single word had been spoken between mother and daughter since the moment Keisha had introduced Martha to Marlene. Rosalinda had gotten somewhat acquainted with Keisha's mom over the phone, but tonight had been their first face-to-face meeting. Pulling up at a stoplight, Keisha looked over at Martha, who stared straight ahead.

"Was she white?"

"How many black chiefs of police held office back then?"

"Enough said. How did the chief get to Daddy?"

"Through his job. And we had moved away from where it happened. They claimed he was stealing televisions and VCRs out of the warehouse and selling them on the black market. They had a bunch of people lined up to testify against him, or so they said. He pleaded guilty because he knew he wasn't going to beat the rap. That's what happens to a lot of black men today. They're intimidated by the time they might get if they decide to go to trial. Plea-bargaining is nothing more than a well-devised trap. Either way, they're going to get time. It just comes down to a matter of how much. They don't have the money to fight the charge, so they plead out to get a lesser sentence, the innocent and the guilty."

"I know. It still happens a lot. I didn't know that it had happened to Daddy."

"I also believe the chief had Dublin killed. With no proof, or no money to prove it if you have any, you have nowhere to turn."

"Since you and Daddy had moved away from that town, what makes you think the chief was responsible for his death?"

"The arm of the law is a long one, far-reaching. Like I said, we had no proof, but we knew that Dublin wasn't guilty of the crime. We later learned that the chief's brother-in-law just happened to be on the police force in the town we moved to. We also heard that one of the men your daddy worked with was spreading a lot of money around town. He was supposed to have been the main witness. Payoff for false testimony?" Martha shrugged her shoulders. "We'll never know.

Keeping her eyes on the road, Keisha leaned over and put an arm around Martha. "I'm sorry, Mom. I had no idea. I can see why you stay on my case about Zach." For several seconds she toyed with the idea of telling Martha about Zach's involvement with Tammy. She quickly decided against it, only because she hadn't yet determined her future with Zach.

"I know I'm hard on Zach, but I'm deeply concerned about you and those kids. Even though I've never met him, that boy hasn't shown me much since you been with him. It's one thing to make a mistake. But to keep repeating the same one tells me he's not learning anything. I was Zach in some regards. I kept taking your daddy back and listening to his lies that his cheating would never happen again. Bottom line: I don't want to see you end up like me. I don't want the kids to grow up with a father who has no respect for his woman and none for the law."

Keisha parked her car in front of her apartment building. "Mom, let's go inside and get you settled in. You can sleep in my bed. I'll sleep in the room with Zanari since Zach is with Lucian. I want us to really talk, Mom. I want you to be my friend."

Both were crying as Martha hugged Keisha. "I am your friend. You'll come to see that in time. Let's go inside. I'm tired and I know you are."

"Thanks, Mom. I'm glad you're here."

"I can't think of anywhere else that I'm needed more. Thanks for allowing me to stay."

CHAPTER THIRTEEN

The church sanctuary was in an uproar when Marlene walked into the outside vestibule. Voices were loud with anger. Before entering the room, she stood outside and listened. She guessed that the subject matter was Jesse since the special voting session had been called.

"If this board removes Reverend Jesse, I'm gone. This is ridiculous. The man practically built this church from the ground up. God put him here, and He's the only one that can remove him. Who are you to remove what God has seen fit to put in place?"

Marlene recognized the angry voice as that of Sister Bertha Sharpe, one of Jesse's strongest supporters. Jesse just happened to love her cooking even more than he loved his wife's.

"I may not up and leave this church," said Sister Winters, "but I know who my vote won't benefit next time around. This has been my church home for over twenty years. Everyone can't just jump up and leave the church when they don't like what's happening in it. You owe it to the other members to stay around and help make what's wrong right. In my opinion, leaving is not the right thing to do. But it's not right for politics to have a place in the church, either. You wanna-be politicians need to run for office somewhere other than in the church."

"Have mercy!" another strong voice shouted. "Preach to them, Sister Winters."

"Even so," Sister Winters continued, "for those of you that want to remove Reverend Jesse—we voted you in, we can vote you out. And we don't necessarily have to wait for the next election. That's all I got to say on the matter. That is, for right now."

Sister Winters loved the church, Marlene knew. And she also loved its pastor like a son.

"I've been listening to all this carrying on," Sister Gobel voiced, "but none of it's worth a hill of beans. We all can talk until we're blue in the face, but until we put some action behind those words, it's just a bunch of yakety-yak. As members of this church, we have say in what goes on in here. I say stop procrastinating and put the matter to vote. And then accept the outcome, even if it's not the one you desire. I agree with the brethren that the church has to have a leader, but we can appoint someone from within on an interim basis. Reverend Clay Robinson has his hands filled with the youth, so we shouldn't continue to put more and more duties on him. Therefore I suggest that, when we take this vote, we pen in who we'd like to see in the pulpit until Reverend Jesse returns. Or pen in the one to put in charge in place of him. And I do believe he will return to us."

"I promise not to give you all a bunch of yakety-yak, but there are a few things that need to be said. You know me, I'm the one to say them when everyone else fails to do so."

Marlene knew something inspiring was about to take place. Sister Gooden was strong in the word, and she wasn't one to mince them, either.

"I just want this church to remember a few things before we put this measure to a vote. I hope we've thought hard about what we're here for this evening. A man's life is on the line in more ways than one, a man that most of us have professed to love over the years. Let's say, for instance, that Reverend Jesse is guilty of all charges."

"Give it to us straight, Sister," someone shouted.

"I want each of you to take a brief journey back into your past. Many of us won't have to go back too far; some of us just have to go back about an hour or two, to recall the last time that we committed a serious sin. No matter how large or small it might be, a sin is a sin. Say that you've been involved in an adulterous affair in your lifetime, that you've been on drugs, or involved yourself in prostitution, that you stole money or goods from your company, or that you have even committed sins that you can't ever bring yourself to talk about. Should we turn our backs on you? Or should we welcome you back among us with open arms? Do we have the right to condemn you and cast you aside? Or should we meet you right where you are and help you turn your life around?

"If Jesus were to walk through that door right now looking dirty and stinking to high heaven, how many of us would shrink away from him? How many would embrace him? Jesus is a healer; therefore, he intended the church as a place of healing. This is a hospital, folks. What if you were afflicted with a terminal illness and the hospital refused to admit you because you'd been in and out of there facility numerous times—and you aren't getting any better?"

"Hallelujah, Sister. Amen," several members shouted in unison.

"Many of us are just taking up bench space in the church. If you got hips like mine, you're taking up lots of space."

Everyone laughed.

"We're packed in here so tight on the seventh day that there's barely room for visitors to find a seat. But where are we on the other six? On Wednesday night, we can barely fill a couple of pews. When it comes time to volunteering for service, we got too much on our plate already. I don't know where you are on the other six days and nights, but I know where Reverend Jesse was. I know where he was on Wednesday nights. When it came down to volunteer service, you'd find our pastor in the front of the line. I can even tell you where he was on the other six days. He was at the nursing homes, the hospitals, the food banks, etcetera. When he was arrested, he was busy delivering food baskets to the needy. I think you get my drift. In ending this long tirade, I'm going to leave you with this: Do unto others as you would have them do unto you. If you follow just that one rule, you won't disobey the others."

Having heard enough, Marlene stepped into the sanctuary. The room fell silent as all eyes gravitated toward her. Holding her head up high, Marlene moved down the aisle toward the front pews with a strong air of confidence.

"Welcome, Sister Covington," one of the deaconesses said. "We're about to take our vote. Glad you could make it in time."

"Thank you, Sister Rockwell. I see that I've made it just in time. However, before we vote, I'd like to say a few words. May I?"

A round of applause from the members approved her request.

This was an emotional time for her, as well as for the church, but she had to do what she had to do. Taking a moment, she looked each of the deacons in the eye, silently praying away any malice in her heart . . . or any animosity that should just happen to slip out of her mouth.

Smiling, she stepped up to the podium. "I realize this is a hard time for the church. It's also a very hard time for the Covington family. Change is always hard, and it's hardest for those caught up in the changes. I don't need to tell you how much my family loves this church. This is home to us. Malcolm may have lost his way home, since he hasn't been here in a while, but I'm sure the loving memories that he has of this place will one day bring him back," she joked to ease the tension. She saw that it worked when immediate laughter came from the members.

"I've said all that only to say this: I'm not going to ask you to vote your heart or your conscience. That would be wrong of me to do. Because I think I know where your hearts are. I'm going to ask you to vote for what you truly believe is right for this church. The well-being of our church is my main concern, as it is Jesse's. Whatever you feel it needs, let your vote reflect the very same." Jesse didn't even know what was going on with the deacons and the desire to remove him—and she hoped she didn't ever have to tell him. It would simply break his heart.

Marlene took a deep breath, but it wasn't enough to calm the butterflies in her stomach. Although she meant every word of what she was saying, it was still hard for her not to fall down on her knees and beg them not to remove Jesse. To remove him would damage his heart, strip his soul bare, and dash away whatever remaining hope he may have had. She couldn't stand for that kind of pain to be visited upon him. Enough trauma had already occurred in his life.

"Before I close, I have something to say to the deacon board. Gentlemen, I very much understand your reasoning for wanting to remove Jesse Covington as pastor. It's your methods of doing so that I question and disapprove of. When you came to me with this, you had already made up your minds about what you were going to do. And you were going to do it without full approval of the church. That's what I objected to, strongly. I've asked God to forgive me for my reactions to your actions. And now I ask the same of you. Please forgive me for anything that I said out of anger and hurt, including the vengeance I felt in my heart during that time."

Marlene looked out at Sister Wylie and smiled. "If you can't forgive me, I understand that, too. But in reality, Jesus' is the only forgiveness that really counts. In fact, He's the only one that can forgive our sins. However, I'd like your forgiveness. I want this church to thrive, not to just survive. Only glorified ascension, not dissension, has a place in God's house. Thank you for your undivided attention. May God be with each and every member of this church."

Marlene didn't expect a standing ovation, but that's exactly what she got. Everyone stood but the opposing deacons. Their expressions showed that they could clearly see they were outnumbered by a wide margin.

The church vote was conducted in a quiet, orderly manner. The count was done in the same way. Marlene sat quietly as a special selected committee polled the votes. Her thoughts were with her husband. She couldn't bear to think of the outcome being anything other than the one in which she had put her faith and trust. She'd said her piece, and now it was time for the members of the church collectively to voice theirs.

Thirty minutes later, Deacon Willie Bowen stood at the podium. With all eyes eagerly on him, he had the urge to keep this impatient group waiting a bit longer. He laughed inwardly, glad that he wasn't on the opposing side. He'd hate to come up against this group of headstrong sisters. Not one of them was the type to take any stuff from anyone, especially a man. That was probably the reason why none of the men, for or against the measure, hadn't gotten up to speak during the entire process. He knew firsthand what the sisters were capable of since one of those vehemently objecting to the removal plan was his wife, Laura.

"Members, I'm extremely pleased to announce that the votes to keep Reverend Jesse on as our pastor have greatly surpassed the nays." Loud cheers and claps filled the air. "However," he shouted above the noise, reclaiming their attention, "it has been voted that a temporary leader should be appointed. In counting the names written in on the ballots, the special committee has reported to me that Sister Marlene Covington has won hands down."

Loud shouts of approval went up.

"Sister Covington, you have been voted in as the church's interim leader for the next six months. As you've so stated before the board, this is Reverend Jesse's church. It will remain so under your leadership. We've all had an occasion to hear your passionate sermons, and we've all been richly blessed for having done so. As this church is independently run of any conference, all the members of First Tabernacle Church have had their say. May the Lord add His blessing to this jubilant announcement."

A multitude of thoughts went through Marlene's head, but none of them as important as thanking the heavenly Father, the only true head of the church, for answering her prayers.

With tears in her eyes, Marlene walked to the podium. Her hands trembled as she adjusted the microphone. "I promise not to give a sermon or even a sermonette today." Everyone laughed at her comment. Everyone except the sore losers, she noted.

"I thank each and every one of you that voted to keep Reverend Jesse on as your pastor. I'm overwhelmed by the vote for me as the church leader, but I can't do it without the members. I may not be educationally qualified in the seminary or qualified by definition, but I'm up to the challenge. There's no way on this earth that I can deliver a sermon every week, at least not the soul-stirring way in which my husband does. With that in mind, I'm going to accept the position as your leader, but only on one condition. I need your permission to solicit visiting pastors to fill in the necessary gaps until Jesse comes home. I'm not a preacher, but I am a teacher of the Word. And I will stand before you each week and teach the Word of God. But Saturday and Sunday are the only days that I can visit Reverend Jesse. My commitment to my husband has to come first. I vowed to be there for him, and I must do that. At any rate, I can promise that you will hear from me more often than not. Thank you."

Another standing ovation occurred.

Sister Annie Wylie approached Marlene after everyone had offered her congratulations and sincere words of encouragement, hugging her with warmth. "You are a beautiful piece of work, Sister Covington. And you're certainly a better woman than I. I gave you enough ammunition on that deacon board to blow them to the moon and back." Laughing, she hugged Marlene again. "You're a good Christian woman. Christian or not, I would've blown them old frisky farts sky-high. But you did good, baby. Real good."

Marlene kissed Sister Wylie's smooth but weathered cheek. "You're still crazy as ever, Sister Wylie. Believe me, I had a major boxing match with the devil over using that ammunition. I didn't want to win by default. And I didn't win by much. Not by much at all."

"But you won! If you had let old Satan take over, everyone would've cheered you on, as you called to the carpet a few of those unruly deacons. You still may get the opportunity. They may have lost this round, but they're going to find a new way to challenge you. Those old geezers don't like to lose at anything."

"I hope you're wrong. There were only a couple of opposing deacons, anyway. If I do my job, they're not going to have anything to challenge me on."

"That's the spirit, Sister Covington. Now that we've settled that, can you give me a ride home? I caught a cab down here so I could vote. And you know how hard it is to get a cab in the residential areas of L.A. I wouldn't have missed this special voting session for the world."

"It would be my pleasure, Sister Wylie."

Before Rosalinda could walk away from the office door of Michael Hernandez, he opened it. With briefcase in hand, it looked to her as if he were on his way out. The look of surprise on his face told Rosalinda that she was the last person he'd expected to find on the other side of his office door, especially after his numerous phone calls to her hadn't been returned.

"Rosalinda, what a nice surprise. How are you?"

"I'm fine." She threw up her hands in frustration. "I'm sorry. This was a mistake for me to come here." She turned to walk away.

Dropping his briefcase to the floor, he caught up to her and gently turned her around to face him. "You obviously had something to say, or you wouldn't have come here today. Please come inside my office so we can talk privately." It looked to him as if she was going to refuse him. "Please, Rosalinda."

Reluctantly, yet at the same time wanting so much to do so, Rosalinda allowed Michael to guide her into his office and over to a wingback chair. He sat down in a chair situated less than a foot away from the one she sat in.

"I'm listening, Rosalinda. I'd like to hear what brought you to my office."

Unable to look him in the eye, she fumbled with her car keys. "I just wanted to . . . I shouldn't have come here." She stood up to leave.

He was there beside her in a flash. This time he directed her to the sofa, where he sat down next to her and slid his arm along the top of it. "Let me get this conversation started, since I see your reluctance. I'm sorry about how I went about revealing my personal interest in you. I shouldn't have tested you in that way. It was wrong of me. I'm attracted to your physical beauty, but I'm more enamored with the beauty inside of you. I know your situation."

Her eyes widened. "What do you mean by that?"

"Ric has talked a lot about you to me. Have you ever heard this saying: 'Don't reveal too much about the woman or man you're involved with to a friend, because they'll start to want what you have'?" Smiling, she nodded. "I can't go into any detail about it, but I've heard enough from Ric to know that you're a very special person and you deserve to have a man in your life who really cares about you."

"And I guess you're that man?"

"I could be. How's your mother?"

His question caught her off guard. She guessed that Ric had told him about Paulina Morales's illness, but she didn't expect him to act like he cared. He actually sounded like he did. Or was he using concern for her mother as a way to get next to her?

"My mother is not doing very well. Her kidneys are in really bad shape, along with another serious complication. She was recently diagnosed with lupus. Thank you for asking."

"Do you know why I asked about her?"

"No. But should I care?"

"I asked because I care about the things that affect you. Even though I can't elaborate, I know so much about the things that are affecting you, the things that are important to you. I know that you work two jobs, one as an administrative assistant and the other as a part-time telemarketer. I'm aware that you struggle financially to take care of your sick mother. You have a good heart. That is usually indicative of a good person. Let me help ease your burdens, Rosalinda. Let me be there for you."

"May I call you Michael since you seem to be so familiar with me?"

"Please do. Nothing would give me greater pleasure."

"What exactly are you talking about in regards to me and you? What is it you're looking for from me? What do you see in me that I can't see in myself?"

"All those questions are simple, easy for me to answer. I've already told you that I'm interested in getting to know you on a personal level. I think I have a lot to offer you. What I want from you is friendship to start with. I got a little ahead of myself the night we met at the motel."

She cringed at the memory. "A little ahead of yourself?"

He grinned. "You've made your point. But we can erase all that and start fresh. What I see in you is a pure work of art in slow motion. You're a budding flower that has yet to find the natural sunlight it needs in order to open up to the world. You won't find that sunlight in the darkness behind prison walls. I see inside your heart. And a halo does shine there. Open up your heart and let the light filter through you, so that it radiates to every part of your being."

Rosalinda had to choke back a sob caught in her throat. All she could do was look at Michael. What could she possibly say to the things he'd said? If she did have a halo inside of her, she wanted it to light her up, as well as her dreary days and lonely nights. But was Michael Hernandez serious? Or was he just another player with a smooth communication groove?

In hopes of him mending it, did she dare risk opening up her broken heart to him?

Cautiously, he slid his arm around her shoulder. "Give us a chance, Rosalinda. I won't ask you what you've got to lose, because I know the heavy penalties that sometimes come with personal relationships. And I know that you can only give it a try if you're somewhat attracted to me. With no arrogance intended, I think you are. Am I right? If I'm not, I won't take my pursuit of you any further."

"What about Ric?" She wasn't about to tell him how attracted she was to him. "You're his attorney, for God's sake."

He shrugged. "Not any longer. I took myself off the case."

Sharply, she raised both eyebrows. "You certainly work fast." She looked troubled. "I told Ric about your proposition to me. That could mean legal troubles for you."

"It could, but I'm not worried. I'm more curious as to what Ric said to you about my alleged proposition." Hernandez still wasn't outright admitting anything about his proposition to her, Rosalinda saw by his use of the word *alleged.*

Her laughter was bitter. "What do you think he said?"

"I'm sure he told you to do whatever it took to make his life easier. Rosalinda, I hope you don't take offense. But I deal with lowlifes and scumbags day in and day out. You'd be surprised at what some people behind bars are willing to do to get what they want. What they expect of others is amazing, yet they don't expect the same from themselves. Some of them would sell their grandmothers down the river to have their way. It's their incredible selfishness that put a lot of them where they are in the first place."

"Why do you represent people like that if you think they're so bad?"

"It's not about what I think of them, Rosalinda. It's my duty as an officer of the court. As a defense attorney, I have to see to it that every client gets a fair shake. I don't always have to like every client or even every case, but I do have to uphold the oath I took. Am I right about what Ricardo asked you to do in regards to his legal fees?"

As painful as it was to admit it, she nodded. "The saddest part about it is that I almost did it."

"More importantly, you didn't. You were able to draw the line. Many wouldn't have been able to. There are a lot of reasons that women stick to or get involved in supporting men in prison. It also happens the other way around. Just as many men are supporting women in jail. There are both men and women who have legitimate reasons for doing so. I've seen all sides. It's mind-boggling at times. Other than the legit cases, a lot of people that get involved with inmates are searching for something that's missing from their lives. Most of the time, they can't even define it. They either wake up to the disturbing facts, which I hope you've done, or they never see the light at the far end of the tunnel."

"I'm getting threatening letters from Ric."

"Really? Do you have them with you?"

"Yes." She took the letters out of her purse and handed them to him.

"I'll take care of this."

Rosalinda got up and walked around the room. Stopping at the large window, she looked down at the busy streets below. She now felt at peace . . . something she hadn't felt in a long time.

Michael walked over and stood beside her. "You came here today to say something to me. We've talked about everything but that. I still want to hear what you have to say. As long as you're not going to tell me that you don't want us to get to know each other better."

She smiled. "I've done nothing but think about that very thing. I'm not so sure that we can go there. Talk about complicated. However, I want to thank you for giving me so much to think about. I've changed because of you and another person that recently came into my life. Whether it's a halo, or only just a little light, it's mine to claim—and I want to let it shine. Thank you, Michael, for helping me to see the light within." Surprising him, she hugged his neck and pecked him lightly on the cheek.

Just before she closed the door behind her, he called out to her. She turned to face him.

"What about dinner, Rosalinda, later in the week? As friends, of course."

She smiled. "But of course. Give me a call, friend, when you come up with a specific date, time, and place."

With that said, she closed the door in Michael's smiling face.

Reading in Spanish the numerous afflictions of Job from the Book of Job, a story from the Old Testament of the bible, Rosalinda sat at her mother's bedside. Paulina spoke English, but she liked to hear Rosalinda read to her in their native tongue.

Rosalinda thought Paulina looked so thin, so very different from the robust woman she'd been before taking ill. Her long black hair, peppered with innumerable strands of silver, was woven into one thick braid. Rosalinda had just finished caring for Paulina's hair, brushing it until it looked less dull. Her hair was still beautiful, but not as healthy as it used to be. Medications had caused some damage.

Even though she felt weak, Paulina tried to sit up. To assist her, Rosalinda propped pillows behind Paulina's head and then used the remote to lift up the head of the bed.

"Are you comfortable like this, Mommy?"

Paulina nodded. "Sit back down, Rosalinda, and relax. I'm okay. Now that you are finished with the bible story, I want to hear more about this lawyer you've been talking so much about."

Rosalinda wanted to smile at her mother's reference to Michael Hernandez, but she refrained. She didn't want anyone to know how thrilled she was by Michael's attentiveness. She still didn't see that a personal relationship was possible for them.

"He's very nice, Mommy. Which is totally opposite of what I first thought about him."

"What was your first impression?"

"That he was evil, through and through. I didn't trust him in the least."

"With him representing Ricardo, I can understand that." Paulina put her hand to her mouth. "I'm sorry. That wasn't a kind thing for a mother to say about the man her daughter loves. Please forgive me."

"I'm not in love with Ricardo, Mommy. In fact, I'm through with him."

Both of Paulina's eyebrows lifted. "What?"

Rosalinda smiled. "Don't try to hide your joy over it. You never did like Ricardo. I understand all your reasons. Mommy, I'm a different person now."

"That beautiful Mrs. Covington has really worked her magic on you. I'm so glad she came into our lives. The flowers she has delivered every week keep my spirits high. It seems that she's been able to get you to see that which I couldn't."

"That's not entirely true. I saw what you were talking about in regards to my relationship with Ricardo. I just didn't think I could do any better. I didn't have any confidence in myself. I accepted bad treatment from him because I somehow thought I wasn't a good person, one that didn't deserve to be treated with love and kindness. I just know better now."

"How is Ricardo taking your decision?"

"Not very well. Before I got my number changed, he called constantly. But I wouldn't accept the charges. The letters came next, full of threats against me. I didn't respond to them. I kept thinking of going there and telling him face-to-face why it's over between us, but Marlene told me it might not be a good idea. I was too weak to face him in the beginning. I was afraid of succumbing to his charm or to give in to his threats of violence."

Paulina's warm brown skin grew pale. "Rosalinda, you know what type of man he is. You also know he's capable of violence. Your face and body have met with his hands on numerous occasions."

Rosalinda looked stunned. "How do you know that?"

"I lived in the same apartment with you for several months before ending up in here. How could I not know?"

"But you never said anything."

"I said plenty to him. But he threatened me something awful." Rosalinda gasped. "I became afraid for both of us. I remember all too well the things my father did to my mother, and the things your father did to me before he passed on. I'm sure you remember what went on in our home back then. That's why you've accepted the same type of behavior from Ricardo. You did exactly what I taught you to do. Shut up and take it or end up losing the man you love. You were just living the things you learned from me. I'm so sorry I couldn't have taught you better lessons in life, *hijah.* I have deep regret over these things, deep regret over not being able to protect you."

As Paulina began to cry, Rosalinda hugged her. "Don't cry, Mommy. It's all good. We're going to be okay."

"But what about the threats?"

"When I shared the letters and threats with Mr. Hernandez earlier today, he told me he'd handle it, that I shouldn't worry. I was sure Ricardo's boy would've come after me by now. Thus far, my life has been relatively calm." *Except for the heart-warming excitement that Michael has brought to it.*

"I somehow get the impression that this lawyer has a personal interest in you. If so, won't that cause him problems as Ricardo's attorney?"

"You are very perceptive. You've gotten the right impression, though I didn't intend for that to happen. I was also worried about the conflict of interest. He's taken himself off the case. He's also informed me that there's nothing to worry about. I was assured that he'd take care of things. Although he's interested in me, I don't see us becoming anything more than friends." *But my heart totally disagrees with me.*

"That doesn't make any sense to me, Rosalinda. In listening to all that you've said, I think you feel something more than friendship for this man. Am I right?"

Rosalinda's eyelashes fluttered and her cheeks grew stained with a rosy blush. "You're right. But, Mommy, it can never be. We're from two different worlds. No, I'm even scared to daydream about it, but there are times when I can't help it."

"Dare to dream, *hijah.* Sometimes our dreams are all we have in a world filled with pain, suffering, and unspeakable uncertainties. Dreaming can be a wonderful thing. One of life's few certainties is prayer. That's why we should always pray constantly."

Tears of mother and daughter mingled as they embraced and Paulina rested her cheek against her daughter's.

CHAPTER FOURTEEN

Crying softly, Alexis hugged Clara and Jacob Gautier as she warmly welcomed them into her posh Bel Air home. Her nerves were on edge, but she tried not to show how scared she felt inside. It had been a long time coming, but it was here now. Her parents were visiting her in her home for the first time ever. During the limousine ride from the airport, they'd talked about a lot of things—mostly insignificant things, but there hadn't been any in-depth conversation about R.J. In fact, they hadn't even asked why he hadn't come with her to meet them at the airport.

Alexis showed her parents into the plush living room, decorated all in white, accented with subtle shades of winter and mint green. While Alexis made them comfortable, the limousine driver, Timothy Scott, deposited their bags in the guest room that Alexis had pointed out to him. Although he was employed as a chauffeur, he also performed many other important duties for the Du Boises.

Jacob wiped Alexis's tears with his handkerchief. "Oh, baby, you're still beautiful as ever. Daddy has surely missed his little girl. When Clara told me you had called, I couldn't stop crying and laughing at the same time." His golden brown eyes had grown misty.

Because of his height of over six feet, Alexis had to stand on her tiptoes to hug Jacob again. Smiling, she pushed her fingertips through his unruly, silky white curls. "I've missed you, too, Daddy. I'm so glad I was finally able to convince you to come to California for a visit."

"Well, when you called and said you might not be able to make it for a couple of months, your momma was highly upset. Then you started pressuring me, so I didn't have much choice."

When Marlene couldn't make the trip because of the emergency situation at the church, Alexis had felt compelled to change her plans. Keisha and Rosalinda hadn't been able to make the trip either. Without R.J. or some other backup, Alexis had let her fear of her siblings change her mind about the homecoming. While she was glad her parents had accepted her invitation to visit her home, she was still fearful of them finding out that R.J. wasn't away on business. That's what she'd told them before they'd left home. Still, she would have to play things by ear.

Clara's doe brown eyes, the same color as her daughter's, shined brightly with glee. "When your daddy saw how agitated I was about not seeing you right away, he changed his mind about coming out here to California. It was important to both of us. So we put everything else aside and came. Jacob wasn't fooling me with his reasons for not coming, though he thought he was. After being married all this time, I'm just now finding out for sure that your daddy's scared to death of flying. I used to wonder about it, especially when he wanted to drive or take the train everywhere we went, but he finally broke down and told me about his fear of flying."

"Why fly when I can take the train for free? I didn't work for the railroad all those years not to use my benefits. I admit to being somewhat fearful of flying, but trains can jump the tracks just as easily as one of them big birds can fall from the sky. Now, if it goes off the tracks high up in the mountains, while crossing one of those endless chasms, you may as well be flying. Those train cars are surely going to end up airborne."

"You're both here now, so all of that other stuff no longer matters. Can I get either of you something to eat or drink? Marietta fixed a wonderful meal for you to enjoy after such a long journey to the West Coast."

Clara looked puzzled. "Who's Marietta?"

Alexis lowered her lashes. "She's our housekeeper, Momma."

"Housekeeper! I'll say. You and R.J. have really come up in the world. I should've guessed you'd surely have a housekeeper when you brought us out to that waiting limousine. And when we entered those security gates leading up to this property, I knew you were living high on the hog. This certainly is a beautiful home. You have a great eye for magnificent things. For a little poor girl, you haven't done bad for yourself."

"We're proud of you, Lexy." Jacob affectionately squeezed his daughter's hand. "Your momma's comments are harmless. Don't take offense. We're both just a little surprised at how well you're living after growing up the way you did. Momma and I are proud of your success."

"R.J. is the successful one." *I'm just the beautiful hood ornament on the top of his success, a trophy, so to speak.* Alexis regretted her thoughts. She couldn't in any way make her parents think her unhappy. But duping those two wasn't going to be an easy task by any stretch of the imagination. Clara and Jacob Gautier had extremely keen senses.

"Lexy knows I don't mean her any harm. Don't you, baby?"

"Yes, Momma, I do. I understand that the way I live might be a shock for you and Daddy. There are times when it's still a shock for me. R.J. has done very well for himself."

Clara crossed her arms across her chest. "Where on God's green earth has R.J.'s business taken him now? You must forgive us for not asking about him sooner. We were hoping he would've returned from his trip—and that he just might show up at the airport with you."

The moment of truth had come, but Alexis was in no way prepared to cough it up. *There was no greenery where R.J. was holed up, no business either. The business part she wasn't so sure about. If there were means to hustle or run scams in prison, R.J. would find out about it. If only her parents knew. But she was glad that they didn't. After finding out what he'd done in their very own home, she wouldn't put anything past him.*

"When will R.J. be home?" Jacob interrupted her thoughts.

Alexis smiled weakly. "To answer Momma's question first, he could be anywhere right now. I'm waiting to hear from him. He always has several stops on his itinerary, but he calls me every night. When he does call, I'm sure he'll be eager to talk with you both."

Jacob stroked his chin. "I'm sure."

Alexis didn't know what to make of her father's last sarcastic—sounding comment, but she definitely wasn't going to ask him to expound upon it.

"You mentioned something about a wonderful meal, Lexy, and I'm about ready to chow down hard on something tasty. You can't even call what they served on that airliner a meal. Snack is a better word, a tiny little snack. What you got good for us, baby?" Rubbing his stomach, Jacob got to his feet.

Clara stood, too. "I'm more sleepy than I am hungry, but I'm sure that once I get to the table my appetite will kick right on in."

Alexis hugged Marietta to her as she introduced her to Jacob and Clara. "This here lady is a genius in the kitchen. Much like you, Momma. As Daddy would put it, Marietta knows how to throw down. Tell us what you've created especially for them," Alexis encouraged Marietta.

"Why don't I just put it on the table so they can see for themselves? Everyone have a seat. I'll have the meal on the table in no time at all."

An eerie feeling washed over Alexis when Jacob sat in R.J.'s seat at the head of the table. It was strange seeing another man sitting there. Many men had graced their dinner table, but no one had ever sat in that seat but R.J. He had controlled many a conversation from his imperial position as the man of his house, the head of his household, from the head of his table.

Marietta had gone out of her way to prepare a magnificent New Orleans–style dinner for the visitors. Red beans and rice were one of Jacob's favorites. Shrimp creole, a sautéed mixture of shrimp and spices served over cooked rice, was Clara's favorite. Both the fried catfish and crawfish étouffée looked mighty tasty.

Alexis had requested grilled swordfish and sautéed vegetables for her main entrée. She loved Louisiana-style foods, but her stomach had been giving her problems ever since the trouble with R.J. had first begun. She didn't think spicy foods were a good thing to add on top of the existing problem. She wasn't certain, but she thought her stomach might be entertaining an ulcer.

"Everything looks so good, Marietta," Jacob praised. "Let's have prayer so we can begin the fun of eating all these wonderful delicacies."

"You don't have to say that twice. For a woman who wasn't very hungry a couple of minutes ago, I suddenly find myself starving," Clara said.

"Marietta, we'd love for you to join us," Jacob said.

Marietta looked to Alexis to lay down the law. The new changes in her employer were something else, but she wasn't so sure about an invitation for her to dine with Alexis's family.

"Please join us, Marietta," Alexis voiced softly. "It would be our pleasure."

Once Marietta was seated, Jacob delivered the blessing. Silence ensued as platters and bowls were passed around the table and plates were filled with the delicious-looking meal. Marietta took the pleasure of filling up everyone's ice-filled glasses to the brim from the crystal pitcher of passion fruit punch she'd made.

Clara looked across the table at her daughter and smiled. "In all our excitement, we forgot to tell you that you're an auntie times four now."

Feeling sick at the news, Alexis looked surprised. "Who, when?"

"Nicole's first child, beautiful Zanobia, is the newest addition to the family. She just happens to look just like her Auntie Alexis. Zanobia was born ten months ago."

Alexis couldn't believe all that had transpired in her family since her absence. She blinked back her tears, wondering if Nicole hated the fact that her daughter looked like her runaway sister, and if she'd had a big wedding. Alexis marrying before her older sisters, Carolyn and Tracey, had also been an extremely sore issue within the family. They'd thought that Alexis should've waited until the older girls had gotten married first.

"Has Zanobia been christened?" Alexis asked.

"Each and every one of our grandchildren has been christened," Jacob responded. "Everyone had hoped you'd show up for Nicole's wedding and the christening ceremony."

"Why would anyone expect me when I didn't know about either of the events?"

"Invitations were sent to you and R.J. I know that for a fact because I addressed envelopes and sent them out to you long before each event. We never dreamed that you hadn't gotten them. I'm really surprised to hear that, since you're still at the same address they were sent to. I guess we'll never know what happened to them. They were never returned to us," Clara informed Alexis.

"I'm just as surprised as you are. I would remember if I had received them. And I would've responded even if I couldn't have come home to attend."

"Oh, well, that's all water under the bridge now. A lot of time has passed us by. But we're together now. And your siblings are all hoping that you will soon come to New Orleans for a visit. They were very disappointed when they learned we were coming here instead of you coming there," Clara remarked.

I'll just bet they were. Alexis still wasn't convinced that her siblings cared about her absence from the family, one way or the other.

Marietta got up from the table. "I'm going to go out to the kitchen and bring in the dessert. I hear peach cobbler is a Gautier family favorite."

Jacob and Clara smiled at the lengths Marietta had gone to in her efforts to please their palates. They thought it was such a beautiful gesture from her.

Alexis nodded her approval, but she was sure Marietta thought the conversation was too personal for her to be sitting in on. It was embarrassing, to say the least. Her youngest sister making her an aunt times four was the most humiliating. That she didn't know one thing about the major goings-on in her family was rather pathetic. She only had herself to blame, even though she couldn't help wondering if R.J. had withheld the missing correspondence. She would've done everything in her power to attend Nicole's wedding. After all, Nicole was her baby sister, and they'd been close at one time.

"Are you okay, Lexy?" Jacob inquired with concern. "You're mighty quiet over there."

Alexis looked up and smiled, but weakly, at best. "I'm fine, Daddy. I just feel bad that I've missed so many of the family events. I'm sorry. I don't have any excuses for not staying in touch, and I'm not going to try and make up some. It was downright insensitive of me to neglect the very people who gave me life. Can you ever forgive me, Momma and Daddy?"

Clara was out of her seat and had her arms around Alexis before her daughter could take her next breath. "Darling, that's all in the past. We didn't come here to make you feel bad about anything. What's done is done. Promise me you won't fret over this any longer?"

"I promise, Momma."

Marietta came into the room with the dessert tray only minutes after things were settled between Alexis and her parents. Alexis wouldn't have been surprised if Marietta had purposely timed her reentry. She appreciated her employee's sensitivity toward her situation with her family. Marietta had already proved herself as an anchor in the recent storms of her employer's life.

Alexis and her parents had retired to the living room, and Marietta had gone to her living quarters for the evening. As she sat quietly, listening to her parents bringing her further up to date on family and friends, Alexis's mind kept wandering to the secret room and R.J. It still baffled her how so much had gone on inside her house without her knowledge. What baffled her even more was how to clean out completely the room that could bring more charges against her husband, which could mean more time for him behind bars. The biggest concern for her was finding someone she could trust. When her three new female friends came to mind, she wondered if the four of them could do the job. They were a feisty, courageous bunch. Realizing that her thought was a ridiculous one, she abandoned it altogether.

Jesse watched as R.J. made his way across the cafeteria. He walked with confidence, but Jesse thought that his swagger just might be a front. Richard James Du Boise wasn't as tough as the image he projected. But he was shrewd. All his talk about money and power had earned him quite a following inside the concrete jungle. It seemed that his hustles had become his ally. There were even those who appeared willing to protect him. Many of the inmates wanted to learn all he knew about making money, legal or illegal. Every day during mealtime, Jesse heard someone talking about R.J. and how smart he was. None of them seemed to realize that R.J. couldn't have been all that smart, especially since he was locked up, too.

"Reverend Jesse, how are you? Mind if I join you?"

"Not at all, brother R.J. I'm doing just fine. How are things going for you?"

R.J. lowered his head. When he looked up at Jesse, he had tears in his eyes. Considering where he was, in the dining hall, he quickly wiped them away. "I'm in neck-deep doodoo, Rev. How does a man like me get salvation? If I died tomorrow, I don't think that I'd get an upstairs vacation. A room is probably already reserved for me downstairs. Is it too late me for to secure an upstairs reservation, a room with a beautiful view?"

Thoughtfully, Jesse stroked his chin. "Claim Jesus Christ as your Savior. It's never too late for you to accept what was sacrificed for you on the cross: eternal life. Prayer always works if you trust and believe. R.J., if you want to be forgiven, all you have to do is ask for forgiveness. The price has already been paid for you. You just have to claim the kingdom that's already yours to inherit. It's yours for the taking."

"That simple, huh?"

Jesse laughed. "There's nothing simple about it. Obedience is a very difficult thing to handle day in and day out. Life has a way of getting even harder when you decide to pick up and follow after the Master. Satan will challenge you at every turn. It is his desire to lose no one to Jesus or to go down in any battle with Him. But he's already lost, a long time ago, and he knows it. Still, he plans to take as many followers to hell with him as he can. Justification is instantaneous. Sanctification is a work of a lifetime."

"Sounds like I have a lot of work to do."

"Hard work! It's hard work that can be made simple when you learn to lay down all of your burdens at his feet. Changing oneself is very hard work, but it can be achieved. All you have to be is willing. Internal changes reflect in outward appearances."

"There are many questions that I would like to ask of you, but there are two specifically that always seem to burn brightly inside my mind. I hope you can give me the answers. If you preachers believe that God provides for your every need, why aren't you ever satisfied with the first offering? Why do you keep coming back asking for more when the goal—which seems to me is man's goal, not God's—isn't met? Two, if the Sabbath is a day designated for rest, why does the church organize and have meetings, choir rehearsals, as well as performing many other official church duties on the day of worship? Rest means rest, doesn't it?"

"It does." Jesse looked at R.J. over the rim of his glasses. "You've asked two reasonable questions. At my church, we are satisfied with the first offering. And we do believe that God will supply our every need. As I mentioned to you before, we don't pass the offering plate. We survive on what is given because we're independent of any conference. We use God's money in our own church. We don't send money to a conference and have them decide how we're supposed to use it and how much of it they're going to send back to us for us to use. The offering receptacles are chock-full every week. Now, I do have an occasion to ask for a special offering for a special need. Those needs are most always met. However, every now and then, I do remind the members that their support is needed. There are times when I preach on tithing."

"I'm sure yours is an exception to the rule. Every church I've ever been in has a tendency to constantly beat you to death about money. They go on and on about the tithe and the offering."

Jesse took his glasses off. "The instructions on the tithe and the offering come from God; not man. A tithe is a tenth part paid or given for support of the church. Read what God has to say about it for yourself, and you'll see. To put it in simple terms, He's only asking for a dime out of every dollar. We're talking about a mere ten cents. You walk away with the remaining ninety. How much fairer can that be? His words on tithing are clear and precise. Read Genesis 14:20, Genesis 28:22, Leviticus 27:32, and Malachi 3:8–10. There are other scriptures that relate, but those four should be enough in helping you to get an understanding of His Word on tithing."

"I'll keep them in mind. I will do a little reading this evening so I can see it in black and white for myself. I've been studying the bible a lot in recent days."

" 'Study to shew thyself approved unto God,' 2 Timothy 2:15. The bible seems to be read a lot inside of here, but it is often a forgotten book when one is thrust back into the outside world. As for your second question, you're right about the Sabbath being a day of rest. That day should not be used for choir rehearsals or any other church activities. We have six other days to do all our business in. Nowadays it's simply called a convenience. When we can't get the members to convene at any other time, we start doing what's convenient for them instead of what God commands us to do. It's often practiced, anyway, even when it means breaking the Sabbath. That does not go on in my church any longer. What we can't get done in six days doesn't get done until the next week."

"Have you always run your church this way?"

"No," Jesse said emphatically. "You tend to do better when you know better. I've made numerous administrative errors in my ministry over the years, and I was still making them before I got thrown in here. It's when you don't learn from your mistakes that you keep making the very same ones. I try very hard at not repeating the same mistakes over and over again."

"I just thought of two other questions. Mind if I ask them?"

"You have my undivided attention, Brother R.J."

"There are many churches that worship a different day from others. Why do the ones who worship on a particular day rent the church out on the other day? If you believe the Sabbath is the Lord's day, why would you encourage someone to worship on another day?"

"We encourage all people to serve God, every day. People do what they do because they believe in what they're doing. They believe in their day of worship. The question that pertains to renting out the church on a different day from the one they worship on is a question you'll have to ask of those who do it. I don't have that answer. You have to keep in mind that there are countless denominations in the world today. John 10:16: 'And other sheep I have, which are not of this fold: them also I must bring, and they shall hear my voice.'

"Who's to say who is right and who is wrong as it pertains to worship? The problem comes when we don't respect a person's right to choose his own method of worship. We don't necessarily have to agree with another method of worship, but we do need to respect it and also that person's right to choose. Think of so-called holy wars. There are so many horrific things done in the name of God and religion that have nothing to do with either. We want everyone to see it our way. It's not going to ever happen. To end this, we don't rent our church out, period. Is that your two questions?"

"No, that was just a two-part question."

"Let me say this before you ask the next question, Brother R.J. I don't have all the answers. In fact, no one does. God reveals to us those things He wants us to know at an appointed time. His time. Deuteronomy 29:29: 'The secret things belong unto the Lord our God: but those things which are revealed belong unto us and to our children for ever, that we may do all the words of this law.' We need to learn to separate our wanting to know from our need to know." Jesse grinned. "I'm ready for the second question. Are you?"

R.J. shook his head. "Reverend Jesse, you're quite inspiring. I'd like to have exactly what you have, whatever that is. You seem so peaceful. Does anything ruffle your feathers?"

"Is that your second question?"

R.J. laughed. "Okay, Reverend, I hear you. There's this thing about wearing jewelry that also has me baffled. There are a number of religions that practice this sort of thing. I've gone to some of those churches, but I've seen women wearing fancy pins, brooches, diamond watches, and large decorative hatpins. Aren't all those things considered jewelry?"

Jesse hadn't expected that question, but he had an answer. Whether his answer would be acceptable to R.J., he didn't know. "Again, that's something you need to ask of those involved in that particular practice. However, there are many false idols in the world, the same idols that many people have a tendency to worship. Cars, houses, money, and even our children, can be idols. Anything you put before God is a false idol. 'Thou shalt have no other gods before me,' Exodus 20:3, is the first of God's Ten Commandments. Jesus said, 'I am the way, the truth, and the life; no man cometh unto the Father, but by me,' John 14:6."

R.J. appeared to be somewhat amazed at the things he'd just heard. "I've got a lot of serious work to do. I want to change. When I get out of here, I want to be renewed in body and in spirit. This is what I want to do for Alexis, my wife. But I know that I must want to do this for myself in order to succeed at it. I do want it. I want the assurance of blessed hope."

" 'And I say unto you, Ask, and it shall be given you; seek, and ye shall find; knock, and it shall be opened unto you. For every one that asketh receiveth; and he that seeketh findeth; and to him that knocketh it shall be opened,' Luke 11:9–10. 'If we confess our sins, he is faithful and just to forgive us our sins, and to cleanse us from all unrighteousness,' 1 John 1:9. Confess your sins to God, R.J., and ask him to cleanse you as white as snow. Only He can do that for you."

"Confession." R.J. took a brief moment of consideration. "What a humbling word that is. I have so much to confess to. You see, Reverend Jesse, I'm not guilty of all the crimes I was charged with and sentenced for. But I'm guilty of being a greedy man, guilty of being an unscrupulous man, guilty of a multitude of sins against the laws of God and man. Plain and simply put, I'm a thief. But I didn't rob my clients. Am I guilty of robbing the government? In my opinion, that depends on whether or not the government has a right to what I break sweat for. Am I guilty of obtaining monies by illegal methods? Again, that depends on how an individual looks at it. How can some-

thing be legal for some and illegal for others? Take gambling, for instance. It's legal in some instances and illegal in others. If it's legal or illegal for some, shouldn't it be legal or illegal for all? Who's to say for sure?"

"Since you've referred to yourself as a thief, let me tell you the story about another thief, the one who was crucified on the cross alongside Jesus. When I'm finished telling you this story, you can read about it for yourself in Luke 23:39–43. Mark 15:27 will identify those who were crucified at the right hand and the left hand of Christ."

CHAPTER FIFTEEN

Marlene had given Major Townsend the astonishing chunks of information that Malcolm had given her. Jesse's attorney seemed to think that it just might be the right information, and enough information, to start turning things around in the appeal process. He seemed very optimistic about securing Jesse's release after he'd heard all that she'd told him.

Marlene couldn't help humming the tune to "Blessed Assurance" as she sat in the family room folding the clean clothes she'd just removed from the dryer.

Although she'd promised herself not to think about it, she couldn't stop her thoughts from turning to her best friend, Myrna. They hadn't talked since Marlene had first told Myrna about her son's suspected involvement in using the van in the robbery. Marlene had called and left a couple of messages for Myrna, but they'd gone unreturned. She didn't know if Myrna had been coming to church, since she'd been absent while visiting Jesse the last couple of weekends. All she could do about the situation was pray.

A lot of unpleasant things could unfold in the next few weeks, unpleasant for all concerned. Todd was her godson, and she loved him dearly. But if he had something to do with the robbery that had put Jesse unjustly behind bars, he'd just have to face the music. The most unpleasant things for her could come when she had to tell Jesse the truth about everything.

The truth was supposed to set you free. In this case, her husband might be the one to set himself free of his beloved wife. Jesse's desire for a divorce because of the lies and the all the other things she'd kept from him regarding Malcolm would be a hard pill to swallow . . . a poisoned pill, at that.

In her mind, Marlene still hadn't exonerated Malcolm from involvement. Myrna had been right about Malcolm being a habitual liar. It was still very possible that Malcolm had just as much to answer for in this case as Todd Jacobson did.

The doorbell rang, yanking Marlene from her thoughts. She finished folding the silk slip she held and then set the basket of clothes aside. Wondering who'd come by without calling first, she rushed to the door and opened it. Finding Myrna and Todd on the other side came as quite a shock. They were the last visitors she would've expected to see on her doorstep.

"Hello," Marlene enthused, trying to sound upbeat. "It's nice to see both of you."

Myrna scowled. "Save the phony pleasantries. This not a social call by any stretch of the imagination. We only came here to get a few things straight."

Marlene swallowed the acid retort stinging the tip of her tongue. "In that case, let's all go into the family room and sit down. How are you, Todd?"

He looked nervous. "I'm okay, Aunt Marlene."

Once everyone was seated comfortably, Myrna nudged her son. "Go ahead and tell her what you've told me," Myrna encouraged her son in a no-nonsense tone.

Todd looked scared. When he took to biting his nails, Myrna slapped his hand away from his mouth. "You're wasting time, boy. Get this thing going so we can get out of here."

"He's nervous. Give him time, Myrna. Don't be so hard on him."

Myrna glared at Marlene. "Don't tell me how to deal with my son. If you had dealt with your son the way he needed to be dealt with, we probably wouldn't be sitting here with our relationship under so much strain. Hello!"

Marlene also ignored those barbed comments. "Todd, I'm here to listen to you. It's going to be okay, but I need to hear what you know about this case."

He fidgeted in his seat. "Uh, the night Malcolm let me use the van, I didn't go to the 7-Eleven store. All I did was pick up my girlfriend. We were about to go over to Sheila's house, where Malcolm was, when Arlissa's oldest brother, Latrell, came outside and asked me could he use the van. I didn't want to let him, but then he offered me fifty dollars. I took it when he said he promised to bring the van right back. But he didn't keep his word. If he used the van to rob the store, I didn't know anything about it. I swear, Aunt Marlene."

Marlene looked extremely relieved. From what was just said, it seemed that neither Malcolm or Todd had been involved in the actual robbery. But she had more questions. "Todd, why didn't you tell me this when your uncle Jesse first got arrested?"

He shrugged his shoulders. "I didn't even connect Uncle Jesse's situation with me letting Latrell Johnson use the van that night. Weeks had already passed since then. I only thought about it after Mom told me what you thought about me being involved in the robbery."

"I'll say." Marlene sighed, dizzy with disbelief and the stress of it all.

Marlene felt worse than she had before. Even though she'd only recently found the 7-Eleven bag, she still thought perhaps all of this could've been settled a lot sooner if she'd pressed Malcolm a lot harder in the beginning. She thought she'd heard loud music in the driveway the night in question, but she hadn't even gotten up to look out the window. Now she wished that she had. Then she would've known for sure that Malcolm had been in the van that night. And perhaps she wouldn't have had to do so much struggling with the horrendous thoughts of her only child replacing her husband in prison.

"Did Malcolm know you'd lent the van to your girlfriend's brother?"

"No. He would've gone ballistic. He really didn't want to loan it to me, but he wanted some time alone with Sheila, before Arlissa and me came over. If I'd told him about the money, he would've wanted half of it, and I needed all of it to pay my pager bill. That's why I took the money in the first place. Malcolm and I have never even discussed any of this."

"Have you talked to Malcolm?" Marlene was curious as to where Malcolm was living.

"He called me a couple of days ago and said that he had something important to talk to me about, but he never came over to the house like he said he would."

Marlene could feel the hostility coming from Myrna. She could also hear Myrna's hard breathing. It sounded as if Myrna was breathless from anticipation. But there wasn't anything she could do about it. In view of the information she'd just received from Todd, Marlene thought that Myrna had every right to be hostile toward her. But all of it was a big misunderstanding.

"Has Arlissa's brother been in trouble before?"

"He was on parole, but he's back in jail now, Aunt Marlene. I think they violated him."

Marlene raised an eyebrow. "Violated him? Who violated him?"

"No, not like that. Latrell violated the conditions of his parole. So his parole officer violated his conditional release. I don't know what he did to get thrown back in jail."

Marlene put her arms around Todd and hugged him. "Thank you for being so forthcoming. I know this was hard for you. I'm sorry for thinking you had something to do with a robbery. But all the facts were pointing to you. I'm very sorry, sweetheart."

"Facts or lies?" Myrna interjected.

"I knew you weren't going to be able to keep quiet much longer, Myrna Jacobson. Take another deep breath before you burst wide open from all the anger inside of you. I've apologized to Todd, and I'm apologizing to you. I'm very sorry about everything. It's up to you whether you accept it or not. I'm not responsible for you or for how you decide to handle things from here on in. I'm sorry for what I thought and for hurting you. But I am your friend, and I do love you. I've made a mistake, a tremendous one. And for that, I'm truly sorry."

Looking like she wanted to blow the entire house down, Myrna huffed and puffed as she struggled to get to her feet. "With friends like you, who needs enemies? Let's go, boy. We've done what we came here to do."

Without another word, Mryna turned and headed straight for the front door.

Wishing his mom would lighten up a bit, Todd shrugged. "See you, Aunt Marlene."

"See you, baby. Oh, Todd, do you know where Malcolm's actually staying?"

Todd shuffled his feet. "I'm not supposed to tell you this, but I know you have enough to worry about already. He and Sheila got an apartment together. It's down in the jungle. Please don't tell Malcolm I told you."

"You have my word on that."

When Myrna shouted for Todd, in an angry tone, from the front entryway, he gave Marlene a quick peck on the cheek and rushed away.

In looking at the wall clock, Marlene realized she didn't have time to ponder the events that had just occurred. She was expecting Keisha and Rosalinda within the hour. While considering the position in which she now saw herself, she knew it was time to talk with the two young women about the secret she'd been keeping. She'd deal with that when they got there, but a hot shower was what she needed right now.

"Rosalinda, you've changed somehow. You're glowing all the time. What's up with you?" Keisha asked while pouring more Coca-Cola into her glass. Waiting for an answer, she set the Coke can back down on the table.

Marlene laughed as she set a tray of cold meat sandwiches in the center of the table. "I thought I was the only one who had noticed the constant rosy blush in her cheeks. Something tells me you're happier than you've been in a long time, Rosalinda."

Rosalinda giggled. "You guys have to promise not to kill me for holding out on you. I've been so afraid of breathing a word of this to anyone. I still can't believe what I'm about to tell you. It's way too awesome for anyone to believe!"

"Hurry it up, already," Keisha demanded. "I'm on pins and needles over here."

"Okay." Rosalinda took a deep breath.

Eagerly anticipating what Rosalinda had to say, Marlene dropped down into a chair.

"Michael Hernandez, Ricardo's lawyer, is interested in me on a personal level. He wants to have a romantic relationship with me."

Rosalinda went on to share all the details with the two women, whose eyes were nearly bulging out of their heads. Marlene's hand went straight to her heart as Rosalinda began to weave the magic of her unbelievably romantic saga.

Keisha leapt out of her seat. "You're not kidding, are you?"

"The girl is dead serious," Marlene interjected. "That's what the *glow* is all about. This is great news, I think. But what about the ethics involved here? He's Ricardo's legal counsel."

"Not anymore. He took himself off the case. But he recognized his feelings for me a long time before he did it. Michael has obviously seen things in me that I haven't seen in myself. He also thinks I'm beautiful, inside and out."

Keisha looked genuinely hurt. "You aren't supposed to keep things like this from your best homie. Don't you trust me anymore?" Her lower lip quivered from the toll on her emotions.

Shaking her head, Rosalinda waved her hand in the air. "It's not like that. I thought you would think I was seriously stupid for even believing that a man of Michael's status might be sincere. And then I thought you'd think I was crazy if I decided to even consider a relationship with him. I've been scared of everything about this, especially what might happen if Ricardo found out. He does know that Michael propositioned me."

Marlene whistled. "This is a serious situation you're in. But is Michael really serious about you?"

"I think so. I know I'm not such a good judge of character, but he seems genuine. We've agreed to become friends for now. There seems to be some kind of magical intrigue going on with us. You know, the kind of stuff you read in romance novels, the kind of love that's never going to happen for you. I know I could get hurt, but I'm dying to see where this will go."

Keisha hugged her dear friend. "So do it. Is Hernandez the real reason you decided to break it off with Ricardo?"

"Ricardo is the reason I broke it off with him. Him asking me to sleep with Hernandez was the last straw. I just couldn't stomach that. He has to be sick to expect something like that from a woman he professes to love. He doesn't know about Michael, but he's been sending me threatening letters. He can't believe I'm over him, that I'm moving on."

"I can't believe it, either. You used to love Ricardo's dirty drawers. When you told me you'd changed your phone number, I was really shocked. Wow! I'm happy for you, happy that you're finally finding some happiness. Have you and Hernandez done the nasty already?"

"Keisha! I just told you we are only friends. I came close to it that night in the motel, for the wrong reasons, but I won't make that same mistake again. I'm not sleeping with anyone again. Not until I'm married."

"Whoa, girl. Miss Rosalinda Morales done gone out and found Miss Rosalinda Morality." Keisha leaned across the table and kissed Rosalinda's cheek. "Not that you were ever immoral. I know Ricardo's the only man you've ever slept with. The same as it is with Zach and me. We're nobody's tramps."

"We've gotten to know each other pretty good over the past couple of months, but I've never asked how you two became best friends," Marlene remarked.

Keisha and Rosalinda laughed.

"Pretty much the same way we became friends with you. When our guys were in the county jail several years ago, Rosalinda gave me a ride home, after I missed the last bus. My car had broken down the week before, and the kids and me had to take the bus when I wanted to visit their daddy. Zach and Ricardo have known each other for a while. Rosalinda and I didn't know each other before the guys landed in jail at the same time for different reasons. We started to get to know each other after Rosalinda offered to come pick me up when she went downtown to visit Ricardo. We've been doing this ride-sharing stuff off and on for a few years now. We were so young when we started visiting those hardheads in jail. Through the ups and downs, we all became best friends."

"That's an interesting story." Marlene put her arm around Rosalinda. "I hope you find all the happiness you deserve. I'm proud of how you've handled yourself in this situation. I'm proud of you, period. Take things slow with this new friendship. If you and Michael are meant to be, it will happen. Don't rush into anything. Take your time. Love can arrive when it's least expected. You are worthy of the very best of everything. Don't sell yourself short, Rosalinda."

"Talking about rushing into things! No one said anything about love. I repeat: This is only a friendship. I won't sell myself short again. I've already done that too many times with Ricardo. Although I've never slept with anyone but Ric, there have been a few other guys with questionable character in my life. No more of that for me. Keisha, what have you decided about a future with Zach?"

"Just continue to love him like I have been. I'm not doing it just for my kids, either. Only this time, there will be enforced boundaries.

Zach is the man I love and the only man for me. Even though I know he's used a lot of women, including me, I'm going to hang in there with him. But Tammy and I are still going to bust his black behind. I think he's just lost track of who he is by trying to fit in with the home-boys. He's going to have to start acting responsibly, or I'm out. Now that I know what happened with my daddy, I can be stronger in my convictions.

"My mother being here has helped me a lot. She's even thinking about moving here. The kids love having her around. She's as good at being a grandmother as she is at being a mother. Having her to baby-sit allows me a little more of life's freedom. Like getting to spend more time with you two, like now. But I don't plan to take advantage of her in that way."

Marlene cleared her throat. "Since everyone is revealing the burdens of their souls, I have some soul-baring to do myself. You said something a short time back, Keisha. And you were right. We're all so much better than what we've accepted from some of the men in our lives." She got to her feet and began to pace back and forth.

Keisha and Rosalinda exchanged puzzled glances because they had no idea what Marlene was talking about. When Marlene didn't elaborate on her statement, they let it go by without comment. Then Marlene started to cry.

Keisha was the first one who leaped to her aid. "What is it, Marlene? What has you so upset all of a sudden?"

A faraway look settled in Marlene's eyes as she thought back on some of the things in which her only son had been involved. She couldn't help rehashing the memory of finding the 7-Eleven bank bag in his gym bag when washing his clothes. Keisha and Rosalinda sensed that Marlene didn't want to go any further into her story, which made them highly curious about the preacher's wife—just another one of the ladies in waiting, even if she was a special one.

Marlene wrung her hands together as she sat back down. "What I've got to say has caused me to develop ulcers. I been wondering for a couple of months if Malcolm had anything to do with the bank bag found in the church van." She went on to tell them a few of the bad things in Malcolm's past that she'd kept from Jesse, and then on to those troubling things she'd recently discovered.

Keisha and Rosalinda watched with anguished eyes as their guardian angel fell down from grace, right before their very eyes. Immediately, they saw that Marlene also had a weakness for a man—her son and only child, Malcolm Covington.

Keisha slapped one hand on her hip. "I don't believe what I'm hearing. You've been on our case since day one—and here you're telling us that you're guilty of the same things we are. You obviously don't practice what you preach. You need to set the record straight in this case. How can you let a man you profess to love sit in jail for a crime you know he didn't commit? You know who the real criminal is—and that makes you just as guilty as your son."

Marlene flinched at the bitter disappointment in Keisha's tone. "I have every intention of setting the record straight, but I had to gather all the facts first. Major Townsend, my husband's lawyer, is helping me sort everything out. If I can believe what I just learned today, Malcolm may not have had anything to do with the crime."

Marlene went on to tell them the rest of the story, and how it involved her best friend, Myrna, and her godson, Todd.

"I've only been able to see my own shortcomings through the scenario that you two have painted for me with such brilliant colors. I've seen my own troubles in witnessing yours. I thank God for sending you young people to me to help me see the light. All this time I thought it was the other way around. I thought I was supposed to be helping you see the light. God works in mysterious and wondrous ways."

Keisha was not moved by any of Marlene's inspirational speech. She was too angry to hear and accept the truth about the woman she'd come to love like a second mother. She felt duped in many ways, somewhat betrayed. The one person she thought could do no wrong had proven herself to be no different than most hypocrites. She was aware that she might hurt Marlene's feelings, but she wasn't going to pass up the opportunity to let her know just how bad she'd made her feel. Marlene was the closest thing to a saint Keisha had ever met.

"I'm trying to hear you, but I have to admit that it's hard for me to get past all the crap you've been feeding Rosalinda and me. Do you even see that your son is still at the root of the major problems brought into you and your husband's lives? If he hadn't taken the van that night, your husband wouldn't be in jail. Your son is responsible for the entire outcome of the situation with your family. Malcolm is extremely manipulative. I saw that the first time I met him."

"I know what you're saying. I understand what you mean. Malcolm is the reason Jesse is in jail, no two ways about it. In stealing the van that night, he became solely responsible for everything that followed his unwise decision. But I can't change any of that now."

"But you could've changed it, and didn't. That's the whole point. You said you found that bank bag some time ago, but you didn't do anything about it until now. I would like to know how you're going to explain that to your husband, who's been sitting in prison for months. I'm happy that I don't have to walk in your shoes. Like my mother said during the support meeting, those shoes aren't fit for anyone to walk in. I'm glad you've decided to take them off. Now you need to get rid of them. I just hope you don't have to throw away your future with your husband along with your worn-down, turned-over shoes."

"Keisha, give her a break," Rosalinda pleaded. "Nobody is perfect, not even the preacher and his wife. You're acting like she knew about the bank bag all along, but she didn't."

Now that Marlene had seen the light, she knew that she had to ask God to give her the courage to tell her husband the truth about everything. She also had to ask for the courage to face the fact that her husband just might divorce her over this latest episode of rescuing Malcolm. Only this time, she'd done the rescuing but at the expense of her loving husband.

Before Marlene could offer her intended apology, the phone rang. She excused herself from the kitchen table and picked up the wall extension. She was surprised to hear Malcolm's voice on the other end. Her heart melted right inside her chest. She hadn't heard his voice for far too long. Another prayer had been answered. At least he was alive and well.

"Hello, son. How are you?"

Keisha and Rosalinda exchanged knowing glances. The delight in Marlene's voice was easily recognized. The light in her eyes was near blinding. Even a slight smile tugged at the corners of her generous mouth.

"When?" Marlene listened to her son's response. "Okay. I'll see you shortly." She hung up the phone and returned to the table.

'That was Malcolm."

"Yeah, and we can see that he's already done his usual number on you. Rosalinda and I are going to go. You don't want me around if he's coming over, because I got something for his narrow behind. He is coming over, isn't he?"

"He wants to talk. But you two don't have to leave. He and I can talk in his bedroom."

"No, it's better if you and your son have privacy," Rosalinda said. "I understand, and so does Keisha. She just has to be difficult. You should know that about her by now."

Keisha bumped Rosalinda with her hip. "I ain't got nothing to say to that. It's kind of hard to argue with the truth. But, Marlene, in keeping it real, you shouldn't let Malcolm reel you back in so easily. He's probably hungry and doesn't have any money to buy something to eat. He's coming over here 'cause he's wants something he probably can't get from the woman he's living with. I know you can't let your child go hungry, but just fix him a hot meal and then tell him to step. The boy will only hurt you again. Look at me and Rosalinda and think of all we've been putting up with. Look at the hurts we've endured. Watch yourself now!"

Keisha was still disappointed in Marlene, but she gave her a hug anyway. "Call me later, Mizz Marlene, if you need to talk. I still love you."

"Me, too," Rosalinda chimed in. "I'll call and check on you later."

Malcolm looked like he hadn't slept since he'd left home. His hair was longer than he normally wore it, and he had a heavy growth of hair on his face. He'd never worn a beard before. He looked so sad to his mother. She felt sorry for him from the moment she opened the front door to him. The effort to keep herself from slipping back into a familiar pattern was working her over. She could remember a time when Malcolm could get on her last nerve, but it had only gotten worse. She didn't have to worry about him getting on her nerves any longer. For the last couple of years, he hadn't gotten off of them. It was like he'd set up permanent housekeeping there.

"Mom, could we sit down? I need to talk with you."

"You go ahead and sit. I've been sitting on my duff most of the day."

"I'd feel more relaxed if you were sitting."

"Malcolm, honey, it's not about what you feel anymore. Now, if you have something to say, you better go ahead and say it. I've got a million and one things to do."

The sweetness in his mother's voice was what he'd missed most, but he didn't like her not doing what he wanted. She'd always tried to please him before, but now it didn't seem to matter to her what he needed or wanted. Could someone really change that much in just a couple of months? It was possible, because he had also changed.

"Mom, I'm really sorry for all the trouble I've caused. I didn't mean to make you and Daddy's life so miserable. All I was thinking about was myself the night I took the van. I knew Daddy wouldn't let me take it if I'd asked, because of the two speeding tickets I'd gotten. If I'd known that robbery was going to happen, I would've never taken it."

"That's a large part of your problem. You don't think about the consequences of your actions before you put your plan into action. In all honesty, you've never had to suffer the consequences for your actions. I take full blame for that. We don't ever know what's going to happen from day to day. That's why we shouldn't take unnecessary risks. As old as you are, it should've at least crossed your mind that something bad could happen if you took the van without permission. As an adult, you should've known better, period."

"Mom, could you just listen? I know all that already. You can't beat me up any more than I've beat myself up, since you told me about the bank bag you found in my gym bag. I feel horrible that Daddy is locked up from something stupid that I did. I just don't know what to do about it. Is there a chance that he could get out of there if his lawyer can find a way to present all this new evidence? Do you think the courts will listen?"

"Major Townsend is working on it. We'll have to wait and see. Malcolm, I've listened to you, and I hear what you're saying, but you and I both know that you have another agenda. What is it that you really came here for? I'm afraid that your newfound concern for your dad's legal situation just isn't working for me. These are the types of things you should think about before you do something stupid, not after you've already done them."

"I don't know why you're being so cynical. I do care about Daddy. I even want to go visit him the next time you go. Is that possible?"

"Anything's possible, Malcolm. Feasible? I doubt it. I don't think I could stand to be around you for that length of time. It's almost a two-hour drive out there. Like you've already expressed, 'I don't want to take that long ride out there to that hot desert.' Well, I don't want you to take that long drive, either. At least, not with me."

He jumped to his feet. "I don't see why you're making this so hard for me. I came here to apologize. I came because I miss you. I miss the good times we used to share—"

"You and I haven't shared in many good times in the past two years. All we've done is fight over what you believe is right versus what I believe is wrong. We constantly do battle about your dirty room, your lousy grades, and your lack of drive in finding a decent job. In my opinion, those aren't good times. You need to understand that things have changed around here. I've changed. This is a new day, boy."

"I got a job."

"And?"

Her uncaring attitude really stunned him. He'd just about played all the hole cards he normally used when trying to get back on her good side, but none of them had worked. What was he to do next? In one last attempt to win her over, he put his arms around Marlene and hugged her tightly. "Mom, please cut me some slack. I want to come back home."

She pushed him away from her. "Okay, now we're getting there."

"Getting where?"

"To the truth of why you're here. You want to come home. Well, that's too darn bad! This is no longer the place where you abide. You have a new permanent address now. But you'll always be able to call this home, son. You just can't physically live here."

"But, Mom, I can't live where I'm staying right now. I can't deal with having somebody jock my every move. Sheila's always in my face about one thing or another. When she's not cursing me out about some other woman, she's telling me that I'm lazy and worthless. I don't need that. What I need is my freedom."

"Ah, freedom. My husband needs the same. And it was you that took it away from him. You didn't commit the robbery, but you're totally responsible for what happened that night. So I don't want to hear about your sad, pathetic-sounding domestic situations with Sheila. You got yourself into this mess, and you can get yourself out of it. Are you feeling me yet?"

"Mom, I got a job now. It pays decent money and I can start paying rent."

"Good. There are plenty apartments around for you to pay rent on. You need to be on your own. That way, you don't have to worry about anyone being up in your face, especially me. You'll be responsible for you, and you alone. You need to have your own place. You just can't live here. Have you ever thought about the fact that I might have to come live with you?"

He frowned. "Why would I think that?"

" 'Cause I may not have anywhere to live once Jesse finds out you took that van. He's warned me too many times about rescuing you from situations that you get yourself into. Rescues without any consequences for you to pay have resulted in my husband's undoing. Now, you just might have to rescue me. I'm through trying to save your butt from yourself. We've given you all the tools you need in order to have a successful life. It's up to you to use them."

With a breaking heart, she watched as Malcolm stormed out of the house. Quietly, she thanked God for keeping her strong, for giving her the strength to resist her son's beautiful but sad, droopy eyes and his pretty but unhappy face.

CHAPTER SIXTEEN

Keisha and Tammy looked at the black female guard who needed a serious attitude adjustment. Both women shook their heads in disbelief at the rude comments the guard had made about Zach's numerous female visitors. The guard, asking them if they were also in Zach's stable of "pay-like-they-weigh" women, had Keisha wanting to knock her nappy head off, since there wasn't an ounce of fat on either her or Rosalinda. She'd even had the nerve to refer to the heavy women that visited men in jail as "big packages."

"What do you ladies want to do? You can't just stand here and hold up the line."

"We're going in," Keisha said, rolling her eyes at the guard.

The fact that Zach already had another female visitor inside with him sparked an anger so deep in Keisha that she felt it burning within. Zach's black behind was going to feel the incinerating heat of her anger. "We're going in, one at time, just as we originally planned. There's going to be some casualties up in here today," Keisha mumbled under her breath. Mad as a wet hen, she stepped away from the window.

Keisha took a seat to wait until Tammy processed through. She was so glad that the kids weren't with them. Her mother had insisted on taking them to Atlanta with her for a while, since she hadn't quite made up her mind about making a permanent move to California.

She now saw that letting them go home with Martha had been one of the smartest things she'd done in a long while. She missed them, but they were in a good place. Allowing her mother to keep them for a while would give her the opportunity to pull herself together. Even though she knew that there were other women involved with Zach, she still hadn't decided their future as a couple. She couldn't get past the fact that she loved him, that he was the father of her children.

It never dawned on her that Zach might be the one to decide their future.

Tammy started crying the moment she sat down next to Keisha.

Keisha put her arm around Tammy's shoulder. "You got to be stronger than this, girl. You can't let Zach Martin know that he's upset you. If you do, he'll try to play you even harder than he already has."

Tammy lifted her head and looked at Keisha. "I'm not crying for me. I'm crying for you and your kids, Keisha."

Tammy's pointed comment stung Keisha hard. It even left its stinger planted deep inside her heart. "What do you mean by that?"

"I have everything to gain at this point, Keisha. My money will stay in my pocket. The phone bills at both the shop and my home will go down immediately, and my gas card will go back to being reasonable. Zach is not worth all this to me. Thank God they don't have conjugal visits up here, even if they are just for married people. I wouldn't just be going half on a baby. The baby would end up as mine alone. I can see that now."

Keisha looked amazed. "You really wanted to have a baby with him?"

"Didn't you? Don't answer that, since it's quite obvious that you did."

Keisha laughed. "You got a point. But I'm curious. What made you want to have a baby by a man already in prison?"

"I know you're not trying to tell me that you didn't fall for Zach's BS. You're still falling for it, and you're a great-looking woman, thin and sassy. I'm fat and unhappy. That's a perfect combination for a man when he seriously wants to play someone. You heard the guard. 'Pay-like-you-weigh.' 'Big packages.' She was only saying that the fatter you are, the more money you pay out. That had to come from the inmates. She just didn't sit around and think that up. The women who keep the inmates in money and goods are nothing more than jokes to their so-called men. I've been nothing but a joke to Zach. But if things go as planned, I'll have the last laugh."

Keisha took ahold of Tammy's hand. "You're so much more than what you've just suggested. You don't have to look a certain way for people to try and take advantage of you. Fat, thin, pretty, ugly, it doesn't matter. People will try and disrespect you, no matter the type of packaging you're wrapped in. Zach's been using me just like he's using you—and I'm the mother of his children. The only thing that's wrong with you and me is that we don't think we can do any better than that hardhead that's locked up in prison. But we can. We just don't have all the tools yet."

"If you know Zach is using you, and so many others, why do you still come way out here in the middle of nowhere to see him?"

Keisha's expression softened. "Because I remember when. When he was the kindest, most considerate man I've ever known. I guess that I'm still hoping that that person will show up one day. Maybe I'm fooling myself, but I believe he can change back to the person he once was. I sometimes hold myself partly responsible for the way he is now."

"How's that?"

"Because I also changed. In the beginning, I didn't take any stuff off of him. I made him respect me. The first time I let him get away with something, he started testing me right after that, at every turn. It was like he wanted to see how far out into left field he could go. I'd bust him for something he'd done, but there were never any serious consequences. The more he got away with, the more he pulled on me. Just like Dr. Trapp said at the support-group meeting, I gave him permission to treat me that way. I hated myself each time I let him get away with something. More than that, I feared losing him altogether if I didn't let his misdeeds go unpunished. Losing him scared me, especially after the kids came."

"I guess you didn't want to be alone."

"But look at me now. I ended up alone, anyway. I haven't told anyone this, but I'm going to tell you because I need to share with someone. When Zach's mother was keeping my little boy, I just happened to see a bankbook on the table. It had Zach's name on it, along with his mother's name. Nosy as I am, while knowing it was wrong, I opened it. The amount of money Zach has in that account astounded me. He has close to four thousand dollars in the bank. I couldn't believe it. I can't tell you how many times I had to borrow money to buy milk and diapers for my kids. I was always short of money 'cause I was putting money on his books."

"I guess my dollars are in that account, too. In the short time I've known him, I know I've sent him at least three hundred dollars."

"This Negro has been saving the money that I practically took food out of my kids' mouths to give to him. I didn't even bother to confront Lucian Martin, 'cause we would've really gotten into it over the money. She would've lied and said it was all hers. But Zach is the primary owner on that account. And he's going to pay me. I wrote the account number down, and I already have his social security number. I'm getting paid, one way or the other. Are you ready to do this, Tammy?"

"Yeah, let's do it, Keisha. As planned, I'll go in first. Then I'll watch for your entry."

"As you know, there's already another woman visitor in there with him, Tammy. Can you handle that? Maybe I should go first."

Tammy took a second to think about Keisha's suggestion. "I think we should go in there together, since he's already got a visitor. I think it'll have an even bigger impact."

Keisha shrank inside. Zach had totally disrespected her, yet she wasn't feeling so good about setting him up this way. She and Zach had serious problems, but she wasn't so sure that they should be handled in this manner. These were private issues, and they should be handled the same way, privately. Especially since a new player had been added to the unfair game.

She looked at Tammy, who looked as depressed as Keisha felt. The forlorn expression on Tammy's face quickly settled Keisha's inner battle. Zach simply couldn't get away with these kinds of things—mean things, hurtful ones, and all of them done to people who really cared about him, people who had sacrificed much to try and help him.

A face-to-face confrontation was called for.

"This is mind-boggling," Jesse snapped, " that you've been holding evidence back all this time. I can't believe you didn't tell me what was going on with our son at the time it was happening. If I had known what was going on, maybe this incarceration wouldn't have ever happened. You've betrayed me, Marlene."

"That's not fair, Jesse. I did the best I could."

"Yeah, I just bet you did. Look how long it has taken you to come to the realization that Malcolm is responsible for the things that have gone on. As you said, you've always suspected that he might know something about this crime."

"I was scared to face it, Jesse. But I acted on it as soon as I found concrete evidence."

"Scared of Malcolm going to jail is what you were. But not fearful enough of sitting on something that could've gotten me out of being locked up in here in the first place. As his father, I had the right to know what was going on in his life. He deserved to have me in his face constantly about his wrongdoing. But you couldn't see that. I'm still not sure you see it."

"I had to make sure that I was right about everything. As it turned out, I wasn't."

"You could've found that out soon enough had you pursued it. Malcolm coming between us doesn't shock me. I've always taken a backseat to our child. It's been okay in most instances. I've tried being understanding with you because of what the loss of our first child did to you. But I don't know if I'll ever understand you letting Malcolm come between us like this. To think I was dispensable in your life frightens me. You were sacrificing me to save a son who couldn't care less about either of us. That's a horse of a different color. That's a horrible truth to accept."

"Malcolm does care about us. He's young, Jesse."

"Youth without priorities is dangerous. An idle mind is the devil's workshop. Malcolm had no game plan, still doesn't have one. I'm disappointed in him—and in you, Mar."

"Please don't say that, Jesse. It hurts."

"Hurts! Woman, you don't know the meaning of that word. I guess you think it feels good being locked up in here like a wild animal. Well, I'm here to tell you that the hurt I feel is so deep, deeper than anything you can ever imagine." Jesse stood up. "This visit should come to an end. I don't want to hurt you in retaliation for you wounding me so deeply. That won't salve my soul in the least. God forbid that I should turn this into an eye-for-an-eye scenario."

"Wait, Jesse. Please don't let our visit end like this. I need you to understand a few things before you decide to cut me out of your life. I'm hurting, too, you know. This has been so hard on all of us."

The rage in his eyes didn't diminish one iota, but he sat back down. "I know you're hurting, too, wildflower. Tell me what you need me to understand."

Tears welled in her eyes at his tender voice. Still, there was nothing tender about the look in his eyes.

"I've always tried to handle Malcolm's numerous afflictions without you. You were always so busy with the church, so I tried not to bother you with the things going on at home. They almost seem trivial next to you conducting funerals, your ministry to the homeless and the incarcerated, visiting the sick and shut-ins, food and clothing drives for the needy, and so many other important duties that you performed regularly. You traveled extensively for speaking engagements and church conferences while I stayed home with Malcolm—"

"I'm sorry. I had no idea that my schedule was upsetting to you," he interjected.

He sounded resentful of her bringing it up, and that was unsettling to Marlene.

"You had no idea because I never told you. I understood what you do and why you do it. Still, there were distressing times for me. But how could I complain, especially knowing all the good you do for others? The times I did come to you with the problems I was having, you told me to have a little more faith, and to turn it over to the Master. 'Prayer works, Marlene, if you work it,' and so on and so forth. I simply did what you've been telling me to do for years and years. I turned this evidence over to the Master, and I waited on Him. I waited and let Him guide me to the truth. That doesn't mean I didn't get impatient, because I did. So impatient that I thought I was going to shrivel up and die from the exhaustion of just waiting for the Lord to answer me. I'm sorry it took so long, but you'll have to take that up with Jesus. His time, not ours. How many times have I heard you say that, Reverend Jesse?"

Unable to contain his anger, he slammed his open palm down on the metal table. Momentarily, the sound drew unwanted attention from the guards and other inmates.

"Does it make you feel good to say these things to me, Marlene? Have you any idea how angry I am with you right now?"

"Good!"

Stunned at her response, he lifted both eyebrows. He'd never raised his hand to a woman in his entire life, but the itch to slap her across the face was testing him something awful.

"I'm glad you're angry. Now I know you're really human. You've walked around cool, calm, and collected every day of your life since you entered into a personal relationship with the Lord. Nothing shakes your tree. Nothing disturbs your peace. That's all well and good. But we're not all where you are in your faith and in your beliefs. You've told me there are times when we have to meet people right where they are, to take their hands and lead them onto the paths of righteousness, and to show them by example the goodness and mercies of our loving God.

"I'm not in a very good place today, Jesse, but I desire to be, should tomorrow come. You've often said that I complete you. I've never wanted to be the reason for you to ever feel incomplete. Jesse, I need you to meet me right where I am today. I need you to take my hand and lead me back to the path from which I've lost my way."

His eyes filled with tears. It didn't matter to him who saw him cry. He didn't care who might think of him as a weak man. God knew his heart. What God and his earthly family thought of him were all that mattered.

"How can I deny your request? I don't think I can." A tear ran from the corner of his left eye. "As a follower of Jesus, I can't turn my back on you. As your husband, I love you, and I vowed to love you through the best and worst of times. We're in our worst of times. I'm sorry if I've somehow failed my family, the very ones who mean the most to me. I'm sorry, Marlene."

"You haven't failed us, Jesse. There were just times that I needed your strength, needed the wisdom of your ways. We're so close to getting you out of here. Please tell me I'll be included in your future. Please tell me that this sorrowful episode in our lives shall pass, too."

He winced from the pain of those heartfelt remarks. "I'm angry. But our future was never in question. Our future is not in doubt. Whether you know it or not, you keep my feet firmly planted on the ground. I don't ever want you to feel doubtful about us. If I'm about to come through the fire, I need you there to cool my brow with your sweet breath when I step out of the fiery furnace. You are my future, Mar. This deeply troubling situation shall pass, too."

Once calm had been regained, and it seemed that Jesse might

come to understand things, Marlene went on to explain to her husband the information she'd learned from Todd.

Now that Major Townsend had all the facts as Marlene knew them, all they had to do was sit back and wait for the end results. Jesse's lawyer felt confident that Jesse would be released, but it was a matter of how much time it would take to achieve the desired outcome.

She told Jesse that the person suspected of committing the crime, Latrell Johnson, was already behind bars for parole violation. The lawyer felt sure that they could get a confession out of Johnson, since he had to do the remainder of his time, anyway—a long time.

According to Todd, the van had exchanged hands many times that night. While Marlene held Malcolm totally responsible for it falling into the wrong hands, she let her husband know that she was totally relieved that Malcolm and Todd had nothing to do with the actual crime.

"Myrna hasn't spoken to me since the day she brought Todd over to the house to explain his part. They haven't stopped coming to church, but I only know that from conversations with other members. I haven't seen them because I haven't been there lately."

"I'm happy they haven't left the church. We'll just continue to pray daily that your friendship will eventually survive this very personal setback, Mar."

Keisha and Tammy went straight to the table where Zach was busy entertaining his other lady. He was so engrossed with the obese white girl sitting across from him that he didn't even see Keisha and Tammy approach. Keisha sat down next to him, but she had to call out his name before he looked at her. The horrified expression on his face was priceless.

"Who's your friend, Zach?" Keisha asked, keeping her eyes on the white girl.

Before he could answer, Tammy dropped down on the other side of him.

"Yeah, who's your girlfriend, Zach?"

Unable to comprehend what was happening, Zach turned his head from side to side. He couldn't believe his own eyes. With Keisha and Tammy sitting on either side of him, he wished he could disappear into thin air.

"We're waiting to be introduced to your friend, Zach," Keisha urged.

"Uh, uh, this is Celeste Powers," Zach stammered.

"One of your homeboy's girls?" Keisha prompted. "Hi, Celeste, I'm Zach's girlfriend, the mother of his two children."

"Yes, and I'm Tammy, the future mother of his baby. We're going to go half on a baby when he gets out of here. Ain't that right, Zach? Where do you fit into Zach's life, Celeste?"

Celeste's green eyes narrowed to thin slits of anger as she looked at Zach. The vehemence in her eyes was apparent. "Maybe Zach should answer that question. How do I fit into your life, Zachary Martin?"

Zach looked nervous. "You're my friend."

"Is that what I am, Zach? According to your letters, I'm the woman you're going to marry when you get your freedom."

Keisha laughed and Tammy followed her lead.

"Married! "Zach can't even commit to a monogamous relationship, let alone a marriage. Girl, you'd better run while you still got legs. Zach's been known to cut women's lower extremities right out from under them," Keisha warned Celeste.

"Enough of this BS," Zach said between clenched teeth. "You all know what the deal is. I ain't marrying nobody right now. When I do get married, I'm marrying the mother of my babies, Keisha. You other two tramps ain't nothing but tricks. I played you both. Now what?"

Keisha rolled her eyes at Zach, but she really wanted to hit him upside his head. "In playing them, you played yourself, Zach. And you been playing me, too."

"How's that, Keisha?"

"How much money do you have in the bank?" Keisha asked.

"I ain't got no money nowhere."

"Don't lie. I saw the bankbook at your mother's house," Keisha remarked. "You have quite a bit of money saved for someone who's always hollering broke."

"Oh, that."

"Yeah, that. And I want back every dime I put on your books, with interest. Every red cent. I've had to borrow money to meet the kid's needs while you've been stockpiling our hard-earned money. I don't know about Tammy and Celeste, but I ain't going out like that."

"Me, either," Tammy chimed in. "I want back my money, too."

Zach kept looking around the room. When it appeared that no one was paying any attention to his situation, he relaxed a bit. Still, he knew he might get teased later. This was embarrassing, 'cause everyone knew that he had more than one woman visiting him. They'd seen him hugging each of the three women. Zach wasn't sure if Keisha had also found out about the other two women who visited him. He wouldn't be surprised if they showed up, too.

"Well, since Zach is handing out money, I guess I'll take mine back also," Celeste said. "What do you say, Zach? Think I can get my thousand dollars back?"

"A thousand dollars!" Keisha and Tammy said in unison.

Celeste glared at Zach with open contempt. "Yeah, a thousand dollars, if not more. Zach, you're a lousy piece of mouse dropping. I hope you rot in this stinking prison."

Before Zach could open his mouth, Celeste was across the table, clawing away at his face. Her hands tore at every part of his anatomy. Keisha looked over at the guards, who were making no attempt to come to Zach's rescue. Practically everyone in the room was laughing his or her head off. Keisha might have thought it was funny, too, if it wasn't coming at her expense and the expense of the other two women. The guards looked on in amusement while Celeste continued to throw Muhammad Ali–like body blows to Zach's midsection. Only after Celeste's big foot connected with Zach's private parts did the guards come running.

Doubled over, Zach fell to the floor with a thud. While writhing around in pain, he called Celeste all sorts of names. Highly offended by the filthy names he spewed out, Celeste broke free of the guards, and kicked him in the behind. Before the guards contained her, she kicked Zach several more times. With one guard on each side of her, they immediately marched Celeste out of the visiting room. Keisha could see one of the guard's shoulders shaking from the force of his laughter. Tammy was also cracking up as she sat back down at the table.

Keisha bent down next to Zach. "Are you okay?"

All the brother could do was moan. He was in serious pain. Celeste's foot had done some damage, but Keisha suspected that Zach was more embarrassed than hurt. This was something the other inmates weren't going to let him live down. A brother having his behind kicked was one thing. But to have a woman take him out—a white woman, at that—was downright scandalous. Zach would never hear the end of this soap opera–style drama.

"Keisha," Zach whispered, "don't listen to them other hos. Baby girl, you're the one I want. I promise to turn everything I have over to you." He moaned. "You and the kids are all I want. Please forgive me. I love you, Keisha, girl. I promise to change. You can have all the money I have in the bank. Just don't leave me out here in this desert alone."

One of the guards came back and told Zach that he'd have to go back to his cell because of all the disruption he'd caused. He then informed the two women that their visit was over.

Keisha didn't know what to do or say. She'd never seen Zach so vulnerable. Though he'd been careful in not letting the others hear his pleas, she felt his sincerity. Keisha watched as the guard assisted Zach out of the room. He was still doubled over in pain.

Tammy stood up and took Keisha's hand. "Let's go. We can't do anything else in here. This visit is history."

"Yeah, I heard the guard. I can't believe we did this, Tammy. I feel so bad."

Outside in the lobby, Keisha surprised Tammy when she started laughing uncontrollably. "Did you see homegirl come across that table? That girl did what we should've done, what another type of sister would've surely done. Celeste came at Zach like white lightning. I wish I'd had the nerve to take him out like that in front of everyone. Zach got his just rewards. Give me five, Tammy. We busted his black behind good. We make a great tag team."

"Just like we had planned," Tammy sang out. "But I won't feel totally avenged until we get our money back."

"Oh, we're going to get all that back! You can believe that," Keisha assured Tammy.

"How was your dinner, Rosalinda?"

"Very good, Michael. This place is so nice. In fact, it's beautiful. This setting is rather romantic for a friendship date. It's much like the place you took me for our so-called business lunch a few weeks back."

"I'm a romantic guy, Rosalinda. What can I say? I think a woman should be treated like a goddess. I'm the kind of man who tends to put his woman upon a pedestal. Unfortunately, the ones in the past have all come tumbling down. Somehow, I don't think that will happen with you. But since you're not my woman, I'm saddened that you'll never know my romantic side."

"You wouldn't be trying to entice my heart, would you?"

"In every way that I can think of."

Rosalinda blushed. "I like you a lot, Michael. The one thing that still concerns me is Ricardo knowing of the offer that you made me. If he can hurt you professionally, he will."

"Ricardo can't hurt me. He's a two-bit punk. He's not smart enough to come up with something as complex as suing me for conflict of interest. Besides, he doesn't know about my feelings for you. Does he?"

She shook her head. "Not from me, he doesn't. I'd never tell him something like that now. All he knows is that I'm through with him."

"Have you seen him lately?"

"No, but he's still writing. I finally wrote him back. That was a mistake, because he's still making threats of violence against me. I'm fearful of what I know he can have his boys do to me. I wanted to go see him, but my friends don't think it's a good idea."

Michael's face turned red from the anger he felt. He was sure Ricardo had gotten the earlier message. "Do you have any of the recent letters with you?"

"I brought a couple of the latest ones along so you could also see them. I'm hoping you can tell me how to stop them from coming altogether."

"Have them remove your address from Ricardo's mailing list. You can request that through the administration offices at the prison. And then you can always physically move. I have a great guest house on my property. My friends are always welcome."

Blinking uncontrollably, Rosalinda swallowed hard. "I could never do that."

"Why not?"

"When my mother comes home from the rehabilitation center, she'll be living with me."

"The guest house just happens to have two bedrooms, two full baths, and a fully furnished kitchen. If it would make you feel better, I'll even rent it out to you."

"That's very generous of you, but I couldn't."

"You won't is more like it. At any rate, I'm only trying to ensure your safety. No one can get to you where I live. The property is behind security gates."

"I do have to go to work. I won't have protection there."

"If you accept a job in my office, you will. I'm willing to do whatever it takes to see you happy and out of the dangerous environment you've been in. Those are the sort of things friends do for one another."

"I'll think it over." The trembling of her heart made her dizzy. His offer had her mind caught up in a whirlwind, even if she didn't have any intentions of taking him up on it.

"Good. About these letters, I want to take them and keep them with the others. I also want to read them over, the same as I did with the last ones. Leave Ricardo up to me. There are many ways to handle him, within the system and out of it. I think Ricardo and I can come to an understanding. He does want to get out of jail at some point in his life. I'm sure of it."

"What are you talking about doing?"

"It's better that you not know. I may not have grown up on the tough streets in Los Angeles, but I know how to speak the language—and in no uncertain terms. The type of language that Ricardo will immediately understand."

"I hope you're not talking about violence. I don't want that. Please don't do anything that would bring harm to him."

"There are times when talk is enough. Talking should do it when he gets the new message that I plan to have delivered. Trust me. This matter of him continuing to threaten you can be handled. Perhaps a little more pressure needs to be applied. No violence, okay?"

"Okay. But there is something else I'd like to say. Will you listen?"

"Most definitely."

Rosalinda took a second mentally to collect her thoughts. She didn't want to come off as an inexperienced woman or to have him think that she'd be as stupid in another relationship as she been in the one with Ricardo. That wasn't ever going to happen again.

"Is it just sex you're after with me?"

Her question thoroughly surprised him. "I thought I'd made my intentions clear."

"Obviously not clear enough. But let me make myself crystal clear. If it's only my flesh that you're pursuing, I want you to know that the next time I lay down naked in bed with a man, I'm going to be the missus. I'm not a virgin, but Ricardo is the only man I've ever been with. I intend to take my life seriously. I have two jobs and a sick mother to take care of, and I don't have time to waste with someone who's only interested in the hit-and-run. So if you think this is a game you're playing, you better find yourself another opponent because I won't be participating.

"I'm too young to have gone through so much already. Most of it I've put myself through by not setting boundaries in my relationships and not having a clear understanding of what I want out of life. I don't know all of what I want for myself, but I do know that it's not some frivolous relationship that only has a snowball's chance in hell of surviving. Please don't step to me in a personal way, Michael, unless you plan to come correct."

He studied her intently, totally impressed with her comments. They and the unexpected mature stance she'd suddenly taken on surprised him. Without any expression, he kept his dark eyes riveted on her lovely face. She had certainly presented him with a bold challenge . . . a challenge on which he'd just have to take her up.

Reaching across the table, he took her hand. "Making love to you has crossed my mind a zillion times. I'd be lying if I said I didn't think about us in that way. But sleeping with you is not my objective in pursuing this relationship. Thank you for setting the record straight. I'm crystal clear on the issues. Now, what about dessert for my lovely companion?"

"Sounds nice."

His unrevealing answer wasn't what she'd hoped for, but she'd have to accept it, just as he'd have to accept her for who she was. There wasn't going to be any more game-playing in her life. From now on, things involving her personal life were going to be her way or no way. If Michael chose to continue in his hot pursuit of her, the boundaries were already firmly in place, boundaries that were not to be crossed under any circumstance.

CHAPTER SEVENTEEN

Marlene helped Malcolm through the visitor processing session by telling him what he needed to do in order to get in to see his dad. The recent changes in Malcolm, changes for the better, had come as quite a surprise to Marlene. Because of those changes, she thought she should begin to reconcile her differences with her and Jesse's only child.

A few weeks back, she hadn't even wanted to be in the same car with Malcolm on such a long drive. Though she hadn't let him move back into home, she and her son were finally becoming close again. He had started coming over to the house to cut the lawn every week and to tend to some of the other heavier chores. Malcolm was also helping his mother with some of Jesse's church duties—and he'd even started attending church services pretty regularly again.

Marlene was impressed with all the changes, but she still kept her guard up. She wasn't going to give Malcolm a license to start trying to manipulate her again. Once she'd begun to stand firm with him, she'd seen that he had actually wanted her to be that way with him. He seemed to have more respect for her and himself.

Jesse seemed so happy to see Malcolm. It was a pleasant surprise for him. Marlene hadn't told him that their son had planned to visit.

When her two men embraced, Marlene had to fight back her tears. Marlene and Jesse sat down next to each other and Malcolm chose to sit across from his parents. Jesse took a good look at the son he hadn't laid eyes on in months.

"Dad, you look so good. I don't know what I expected, but I didn't expect to see you looking so fit. I'm sorry I haven't been out here before now to see you. I just didn't think I could stand seeing you locked up like this. How are you?"

"I'm fine, son. I'm doing even better after the news I received today." Jesse took his wife's hand. "I may be getting out of here very soon. Major was here earlier. He told me that the DA is willing to listen to him and take a look at the new evidence without waiting for the appeal process to run its course. According to Major, Latrell Johnson has agreed to talk with him about the case. It seems that Latrell's mother convinced him to talk with Major."

Jesse put his arms around Marlene when she began to cry. She couldn't have been any happier. Jesse never did belong in prison. She couldn't wait until he walked out into the sunshine. She'd be right there at the exit gates of hell, waiting to take him home.

"That's great news, Dad." Malcolm had tears in his eyes. "This all happened because I acted irresponsibly. When I took the van that night, I didn't consider anything but my desire to see Sheila and to hang out at the basketball court. I have violated every trust you and Mom have ever put in me. I'm sorry for everything. I hope you both can forgive me."

"Forgiveness is a must when you're a Christian, Malcolm. I forgive you, and I'm sure your mother does. Have you asked God to forgive you? And have you forgiven yourself?"

"I have asked God to forgive me, but I am having a hard time forgiving myself. Sometimes I think I hate myself for what happened to you, knowing it was my fault. I struggle with the truth of what I did every day. My selfishness is to blame for all of this."

"Malcolm, you can ask God to forgive you, but if you can't forgive yourself, what's the point? When you turn over something to God, and then ask His forgiveness, you have to let go of it completely. If He can forgive you, who are you not to forgive yourself? The price has already been paid. Accept that He has forgiven you and move on with your life. You can't go back and change a thing that you've already done, but you can make sure that you don't continue to do these same kinds of inconsiderate, selfish things."

"Listen to your father, Malcolm. He's never told you anything that's wrong yet, and he never will," Marlene told her son.

"Malcolm, it seems that everyone but you has had to pay for the consequences of your actions. I hope you've learned something from all this. This has been a very unpleasant experience for everyone but you. This injustice that's been visited on me is the result of you taking the van without permission. You've made some very unwise choices, son, but I hope you have truly learned something as a result of all this emotional pain that not one but two families are going through. The Jacobsons are hurting, too, just like your mother and me."

"I have learned a lot, Dad. I'm doing good on my job. Been there almost a month. Now, you know that's a record for me." Marlene and Jesse laughed. "The boss says I'm doing good. I like working with the kids. Maybe I can keep them from doing some of the dumb stuff I did. I help run the sports program with the Los Angeles County Department of Parks and Recreation. It pays really well, too. I'm saving for a down payment on a car."

"Malcolm has also been helping me out a lot around the house, inside and out. He takes care of the lawn every week and runs a few church errands for me. I must admit that he's changed for the better. Our relationship is also getting back on track.

"Jesse," Marlene said breathlessly, "you're coming home. I can feel it. I can't wait. Getting you home is a prayer that's about to be answered. God does deliver."

"Always. God is good. His wonders to perform.

"Malcolm, your mother tells me you and Sheila are living together. That's not the way we've taught you to live your life, but it's your life to live. How's it working out?"

Malcolm shrugged. "Not so good. I didn't realize how good I had it at home until I got tossed. I thought Mom was on my case all the time, but Sheila is ridiculous. She rides me all the time, morning, noon, and night. I can understand why she can't trust me, but I can't get her to see that I've changed, that I'm not like I was before. I guess it's going to take a while to regain her trust. I've hurt her a lot, too. I'm trying to hang in there, but I am seriously looking for a place to rent on my own. I just don't know how to tell her I want to move out. Her trust in me is zero."

"Trust is a delicate thing, son, especially between a man and a woman. Once you violate that trust, it's hard to regain it," Jesse advised Malcolm.

"Amen, Jesse. You see, Malcolm, I didn't trust enough that your daddy would understand, so I didn't tell him about what I thought I knew. I also have to regain his total trust. Trust is so very fragile. When someone puts their trust in you, be extremely careful with it. It can be a long way to getting it back once the bond of trust has been broken. I know firsthand. I have a long way to go to get back the trust your aunt Myrna had put into me and in our friendship. She feels betrayed by me, though I don't think I'm guilty of betrayal. Because she was my good friend, I went to her with the only information that was available to me at the time. I don't know how else I could've handled it. But I can't discount what she may have felt. Therefore, I'm going to have to try and rebuild what we had. I intend to ask for her forgiveness."

"I was real angry with your mother when she told me about you taking the van. I wanted to hurt her just like she'd hurt me. Then she said some things that make me stop and think about why she'd do such a thing. First, Marlene, I want to apologize to you for my initial reaction. I've had time to think things through. I'm sorry for not taking care of my responsibilities where my family is concerned. I should've been there for both of you. Your mother pointed out to me how she had to deal with family issues all alone. A boy your age needed your father to be there. I wasn't—and we're paying the price for that."

"But, Dad, I didn't do the things I did because you weren't there. I did them because I wanted to. I'm a fairly intelligent guy. I knew you were busy doing God's work. I knew that there were people that needed you more than I did, but there were times when I really did need you. You were there when it counted the most. You took a lot of time with me in my early years, and you always instilled the right things in me. As you've said many times, it's all about choices. I could've done right as easily as I did wrong. I don't blame you for anything that's gone wrong in my life, Dad. I only have myself to blame. That goes for you, too, Mom. A guy couldn't ask for better parents than the ones that God gave me."

Marlene's eyes grew watery. "Thank you for that, son. It's nice to hear you say those things. But we've all made some bad choices in this deal. Mine was covering for you all the time and not sharing the serious problems with you, Jesse. I tried to take care of everything myself, forgetting that this is a partnership. We're all going to have to work on our shortcomings. I apologize to both of you for my part in not communicating the issues effectively."

"We've all apologized to one another. Now we have to move on. This all happened for a reason, a reason that God has yet to reveal. He will. We just have to be patient a little longer."

"Since we first started this support group, there have been good and bad times for all of us. Those of us who manned the phones this week have received all sorts of calls from our members. I logged in over twenty-five calls myself. Some members have had good news, while several others are dealing with further devastation in their lives. I, for one, have some good news, so good that I'd like to share it with you. It's very possible that my husband may be released in the next couple of days. . . ."

Teary-eyed, Marlene had to wait unit the cheers and clapping died down to continue.

"The person who actually committed the crime has confessed. It seems that he was already behind bars when his identity was uncovered—"

"It was my son that committed the offense," a strong voice interrupted. A black lady seated in the center aisle of the church stood up. "I came here tonight to tell you how sorry I am that my son has caused your family such grief, Mrs. Covington. I thank God that I was able to talk him into confessing. After my daughter's boyfriend told her what he thought Latrell may have done, she came to me with the story. Latrell has been in and out of trouble since he was fifteen. He's now twenty-five. For ten years I've been a lady in waiting, waiting for him to turn his life around. Because of the way I raised him, I still believe that he can do it. In some instances, the system is too harsh. In other instances, it's too lax. Latrell never got the type of help he needed with his addiction to drugs."

Marlene was astounded by the courage this woman had shown. If only every woman and man could learn how to face their trials and tribulations with such valor. Todd Jacobson had a lot of courage, too. By telling his girlfriend of Latrell's possible involvement, he'd helped Jesse out.

"Throwing drug-addicted people into jail is not the answer. If they don't get proper treatment, their crimes against society are only going to increase. My son needs lots of help in many areas of his life. Mrs. Covington, I'm here to ask that you and your husband pray for my boy. He's to be pitied, not censured. He doesn't need further condemnation. He's already condemned himself more than anyone ever could. Thank you for hearing me out."

"Thank you for that, ma'am." Marlene's voice trembled with emotion. "I'm happy to report that my husband and I are already praying for your son. More than that, we owe him a debt of gratitude. Had he not confessed to the crime, my husband and I wouldn't be hopeful about him coming home. Also, Reverend Jesse plans to visit Latrell. If it's any comfort to you, we don't intend to condemn your son. Jesus commands us to forgive to be forgiven."

Marlene fixed her eyes on the back of the room when she saw movement there. As the very attractive-looking woman came into her line of vision, Marlene thought her face looked familiar. Then she placed her. It was the woman who'd been beaten up by her husband in the prison visiting room. She looked much different. She was all dressed up and wearing makeup.

"Do you remember me?" she asked Marlene.

"I certainly do. How are you?" Marlene blinked back the tears at seeing such beauty.

"I'm getting along okay. I saw your picture in the paper this week. There was an article on you regarding this support group. I can't tell you how happy I was that I was going to be able to make contact with you again. I've often wondered about you over the past few months. I came here to thank you for helping me that day. I'm not going to go into any details of what happened. But you helped me change my life, of which I'm in total control now. Your kindness and soothing words that day went a long way in helping me to see that I needed to make changes, and that I was the only one who could make those changes. I'm no longer a lady in waiting, just a happy lady, period. I'm in the process of getting a long overdue divorce and getting back to being busy about the Lord's work. My baby is also doing very well. Her future and welfare figured in heavily when weighing my decisions. We're truly on our way to a much brighter future."

No one knew the nature of this woman's business with Marlene, but it was easy to see that the support-group leader had somehow touched this woman's life in a special way. It seemed that something extraordinary and spiritual had brought them together.

"Welcome! We're glad to see you here, glad that you've been able to change your circumstances. God bless you, my sister. May you keep walking in the light."

Loud applause came once again.

"Is there someone that would like to share with us this evening?" Marlene asked of those in attendance.

The woman who got to her feet was easily recognized by Marlene as the older woman who had embraced the young woman inflicted with the AIDS virus who'd spoken during the first support-group meeting.

"I just want to bring you up to date on the young lady who spoke out so bravely at the first meeting. I'm sure many of you remember the young woman with AIDS. She and I exchanged phone numbers after the group session was over that evening, and we've been keeping in touch on a regular basis. I'm saddened to report that she is currently in the hospital, fighting for her life. I visit her as often as I can. I'm standing here to ask you all to remember her and her young son in prayer. She's doesn't want visitors, because she's so weak, but she does want and need your constant prayers. Thank you."

"Thank you for the updated information. Please, let us close our eyes for a moment of silent prayer," Marlene requested.

When Marlene opened her eyes, another person was already standing.

"You have the floor," Marlene told the middle-aged black woman.

"Marlene, I just wanted to stand up here and thank you and your two lovely assistants for starting this group. I had nowhere to turn before this group came into existence. I'm sure many of you were like me, too embarrassed to talk to people about having a loved one behind bars. It's not something you want to share over lunch with a friend or a coworker, or while you're having your hair done at the salon. It's not something you want to talk about, period. But I'm learning that talking about it helps. Especially when you can talk about it with people in similar situations.

"If I don't take another thing away from this group, I've already walked away with the fact that I don't have to be embarrassed by what my loved ones do. We don't raise them to become criminals. I've learned that these are our loved ones' choices, not our choices for them. Mrs. Covington said her husband told her that parents are not responsible for who their children become as adults, because it's all about choices. In having it put that way to me, I began to see the light. And I've been able to rid myself of the burden of guilt I've often felt over their wrongdoing. I will continue to love and support my loved ones, but I no longer hold myself responsible for their actions. I hope you can unload the guilt, too. That's all I have to say."

"Those were some powerful words, my friend," another woman said as she got to her feet. "In dissecting those words, some of you should be able to unload the guilt. I feel responsible for my son getting into trouble, because I wasn't home where I belonged. I had my son at an early age. He had no father in the home and a mother who thought partying was more important than spending quality time with her child. Had my mother lived, he probably would've turned out okay. You see, she took much better care of him than she did me, because she'd grown older and wiser. I became my mother. Everything I learned about not being a good mother, I learned from her. But what I've learned from coming here is that I didn't have to follow in her footsteps. I chose to do as she did. I didn't understand that I had choices back then. And many of our young people don't understand that today. If we all take a look around the room, we'll see that the majority of the women in here are under thirty. A lot of them are here because they want to choose another path. It's up to us who've been there and done that, the veteran ladies in waiting, to take them under our wing and show them a better way. We can't change the darkness of their past, but we can help them choose a better, brighter future. Can I get an amen, sisters?"

She got more than her request, when everyone stood in ovation.

Marlene came back to the podium. "Thank you for sharing. Now my assistants have something they'd like to say. It's hard for them to get up in front of this crowd. They've never done any public speaking, so let's try to give them our undivided attention. Keisha, you're on."

Keisha wrung her hands together as she came to the podium. "Hi, everyone. It's nice to see that so many of you keep coming back. We've lost a few of the women, but most of you have become regulars.

We've worked hard for you to have a place to come and share. We will continue to do so. Suggestions are always welcome."

Keisha looked at Marlene for encouragement. Marlene simply nodded.

"As you can see, I'm one of the younger women. Both my best friend and me are under thirty. We've both been supporting our boyfriends, who are up at CCF. Before we met Marlene, we had no self-esteem whatsoever. The truth is, we didn't know what our problem was. We didn't know that we lacked self-esteem. Didn't know what the word really meant. That's how pathetic we were. We thought we were grown, doing our own thing, with no one to answer to."

Keisha looked at Rosalinda and smiled. Her friend's return smile gave her the courage to keep talking. Although she was extremely nervous, she knew her comments might keep someone from making the same mistakes she'd made.

"We've been doing this so long that we've forgotten what it was like before we started visiting jails. This has been our whole life since we were eighteen. Every weekend we drive up to the desert like we're going on holiday. After working all week, we get our hair and nails done on Friday night. Half the time, the guys don't even notice. The next morning we pack the car with the kids, plenty of sandwiches and cold drinks, and an overnighter just in case a lockdown occurs or visitation is canceled. We spend our hard-earned money on rental cars and hotels. Then we have to struggle to make ends meet throughout the week. My phone is cut off more than it's turned on, and I have little babies at home. I don't want to see anyone else go through this.

"There are various reasons that we support men in jail, but still, we need to act more responsibly. We can't let our lives and the lives of our children go to the dogs to supply someone on the inside with things that we have to do without so our inmates can get what they want. If they can get on the inside everything we can get out here, what's the point of them being there?"

Rosalinda came to the podium at Keisha's summons. "She's going to take up where I left off. Thank you for hearing me out."

Keisha received a healthy round of applause as she left the podium.

Rosalinda cleared her throat. "Preparing for our weekend visits has become a regular routine. I can't remember a time when we didn't roll up there early on Saturday morning to see our men. Keisha said all that to say this. It's expensive being a lady in waiting. But when what you do is not even appreciated, and never enough, you need to check yourself. When you and your kids are doing without so that someone else can live good, you need to take a hard look at the way you're doing things. Don't get caught up in the game like we did. A learned behavior can be unlearned. As Keisha said, we have to act responsibly. Keisha and I both want to thank Marlene for pointing out to us what should've been obvious. She's helped us in ways that we can never repay her. All I'm going to ask is that you keep coming back to the meetings until it clicks for you like it has clicked for Keisha and me. Thank you."

Rosalinda received the same show of support as Keisha had.

Beaming from head to toe, Marlene came back to the podium. "Let's give our young people another round of applause. They're doing a tremendous job for this group."

Much to her surprise, since she hadn't even noticed her come in, Marlene saw Alexis coming toward the podium. The three women were supposed to meet up with Alexis for a late evening dinner. Alexis hadn't been able to get away much because of her parents' visit, but she had called earlier to see if they could get together for a couple of hours after the meeting.

Marlene moved aside to allow Alexis access to front and center.

Alexis swallowed hard. This was so difficult for her. *Go with your heart. No one is here to judge you. Do this for yourself. It's okay to release the poison from within in this manner. You'll probably feel much better once you've gotten it out of your system.*

Quieting her thoughts, Alexis came up to the microphone and picked it up. "I'm Alexis. I'm glad to be here among you. I've heard so many stories that have touched me. It has taken a lot of inner coaxing for me to get up the nerve to stand before you and tell mine."

Alexis stated her name and then began by talking about why her husband had been arrested and the profound effect that his sentence had already had on their lives. "Never in a million years would I have thought that this would be our lot in life. It never crossed my mind that one day unconquerable metal bars would stand between me and the man I love."

She took a moment to ponder her next comments and to muster up more courage.

"Although I came from a very poor background, I began living an extravagant life of privilege not long after I got married. My husband amassed a fortune within the first couple of years of our marriage. But it doesn't matter who you are or where you came from, or how much money you have, especially when you find yourself accused of breaking the law. Someone very young but very wise once told me that my husband was behind bars and subject to the same conditions as every other inmate, regardless of how rich we were. That was a bitter pill to swallow, but swallow it I did."

Alexis turned, looked over at Keisha, and smiled. Keisha acknowledged Alexis's comments by returning the smile.

"It was money that got him into this mess, but money couldn't get him out of it. I live in Bel Air and I drive a Rolls-Royce. But what does that mean when your husband's been sentenced to time in prison. Our men are not doing this time alone. We ladies that are standing by our men are doing time right along with them. What I've learned from this ordeal is that there are many reasons for women to support their incarcerated men. I've learned that no one should judge another's reasons for doing so, especially when you don't know all the issues. I'm guilty of doing that. I now know that I was wrong. I've learned to ask for divine guidance, and I've found a true friend in a very dear lady who is helping me find my way back to God. I've learned courage in the face of adversity from another. And I was taught basic truths from yet another. After all that I've learned, I've made the decision to stand by the man I love. Until death us do part."

Alexis pointed to the three women she'd come to care so much about, Marlene, Keisha, and Rosalinda. "Thank you for the lessons you've taught me. Thank you for being my friends. With that said, I surrender the podium."

Now that Alexis had had her say, Marlene read the minutes from the last meeting. She then talked about future seminars and other things that were being planned for the group.

An hour later, the meeting was adjourned.

Marlene, Rosalinda, and Keisha hurried out to Marlene's car. They were still going to have dinner with Alexis. Marlene didn't want to be out too late because tomorrow was her turn to teach the lesson at the church.

The three women discussed the support-group meeting on the way to Roscoe's Chicken and Waffles store located on Pico Boulevard in

Los Angeles. Each was extremely delighted by how many women had come out again and how the meeting itself had turned out. Marlene still couldn't believe that Alexis had shown up. Neither could she believe how Latrell Johnson's mother had shown such bravery in encouraging her son to step forward and accept responsibility for his crime. Had Marlene shown such courage in informing her husband of the things that were happening in Malcolm's life—and then later aggressively confronting Malcolm with her suspicions—Jesse's incarceration might not have ever happened.

Alexis had already parked her car in the parking lot by the time the others arrived. After exchanging hugs and pleasant greetings again, the women went inside, where they were seated in a booth that looked out onto the still-busy streets. When the waitress asked if they wanted to order something to drink before ordering their meals, in consideration of their limited time, they decided to order both while they had the waitress in front of them.

"So, Ms. Alexis," Keisha began, "how's the visit coming?"

Alexis laced her fingers together. "It's going very well, thank you. My mom and dad are so happy they decided to come to L.A."

"Have they asked about R.J. yet?" Marlene inquired. "How is he doing? We don't get the chance to see him unless you're there to visit."

"R.J. is fine. And yes, they've asked about him, but they haven't probed too deep into his whereabouts. I've told them he's away on business. We all know that's a bald-faced lie. They're more excited about spending time with me than worrying about where R.J. is. It's no secret that they don't care for him. They're probably more comfortable in our home without him being there, if the truth be known. So how are all of your guys doing?"

"Zach is still a buster. But he got his, real good." Keisha went on to relay to Alexis what had happened at the prison. Even though Marlene and Rosalinda had heard the story before, they couldn't hold their laughter when Alexis busted up.

Marlene thought it was nice to see Alexis really let go. It was a refreshing change. Alexis also seemed more relaxed and more accepting of the other women's sincere offer of friendship.

Remembering that she had something she'd been wanting to ask

Keisha for a long time, Marlene snapped her fingers. "Keisha, I need to know something. How did Zach get that gash in the back of his head? I forget to ask you that every time we're together."

Keisha sighed. "One of his homeboys cut him over some rap music they were putting together. It was serious. Zach could've died had the knife gone in any further. It happened in my apartment while I was at work. They got into an argument over the music after smoking a blunt. The guy grabbed a steak knife out of my kitchen and went to cutting on Zach."

Marlene cringed. "Maybe I was better off not knowing."

"And your guy, Rosalinda? How's Ricardo?" Alexis inquired.

"Ricardo's history. He's no longer in my life."

"What?" Alexis's eyes widened in disbelief. "When did all this happen?"

"When he asked me to sleep with his lawyer to pay off his legal bills. That was something I just couldn't get past. It was a real eye-opener."

"I would say so." Alexis looked shocked. "I can't believe he'd even ask something like that of you. I guess he has to be pretty upset about this. Is he still in contact with you."

"I changed my phone number. But I got a three-way call at work the other day. Ricardo was on the other end. Usually if you use call-waiting or any other calling feature, the connection gets broken. But it didn't happen this time for whatever reason. Ricardo groveling on the phone came as a surprise to me, since he'd already started sending me threatening letters. But now the letters and the phone calls have stopped altogether."

"Thanks to Michael," Keisha chimed in.

"Who's Michael?" Alexis looked puzzled.

"Ricardo's lawyer," Marlene enlightened.

"Michael and Rosalinda have become close friends," Keisha offered, raising her eyebrows suggestively. "Michael has become her swarthy, Spanish hero."

Alexis rubbed shoulders with Rosalinda. "What's going on, girlfriend? Sounds like you have moved on. Extra, extra, I want to hear all about it," Alexis sang out.

"Well, since your inquiring mind wants to know, it's like this," Rosalinda quipped.

Roslinda began smiling all over herself. She was eager to share her good news with Alexis. It was times like these to which the four women had come to look forward. Relaxing and sharing with each other away from the prison setting did all of them a wealth of good.

"I want to tell you all the good stuff, Rosalinda began, but I have something else I need to say first. I don't want anyone to think it was easy for me to cut Ricardo off. It was really hard. Before my number was changed, I came so close to accepting the charges from him on numerous occasions. I fought a hard battle with myself to stay away from visiting him. I really cared about him. I probably would've eventually married him. But I know now that Ric is not the only one to blame for how bad things were going for us. I'm equally responsible."

"How's that?" Alexis asked.

"Ric and I were both pitiful creatures who didn't believe that we deserved love. I still have a soft spot for him despite his disrespect for me, but I truly have moved on. What Ric and I had wasn't love. In fact, it was rather sick. We simply fed off of each other's insecurities. But since I've learned to respect myself, I can now demand it from others. Now for the juicy part: Michael Hernandez. Who would have ever thought it? We are actually trying to build a solid personal relationship, starting with friendship."

Rosalinda couldn't stop smiling as she filled Alexis in on all the details.

As Marlene had been voted in as interim head of the church, she stood before the members of the church school class to give that which she hoped would be an arousing bible study. Although she'd continued to play her appointed role, it was mostly done from behind the scenes. On most weekends she was at the prison, but she'd kept up with her duties, as promised. In Jesse's absence, Marlene had filled the pulpit with a dynamic speaker every week since she'd been given control. The flock always left filled up to the brim after receiving no less than a five-course spiritual meal served up by the visiting pastors.

Marlene looked out over the study-group members. Seeing Myrna sitting out there caused her heart to palpitate. She hoped that her best friend wouldn't misconstrue her lesson study on forgiveness. Though she hadn't expected Myrna to attend her class, she was thrilled to see her among the church members. She was also ecstatic to have Keisha and Rosalinda present.

"Let me start my lesson off with a simple question. What does WWJD mean?"

"What would Jesus do?" someone responded.

"Exactly. What would Jesus do? That's a question every Christian should ask themselves before responding to situations that cross their life's path each day. How would Jesus react or respond? Let me give you an illustration. The story is told of a woman that was brought before Jesus by an angry mob, demanding that just punishment be administered under the law. The woman was accused of being caught in the very act of adultery. How many of us know this story?" Hands went up everywhere. "Any comments before I move on?"

"Now, I personally have a problem with that specific story," a young woman said. "If adultery was a sin punishable under the law, and she supposedly was caught in the very act, shouldn't both people involved be equally charged?"

"That's what I call a question! It's something for all of us to think about and ponder. The answer depends on how each individual feels about the law. Therefore, I'm not going to interject my opinion. We could stay stuck on that subject all day long. But we have to keep in mind that everyone is not going to feel the same way that you or I may feel. But to continue, Jesus was asked what should be done with her. If anyone knew if the charges were valid or not, Jesus knew. He responded to the mob with a soul-searching statement: 'He that is without sin among you, let him cast the first stone.' Then He bent down and started to write in the sand."

"Do we know what was written in the sand?" someone asked.

"What He wrote is not recorded in the bible. Whatever it was, it caused the crowd to slowly disperse. When only He and the woman remained, Jesus asked the woman, 'Where are those thine accusers? hath no man condemned you?'

"She responded: 'No man, Lord.'

" 'Neither do I condemn thee; go, and sin no more.'

"Wow! What a statement! He knew she was guilty. He knew justly that she should be punished under the law, but He showed mercy. 'Go, and sin no more.' John 8:1–11. What a loving and merciful Savior is Jesus, my Lord! Cloaked in those very words was also the spiritual act of forgiving. Forgiveness! Now that's another word for you, a word many of us don't fully understand. Let's explore that word together. Who can define for me the word *forgive?*"

"To pardon. To absolve," came the first response.

"To grant relief from," an elderly woman voiced.

"To give up resentment."

"Thank you. While *forgive* means all those things mentioned and more, *forgiving* means to allow room for error and weakness by one of many definitions. Error and weakness are both just signs of human frailties.

"Church, we've all done something we want to be forgiven for, and we've all had something done to us that needs to be forgiven. In forgiving others, we set our spirits free. It's a form of cleansing the soul. There are times when we need to seek forgiveness, even though we don't think we did anything wrong."

"Well, if we don't think we did anything wrong, why would we ask for forgiveness?" a church member inquired.

"The answer for me is this. It's not always about what we think we did or didn't do that's at issue. It's about what the person we're seeking forgiveness from is thinking. It's about what that person may feel regarding something we've said or done to them that caused pain and suffering. It may not have been our intention to inflict pain, but pain was nonetheless inflicted. No matter our intent, good or bad, we can't perceive how someone else is going to feel about the things we say or do. If someone else is affected badly by something we did or said, we need to seek forgiveness regardless of our intent. If we are affected badly by something someone did or said to us, we need to offer forgiveness regardless of what we think was their intent.

"That takes us back to the question of what would Jesus do? WWJD? In confronting life's numerous ups and downs, just ask yourself, what would Jesus do?"

Myrna raised her hand and Marlene acknowledged her immediately.

"In forgiving those who have hurt us, don't we have to heal from those wounds first before we're even capable of forgiveness?"

Knowing the question was centered on their particular situation, Marlene took a moment to ponder. "I could answer that by simply saying WWJD. But what if tomorrow never comes for us? Although we're promised eternal life, we're not promised tomorrow. But if we don't forgive today, how can we be assured of the blessed promise of eternal life. If we die tomorrow, without forgiving those we believe have harmed us in some way, how can we claim the promise of life after death? How can we claim the right to spend eternity in the glorious kingdom? The answer is a simple one. We can't."

"What do you do when a person hurts you so deeply, repeatedly?" another person asked.

"The Lord's prayer can be found in Matthew 6:9–13. Do these words from the Lord's prayer sound familiar? 'And forgive us our debts, as we forgive our debtors.' Also, in versus 14 and 15 of Matthew 6, he goes on to say, 'For if ye forgive men their trespasses, your heavenly Father will also forgive you: But if ye forgive not men their trespasses, neither will your Father forgive your trespasses.'

"When Peter asked the Lord how many times should we forgive, he also asked, 'Is seven times enough?' Peter's question can be found in Matthew 18:21. Can someone tell us what was the Lord's response?"

The hand of a young man waved wildly in the air until Marlene called upon him.

"In Matthew 18:22, the Lord answered this by saying seventy times seven. Also, on the cross, just before dying, Jesus said, 'Forgive them Father, for they know not what they do.' Luke 23:34." The young gentleman had responded with deep emotion.

"Exactly! Thanks for your input, kind sir. Now, ask yourself whose salvation is at stake here? Who's doing the hurting? Who's it on? But when we respond to that hurt in a retaliatory manner, we're guilty of putting our own salvation at risk. Forgiveness is not something we have the luxury of considering on a case-by-case basis. Forgiving is a requirement of God in order for us to seek forgiveness from the Father. There are no ifs, ands, or buts about it. God's law on forgiveness is not up for compromise.

"None of His laws are open to compromise," Marlene went on to say. "We either obey His law or we don't. Just remember that there are consequences in both choices. It's up to us individually to decide what path we want to choose. No one can decide our paths for us. We're the only living creatures that God gave the freedom of choice. There are times when I think we are the very ones that He should've kept the freedom of choice from. And to think that God's animals are the ones that are often referred to as dumb!"

Her comment drew a roar of laughter.

A hand went up from the center pew. "I have one more question, Sister Covington."

Marlene nodded her approval.

"When it seems that our hearts have been broken beyond repair, and when all hell breaks loose around us, in our homes and in our families, and we feel that we've done all we can do, what should we do next?"

"In the word of the good Brother Donnie McClurkin: 'Stand'."

Loud amens and hallelujahs came from all around the room.

"I want to thank you for your participation in the lesson study. I pray that we'll all leave here filled up with a dish of delightful food for thought. Before my final remarks, I want to give you a few things to consider: God loves us. God wants us to be with Him. God offers us a plan of salvation through Jesus. God wants us to work for and with Him. We are justified through Jesus. We are saved by grace, simply by believing. If we truly believe, we will confess this belief to all we come in contact with by the way we live. WWJD.

"My closing text and statement: Jesus left an example of how we should live and how we should act. We Christians are sinners saved by grace, confessing our love for the Savior through our interaction with mankind. A Christian should be Christ-like, a reflection of His love. Let us bow our heads for closing prayer."

CHAPTER EIGHTEEN

"How are you, Alexis? And how are things going with your parents' visit?"

"I'm fine, and our visit is going just great, R.J. What about you, how are you doing?"

"Okay. Been thinking about some of the things you said on your last few visits. I didn't realize how successful I'd been in isolating you from your family, even though it was my every intention to do so. I also know that was wrong of me. I was sure you were still calling them every chance you got. I didn't know you had stopped calling them altogether."

"Why did you want to do something like that in the first place? They've never done a thing to you. Our family was close, but after you and I got together . . . well, you know the rest."

"I knew they didn't like me, didn't trust me, and never thought I was good enough for you. Your father and brothers never tried to hide that fact. In paying them back for hating on me, I did everything I could to keep you away from them. I'm sorry. I only hope that one day I'll get to make it up to you. Have they been asking you a lot of questions about my whereabouts?"

"Get off the damn phone. You're way past your limit, dog," an inmate shouted at R.J.

Alexis grew frightened when she heard loud shouting in the background.

"I'm only two minutes into my conversation. I'll hang up when my time is up," R.J. shouted back.

"What's going on, R.J.? Are you having an argument with someone?"

"Calm down, baby. I can hear the anxiety in your voice. It's just some punk trying to control usage of the phone. He's next in line, but all the other phones are also in use. I don't know why he chose me to hassle. Just another frustrated loudmouth."

"Be careful, R.J. You know how easy fights get started in there. I hope he didn't hear the things you just said to me about him."

"It's okay, baby. You can't let these people in here intimidate you. I love you, Lexy. I'm looking forward to seeing you at the end of the week. It's tough not being able to hold you every night. I miss that so much."

"Me, too. The bed is so cold. A lot of times I fall asleep in the audio-visual room. The television or the music stays on all night when that happens. I can't even stand to listen to our favorite songs, watch our favorite programs, or special movies. I miss you, badly.

"I miss you, too, Lexy. Like crazy."

"Mama and Daddy being here isn't squashing my need for you to be here with me. To answer your earlier question, they've asked about you, but they're not pressing the issue. I believe they think you're staying away intentionally. They know you don't like them, either. I wish things were different between you and them."

"I'm going to work on that when I get out of here, Lexy."

"I need to ask you something, R.J."

"I'm listening."

"Have you been withholding any mail that my family sent to me?"

A few moments of silence answered the question for her.

"How could you do something like that? All this time I thought my parents didn't want to have any contact with me. I missed my youngest sister's wedding and the christening of her first child. Keeping my mail from me was an evil thing to do. I never thought you were capable of something so underhanded against my family and me. I don't know what to say."

"Would it help if I talked to them and apologized for those things?"

"It wouldn't hurt."

"I'll call and talk them to tomorrow. I promise you that, Lexy. There's not enough phone time left for me to speak with them now."

Alexis heard more yelling in the background. "What's all that noise about? It keeps getting louder and louder."

"Same guy, same scenario, baby. When my time is up, the phone will automatically go dead. That's how I know I haven't gone over. Partner knows the drill. I want to get back to talking about us before the time is up. There are a lot of things you and I need to discuss when you come out here again. I have so much to tell you, Lexy, so much that I've kept from you. So many things that I deeply regret. I promise to answer all your questions."

She couldn't believe her ears. It surprised her that he was talking about being up front with her. How many times had she begged him to do that very thing? "Are you serious? If so, I hope you really mean it when you say you're going to answer the questions I've been dying to have the answers to. There are so many things I need to know."

"Dead serious, baby. There are things you should know just in case I don't win the appeal. I wrote . . . ugh . . . damn, oh, my . . . God . . ."

"R.J., what's wrong? You sound like you're in pain." Nothing but silence answered her. "R.J., are you still there?" Close to hysteria, she muffled her screams with the pillow. She didn't want anyone to hear her crying out for fear they'd come running. "R.J.!"

Fear gripped her insides. Grasping the phone tightly, she listened intently. She only heard more shouting, loud cursing, and what sounded like echoes of several pairs of feet stampeding across the floor. Pressing the phone even closer to her ear, she listened for any signs that might tell her what was going down. The sounds of feet striking the floor were coming in clearer.

"Get someone down here, now!" she heard someone yell. "Holy hell, hurry. He's bleeding. . . ."

Suddenly, the phone line went dead, leaving Alexis in a state of panic. Something bad had happened—and she felt sure that it had happened to her husband. Someone was bleeding. Was it R.J.? She prayed hard that it wasn't her husband who was hurt.

After taking a few minutes to calm down, Alexis looked in her personal address book and came up with the main number to the prison switchboard. Her fingers trembled violently as she punched in the numbers. Her knuckles had already turned white, and she actually felt sick to her stomach. As she looked into the mirror on her dresser, she saw that her skin had even paled.

The inner fear she felt quadrupled when no one answered the switchboard. A melee of scenarios played in her head, but she couldn't imagine what would shut down the entire communication system. Something was wrong, terribly wrong.

It was late, she reasoned. Thinking R.J. might be trying to call her back, she hung up. She gave no thought to the call-waiting feature, which would've allowed her to receive another call even though she was on the phone.

The prison's phones continued to go unanswered for the next thirty minutes. Alexis's nerves had already been stretched to the absolute limit. She'd popped three five-milligram pills of Valium, but there hadn't been any calming effects thus far.

When Alexis finally did get through to the switchboard, she wasn't able to find out a single thing. R.J.'s counselor told her that he'd check to see that her husband was okay, but Alexis sensed that he already knew something—something that he couldn't or wouldn't share with her. The next call she placed was to R.J.'s attorney and longtime friend, Tom Goldstein.

Tearfully, Alexis explained to Tom what had happened.

"Stay calm, Alexis. I'll see what I can find out. But I have to warn you. I may not be able to get any decent information until normal business hours tomorrow. I'm sure everything is okay. If something really bad has happened, someone from there will be calling both you and me. Please call me back if you hear anything before I do. Try to get some rest. I know that this whole ordeal has been really tough on you."

"Not as tough as it is on R.J. Please call me as soon as you know something. I don't care what time it is. I can't imagine going back to sleep until I know that R.J. is okay."

"You got it."

"Thanks, Tom."

As she thought about it, Alexis realized that she had timed her parents' visit badly. Everything seemed to be coming down on her at once. All these bad things just kept on happening. And there didn't seem to be any relief in sight. She then thought of another big problem. How was she going to get away over the weekend for the next visit without arousing her parents' suspicion? She prayed that there would be a next visit.

Feeling the nerve medication taking hold, Alexis threw her bead back on the pillow. Moaning with despair, she felt her body fall limp. Responding to her body's urgent demand for sleep, she closed her tear-filled eyes.

Standing at the entrance to Marlene's home, looking like the ghost of Christmas past, Alexis embraced Marlene and then Keisha and Rosalinda. The four women entered Marlene's family room. With the exception of Marlene, they seated themselves on the gray leather sofa. Marlene sat in Jesse's favorite chair, the matching gray leather recliner.

"We're all deeply sorry for your loss, Alexis. When we heard about the incident on the news, they hadn't yet identified the person who'd been hurt. I was so scared that I immediately called Jesse's attorney to see what he knew. He called me back later and told me the name of the person who had been injured. It was then that I learned the wounds had been fatal. Major Townsend had no idea that I knew you. He was just letting me know that Jesse hadn't been involved in the incident. Rosalinda and Keisha came over here as soon as they heard about R.J. We've tried to call you to see about coming to you, but there wasn't an answer."

"I was actually on the phone with R.J. when it happened. That man stabbed him in the stomach while he was talking to me. Then I heard a lot of shouting and what sounded like scurrying feet. The line went dead a couple of minutes later. I didn't know exactly what was happening at the time, but I knew it was happening to my R.J. The last words I heard from him were 'Oh, my God.' Then the sounds of agonizing pain followed. I can't believe I won't ever hear his loving voice again."

Wailing like a wounded animal, Alexis collapsed in Keisha's arms, stunning her in the process. "It's okay, Alexis, we're all here for you. You don't have to go it alone," Keisha soothed, wiping the sweat from Alexis's forehead with a paper napkin.

While Marlene helped to get Alexis calmed down, Rosalinda hurried out to the kitchen to get a glass of cold water. Marlene placed a pillow behind Alexis's head and had her stretch out on the couch.

She was still pretty broken up when Rosalinda returned with the water. Her hard sobs had turned to soft moans of torment. It was easy to see that she was utterly distraught, but understandably so.

Suddenly Alexis jumped up from the sofa. Once again her haunted wailing filled the air. Like a rabid animal, she practically foamed at the mouth as she paced back and forth across the room. "This isn't supposed to happen to me. I'm the one who has it all: good looks, power, stocks, bonds, real-estate holdings, a yacht, a Rolls-Royce, a heralded position in society, more money than you could count in a lifetime. Tragedies like this don't befall people like us, rich people. We're invincible. Money helps keep all the bad things at bay. This is nothing but a cruel twist of fate," she mocked in her husband's voice.

Hysterical, Alexis began to laugh and cry at the same time. "Don't you know who I am?" she asked the others. "I'm Richard James Du Bois III. I'm a self-made man. I don't need anything or anyone. The entire world is my playground!"

Sobbing softly now, she threw her arms open wide and looked up to the ceiling. "None of what he said means anything. But that's what R.J. believed. He said those very words too many times for him not to have believed them. He said them so often that I also began to believe them. Lord, can You forgive me for believing in everything but You? For believing in false idols, for heeding unto the call of the unrighteous?"

Marlene walked up to Alexis and put her arm around her waist. "Come and sit down. You're wearing yourself out. You're also sweating profusely, ruining that lovely silk dress."

Determined to have her say, she forcefully pulled away from Marlene. One by one, Alexis pointed at all three women.

"Money is nothing. The three of you are much richer than I could ever be simply because money does not rule your world. It does not control your every move. It's not your God. If you know what I know, you won't ever let it become that to you. Don't let its green-with-the-color-of-envy greediness get inside of you and bleed you soulless. What can money do for me now? Give my husband a decent burial? Perhaps. At any rate, he won't know whether he's been buried in style or burnt to a crisp. I once heard that the dead know nothing. But if he's to burn in hell for all eternity, he'll surely know. Don't you think? Will money help him then? Does he have a ghost of a chance to get into heaven? I would say not. . . ."

Falling back down to the sofa, Alexis buried her head into the pillow to muffle the sound of her shrill screams. The thought of R.J. burning in hell was too much for her to bear.

The others could clearly see the last traces of her energy slowly draining right out of Alexis's body as her screams grew weaker and weaker.

Hurrying across the room, Marlene took both Keisha's and Rosalinda's hands. Using her free hand, Keisha took hold of Alexis's which had gone limp. While kneeling in front of the sofa, Marlene massaged Alexis's neck and back as she prayed. After asking God to bring mercy and solace to Alexis, she prayed for R.J.'s soul to find peace in the valley of the shadow of death.

Before closing, Marlene recited the 23rd Psalm.

For several moments, everyone just sat in silence. Alexis had stopped screaming and crying, but she still looked thoroughly distressed. When she stood up again, everyone braced for another emotional eruption.

Surprisingly cool and calm, she looked at each of her new friends. "I want to thank all of you for being such a comfort to me. If I never learn another thing in this life, I've learned that it's extremely important how you treat others. You never know when you might need the very person whose feelings you've trashed at one time or another. I need all of you. But I'm constantly reminded of when I first met you, when I didn't think I needed anyone or anything, of how I treated you, as if you were beneath me. I pray to never act and think that way again."

Alexis turned to Marlene. "As you've probably already guessed, we don't have a church home. In fact, we aren't involved in any type of ministry, period. Can you help me find someone to conduct the burial service? Perhaps someone at your church? I want to do this right, but I'm afraid I don't know how. You don't read about these sort of things in *Money Market.*"

Though she felt like breaking down, Marlene smiled instead. "You leave everything to me, Alexis. I just need you alongside me to tell me what services you want and at what cost."

Alexis nodded in agreement. "First off, I need a mortuary right away. The prison is awaiting word from me regarding the arrangements for the removal of R.J.'s remains." At the word *remains,* Alexis looked like she was going to crack again. The squaring of her shoulders was a visible gesture of willing herself to remain calm.

"Braxton's is a fine place to have your loved one," Marlene assured her. "I'll take you over there first thing in the morning. In the meantime, we can make the arrangements for the mortuary to transfer R.J. What about his family? Are you going to get any input from them?"

"R.J.'s an only child. Both parents are deceased. He's always been somewhat of a loner. I don't think R.J. has a single true-blue friend. When you set yourself aside from the world, or on top of it, this is what you can expect to happen. Too bad I'm finding it out so late, and alone. I thought we'd always be together, that we'd walk through all the sunsets in our golden years. Although I'm able to purchase the finest in funeral arrangements, I want to keep it simple. Very simple. The same way I hope to live the rest of my life. Wealth be damned!"

"Whatever your heart desires," Marlene said. "We'll be here to see you through to the very end of this sad occasion—and beyond."

Alexis chewed on her lower lip. "I've got a big problem, ladies. As you already know, my parents are here visiting, and they don't even know R.J. was in prison. And now I have to tell them that he's dead. They think he's away on business."

Alexis had once again managed to floor the others with another surprise from her cachet of secrets. It seemed that she had just as many secrets as she had accused her husband of having. It sounded like Victoria had nothing on either one of them in the way of secrets.

"Yes, I can see how that could be a problem. It's getting late. Where do they think you are at this hour of the evening?" Marlene asked.

"I told them I had an important matter to handle. They're not expecting me back until late. Marietta is entertaining them while I'm gone. She has taken them out to dinner and I heard them talking about seeing some of the nightspots in Hollywood. Marietta is another problem."

"Why do you say that?" Rosalinda asked.

"She doesn't know that R.J. has passed away, either. It's going to break her up terribly. She loves him like a son. To be honest, I couldn't handle her grief and mine at the same time."

"Wow! When you keep a secret, you seem to do it so well. Also, it seems to me that R.J. does have at least one true-blue friend: Marietta," Marlene offered.

"Alexis," Keisha interjected, "don't you think you should tell your parents everything? The only way you're going to keep your life simple is to settle all the complications of the past. I think you should pour your heart out to your family and let the chips fall where they may."

Marlene gave Keisha a look of admiration. For one so young, she had a lot of courage. Not enough to extricate herself from Zach, but more than enough to bravely fight her battle—and to help others fight theirs. "I agree with Keisha. They should be told. This tragedy is already on the news. It has probably hit the newspapers as well, especially the ones in the area you live in."

Alexis spun around on her heels. "Oh, no, the papers. I didn't think about the newspapers. Daddy loves to read it, front to back and all that's in the middle." She looked at her watch. "The paper has long since been delivered. I've got to get home. Marlene, I'll call you later on tonight. Give the mortuary my phone number so they can contact me for payment arrangements."

"Go ahead on home. I'll call them. Do you want them to go forward and pick R.J. up?"

"As soon as they can. Don't worry about the expense. I've got it covered. Good night, everyone. Thanks again."

Marlene watched from the doorway as Alexis ran to a flashy car that she hadn't seen before, a dark blue Jaguar convertible. It looked brand-new. As she pulled away, Marlene noticed that it didn't have any license plates on it. It *was* brand-new. She looked after the car until Alexis turned at the corner.

"And I've always thought of how good the rich have it, often wishing I had just a fraction of what they have. Alexis Du Boise is one wealthy woman. But the sister has got some serious issues," Rosalinda exclaimed. "I can't believe the number of secrets they both had."

Keisha shook her head. "I know what you mean. Money can't buy her beautiful behind a way out of this horrific tragedy. I'd hate to be in her shoes, especially having to face her parents with the truth of how they got what they have so much of. It probably won't be pretty."

Marlene came back into the room. "What's not going to be pretty?"

"Alexis facing her parents with the truth," Keisha responded.

"Her parents will embrace her, just like they did after she failed to stay in touch with them all these years. Nobody but Jesus can beat black folk in giving and forgiving," Marlene said. "We are definitely a forgiving people."

"I heard that!" Keisha remarked. "Even with all the forgiving we've done, I would've been one dead sister back in slavery time. If I'd had the opportunity to be in the kitchen, there would've been at least one dead family member a year. And I ain't talking about my family. I would've been growing my own oleander bushes. And you know how we like to cook with herbs and spices. Their food would've been doctored up really good! A slow death but a sure one."

"Ooh, Keisha Reed, you better hush your face, child," Marlene said, laughing along with Rosalinda. "All joking aside, we have to be here for that woman. She's going to need us."

Keisha scowled. "You got that right. But don't be surprised if she turns on us again. She hasn't really convinced herself to live like real people yet. It's going to be real hard for her to live simple. Hell, it would be hard for me, especially after having all the money she's used to."

Rosalinda couldn't help thinking about her mom, and how she couldn't bear to lose her. But she had to face the fact that her mother wasn't doing very well. Alexis's reality of losing a loved one could very soon become her own. "I'll do all I can to help her."

"I'm glad we're all going to do our part. We'll have to keep her and her family in prayer. I'd like for you both to help me with the funeral arrangements. We can start by calling Braxton's Mortuary."

Keisha and Rosalinda nodded in agreement.

The house was bathed in silence when Alexis returned home. Glad for the temporary reprieve, she went straight to her room and prepared herself for bed. Her courage had been high on the road home, but the closer she'd gotten, the more and more it had weakened. Telling her parents about R.J. wasn't something to which she looked forward. What would she say? How did she begin?

She looked into the mirror. As beautiful as she was, the sorrow in her eyes seemed to completely obliterate any loveliness. *Beauty is only skin-deep*, she'd been told as a child. *Pretty is as pretty does.* Now she knew why she hadn't been able to see the beauty about which people raved. Her despicable behavior had made her feel and look ugly. Most of the people who went on and on about her looks usually weren't around long enough to discover that her outer wardrobe hardly matched the obnoxious inner clothing in which her heart was cloaked. To change her outward appearance, she had to work extremely hard and change the inner workings of self. That was not to be an easy task, no matter how one looked at it.

Yet she vowed to do just that.

"Well, Mom and Dad, R.J. went to prison for embezzling money from his clients. And now he's dead, stabbed to death by another inmate."

She cringed at the sound of that. So would they. She would have to start from beginning to end, revealing so many lies in between. Even though she knew a lot of lies had been told, she didn't know the truth about a lot of things that had gone on in R.J.'s private world. It now seemed as if their whole lives had been lived as one big, vicious lie.

As grief-stricken as she was over R.J., she couldn't help thinking of the little problem with the gambling equipment in the secret room. Little problem? Hardly! How was she going to get it out of the house without getting herself into serious trouble?

She thought about talking with the chauffeur about it. She quickly figured out that that might be too risky. She even wondered if he might know about the illegal operation. She thought of all the hundreds of people he had driven to the house over the years. How could he not know? Someone in R.J.'s employ had to know. No one person could run a secret operation like that. She deeply regretted that she hadn't gotten the chance to ask R.J. about the gambling equipment. Still, she had to find a way to get rid of it without calling attention to herself, especially with R.J. dead. No one would believe that she hadn't been a part of the operation.

She thought about all the hundreds of men who'd visited R.J. in that room at one time or another, sure that some of them had to be his partners in crime. He didn't run that operation solo. It took a lot of work and physical bodies and brilliant but criminal minds to create and then secret a room like that. An illegal gambling casino with all the alluring trappings of Vegas, minus the showgirls.

R.J. was the only person who knew the truth about everything—and he had now taken it to his grave with him. The mystery wrapped around his life, as might be told in the autobiography of James Thomas Du Boise III, would never be completely solved, never have a happy ending.

The chimes on the alarm system rang, signaling that Marietta had returned home with her parents. While she hadn't expected them to be there when she'd gotten home, she still wished she had more time. But more time wasn't what she needed. Nothing short of a miracle would meet her needs.

Wearing dainty gold slippers and an elegant silk lounging gown, Alexis left the bedroom and went to the front of the house to greet her parents. As they met up in the hallway, she hugged both her mother and father.

"Did you two have a good time with Marietta? By the way, where is she?"

"She's out in the kitchen making coffee. You look mighty comfortable, Alexis. Your daddy and me are going to slip into something comfy, too. We'll see you and Marietta in the kitchen in just a few minutes."

"Okay. See you in a few. I'm eager to hear all about your wonderful evening." *Wish I were just as eager to tell you about mine.*

Slowly, thinking all the while, Alexis made her way to the kitchen. She could smell the wonderful scent of fresh-brewed coffee as she grew nearer.

When Alexis entered the room, Marietta was busy slicing the delicious-looking lemon pound cake she'd baked that morning.

"Good evening, missy." Marietta was in a cheerful mood. "Ready for a cup of coffee?"

"I'll get it." Marietta raised an eyebrow. "In fact, I'm going to serve everyone. Mama and Daddy are changing into nightclothes. Why don't you run out to your quarters and do the same?"

"Are you feeling okay, missy? You sure are acting strange."

Alexis smiled. "I'm fine. I know I've never offered to lift so much as a finger to help you around here, but that's all going to change." Marietta looked worried. "No, I can't do without you altogether. Your job is not at all in jeopardy." Alexis had read her employee's expression. "I'm going to need you a lot more than you think. Hurry and change so we can all have our coffee together." *Then I plan to fill you up with the most bitter-tasting truth of all time: death.*

Marietta looked relieved. She needed her job. "If I go out to my quarters and change, I know I won't want to come back. One look at that bed and I'll be a goner. I'm fine dressed just the way I am. I have no intention of being up too much longer, anyway."

"All right. Have a seat and let me wait on you for a change. Two sugars and a dash of cream, right, Marietta?"

"Right you are, missy."

Clara and Jacob came into the kitchen and took seats at the table. Alexis poured three more cups of coffee and served two of them to her parents. She then placed the cake-filled plate in the center of the table. Before sitting down, she grabbed the napkin holder off the counter, along with the third cup of coffee.

Several minutes slipped by while coffee and cake were consumed. The golden lemon pound cake was moist and delectable. Alexis saw how much Jacob enjoyed it by his expressions. Very few people could outdo Clara in the kitchen, but Marietta could hold her own.

Now, said a little voice inside Alexis's head. *Now is the time.*

"Momma and Daddy," she began, "I have so many things to tell you. Some of them are very unpleasant. I've not been completely honest with you about so much stuff."

"What's wrong, baby?" Clara asked. "You look so distressed."

Sensing private issues, Marietta got up. "I'm going to give you all your privacy."

"No, Marietta, you should hear this, too. Please stay."

Marietta sat back down when she heard the anguished plea in her employer's voice.

"First off, R.J. is not away on business—"

"We already figured out that much," Jacob interjected. "Baby, we know we're not R.J.'s favorite people. We're just glad that he afforded us this time to spend with you. Don't worry about it. We understand."

"No, you don't. R.J. is in prison, but he recently escaped the dark caverns of hell."

"Escaped!" Marietta shouted. "What are you talking about, missy?"

"He has escaped from hell. He's at peace now. I hope. R.J. was killed by another inmate."

Dead silence swooped down around the occupants of the room and covered them like a blanket threatening to smother. Looks of disbelief passed between the others. The desire to fall apart, which would keep Alexis from further explanations, tugged viciously at her resolve to remain strong. Through a moment of silent prayer, she was able to hang tough.

Piercing the air, shrill and sorrowful, Marietta's screams shattered the unrelenting stillness while slicing through Alexis's soul. R.J. was the baby boy Marietta had never had. He and Alexis were like her family. The loss was costly for her.

Looking startled, Alexis got up from her chair and put comforting arms around Marietta, who was now sobbing uncontrollably.

Clara and Jacob sat stock-still in stony silence. Feeling powerless, Jacob covered his wife's hand with his own. For all the bad blood between him and his son-in-law, he would've never wanted something like this to happen to him. Although he couldn't help wondering which of R.J.'s hustles or scams had landed him in prison and then gotten him killed, he wouldn't think of questioning his daughter about it at a time like this. The tragedy that had befallen his daughter's life made him tremble.

Clara's tears finally came, but they were for her daughter. Alexis's unyielding grief was deeply etched in her lovely face. Clara had gotten along fine with R.J., but after a period of time, she had grown to dislike him for alienating her daughter from her family. She was certain that he had purposely orchestrated Alexis's long absences from her family home.

Once everyone gained some semblance of control, Alexis told her parents and Marietta the whole story surrounding R.J.'s death, as she knew it, from the beginning to the bitter ending. As she began to break down, moaning with grief, Alexis found comfort in Jacob's arms as he held her tight. Emotions ran high until the wee hours of the morning, when everyone separated in hopes of getting some sleep to preserve strength for that which was yet to come.

Just as an emotionally exhausted Alexis slipped between the sheets, a gentle knock came on the bedroom door. Marietta entered upon Alexis's soft command.

Crossing the room, she sat down on the side of Alexis's bed and took her hand. "I want you to know that I'm so proud of you. It took a lot of courage to come clean with your parents. I'm sorry things turned out this way for you. I know how much you love R.J. This is a deep loss for us all, especially for you, my dear. I couldn't take this any harder if he'd been my very own. May God grant him peace in the hereafter. I also slipped in here to tell you I love you. I'll be here as long as you want and need me." She kissed Alexis's forehead. "Get some rest now, missy. The storms of troubled times aren't over yet. But soon, and very soon. Good night."

"I know. I still haven't told my parents everything about my life with R.J. But I think they've had enough unpleasantness for now. There's so much more to tell, but I'm not sure it really matters anymore. With R.J. gone, it somehow seems pointless to bring these troubling things to the forefront. If I could just make peace with these truths for myself, I might not need to go any further than that."

"You can make peace with anything, but you need to start by making peace with the heavenly Father, and then with yourself, for yourself. The rest will follow."

Alexis looked deeply troubled. "I want to ask you something. Did you ever notice anything out of the ordinary going on around here?"

"Can you be more specific?"

"Did you ever get the sense that something just wasn't quite as it should be in this house? That something more was going on around here, more than what met the eye?"

"In my line of work, I learned a long time ago to keep my eyes focused on my duties, and to keep my big mouth shut. 'Ask me no questions—and I'll tell you no lies' became the motto that I quickly adopted. That's the only way to play it safe."

"In reading between the lines of your comments, it seems to me that you did know something unusual was happening around here. How did I miss so much, so much of what was obviously going on right under my nose?"

"Missy, just be glad that you did. When you don't know anything, you can't talk about it if asked. There are times when ignorance is bliss. This is one of those times. If I were you, I would stop trying to figure it out. The answers are no longer available to you. I hope you get my meaning. The answers can't be obtained without bringing a heap of more trouble to yourself."

Alexis embraced her employee. "Thank you. I hope you won't ever leave me. I do need you, Marietta. I promise to be more considerate of you from now on. I've taken you for granted. That's just another of my many crosses to bear."

"Not to worry, missy. Just remember that there's no rainbow in the absence of rain."

"Thanks again for such inspiring words of wisdom."

With an even deeper understanding reached between them, Marietta left Alexis alone with her grief and her troubled thoughts—thoughts that would leave her sleepless for many nights to come.

Spiritually awakening thoughts.

Marlene drummed her fingers on the dashboard of her car. With the window down, she heard the distinct sounds of nightfall. She hadn't seen any desert creatures, but she could hear them. It was a different sound out here in the desert, much different from the wailing police and ambulance sirens and the fast-moving cars heard in the city. Blanketed with smothering heat, the desert air was hot and muggy, even in the absence of the burning sun. Marlene would've been frightened to be out here alone if she hadn't known she was covered with the blood of the Lamb.

When her thoughts turned to Alexis, she remembered her request, after she'd told her Jesse was coming home in a couple of days. *Please ask Reverend Jesse if he will conduct R.J.'s funeral in place of Reverend Robinson. That is, if he gets out in time.*

It was close to midnight when Jesse came through the prison gates. Seated in her car, where she'd fixed her sight on the prison entrance, Marlene threw the door open and ran to her husband as fast as her legs could carry her.

Caught up in the emotional release of his first taste of freedom, Jesse swept Marlene up into his arms and swung her around. His lips connected with hers in a fiery burst of passion and heartfelt emotion. "Oh, Marlene," he cried, "we're finally back together." He squeezed her tightly. "It feels so good to hold my wildflower without restrictions. There's no one out here to dictate to me the amount of affection I can shower my wife with. Ah, listen to the beautiful sounds of the desert. This very moment is like heaven right here on earth for me."

"Jesse, you're free. Free at last! Thank you, Jesus."

Unable to contain his joy, Jesse knelt down and kissed the ground. Drawing Marlene down to her knees, he held on to her hand as he led them in a prayer of thanksgiving. Neither of them could dam up their tears for another moment, so they allowed the floodgates to open. Much like Jesse had, the water immediately rushed to freedom.

In the same moment they both said amen, Jesse brought Marlene back into his arms. They kissed each other as if there might not be a tomorrow. Alexis came to mind again as Marlene held onto her beloved husband. While she and Jesse had received a second chance at love and happiness, Alexis hadn't even gotten a chance to kiss her R.J. again—and tomorrow they were to bury him.

"We'd better get going, Jesse. It's very late."

He smiled. "Yeah, but we have no curfew ruling our lives. No more distance between us. That's what I'm talking about!" He grew somber. "Mar, I have to say this, and then I'm going to move on. I was sorely disappointed in how you handled this thing about Malcolm being involved in the crime I was charged with. I'm still having a hard time with it, but I know in my heart that we can get past it. I keep it in constant prayer. But I think my mission for being in prison was accomplished. I'm not sure it would've been had I not been in that place. I just don't know."

He hugged her gently. "However, we're both going to have to take responsibility for how we handle Malcolm from here on in. I promise to be there for you, and I need you to be there for me. We can't let Malcolm play us against one another ever again. Do you think where our son is concerned we can get on the same page and stay there?"

"I know that we can. And I know it's going to take some time for you to fully forgive me, but I'm a very patient woman."

He grinned. "That you are! You've certainly proven that through this ordeal. Patience is a virtue, and you are one virtuous woman."

She kissed him hard on the mouth. "You're not so bad yourself. Job would be proud of the patience you've shown through all this. I know the heavenly Father is proud."

"Let's go home, wildflower."

Seated in the car, Jesse reached across the seat and hugged and kissed Marlene, as if he just couldn't get enough of her. "By the way, where is Malcolm? With it being so late why didn't he drive way out here with you?"

She winked at him. "No Malcolm tonight! This night belongs to us. We have to be totally alone for what I have in mind for you as a welcome-home present. Okay, Reverend Jesse?"

"Okay, Mrs. Reverend Jesse!"

CHAPTER NINETEEN

The First Tabernacle Church was filled to capacity. Marlene had asked everyone in the congregation to come out and support Alexis during this difficult time in her life, even though they didn't know her. As she looked around the church, she saw several other mourners. Many of them were white men and women. They all looked rather well-to-do—and out of place. So, it seemed to her that R.J. did have a few friends. Whether they were true-blue or not, she didn't know, but she was glad they'd come to pay their last respects to a fallen comrade. In her opinion, Alexis also needed to see that there were indeed people who seemed to care about her husband. She hoped it would bring her every comfort.

Jesse stood proudly as he began the service by leading everyone in prayer. This was one funeral service over which he had labored long and hard during his preparation. He had been the one to administer the last prayer that R.J. would ever hear in this life. What had happened that unforgettable day in the prison still haunted Jesse.

The events that had led up to R.J.'s death had been downright chilling. It had caused Jesse to think even harder about his own mortality. Seeing a man lying there in a pool of his own blood had had a profound effect on Jesse that day. It had changed him in many ways. The nightmares that he'd had following R.J.'s murder were no less morbid than the actual scene itself. Jesse was glad that he and R.J. had talked about the Lord, and that R.J. had decided he'd needed to make a definite change in his life.

While he hadn't accepted the idea of religion as a whole, R.J. had believed in God, and he'd also told Jesse that he wanted to receive Him as his Lord and Savior. However, he hadn't believed in the goings-on of the church. He'd detested what he thought the church stood for in today's world. He'd seen it as big business and had referred to a handful of the television preachers as educated pimps.

When Jesse had learned that R.J. was begging to see him, the guards couldn't get him down to the infirmary fast enough. He'd been so glad that R.J. wanted to see him, of all people. Seated at R.J.'s bedside, Jesse had watched R.J. defy death as he told Jesse many things. Jesse had thanked God for not allowing R.J. to be alone in this hour of darkness, for allowing R.J. the time to share his burdens. Almost in the same moment that Jesse had finished praying for R.J.'s salvation, while gripping Jesse's hand tightly, Richard James Du Boise had succumbed to his sunset.

Jesse's mission had been made abundantly clear.

Still ringing in Jesse's ear was R.J.'s last whispered request, while he'd lain there dying, struggling to take each breath. While Jesse had promised R.J. to fulfill his whispered request, he knew that it would be a painful thing for R.J.'s widow. Still, a promise was a promise, one that he had to keep. One that he hoped would eventually bring Alexis comfort.

Jesse opened his bible and began to read 1 Thessalonians 4:13–18. " 'But I would not have you to be ignorant, brethren, concerning them which are asleep, that ye sorrow not, even as others which have no hope. For if we believe that Jesus died and rose again, even so them also which sleep in Jesus will God bring with him. For this we say unto by the word of the Lord, that we which are alive and remain unto the coming of the Lord shall not prevent them which are asleep. For the Lord himself shall descend from heaven with a shout, with the voice of the archangel, and with the trump of God: and the dead in Christ shall rise first: Then we which are alive and remain shall be caught up together with them in the clouds, to meet the Lord in the air: and so shall we ever be with the Lord. Wherefore comfort one another with these words.' "

With deep compassion awash in his eyes, Jesse looked at Alexis.

Then his warm gaze encompassed his wife, who sat next to Alexis, holding her hand.

His eyes returned to the bible. "Ecclesiastes 3:1 makes a simple but very understandable statement about life. 'To every thing there is a season, and a time to every purpose under the heaven.' Solomon further states that 'there's a time to be born, and a time to die.'

"We've come together to put to rest Richard James Du Boise. I personally knew him but a little while, and on that I can reflect. Some knew him longer, better, and on that they can reflect. But when all is said and done—the good, the bad, and the sometimes ugly things in his life—the final saying is up to God, and God knew him best. Our paths crossed under strange circumstances, but just as God would have it be, and for a purpose. We came from different areas, different backgrounds, different walks of life, but we met in a common place, a place where it matters little where you came from or how you got there. The truth of the matter is that you're there for whatever reason God saw fit. Most of you know what I'm talking about."

Before continuing, Jesse waited until the amens and hallelujahs were all said.

"Richard, or let me say, R.J. and I met as guests of this great state of California. Let me break it down a little further for those of you that don't know. R.J. and I found ourselves incarcerated for whatever reason—good, bad, justly, unjustly. And for whatever reason doesn't really matter now; what matters is that we met. Brethren, God knows all, from the beginning to the very end. And in His infinite wisdom, He chose that Richard James Du Boise's path and my path should cross at a preappointed time in our walks along this road we call life. God set it up! It was in His plan! Sure wasn't in mine. Never crossed my mind that I'd ever be arrested, let alone be in prison as an inmate. But God knows best!"

Jesse's emotions were staring to show. For several minutes he paced back and forth across the pulpit before returning to the rostrum. He had regained control.

"If anything good came out of my being incarcerated, justly or unjustly, the good was meeting R.J. and having the privilege to introduce him to my cell mate, J.C. You see, Jesus Christ promised to be with me always. R.J. and J.C. were cell mates, too; R.J. didn't know it, though. It was my privilege and my duty as a child of God to let Richard James

Du Boise know that he was loved by someone who would love him regardless of what he may have done and would be with him through thick and thin. I'm talking about Jesus, y'all. He's the giver of life and holds the key to the gates of hell. He's alpha and omega! He's the bright and morning star! He's the great I am! And He was my cell mate, and R.J.'s, too. Not wanting to tarry too long, I'll quickly move on."

Jesse looked at Alexis again. Knowing he was about to stun her something good, his eyes apologized for what his next comments were to be.

"Richard, by his own confession, was a thief. And the law caught up with him."

As Jesse had expected, Alexis's gasp was an audible one.

"I told him of another thief, a thief that stole heaven. No, let me rephrase that. I told him of a thief who, when dying on a cross next to Jesus, looked over and simply said, 'Lord, remember me. Amen! He said, 'Lord, remember me when you come into your kingdom!' You know the rest. Jesus gave him the promise of eternal life and a place in his kingdom, even as He himself was dying on a cross for humanity. So, he didn't steal heaven. It was freely given.

" 'For by grace are ye saved through faith; and that not of yourselves: it is a gift of God.' Ephesians 2:8.

"I want to tell you here today that there are many thieves who are given heaven. R.J. was given heaven. And that's the good news. His life was taken while incarcerated, but he received freely the blessed hope of eternal life. He made his commitment while on his cross. Let us mourn his passing, but let us more so rejoice in his decision to accept and follow Jesus Christ. Let us bow our heads and pray."

When the casket was opened for one last viewing, Alexis nearly fainted. With Marlene on one side and Jacob on the other, they held her steady while walking her the few feet to where her husband lay still in death. It was Alexis's desire to take one last look at Richard James, who appeared to be only asleep. He was dressed in a fine charcoal gray Brooks Brothers suit; the fashion statement Alexis had chosen for him was typical of the elegant ones R.J. had made throughout his life. Though deceased, R.J. was still matching from head to toe: a charcoal gray suit, white shirt, gray-and-powder blue silk tie, dove gray casket, sky-blue satin pillow.

Alexis swallowed the screams in her throat as she looked down on her husband. Even in death he was handsome. She reached out and touched his hair, surprised to find out that it felt so soft, more surprised that she hadn't ever noticed the silver at the temples. She'd never touched a dead person before, but her hands couldn't be stilled as they touched his face and stroked his fingers. He was so stony and cold. The cool marble feel of him nearly paralyzed her on the spot. She had to bite back another scream as she thought about how his delicious warmth had heated her anatomy up during the night and so often in the early morning hours.

She saw that there were no stress lines in his face. He appeared peaceful. She was grateful for that. She could only guess that the last moments of his life had to have been extremely stressful. The thought of what a horrible death he had suffered made her tremble all over.

The desire to kiss R.J. was so much stronger than her weak will. Perhaps her kiss would awaken her handsome prince. Bending her head, she kissed the lips that used to bring her such infinite pleasure, lips that would kiss hers no more. Unchecked, her tears ran down her face, splashing onto his. When the makeup on his face smeared from the wetness of her tears, her body shook with a tormenting intensity. His name repeatedly arose in her throat, but she gulped it back down each time. The agonizing urge to call out his name nearly took her breath away.

The funerals of her maternal grandparents had been the only ones she'd ever attended, but she'd been very young back then. Clearly, she remembered the mournful wailing and moaning on both occasions. She wasn't going to do that. She had to think of this service as a celebration, as his going home, just as Marlene had suggested to her.

This tragic occasion called for her to show dignity at the highest level.

She couldn't help remembering that a couple of her mother's sisters had turned their parents' funerals into screaming fiascoes. One sister who had done absolutely nothing for their parents had screamed the loudest at both services. She remembered the others talking about what guilt could do to a person during and after a funeral.

Guilt wasn't something she felt in this instance. Had it been one of her parents lying there in that casket, culpability would've brought her down to her knees, too. Thank God she'd made amends before it could come to that. Quietly, she vowed never again to let the distant screams of silence come between them.

While there was no love lost between R.J. and her parents, they were deeply distressed over his death. Alexis had told them that she wouldn't mind if they didn't want to attend the funeral, but both of her parents had insisted on seeing her through to the end. They would never leave her at a time like this.

Her other family members had also offered to come to California, but she'd declined their gracious overture of support. She had more than enough to deal with and so much more that was yet to come. R.J.'s funeral was hardly the end of her troubled times.

Rosalinda looked totally shocked when Michael Hernandez came up beside her and took hold of her arm as they filed out of the church. Not daring to look him in the face, she kept her eyes trained forward. "Why are you here?" she whispered to him.

"I came to support you," he whispered back.

"How did you know where I was?"

"I called your job. I got lucky when one of your coworkers fell prey to my wily charm. Before she knew what had happened, I'd already coerced her into revealing your whereabouts." He grinned, showing off his beautiful white teeth.

"Mary Lou," she said, more to herself than to him. "The modern day Chatty Kathy of the office." The woman talked on and on, hardly ever coming up for air.

Rosalinda clearly remembered telling Mary Lou all the details about the funeral she had to attend. But never in her wildest dreams had she thought it would somehow be relayed to Michael Hernandez. Complicated was turning into downright complex.

"Sounds like you missed your calling, Detective Hernandez."

"Not at all. You can't be in my line of work without having some of the skills that good detectives possess. Intuition for sure. Pleased to see me, Rosalinda?"

"What's your intuition telling you, Michael?"

A roar of thunder kept him from responding. Rosalinda practically leaped into his arms when the offensive sound reached her ears. Silently, he prayed for more rolling thunder.

Keisha had to smile. Seeing Rosalinda with Hernandez did her heart good. Maybe there was hope for her yet, the hope that Zach would one day be released and begin treating her the way she deserved. Her love for Zach was the one thing in her life over which she had no control. But she finally had a game plan where her relationship with him was concerned. Loving him didn't mean she had to live the rest of her life in sorrow. She had laid the law down to him. Zach could accept the changes in her and work on himself or go on with his life without her in it.

Her kids deserved better, and so did she. She and the kids were going to have the kind of life they deserved. True to his word, Zach had turned over to her all the money he had saved in the bank, and he'd also enrolled in a couple of classes. In turn, she'd given back Tammy the money that she'd sent Zach out of the kindness of her big heart. She never saw Celeste again.

R.J.'s untimely death seemed to have everyone rethinking his or her life's goals.

During the internment Alexis wept openly, bitterly, yet she was careful not to lose total control. R.J. wouldn't want that. He had taught her to control her emotions, had taught her not to cry over spilled milk. Only it wasn't milk that had been spilled. Some degenerate had spilled R.J.'s blood, needlessly so. No phone call could've been so important, unless it had been a matter of life and death. On second thought, it had become a matter of life and death—resulting in murder, resulting in the death of her husband.

The death of her beloved husband had occurred over something as insignificant as a lousy phone call. *God, please help those of us who are left to live in this cruel, cold world.*

Operating under her very own power, Alexis walked up and laid a single red rose atop the now-closed dove gray casket. Her parents, Marietta, and her three newfound friends followed suit by placing long-stemmed white roses next to the red one. Forgetting dignity for a few brief moments, Alexis fell to her knees. It was all she could do to keep from throwing herself across the top of the casket as it was slowly lowered into the darkened depths of the unknown.

Still on her knees, moaning and groaning, she rocked herself back and forth, doing her very best to quiet the frenzied screams stuck in her throat. “Lord,” she murmured, “Lord, R.J. now has Your saving grace. And I also need Your saving grace. Lord, I need You.”

Unable to remain in control for another second, Alexis released the torrent of screams that she'd held back for far too long. This wasn't about what R.J. wanted. This was about what Alexis wanted, what she had to do . . . about what Alexis needed to do.

And right now Alexis wanted and needed to scream at the top of her lungs. . . .

Every food imaginable was served at the repast. The women of First Tabernacle had taken on the task without so much as a hint from Marlene. Although Marlene had asked the church members to attend the funeral, she hadn't asked for any further assistance. She had intended to cook the food herself, before she got a call from one of the deaconesses telling her that the various church groups were coming together in planning, cooking, and serving all the people who attended the repast.

Marlene thoroughly enjoyed watching Alexis and her upscale white friends tackling the soul food, especially the barbecued ribs and chicken. The collard greens, black-eyed peas, and corn bread were cooked the way only black folk knew how to prepare them.

Marlene, Rosalinda, and Keisha had a good laugh at one puritanical-looking woman. Giving no thought to her expensive silk suit, the sophisticated woman was actually licking her fingers clean of the barbecue sauce.

Happy with Jesse's sermon for her husband, Alexis approached him. Because she hadn't officially met him, she felt a little timid stepping up to what R.J. would've referred to as “a man of the cloth.”

“Reverend Jesse,” she said softly.

He turned around and smiled. As his wife had said to him many times, Alexis Du Boise was one beautiful woman.

“Hello, Mrs. Du Boise. It's a pleasure meeting you face-to-face. I've seen you many times in the visiting room at the prison, but I never got the opportunity to make your acquaintance. I'm happy to see how well you're holding up. R.J. would be proud."

"Thank you. It's been hard, but I've done my best. I came over to thank you for such an inspiring message. R.J. would've been pleased with everything. If it were possible, I'm sure he'd be smiling down on us."

"I'm sure. I was with your husband when he passed on from this life. In fact, he was holding on to my hand when he took his last breath."

That remark brought burning tears to her eyes. "I'm glad he had someone to hold onto. That must have been a horrible time for him."

"Maybe it wasn't as bad as you might think. He was at peace with himself. And he'd made peace with his Maker. Don't worry about him. He's at rest now."

Alexis felt like crying out loud but she held back. She wouldn't be able to find out what she needed to know if she fell apart. "Are you saying R.J. talked to you about God?"

"Yes, ma'am. But he talked even more about the modern-day church, and what he didn't like about it." Jesse chuckled.

"Uh-oh, it sounds like you got an earful. He did have issues with the church. Many issues, especially about money. He could go on and on about that."

Jesse grinned. "He did go on and on. R.J. spent his last days searching for truth. He asked me so many questions. He was certainly curious about the man in power, the man upstairs. R.J.'s going to be just fine."

"In all his searching, I can't help wondering if he'd asked to be forgiven. After all, he was responsible for so much wrongdoing in his life."

"I don't know all that has taken place with R.J. in this life, but I do know about God and His divine forgiveness. I'll tell you what I told R.J. The price was paid to save mankind at the cross. I believe he came to understand that."

"Do you think he asked for forgiveness, Reverend Jesse?"

Marlene walked up and took her husband's hand. "I see you two have already met. Normally Jesse would meet with the family before performing a funeral service, but time hadn't allowed for that."

Jesse was glad for Marlene's appearance. There were things he didn't want to get into with Alexis. He'd made R.J. promises about certain things, and he had to keep them. Besides, Alexis wasn't ready to receive the secrets Jesse knew about R.J. At least, not yet.

"We were blessed to have him at all. The fact that he was released only last evening is amazing in itself. Was Reverend Clay Robinson upset when you told him what I wanted to do about the services, Marlene?"

"Not at all, Alexis. He was glad to have Jesse take over the service. We have stretched that brother to the max over the past few months. He was eager to have Jesse do it. He knew your husband and Jesse were in the same prison."

"Excuse me, ladies," Jesse interjected. "I'm being summoned by the head deacon. Mrs. Du Boise, we will meet again. I'm sure of it."

"Thank you, Reverend. Before we leave, I'd love you to meet my parents. We're sitting at the receiving table."

"I'll make it a point to drop by. Until later, Mrs. Du Boise. Mrs. Covington, I'll definitely see you later." He winked at Marlene as he walked off. That made Marlene blush.

Alexis took Marlene's hand. She then asked Rosalinda and Alexis to come over and join hands with them. "I know what you all were laughing about earlier, and you should be ashamed of yourselves," Alexis teased. "No so long ago, I wouldn't have dared to eat soul food around R.J.'s friends and acquaintances. Even though I never liked to hang out with them, I'm glad to see that they cared enough about R.J. to attend his funeral. He would be very pleased about the entire service. Everything was wonderful. Jesse preached a dynamic sermon."

"We're glad that you're pleased with everything," Keisha said.

Alexis embraced the three women for a brief moment. "I've come to love each one of you. I can't thank you enough for being my friends, for sticking in there even when I was at my worst. I have to smile as I think how things have turned out for every one of you. Marlene, you've got your husband back home. I'm so happy for that, happy that you didn't have to go through the entire appeal process, thrilled to know that Malcolm wasn't involved."

Turning to Keisha, Alexis squeezed her hand. "Who would've thought that we'd ever become friends? I'll never forget our first encounter. I'm sure you won't, either. It probably would've been easier for you to pull my hair out than for you to be nice to me."

Everyone laughed at that. Alexis didn't know how close her statement was to the truth. Keisha wanted very much to pull her hair out the first day they'd met outside the prison.

"I'm also glad you've come to terms with the relationship between yourself and Zach. It takes a lot of courage to hang in there. I just hope Zach keeps all the promises he's made to you."

"I'm sure he will. He never again wants to come that close to losing me. No more placing singles ads in the newspapers for him. Instead of continuing to lie about being on a waiting list for school, he's really working hard in the classes he finally signed up for. Zanari's sudden illness also made him start looking at things differently. Your husband's death really shook him up, more than anyone can know. If Tammy and I hadn't busted him the way we did, I don't know what would've happened to our relationship. Now that everything is out in the open, we should be okay."

"I hope so." Alexis pulled Rosalinda close to her. "And you, I can't believe what's happened to you. At long last, you have found someone who genuinely cares for you. Michael seems like a wonderful man. Be happy. You deserve it."

Rosalinda giggled softly. "I know that now. Thanks to all of you, I have survived. My mom is also doing so much better. Ricardo isn't writing to me or trying to call me anymore. Michael and I are taking our relationship extremely slow. Things are really coming up roses for me, finally. What about you, Alexis? Have you decided what you're going to do?"

Alexis smiled gently. "Not really, Rosalinda. It's still too soon. As for my personal outcome, I'm finding myself. I won't ever again make the mistake of allowing myself to be defined by another's idea of what they think I should be. I don't think I can ever love again, not way the way I love R.J. He'll always be in my heart. I have a lot of healing to do yet. I especially have to learn how to deal with the way he died."

"How long are your parents going to be here?" Keisha asked.

"I'm not sure. They want me to move back home. Back to New Orleans? Or stay in California? Haven't come to any conclusion on that one. But I think it will be hard for me to leave my new friends. I like hanging out with you all. It's kind of nice being a down-to-earth homegirl again. I haven't forgotten the days when I lived among the real people of this world."

Alexis looped her arm through Marlene's. "I want you to come over and meet my parents before we leave. Can you spare a moment?"

"I can spare a few moments. I wouldn't miss meeting your parents for anything. Have you introduced Keisha and Rosalinda to them?"

Alexis smiled at the two younger women. "Yes, I have. Both of them were very sweet to my mom and dad. You guys have really matured under Marlene's direction. You've changed so much."

"We've all changed, Alexis. Because we all had a lot of changing to do," Marlene quipped. "I think you've changed more than any of us, Alexis."

"I think you're right. You all had less to do. I needed a major overhaul in every aspect of my life. While the changes in me have been phenomenal, I have a lot more changing to do."

The four friends laughed as they embraced one another. After a few minutes more of emotional spillage, the foursome walked over to where Alexis's parents were seated. Jesse had already joined them and was in the process of making his acquaintance with the Gautiers.

Alexis undressed and slipped into a champagne-colored silk gown and robe.

Inside of R.J.'s walk-in closet, she looked at all the dozens and dozens of designer suits and sport jackets hanging neatly on wooden hangers. Crisp shirts had been hung and sorted by style, color, and sleeve length. Highly polished boots and shoes rested on a large shoe stand. Hundreds of silk ties were neatly placed on tie racks. The matching silk handkerchiefs were stacked by color in clear plastic containers. Suspenders, socks, and silk underwear occupied another set of clear containers.

Charity was her first thought. Then Marlene's church came to mind. Dividing them evenly among the two entities was her final conclusion.

As she walked down the hallway toward the kitchen, something compelled her to the secret room. Returning to her bedroom, she retrieved the keys from the top dresser drawer and went back to the other room.

When she inserted the key, the door came open, even before she'd released the lock. Much to her shock, the room hidden behind the wall was in plain view, but completely emptied. All of the gaming machines had been removed, but the other furnishings had been left untouched.

After taking a quick inventory of what she remembered as having been there, she realized that nothing was missing but the gaming tables. The pool table, pinball, and other arcade-style machines remained in the outer room. All the fine black artwork still hung on the walls in both of the rooms. The expensive audio-visual equipment was still in place.

Alexis actually felt relieved to see the illegal stuff gone, until it dawned her that someone else had keys to her home. That unnerved her considerably. But then she decided that changing the locks was an easy enough remedy. The person or persons responsible had taken exactly that for which they'd come. They could've wiped her out had that been their intention. With everyone at the funeral, they would have had plenty of time to empty the entire house.

As she stepped farther back into the secret room, she saw a door she hadn't noticed before. Before fumbling with the keys to see which one fit, she turned the knob, and this door also came open. Behind the entry was a long hallway. Though somewhat fearful, she followed the carpeted passage and discovered that it led out to the unused set of garages at the back of the property. So this was how entry was gained to the secret room, she mused.

She breathed a deep sigh of relief. The problem of how to get the equipment out of the house had been solved. Thinking that she'd never have any peace or security within herself, at least while living in this house, she made the snap decision to list the property for sale.

Alexis had just made it to her bedroom when a knock came on the door. She tightened the belt on her robe as she walked across the room. It was her mother who stood there. Alexis embraced Clara with warmth, glad that she had the comfort of human contact. "Do you and Daddy need something, Momma?"

"No, but we thought you might be needing something. Care to join us in the kitchen for a cup of coffee? Marietta has it already made."

Alexis smiled. "I think I'd like that. Let me put my slippers back on."

Clara waited until her daughter slipped her tiny feet into satin slippers that matched the silk gown and robe she wore. Hand in hand, daughter and mother made their way into the kitchen, where Jacob and Marietta awaited their arrival.

* * *

A couple of weeks had already passed since R.J.'s funeral. As Alexis sat in her living room, her thoughts were riddled with guilt and deep regret. Her parents had returned home. They'd begged her to join them up until the last second before they'd boarded the plane at LAX.

Marietta had decided to take a much-deserved and needed vacation to the Caribbean. She had invited her employer, but Alexis had thought it was much too soon for travel excursions. Besides, there was a lot of business that had yet to be wrapped up before she could think of leaving town. Insurance matters were still pending since R.J. had been killed while institutionalized for a criminal act. Supposedly, there was a clause that prevented payment in the event an inmate met with his demise while incarcerated.

Alexis's grief hadn't eased one bit. She missed R.J. like crazy, missed the times that would be no more. Although she hadn't come to any final conclusions about her personal life, she desired to live a more modest lifestyle. With the nice chunk of money she would receive from the sale of the house, she planned to purchase a reasonably priced town house or condo. The days of living high on the hog were over for her, but she had no thoughts of totally depriving herself of the many good things life had to offer. R.J. wouldn't want her to do without. He'd already paid the ultimate price for his lavish lifestyle.

Marlene had called several times, and so had Keisha and Rosalinda. They had offered to come and sit with her, but she'd declined to have them to come to her home, separately or all together. She had even lied when Marlene had called to have her mark her calendar for the upcoming celebration in honor of Jesse's homecoming. She'd told Marlene she had decided to go to Europe for a month and would already be out of the country on that appointed date.

The doorbell startled Alexis. She couldn't imagine who it could be. In a way, she hoped the girls had ignored her pleas for privacy. She was lonely and despondent. A visit from them could only help.

Surprised to see Reverend Jesse Covington through the peephole, she quickly threw off the extra new precautionary locks she'd had installed right after finding that the secret room had been emptied of all its illegal contents. The old locks had also been changed.

"Reverend Jesse, what a pleasant surprise. Please come in."

"Thank you, Mrs. Du Boise. How are you?"

"I'm not going to say I'm doing okay, because I'm not. I still have a lot of things to work through. Reality is just beginning to set in. Please come into the living room. Can I get you something to eat or drink."

"Not a thing, thank you. I came to deliver something from R.J." He handed Alexis a bloodstained envelope.

Upon seeing the bloodstain, sure that it was her husband's blood, she slammed her eyes shut. She kept them closed for several seconds. Finally, after taking several deep breaths, Alexis opened the envelope that Jesse had given her. Inside was a letter from R.J., which was also splotched with his blood.

"R.J. had the letter in his pocket when he was stabbed. It had already been sealed and stamped for mailing."

"How did it come to be in your possession?"

"Your husband gave it to me during the time we spent together before he passed away. R.J. was determined to hold on to life until he said all that he needed to say. His courage was very strong during that time. R.J. wanted me to promise that I would mail this letter for him. I made that promise to him along with a couple of others. In learning that I would be released in the next day or so, I decided to deliver it to you in person. The funeral wasn't an appropriate delivery time in my opinion."

Her hands trembled. Her breathing came rapidly, unevenly as she unfolded the letter and began to read. Immediate scalding tears ran down Alexis's face as she quickly scanned the contents of the letter. She then decided that this was something she needed to do in private. After folding the letter, she placed it back inside the envelope.

"Thank you for bringing this to me, Reverend Jesse. I've decided to read it through when I'm alone. I hope you understand."

"I understand perfectly, Mrs. Du Boise. I would want to do the same in this instance. How are things here at your home?"

"Things are just fine."

"Are they?"

"Yes. Why do you say it like that?"

"Is everything as it should be? The same as you thought it was before R.J.'s imprisonment?"

"I don't understand, Reverend Jesse."

"There is nothing to understand. Just making sure that all is like it should be. R.J. would want me to make sure that everything was fine, that everything was back to normal."

Alexis thought about the things he was asking. There seemed to be a hidden meaning in his questions and comments. *Making sure that all is like it should be. That everything was back to normal. I made that promise to him along with a couple of others.*

Then it hit her. Was he talking about the gambling casino? Could R.J. have told him about it? Had R.J. instructed Reverend Jesse on whom to contact to have the secret room cleared?

Sure that she now understood his line of questioning, she smiled knowingly. "Everything is back to normal. It is as it should be."

As he got to his feet, he nodded. "Then my mission here is completed. Take care of yourself, Mrs. Du Boise. It has been a pleasure. My promises to R.J. have all been fulfilled."

"Thank you, Reverend Jesse. My friends call me Alexis."

"My wife's dearest friends call me Jesse."

"Thank you, Jesse. That Marlene considers me a dear friend is indeed an honor."

CHAPTER TWENTY

In honor of Jesse's homecoming celebration, the First Tabernacle Church choir was in the middle of singing the opening song, Donnie McClurkin's "We Fall Down." Everyone was up out of their seats, moving along with the heart-stirring gospel rhythms. Reverend Jesse's celebration had just gotten underway.

Everyone who really mattered to Jesse Covington was in attendance. He knew that his wife was saddened that Alexis Du Boise wasn't coming to the celebration. But Marlene understood that Alexis had to work through her grief in her own way and in her own time. Marlene had told Jesse that she didn't believe that Alexis was out of the country. She was certain that Alexis was alone in that big house, wallowing knee-deep in self-pity and incrimination of self.

The choir finished two more songs and then Marlene stepped up to the podium. "That was simply beautiful! Thank you, choir. It's only fifteen minutes into the program and we've been inspired already. We have so much more in store for you on this wonderful afternoon. As we have come together in celebration of Reverend Jesse's homecoming, let us thank the Lord for delivering him back to us. Let us give praise to His most holy name. To God goes all the glory."

"Amen, hallelujah," the praises rang out.

Smiling, Jesse nodded his approval of the church coming together in his behalf.

"With that said, I want to thank each of you that are in attendance, as well as those who couldn't make it this evening. Thank you for coming out to honor our beloved pastor. In honoring him, you honor me. Jesse and I are one and the same. As your mistress of ceremonies, I'm going to move this program right along. We have so much to achieve this evening. Then we get to hear from our honoree. But right now, Miss Crystal George is going to sing 'Blessed Assurance' and then she will perform 'His Eye Is on the Sparrow.' Let's give her a warm welcome and a loving hand of encouragement."

With the voice of an angel, sixteen-year-old Crystal George made proud both her biological and church families. The Holy Spirit seemed to be upon her as she commemorated in song Jesse's long-awaited return to the church.

The next entertainers on the program, Malcolm and Todd, made their parents beam with pride as they performed a most appropriate gospel rap, "Late Night Talks," recorded by the new dynamic rapper on the block, Justified.

Seeing Malcolm and Todd performing together made Marlene's heart feel good. The two young men had practically been raised as brothers. She and Myrna had taken the kids everywhere together, from Magic Mountain in California to Disney World in Florida. They'd even dressed them alike on many occasions. With both of their husbands involved in demanding careers, Marlene and Myrna had kept each other company during countless long, lonely evenings. They'd even had meals together at least three to four times a week.

It hurt Marlene that she and Myrna still hadn't made peace with each other. Myrna hadn't returned a single one of the dozens of calls Marlene had made to her home, even though Myrna had received the messages Marlene always left for her. Marlene knew that Myrna had received them because Todd had told Malcolm.

As Myrna was the next person to perform, Marlene glanced in her direction before she went back to the podium. Not so much as a flutter of warmth came from Myrna, even though she'd briefly made eye contact with Marlene.

"Thank you, Malcolm and Todd. You did a beautiful job. Now we will hear from Todd's mother and my very best friend," Marlene dared to say, "our very own Sister Myrna Jacobson. Since we've all heard her sing on numerous occasions, I'm sure you've been anticipating yet another stellar performance from her. I now present to you

Sister Jacobson as she performs an old church favorite, 'Bridge over Troubled Water' ."

Tears filled Marlene's eyes when Myrna took the podium without so much as a friendly nod in her direction.

When Marlene took her seat next to her husband, he took her hand and massaged it gently. Taking a handkerchief out of his pocket, he wiped Marlene's tears away. His smile was reassuring. It hurt him deeply to see his wife so devastated by the broken friendship, but he felt certain they'd find their way back to each other. While their wives' issues hadn't directly affected Jesse's relationship with Myrna's husband, Raymond, there was still a bit of an awkward strain between the two families. However, Malcolm and Todd didn't seem at all affected by the troubles existing between their mothers.

All eyes were on Myrna as she sang from a place somewhere deep inside her heart and soul. Though she kept her eyes closed during the entire performance, the tears running down her face were visible to everyone. Marlene was deeply touched by Myrna's emotional state. It was all she could do to keep from running up to the podium and embracing her while she begged for her forgiveness on bended knee. She missed Myrna more than words could express. As if it hadn't been enough for her to have to live without her husband for several months, she'd also had to go through a part of it without the comforting arms of her best friend.

When Myrna went on to sing "Wanna Be More" by Bebe Winans, a song featured on the *Heaven* CD, both Marlene's and Myrna's tears flowed unchecked. Just as Jesus wasn't a fair-weathered friend, which the song mentioned, neither of them had ever considered each other as such. Their friendship had been solid through and through, which gave Marlene reason to continue to hope and pray for its resurrection.

After several more extraordinary performances were accomplished, Marlene got up and went back to the podium.

"Before we hear from our honoree, we're going to go ahead and serve the delicious meal that has been prepared for us by our church family. We are going to convene in the dining hall. Once everyone is seated, we will call on each table to come forward and pass through the serving lines in an orderly fashion. The lines will operate from both sides of the three serving tables that we have set up. Servers will be at each table to assist you in getting your food and drinks. As we work together to see that everyone is taken care of in a timely manner, we thank you for your patience. Let us now move into the dining area pew by pew. Our deacons and deaconesses will lead the way."

The church members had prepared quite a memorable feast in Jesse's honor. Lots of soul food had been prepared: corn bread, collard greens, candied yams, macaroni and cheese, potato salad, black-eyed peas, okra and tomatoes, fried chicken, grilled chicken and boneless turkey breasts, and baked turkey legs and wings. Huge aluminum pans filled with mixed fresh salad greens were located at the ends of each table, along with a variety of salad dressings. The dessert tables were laden with sweet-potato pies, peach, blueberry, and cherry cobblers, and a large selection of freshly baked cookies and an array of delicious-looking cakes.

The food was served in an orderly and timely manner. Once everyone was seated, Reverend Jesse gave the invocation. Laughter and conversation buzzed about the church's dining hall as the guests visited with each other while partaking of the delicious meal.

Marlene smiled at Jesse before she left her seat. It was now time to hear from the honoree, Reverend Jesse Covington, her best friend and beloved husband, pastor of First Tabernacle Church.

"Our next speaker needs no introduction. As the pastor of this church for the past twenty years, we have come to know him almost as well as we know ourselves. He's one of the predictable saints, a most faithful servant who's always leading the way into the light. Even though his goodness and gentle ways may be predictable, we're constantly amazed at the unpredictable ways in which he finds to serve his Master and the Master's bride, the church. Before I call him up here, I have a couple of things to say."

Marlene swept the sweat from her brow with a lace handkerchief. "Church, when I learned that my husband was coming home, and that I could pick him up within the next twelve hours, I wept like a baby. My prayers had been answered and I fervently thanked the Master for giving my husband back to me. It was close to midnight when he was released, but I was sitting right outside when he came through those fiery gates leading from the dark caverns of hell. No sweeter sight have I ever seen!" Marlene grinned. "I won't share with you how we later made up for lost time once we got back to our home. But I'm here to tell you I'm just so glad that our Malcolm is living elsewhere these days."

Marlene's desire was to ease the gripping emotions brought on by the moment. When everyone laughed, she felt instant relief.

"Reverend Jesse and I have some very personal things to work through, and we need your constant prayers. You see, over the years I've tried to run things at our home, personal issues, family issues, without consulting my soul mate. I'm guilty of keeping a few very inportant troublesome details from the man I vowed to share the good and the bad times with. I thought I was doing the right thing, but I know better now. In trying to be superwoman, there were events that happened that probably could've been avoided had I been a team player."

Loud gasps permeated the air, but Marlene was not ashamed of her admissions.

"Even though I honestly believe that I was waiting on the Master to supply me with the answers, I want to public apologize to my husband—and to all the others who have been hurt by this unfortunate chain of events. I also believe that everything was finally resolved at the appointed time, His time. Jesse was mighty angry with me, but in talking things over, he is also convinced of the appointed time. I also want to publicly apologize to my best friend and her family—Myrna, Raymond, and Todd Jacobson—who have also been affected by these troubling events. Myrna, I love you, dear heart. I miss you more than anything. I just need you to know that."

Myrna looked at Marlene briefly before turning her gaze away. Marlene had to fight hard to keep from breaking down. It looked as though Myrna had no intention of forgiving her, but Marlene wasn't ready just yet to throw in the towel on their relationship.

"Without further ado, I present to you our beloved pastor, Reverend Jesse Covington."

Simultaneously, with everyone getting to their feet, the applause came like rolling thunder. If anyone deserved a standing ovation, Jesse Covington did. He had gone with Godspeed into the heat of battle. In wearing the full armor of the heavenly Father during the conflict of his lifetime, he'd been fully protected from Satan. While touching Jesse soul-deep, the standing ovation lasted for a solid twenty minutes.

Tears clouded his vision as he said a word of prayer before making any remarks. With his head bowed low, he thanked God for making this day possible. In lifting his head, he smiled.

"I want to first begin by giving everyone a warm thank-you for everything you've done on my behalf. And I want to give out a special thank-you for you coming here this evening. It's good to see every one of you. Church, it is indeed a blessing and an honor to stand here before you. It is good to be home and even better to be in the house of the Lord. I also want to thank you for your prayers. I don't know about all of you, but I never doubted that I would return home. For those of you who thought I might not return, I fully understand that you did what you believed you had to do. But when God is for you, who can be against you? Folks, I'm going to answer that for you. No one can be against you when God is for you."

Surprised at Jesse's remarks, which seemed to suggest that he knew of the plan to remove him as pastor, Marlene looked around at the members of the deacon board. It was easy to discern the sheepish looks on the faces of those who had voted for the measure to oust him. She hadn't uttered a word to her husband about the matter, but it appeared that he'd found out anyway.

"My patience was growing thin while locked up behind bars, but my unwavering faith remained steadfast. I worked hard at trying to find the reasons for my being there. Even though I couldn't figure them out until much later, I knew the reasons would be valid ones. I also knew that it would be revealed in His time. I believe that I now know the reason I was there. My lovely wife has already shed some of the light for you. I hope to shed even more light, the light of truth. Some of you might find it hard to believe, but if you read the stories of the bible that relate to incarcerated followers of Jesus, you, too, will come to believe. Jesus still today chooses His disciples from many walks of life. I'm so glad that I am among His chosen ones."

There was an abundance of resounding amens from those in attendance.

"The day my mission on the inside became abundantly clear to me, I was to learn shortly after that, that God had already started working with those on the outside in securing my release. Only God could have secured my release in that short amount of time. My release papers were even signed with His precious blood. Three days after the death of Richard James Du Boise, and on the eve of his funeral, I was released from the dark depths of hell. Released just in time to perform R.J.'s going-home."

Jesse mopped his brow with a handkerchief.

"You see, R.J. came to me one day and asked me how he could find salvation. He then gave me the opportunity to counsel him in depth on that very subject. Would God dare to lock me up just to save one man's soul? I know what the answer is. I'll let you make your own determination, but I will say this: R.J. died a believer. God will use you in any way He sees fit, especially when you've opened yourself up to being used. I am but an instrument of God!

"I'm now going to leave you with this. I want to thank each and every one of you that caught the ball and ran with it in my absence. Running the church is a team effort. You have proven without a shadow of a doubt that we are a team, Jesus' team. Thank you so very much."

As Jesse stepped down from the podium, he received another ovation. Before taking her place at center stage once again, Marlene engaged her husband in a loving embrace.

Just as Marlene presented the Double Rock Baptist Church Choir, she spotted Alexis seated in back of the church. She couldn't help wondering if Alexis had been there all along. She hoped that Alexis had heard everything Jesse had said, especially the things about her husband. To know that R.J. had been saved, by the precious Blood of the Lamb, should surely bring her peace and comfort.

Before the choir began singing, Alexis made her way down to the front pew. Though there was very little space left, she managed to squeeze herself into the pew beside Marlene. Keisha, Rosalinda, and Michael Hernandez sat in the pew across from Marlene. Both women were extremely happy to see Alexis there. Jesse smiled broadly at Alexis when she looked his way. He was also very happy to see her in attendance.

"What a pleasant surprise," Marlene whispered. "So glad to see you."

Alexis leaned over and whispered something in Marlene's ear.

Marlene nodded. "As soon as the choir is finished," she whispered back.

For the next thirty minutes, the Double Rock Baptist Church Choir stirred up the emotions of everyone present while singing the old Negro spirituals that modern-day choirs rarely sang any more. The church was rocking on its very foundation as the choir pulled out all the stops in performing several of the modern-day pop gospel tunes: Kirk Franklin & the Family, popular gospel tunes from the various members of the Winans family, Donnie Mc Clurkin, and a host of other gospels greats. People found it hard to stay in their seats as the choir continued to stir up their emotions, leaving not a dry eye in the sanctuary.

Marlene adjusted the microphone. "All I can say is awesome! Thank you, Double Rock Choir, for being a part of our homecoming celebration for Reverend Jesse. You have done us proud. Your performance was so awe-inspiring and we can't wait to hear more from you."

Marlene looked over at Alexis. "This next event is not on the program, but I think we'll be able to deeply appreciate what our next presenter has in store for us. Alexis Du Boise is the widow of James Richard Du Boise, and she would like to share something with us. Alexis, please come forward."

At the podium, Alexis hugged Marlene. Once Marlene was back in her seat, Alexis unfolded the bloodstained letter and held it up for everyone to see.

"This is a letter written to me from my husband. It's stained with his blood. He had it in his pocket the day he was murdered. According to Reverend Jesse, R.J. found the strength to hold on to life until he said those things that he needed to say. He gave this letter to your pastor to mail to me. Instead, Reverend Jesse decided to deliver it to me in person, once he learned of his pending release from prison. I'm going to read you a paragraph or two so that you can see the state of mind my husband was in before his untimely death. This letter also speaks to the goodness and godliness of your pastor, which is why I've chosen this venue in which to read it.

" 'Dear Alexis, I hope things are going well for you. There's nothing positive to say about the conditions in here, so I won't say anything more than that. I've met a few times with Reverend Jesse Covington, the husband of your new friend, Marlene. He is as generous as you say that his wife is. I really believe that this man is innocent of the charges he was convicted of.

" 'Lexy, in searching for my soul, I'm beginning to find my true self. The self I lost to greed a long time ago. Reverend Jesse has given me insights into many bible truths. I never got them on my own because I wasn't ready to receive that which God had in store for me. How could He give it to me when I was following behind another master? Reverend Jesse taught me that never can there be two masters. I believe that I can now receive God's will for my life and that I understand His will for me.' "

Alexis took a few moments to compose herself. She couldn't be happier that R.J. had changed his worldly ways of thinking and acting. She was just sorry that they wouldn't be together to implement all the new desired changes. Before continuing, Alexis sucked in a deep, calming breath.

" 'I know everyone spouts bible talk when they're locked up, but I'm not just talking. Thanks to the pastor, I'm ready to walk on this journey step by step. Things are going to be different when I get out. I've decided to join you on your shopping spree for a new inner wardrobe. I can't wait until the weekend for your visit. I have so much to share with you. The only thing that I can't hold inside another second is that I'm going to ask Reverend Jesse to baptize me in the prison chapel.' "

With her heart bleeding inside, Alexis had stumbled terribly over the last sentence. It only took her a couple of seconds to regain her composure.

"That's all I'm going to read. The rest is rather personal and somewhat steamy."

Alexis managed to laugh, though her heart was broken into millions of tiny pieces. "We didn't get to have that weekend, because R.J. was murdered over something as ridiculous as the length of a phone call. I don't know why Reverend Jesse was wrongly convicted, but I do know for a fact that he helped my husband convict himself to salvation. This letter proves that. Did Jesus put your pastor in prison to lead my husband to righteousness? I don't know the answer to that. But I'm so glad that he was there with and for R.J. when he took his last breath. It's the one true comfort that I can take out of all that has happened. Thank you, Reverend and Mrs. Jesse Covington, for the dynamic roles you've played in both R.J.'s life and mine. Thank you, church. Marlene, Keisha, Rosalinda, I love you. Reading this letter has brought me toward the first steps in the healing process. Knowing you'll be there with me is what's going to help me get through the rest. May God bless each and every one of you."

The choir began to sing "Don't Cry for Me" as Alexis stepped down from the podium.

Waiting for her with open arms, ready to express the genuine love they've come to feel for one another, were Alexis's three comrades, Marlene, Keisha, and Rosalinda. As the foursome continued to embrace one another, Jesse and Malcolm joined in the touching celebration.

The Double Rock Choir began to sing Donnie Mc Clurkin's "Stand."

Unable to stay in her seat a second longer, Myrna Jacobson walked up to Marlene and threw her arms around her best friend. Their tears mingled as they cried together in each other's arms. Their bodies shook with emotion as the two women squeezed each other tightly. Myrna's husband, Raymond, and their son, Todd soon followed Myrna's lead.

Wanting to be at the side of the woman for whom he'd grown to care deeply, Michael Hernandez joined the group and took hold of Rosalinda's hand. Certain now that Michael was indeed sincere about her—and that they could one day truly have a wonderful personal relationship—Rosalinda squeezed Michael's hand tightly.

As Rosalinda and Michael hugged each other, Keisha gave both of them a smile bright with approval. Keisha could only pray that Zach would join this circle of true friends. For them to finally be a real family was what she prayed for on a daily basis. The kids needed her and they needed their father. And she was now a witness to how a loving God answered prayers.

These four women from four different walks of life had found strength, courage, and the renewal of hope in one another. Each had brought something to the table; each had walked away with both new and worn swatches of material to add to the evolving patchwork quilt being made from the fabric of their lives.

Clearly etched on their faces was their commitment to one another and to the other women who walked in their same shoes. Smiling like a bright beam of light, the four ladies in waiting linked hands with their loved ones while moving to the soul-stirring gospel rhythms.

Through all the tears and emotions, the choir continued to sing "Stand."

Dear Readers:

I sincerely hope that you enjoyed reading LADIES IN WAITING from cover to cover. As this is my first mainstream inspirational novel, I'm interested in hearing your comments and thoughts on the story of these four courageous women whose dedicated love and support for their men gave them something in common. Without the reader, there is no me as an author.

Please enclose a self-addressed, stamped envelope with all your correspondence and mail to: Linda Hudson-Smith, 2026C North Riverside Avenue, Box 109, Rialto, CA 92377. Or you can e-mail your comments to LHS4romance@yahoo.com. Please also visit my Web site at www.lindahudsonsmith.com.

ABOUT THE AUTHOR

Born in Canonsburg, Pennsylvania, and raised in the town of Washington, Pennsylvania, Linda Hudson-Smith has traveled the world as an enthusiastic witness to other cultures and lifestyles. Her husband's military career gave her the opportunity to live in Japan, Germany, and many cities across the United States. Linda's extensive travel experience helps her craft stories set in a variety of beautful and romantic locations. It was after illness forced her to leave her marketing and public relations administration career that she turned to writing.

Romance in Color chose her as Rising Star for the month of January 2000. ICE UNDER FIRE, her debut Arabesque novel, has received rave reviews. Voted as Best New Author, by the Black Writer's Alliance, Linda received the 2000 Gold Pen Award. She has also won two *Shades of Romance* awards in the categories of Multicultural New Romance Author of the Year and Multicultural New Fiction Author of the Year 2001. SOULFUL SERENADE, released in August 2000, was selected by *Romance in Color* readers as the Best Cover for that month. She was also nominated as the Best New Romance Author at the 2001 Romance Slam Jam. Her novel covers have been featured in such major publications as *Publishers Weekly, USA Today,* and *Essence* magazine.

Linda is a member of Romance Writers of America and the Black Writer's Alliance. Though novel writing remains her first love, she is currently cultivating her screenwriting skills. She has also been contracted to write several other novels for BET.

Dedicated to inspiring readers to overcome adversity against all odds, Linda has accepted the challenge of becoming National Spokesperson for the Lupus Foundation of America. In making lupus awareness one of her top priorities, she travels around the country delivering inspirational messages of hope. She is also a supporter of the NAACP and the American Cancer Society. She enjoys poetry, entertaining, traveling, and attending sports events. The mother of two sons, Linda shares residences in both California and Texas with her husband.